T0146496

Victoria Monzelle was one of a kind, without question.

She met his gaze, amusement and a glittering triumph in her eyes. He smiled, wishing they had all day to explore just how *rigid* he could be. But the second he put his hands on her, it was over. He knew it. By the curve of her mouth, she knew it, too. For some reason, she wanted to goad him. She'd misread him if she thought he'd back down. "You really do like playing with fire, don't you?" The irony, considering he could create fire, only amused him more. "I truly do." She moved his way, no fear anywhere in her. "But we both know you're all talk, don't we?"

"The second I stop talking, we're both in trouble," he said honestly. "Yet trouble is something you seek."

She moved into his space, and the scent of wild orchids, the kind growing abundantly around his childhood home, washed over him. "I love trouble."

Wicked Kiss

Realm Enforcers, Book 4

Rebecca Zanetti

LYRICAL PRESS
Kensington Publishing Corp.
www.kensingtonbooks.com

LYRICAL PRESS BOOKS are published by

Kensington Publishing Corp.
119 West 40th Street
New York, NY 10018

All Kensington titles, imprints, and distributed lines are available at special quantity discounts for bulk purchases for sales promotions, premiums, fund-raising, educational, or institutional use.

Special book excerpts or customized printings can also be created to fit specific needs. For details, write or phone the office of the Kensington sales manager: Kensington Publishing Corp., 119 West 40th Street, New York, NY 10018, attn: Sales Department; phone 1-800-221-2647.

LYRICAL PRESS and the Lyrical logo are Reg. U.S. Pat. & TM Off.

First electronic edition: July 2017

ISBN-13: 978-1-60183-517-8
ISBN-10: 1-60183-517-5

First print edition: July 2017

ISBN-13: 978-1-60183-518-5
ISBN-10: 1-60183-518-3

This one is for Gabe Zanetti,
who hits like a truck on the football field,
smashes the honor roll in school,
smiles like a sweetheart,
and loves his mama.

Yeah, you're going to take ribbing
about that last one if your friends read this.
Your friends shouldn't be reading this book.
You're all too young at the moment.
If a girl you like says she's read my book . . .
she's too old for you.

True words.

And I love you, son.

ACKNOWLEDGMENTS

I have many people to thank for help in getting this fourth Realm Enforcer book to readers, and I sincerely apologize to anyone I've forgotten.

Thank you to my husband, Big Tone, for being everything I could ever want in a mate. Thanks also to Gabe and Karlina for being such awesome kids and for making life so much fun;

Thank you to my amazing, talented, and dedicated Kensington editor, Alicia Condon;

Thank you to the Kensington gang: Steven Zacharius, Adam Zacharius, Lynn Cully, Alexandra Nicolajsen, Vida Engstrand, Michelle Forde, Jane Nutter, Lauren Jernigan, Kimberly Richardson, Fiona Jayde, Allison Gentile, and Arthur Maisel;

Thank you to my hardworking and talented agents, Caitlin Blasdell and Liza Dawson;

Thank you to my fantastic Facebook street team, Rebecca's Rebels, and thanks to Minga Portillo for her hard work there;

Thanks also to Jillian Stein for basically saving my sanity and doing such amazing work on my behalf;

Thanks to Liz Berry for her friendship and wonderful insights;

Thank you to all of my writer friends. They mean so much to me, and I'd like to name each one, but my space here is a bit limited;

And thanks also to my constant support system: Gail and Jim English, Debbie and Travis Smith, Stephanie and Don West, Brandie and Mike Chapman, Jessica and Jonah Namson, and Kathy and Herb Zanetti.

Chapter 1

So far, the magical world of Ireland sucked eggs. Her dreams of rolling hills, rugged men, and wild adventures had given way to facts that tilted her universe, spun it around, and spiked it headfirst into the ground.

The world held too many secrets.

Tori Monzelle leaned her shoulders against the cold interior wall of the van and tried to blink through a tight blindfold. Nothing. She couldn't see a thing. The carpet in the rear of the van smelled fresh but was rough against her pants, while she sat with her knees drawn up and her hands tied behind her back.

A metallic taste filled her mouth. Her mind whirled, and she tried to focus, but her breath panted out of her lungs as if somebody squeezed them.

The vehicle hiccuped a couple of times but ran smoothly for now. It would experience a mechanical glitch at some point. Her curse was predictable. At least then she could run.

She cleared her throat. The whole situation was just so surreal. If she could get the two kidnappers to stop the van, maybe she could get free. "Listen, jackasses. I'm done with this entire kidnapping scenario. I promise not to tell anybody that supernatural beings exist. Just let me go."

A snort came from the front seat. "Supernatural," one of the men muttered.

Her chest heated. "So you think you're *natural*. Then how about I refrain from announcing your species even exists?"

Another snort.

Where were they taking her? The sounds of drizzling rain and honking horns filtered in from outside, while the two men breathed loudly in the front seats. She hadn't recognized either of them when they'd arrived at the penthouse an hour before. For an entire week, she'd been held hostage in various luxurious Dublin locales after having been kidnapped from Seattle. The last penthouse where she'd been kept even had a piano. Finally, she'd been able to play music and had created a new score.

Then they'd come for her—again. This was the first time she'd been blindfolded during relocation. That couldn't be good.

Had it only been a week since she'd learned the world wasn't as she'd thought?

Immortal beings existed. As in *really existed*.

"Are you witches, demons, or vampires?" If she had to guess, they were witches. They were just a different species from humans. So far, she'd seen witches create and throw fireballs, and she'd met a demon who'd shown her his fangs. She had to go on faith that vampires really existed, but at this point, why not believe? "Mr. Kidnappers?"

No answer. She'd seen their faces; the only reason to blindfold her now was to keep her lost and confused. So she couldn't find her way back to safety. She shuddered.

The van swerved, and she knocked her head against the side. "Ouch." It was time to get free. "This is international kidnapping." Did witches care about international laws? Her shoulders shook, and a welcome anger soared through her.

The van jerked.

"What the hell?" one of the guys snapped.

The world tilted.

Something sputtered. The engine?

An explosion rocked the van, and it started to spin. Her temple smacked metal. Pain flashed white and red behind her eyes. She rolled to the other side across the carpet. Breath swooshed from her lungs. Blood welled on her lip, and she blinked behind the blindfold.

The van stopped cold, and she rolled toward the front, her legs scrambling. Her forehead brushed the carpet and she shook her head frantically, dislodging the blindfold.

The front doors opened, and grunts sounded. Men fighting. Punches being thrown.

The back doors opened, and light flooded inside.

She turned just as broad hands grabbed her ankles and dragged her toward the street. Kicking out, she struggled furiously, her eyes adjusting and focusing on this new threat. A ski mask completely covered the guy's head, leaving only his eyes and mouth revealed. With the light behind him, she couldn't even make out the color of his irises.

His strong grip didn't relent, and he easily pulled her toward the edge, dropping her legs so her feet could touch the ground.

She threw a shoulder into his rock-hard abs and stood. He was at least a foot taller than she and definitely cut hard.

Everything in her screamed to get the hell out of the area and make a run for it. She was smart, she was tough, and she could handle the situation. No time to think. She leaped up and shot a quick kick to his face. While he was tall and fit, he probably wasn't expecting a fight.

He snagged her ankle an inch from his jaw, preventing the impact. Using her momentum to pull her forward, he manacled his other hand to the back of her thigh and lifted, tossing her over his shoulder in one incredibly smooth motion.

Her rib cage slammed into solid muscle, knocking the wind from her lungs. She stilled in shock. Her adrenaline spiked, and the blood rushed through her ears. Free—she had to get free. This guy was too powerful and way too much in control. She couldn't fight him, and there was no doubt she was outmatched. Fear sharpened the entire day into focus.

She tried to struggle.

One firm hand anchored her thighs, and he turned, moving into a jog. The sound of fighting behind them had her lifting her head to see more men in ski masks battling the two guys from the van. Those two were losing badly. Blood sprayed from the driver's nose, and he went down. Hard.

Then her captor turned a corner and ran through an alley, easily holding her in place.

"Let me go," she gasped, pulling on the restraints holding her hands. Cobblestones flew by below, while cool air brushed across her skin. Rain pattered down, matting her hair to her face. Begging wouldn't work with this guy—she just knew it. What did he want?

"Leave me here, and I won't turn you in."

He didn't answer and took two more turns, finally ending up in yet another alley, next to a shiny black motorcycle. Her hair swooshed as he ducked his shoulder and planted her on her feet. Firm hands flipped her around, and something sliced through her bindings.

Blood rushed into her wrists, and she winced at the prickly pain, pivoting back around. "Who are you?" She set her stance to fight.

He reached out and tugged the blindfold completely off her head before ripping off his ski mask.

Adam Dunne stood before her, legs braced, no expression on his hard face. Rain dripped from his thick black hair, and irritation glittered in his spectacular green eyes. That expression seemed to live on him. She knew he was some sort of brilliant strategist, definitely a brainiac, and he always appeared annoyed.

She blinked twice. "Adam?"

He crossed his arms. "It has been nearly impossible to find you."

His deep voice shot right through her to land in very private places. Then the angry tone caught her. She slammed her hands against her hips. He was the very last person in the world she wanted to see right now. "That's my fault? Your stupid people, the witches, kidnapped me."

Witches. Holy crap. Adam Dunne was a *witch.* Sure, she'd figured that out a week ago, but with him standing right in front of her, she was face-to-face with the reality. The sense of power she'd always imagined in him was real. True power.

The man looked like a badass vigilante and not some brilliant otherworldly being. For this kidnapping, he'd worn a black T-shirt, ripped jeans, and motorcycle boots—definitely not his usual pressed slacks and button-down silk shirt. For once, he appeared just like the criminal she thought he might be.

His sizzling green eyes darkened. "I have about an hour to get you to a plane and out of this country, so you'll be quiet, and you'll follow orders."

She pressed her lips together. No matter how badly she wanted to punch him in the face, she wanted to get out of the country even more. But could she trust him? He was one of the witches. He was probably their leader, and this could be just another part of the whole kidnapping. "Fine."

He lifted an eyebrow. "We're getting on the bike, heading to the airport, and then you're flying to Seattle. You don't know who rescued you, and you haven't seen me in weeks."

She swallowed. Oh, she knew more about him than he could even imagine. For now, she'd play along, especially if it got her out of the country. "How much trouble are you in if we get caught?"

He grabbed a helmet off the bike. "Treason and death sentence."

Right. Like she believed that one. Yet . . . she had a part to play. "Thank you."

He shoved the helmet at her. "Don't thank me. Just do what I tell you."

Man, what a jerk. Nearly biting through her tongue to keep from lashing out, she shoved the helmet on her head. If her intel was right, he might be a killer. A cold-blooded, meticulous, dangerous killer. And here she was, alone with him.

He swung a leg over the bike, holding out a hand to help her.

She ignored him and levered herself over the bike and into place, anger flowing through her along with awareness. She didn't know how to fight like he did. Even without dangerous powers, Adam was solid muscle and powerful strength. Could she escape him?

He ignited the engine. It sputtered. He stiffened and tried again.

No, no, no. She closed her eyes to calm her temper and soothe her fears. Being stuck in the alley with Adam was a disaster. *Work, bike. Damn it, work.* The more she tried to concentrate, the more irritated and breathless she became.

He twisted the throttle again, and this time, nothing.

Why did this always happen to her? What was wrong with her? "It won't work. If it's broken, it won't work." She tugged free of the helmet and shoved herself off the bike. Maybe he'd just leave her alone in the dismal alley. She could get to safety somehow.

He turned toward her. "The bike ran just fine an hour ago."

Her face heated. No way was she telling him about her oddity. She eyed the end of the alley. Could she make it before he stopped her? "I know the sound of an engine that's not coming back to life, and so do you."

He frowned and tried the bike again. No response. "All right." He swung his leg over and stood, studying her. "Are you up to running?"

She blinked. Was that concern in his tone? "Yes. In fact, it'd be better if we separated and ran in different directions."

His lips twitched.

She stared, almost fascinated. Had that been a hint of a smile? While she'd known Adam for months, she'd never seen him smile. "It's a good plan," she asserted, wiping rain off her hands.

"Sweetheart, I haven't spent an entire week scouring the country for you to send you away unprotected." His brogue deepened, and he reached out to tug a wet curl away from her cheek.

Her body short-circuited. From one simple touch. "Why have you been looking for me?" Was he telling the truth?

His pocket buzzed, and he withdrew a cell phone and pushed a button, taking a step back. "Our transport isn't running," he said into the phone, his gaze remaining on her.

"I've downloaded information from the phones on the van you just demolished. The woman has been tagged," came an urgent male voice over the speaker. "There's a tracker planted on her clothes somewhere, and you have about five minutes until the Guard gets there." Keys clacking echoed across the line. "Get rid of the tag and find safety. I'll be in touch with new coordinates as soon as I can." The line went dead.

Adam's expression went hard. He surveyed her head to toe, reaching for her shirt.

She slapped at his hands, adrenaline exploding inside her. "What are you doing?"

He radiated menace. "Your clothing has been tagged, and I don't know where. Strip, baby."

Baby? Did he just call her *baby*? Wait a minute. "Strip?"

"Now." A muscle ticked in his powerful jaw. "Our tags are minute and could be anywhere on you." He dug both big hands through her hair, tugging just enough to flood her with unwelcome tingles. "Not in your hair."

"I am not stripping," she said through clenched teeth, her body doing a full tremble against her will.

He lowered his head until his nose almost touched hers. "Take everything off, or I'll do it for you."

She blinked. Her abdomen clenched. Heat slid through her to land in her core.

He gave a barely perceptible eye roll and turned around, pulling off his T-shirt. "Drop the clothes, and I'll give you my shirt. It'll cover you for the time being." Muscles rippled in his back, moving a jagged tattoo of the symbols CE9 over his left shoulder blade. What did CE9 stand for? The ink was dark and intricate and seemed right at home on him.

Her mouth went dry. Tight-assed Adam Dunne had a tat? Seriously? Who was this guy?

"Now, Victoria. We have to hurry."

"Okay," she whispered, taking a quick look around. Now. It was her only chance to get away from the witches. There had to be an American consulate somewhere. She pivoted to run and made it nearly a foot before his muscled arm snagged her around the waist. She halted mid-stride, and the air whooshed from her lungs. Her eyes bugged out. Whoa. He moved faster than sound.

He hauled her back against his rock-hard bare chest, and his breath brushed her ear. "Don't forget, I gave you a chance." His fingers tangled in the bottom of her shirt.

"No," she yelped, struggling against him, panic hazing her vision.

"Aye," he muttered, easily ripping the wet material over her head. A flick of his finger between her breasts released her bra, and he tugged it away. Rain splashed over her naked skin. His broad chest warmed her bare back.

The gurgle up from her chest held a slight hysterical giggle. Obviously not Adam's first bra. "Damn it, Adam." She kicked back, her heel bouncing off his shin.

He flipped her around to face him, and her hair spun water. "Stop fighting me," he growled.

Her chin dropped as reality splashed in. Red slashed across his angled face, and his eyes burned a fiery green. Danger. For the first time, she would really see the otherworldly predator beneath his smooth veneer. She shivered in the rain, wanting nothing more than to cover her bare chest. But a girl had her pride, and he needed to know he didn't scare her. Her chin lifted this time, and she met his gaze.

Something flickered in those deadly eyes. Admiration? His head cocked ever so slightly to the side, and his nostrils flared. As if accepting her challenge, on his timeline, he slowly let his gaze wander.

Her nipples, the little bastards, hardened instantly just as his heated gaze landed on them.

Tension rolled through the small alley. From him.

She swallowed. "Give me the shirt." A small tremor caught her words.

"The view is too lovely to hide." His gaze lifted. "But as soon as you finish stripping, I will."

Lovely? She clenched her teeth together. Rain and wind whipped into her, and goose bumps rose on her skin. Even so, beneath his gaze, her body warmed. They had to get out of the alley. "Fine. Turn around?"

His lip curved. "I already gave you that chance. Lose the pants and shoes. I'll allow you the count of three."

Her jaw ached, and her temper snapped. "Excuse me?" she said levelly, turning just enough to get a good aim at his balls.

His eyebrow lifted. "I retaliate, Victoria. Don't forget that." There was a sexual undertone to the threat that vibrated through the rain.

Oh, she was out of her depth on way too many fronts right now. Yet nothing in her was about to show vulnerability to this man. Not once. Not ever. "Back off, Adam."

"One."

Her entire body stiffened, and she felt like she grew two inches. "Don't even think about it."

"Two." He didn't so much as twitch, and yet, as prey, she could sense he was about to pounce.

Dropping all pretense of talking to him, she twisted and aimed a side kick for his groin with all the strength she could muster.

He caught her ankle, tossed it down, and grabbed her pants with both hands. A quick twist, and they tore down the middle.

She gasped. The material had been good and strong, and he'd destroyed it with his bare hands. "You jerk." She swung and nailed him beneath the right eye. Pain shot through her knuckles to her wrist. What was his damn face made of?

The sound he gave was much more growl than hiss. He tore her panties in two, and they hit the ground. Less than a heartbeat later, he yanked his shirt down to cover her. The soft material fell beneath her thighs and surrounded her with the scent of male.

Her breath panted and she gasped out, already making another fist. Tattoos covered his chest, too!

He flipped her around, and his palm landed square on her ass. Hard. The sound reverberated through the alley, and pain exploded through her butt. "Retaliation," he muttered, yanking her back around to face him. Her hair spun around. He dropped his face to hers. "We done now?"

"No," she breathed out, the air hot, her mind spinning and her temper roaring.

"Yes." He settled a hand around her throat and drew her even nearer. "Kick. Off. The. Shoes." His face was an implacable mask of determination, and he stood over her like an avenging god.

She opened her mouth to let him have it, and he tightened his hold, almost cutting off her air.

Her eyes widened.

"I see you're starting to understand me," he said, his hold not relenting. "I'm sorry. You either get this, or you don't. We're at a life-and-death moment, darlin'. Obey me, or I'll knock you out just to make sure we both fucking live."

He wasn't bluffing. Everything inside her knew he was giving her the full truth. The witch would actually do it. "You'll pay for this," she sputtered.

"Last chance."

She had to remain conscious. "Fine." She could barely get the word out as she kicked off her shoes.

"Good girl." He leaned down and whipped off her socks, gently placing her feet on the wet cobblestones.

His phone buzzed, and he released her to grab it, pressing the speaker button. "What?"

"They've upped the order on the girl and canceled the 'no harm' directive. It's upgraded to take her at all costs," the same male voice all but shouted. "Get the fuck out of that alley."

The urgency got through to Tori, and she bunched her legs to run. Survival was all that mattered.

Adam took her hand. "Sorry about the bare feet, but we'll get you replacement clothes soon. For now, we don't look back."

A car screeched to a stop outside the alley.

"Bollocks. They're here," he muttered, launching into a run down the alley. "Hurry, and if I stop, keep going."

Panic seized her, and she held tight to his hand, her bare feet slapping hard cobblestones. Her ankles ached. A fireball careened past her, smashing into the brick building above her and raining down debris. She screamed.

Adam stopped and shoved her behind him, dark blue plasma forming down his arms as he pivoted to fight.

She gulped in air and peered around him as three men, all forming different-colored plasma balls, stalked toward them from the street.

"Run, Victoria," Adam bellowed.

Chapter 2

Adam kept his fire up around his face, hurtling ball after ball of plasma at the advancing men. He didn't want to permanently hurt any member of the Guard, the police force for the witch nation, but he also couldn't let them see his identity.

Never once in his life would he have thought he'd commit treason.

Nor had he ever had a plan go so completely wrong. His bike was in pristine condition, and there was no explanation for it petering out. "Victoria? Get the hell out of here," he ordered again.

He'd also never had anyone disobey one of his direct orders during a combat situation.

"And go where?" she demanded from behind him, yanking his gun from his waistband.

What in the hell was the woman doing? Apparently one slap to the ass hadn't been enough to teach her a lesson. "Put that back," he snapped, hitting one of the men center mass with a plasma ball and sending the soldier flying backward into a brick building. Shards rained down, and the guy landed hard enough to bounce twice.

He didn't get back up.

She kept behind Adam and to the right. Green laser bullets flashed by his arm as she apparently fired the gun. "What the hell is that?" she asked, still shooting.

"Laser bullets that turn to lead upon impacting immortal flesh," he muttered. Or human flesh, probably. They didn't normally shoot humans, so who the hell knew?

Did the woman have training? His dossiers on her didn't include that, but since her sister was a cop, maybe there had been a few familial shooting sessions.

She fired again, the bullets going wide of target. Very wide. So . . . no training.

"Stop firing," he said.

"No. You definitely need backup."

Oh, they were going to have to get a few things straight, and soon. He ducked while a blue plasma ball flew by his head, making sure to keep her covered with his body at the same time. Enough. Gathering double his usual amount of power, he used both hands to create a ball and then threw it at the second man's legs.

The impact thundered through the alley, and the guy went down with a shriek of pain. He wouldn't die, but he'd take a few years to recuperate.

Without missing a step, Adam turned, grabbed his gun from Tori, and seized her elbow. "Keep up." He launched himself into a run, noting how fragile her bones felt beneath his hand. It had been a century since he'd touched a human. They were far too breakable.

She ran next to him, her head down, her lithe legs pumping furiously. Her bare feet didn't slow her in the slightest. Man, he had to get the image of her pert breasts out of his damn head so they could survive this. The woman was much too tempting.

So far, nobody had seen his face. They had to get out of there, or he'd be wanted by the ruling witch council, and he wouldn't be able to help his brothers. They were already fugitives. The witch nation didn't take well to subterfuge and disobedience.

His family didn't know any other way. It was a miracle they'd worked within the system for so long.

He turned another corner, easily mapping their escape route in his mind along with their velocity, endurance, and possible hindrances. "Are you doing all right?" he asked.

"Yes," she gasped.

"Almost there, sweetheart," he said, leading her into a darkened alley. A helicopter whirred through the clouds above. Damn it. He reached the end of a rough stone building and jerked Victoria to a stop. He quickly rearranged a series of small stones in the exterior wall, and a barely there green door appeared.

"Wh—" she started.

He planted his palm against the door, right at eye level.

Tori leaned over, hands on bare knees, still keeping the gun clasped tightly in one. Her breath panted out.

The door hitched, shimmered, and then opened. Another helicopter joined the first above them.

Adam grasped Tori's arm and drew her inside the quiet interior. The door closed on its own. Darkness surrounded them and pressed in. Her breathing filled the silence, and he let her adjust while he listened for any threats on the outside. The helicopters hadn't been close enough to see them, but they might have heat sensors that had kicked in before Adam had gotten them inside.

No sounds filtered through the thick walls.

"Where are we?" she whispered.

"Lights," he murmured.

Century-old sconces lit up along a narrow hallway; the walls were stone, the floor dirt. The sense of magic, the real kind, born of physics and the laws of nature, filtered around them.

Tori stood straighter, the purple streaks in her hair almost glowing. "Are we safe?"

"Aye," he said automatically.

She stiffened. "Don't give the little woman assurances. I need the truth. Are we safe?"

Fuck no, they weren't safe. There wasn't a haven on the damn planet for them at the moment. "We're as safe as we're going to get." He shoved his gun in at the back of his waist and then took her hand to move inside the building. "We're in a safe house for now, and our heat signatures are hidden from the outside. We'll hole up here until we can get to the airport."

"Okay." She stumbled and quickly regained her balance, just like a cat.

As they passed each sconce, it sputtered out into darkness.

"Weird," Victoria muttered, her head swinging from wall to wall, her voice echoing. "How do they do that?"

He didn't have time to explain quantum physics and the very real metaphysical world to her. "Magic."

She snorted. "Fine. Don't tell me."

Why couldn't that suffice? They reached the end of the hallway, and smooth stone steps led down to another faded green door.

The second they passed through it, both the stairs and door would disappear.

He moved down the stairs, and his palm opened the door.

"Where are we going?" she asked, her voice echoing off the stones.

"Down," he answered, tuning his senses to the outside world. No shouts or running feet. That had to mean something. He drew her inside, called for the lights, and showed her a plush living room with priceless antiques and velvet furnishings.

Victoria paused and looked around at the two small settees and hand-carved end tables. In his shirt, she appeared small and defenseless. "Have we traveled back in time to a whorehouse?"

He barked out a laugh, surprising humor heating his chest. He paused. When was the last time he'd actually laughed? "Not exactly." The walls were bare rock . . . at the moment. "Watch this." Was he showing off for her? Maybe a little. "Engage," he said quietly.

Three of the walls lit up with screens—modern and very well connected. One displayed a series of camera feeds transmitting from around the local area, one showed satellite imagery, and the other was a blank screen with a cursor, waiting for his command.

"Cool," she breathed, stepping toward the nearest screen, which showed soldiers scouting the neighborhood. Her toenails were painted a wild purple that almost matched her hair. "Are they after us?" Her voice shook.

"Aye," he said, counting the boots on the ground through the screen. At least fifteen fully armed soldiers in combat gear wound through the labyrinth of alleys and streets within the closest seven square blocks. "This stronghold is owned by my family. Nobody else knows it exists." Hopefully. It wouldn't be the first time a family stronghold had been infiltrated.

"Good," she breathed, her shoulders dropping from around her ears to where they should be.

Ah. So he had been able to provide some assurance. Excellent. Scaring her had never been his intention. Not that he had intentions toward her, but something about her free spirit intrigued him.

He'd never felt free. Not really. Duty and family always called. He was a protector of the Coven Nine, of his people, and he lived that responsibility to his very bones. To be on the opposite side of the Guard, even in one campaign, ripped claws through him.

Yet the woman staring at him managed to take him away from reality for a brief moment. God, she was stunning.

The comfortable room glowing with passionate colors seemed suddenly too small. Her feminine scent, one of wild orchids, wound around him, infiltrating his thoughts. He'd know her scent in the middle of Times Square, and sometimes late at night, when he couldn't sleep, he could swear it was near.

That she was near.

He studied her. At least a foot shorter than he, she had classic features set in a stubborn face: straight nose, pointed chin, high cheekbones. What would she look like all flushed with passion?

Her pretty blue eyes narrowed. "Why are you shaking your head at me?"

"It's not at you." He turned toward the cursor and away from her delectable body. He'd always liked curvy women.

Victoria rubbed her chin. "I have *so* fallen down the rabbit's hole."

"Aye," he said, striding toward the small kitchen to the right. "It's past suppertime. Are you hungry?"

"No. Thirsty though." She was right on his heels. "Have a beer?"

"No." He rummaged through ancient cupboards and found a dusty bottle. "How about whiskey?"

She nodded. "Perfect, and now you can tell me what the hell is going on. How are you a witch? How do they even exist? Why have your damn people held me hostage for nearly a week?"

All good questions, really. He took out two lead crystal glasses, wiped them on his shirt, and poured healthy shots for them both. Turning, he handed one to Victoria.

She looked at the honey-colored alcohol, sniffed it, and downed it in one gulp. Color bloomed across her pretty face.

His lips twitched. "That's hundred-year-old whiskey, darlin'."

She hummed. "I like it." She held out her glass again, and this time he gave her a double.

"Sip a bit so we can chat." He added to his glass and moved into the living area, setting the bottle on a carved table before sitting. The woman should be coughing and not humming, although he appreciated the soft sound. "Have a seat."

She sat on a purple brocade chair. "Time for you to talk, Adam Dunne." After the whiskey, her voice had deepened to a sexy whisper.

Rebecca Zanetti

His pants suddenly felt too tight. All right. It had been a while since he'd been with a woman, and this one was completely wrong for him. His body was just reacting like any healthy male's would. He could control himself. "What do you want to know?" He took a big drink, allowing the whiskey to heat through him.

She blinked. "How do humans not know about witches, and can you turn me into a frog?"

He laughed. "Humans don't know about other species, more powerful species, because we don't want them to know." Her blue eyes seemed to darken, and he watched, impressed. "I wouldn't turn you into a frog. A mermaid, maybe."

She leaned back. "You could turn me into a mermaid?"

He couldn't help the smile this time. "No. First, mermaids don't exist. Second, we use quantum physics to alter matter, like to create fire out of air. We can't take a higher being like a human and turn it into anything else. You're safe."

A slight smile curved her pink lips. "Did you just make a joke?"

"I'm very funny," he deadpanned.

She finished her drink. "Why did your people kidnap me? I just don't get it."

He sighed, reaching for the bottle to pour her another. Why not? They weren't going anywhere for a while, and her tolerance was impressive. "You were in the wrong place at the wrong time, and then you saw witches get in a firefight." At that point, her life came into jeopardy.

"That's not my fault," she sputtered.

"No, it isn't. But the Coven Nine, the ruling body of witches, is fractured right now, and they don't want any threats out there. Your knowing about us is a threat." His hiding her from them was treason. He'd always lived in a black-and-white world . . . and now gray surrounded him.

She sipped slowly, her expression smoothing out. "I'm a threat to a bunch of witches. Seriously?"

"Aye," he said, taking another drink. "Consider this: my brothers and my cousins are all going into hiding, temporarily. So, yes, you're definitely in danger. I have to get you to the States and off the grid."

She reared back. "Why is everyone going into hiding? And what about *my* sister?"

Of course she was worried about her sister, who was now mated to his brother. Adam considered what to tell her. "My brothers committed treason the other day by helping one of our cousins go against the sitting Coven Nine members, our ruling council of witches, of which there are now only three instead of the usual nine." He held up a hand to forestall her question. "I can't tell you why or who my cousin is. Just know that we're in, ah, big trouble."

"Was it Simone?" Victoria asked.

Hell. He'd forgotten Victoria and Simone had become friends in Seattle. "Yes. The Council ordered her death. Found her guilty of treason even though she was set up. Right now, she's safe as we try to prove her innocence. I promise."

"What about my sister?" Victoria ground out. "She's dating your brother right now. Is she in danger?"

"They're a little past the dating stage," Adam said dryly. "Kellach *mated* your sister."

Victoria leaned away from him, her eyebrows slanting down. "What the hell does that mean?"

Might as well give her all of it. "Mating is for life. Sex, a good bite, a marking, and aye . . . immortality for your sister. Her chromosomal pairs will increase, which means only beheading or perhaps completely burning will kill her." Adam smiled. "Good news, right?"

Victoria paled. "That's impossible."

He didn't correct her, just waited until she ran the facts through her head. There wasn't time to gently ease her into the knowledge. After seeing witches throw fire, she'd believe soon enough. "Human females, ones who are enhanced, can be mated to immortals. To witches."

"Enhanced?" she asked, her brow furrowing.

"Yes. Psychic, empathic, telekinetic . . . you name it." He studied her. "You're enhanced—I can feel the vibrations." Aye. She could mate an immortal. His breath tried to speed up, and he forced his lungs to behave properly.

"I-I'm not psychic. Or any of those things." She paled.

He shrugged. "You're somehow enhanced. Sometimes empaths don't even realize their gifts. I think your sister is empathic."

Victoria shook her head, looking bewildered. "Why didn't she tell me about witches and this whole mating thing?"

"Treason," he said simply.

"Then I guess I'll deal with my sister later." Victoria looked at him then, her eyes focused, intelligence shining in them. For several seconds, she just studied him. Then she took another deep drink. "Why don't you like me?"

He paused. What kind of a question was that? "I do like you."

"No, you don't." She swirled the alcohol around in the glass. "You're bossy and impatient, and you always look at me like I'm annoying you. Why?"

He sighed and sat back, forcing his body to relax. "I do like you, Victoria. Entirely too much." He appreciated that she didn't ask for an explanation. A stunner like her probably didn't need one. More soldiers came into view on the screens, and he sighed. "Looks like we'll be spending the night here."

Chapter 3

Tori brushed out her wet hair, letting the mass drop to her shoulders. After a very warm shower, a much-needed one, she'd found a pair of running shorts and a tank top in a drawer. They'd do while her clothing dried. The small bathroom sat off a cozy bedroom complete with a queen-size bed. She tried to ignore the red satin bedspread and plump pillows. The place really did feel like a whorehouse from the fifties.

It was one thing to stare at Adam Dunne across a room. Quite another to share a bed with his hard body.

She shook her head and maneuvered past the bedroom into the main room.

Adam overwhelmed one of the two small settees, his boots up on the table, his gaze on the multiple screens. His short hair had dried, but wet patches marred his jeans. He'd hung his T-shirt over one of the two kitchen chairs.

Her mouth went dry—partly in shock as she had time to truly look at him. As she'd noted before, his chest was even better than his bare back. Oh, she'd expected the width of his torso and the chiseled muscles, even the bronzed skin that covered his ripped abs. What caught the breath in her throat was the tattoo, the one inked over his left pec that wound down his rib cage: a series of jagged, sharp swords, all seeming to dance together in what felt like a warning. Words, maybe Gaelic ones, flowed along the design.

Adam Dunne had two tattoos. She would've bet her entire savings account, all fifty dollars of it, that he wouldn't have any tats.

Her borrowed panties dampened. Who was this guy? She faltered and then straightened her shoulders. "The shower is all yours."

"Thank you." Even half-naked, he epitomized class and style, his voice cultured and smooth.

He took a sip of his drink, his dark gaze wandering over her outfit.

She fought the urge to fidget. "These were all the clothes I could find." Darn it. She didn't need to explain anything to him. Why he made her feel like a kid from the wrong side of town, she didn't know. Well, maybe she did. Compared to him, she *was* a kid from the bad end of town. She'd even downed the expensive whiskey like it had been Mad Dog 20/20.

"I just returned to the country this morning, or I would've made sure you had clothing," he said, his gaze thoughtful. "I searched the cupboards, and there's nothing to eat here. If you're truly hungry, I can slip out and secure supper."

The word *hungry* shot unwelcome thoughts of his body against hers through her brain. Man, she needed a nap. She shook her head. "I'm fine. Managed to eat before the last kidnapping attempt."

His cheek creased. "That's good. The Guard is searching every corner, and I'd rather not have to hurt any of them. They're just doing their jobs."

She couldn't help it. "What do the words on your chest say?" It was none of her business, but something in her craved to know.

He didn't look down at the ink. "Family, Fate, and Forever." He tipped back his glass and finished the amber-colored liquid, his jaw visibly tightening. "It's a mantra."

"It's beautiful," she whispered, unwillingly touched by the simple vow.

"Thank you."

She faltered. "You're kind of an all-in or all-out type of guy. Right?"

Now amusement fully tilted his lips, and he stretched to his feet. Even so, tension radiated from him. "I guess you could say that."

What would it be like to have a guy like him, smart and powerful, be totally into her? She shook her head. Impossible, that was what. "Why the Celtic swords all around Family, Fate, and Forever?" The design was stunning, but the choice of deadly and wicked swords had to have been deliberate.

He moved toward her, all grace. "Because weapons are required to protect all three." He reached her, his scent washing over her and weakening her knees.

She cleared her throat. "What's that cologne you wear?"

He brushed a wet tendril of hair off her forehead, his touch gentle yet sizzling. "I'm not wearing any." He towered over her without even trying. "You look about eighteen years old without all the purple makeup."

Her war face? Man, she'd kill to have her face done up right now. Armor to confront him was a necessity. "I'm twenty-eight, Adam," she said, crossing her arms.

"'Twasn't an insult. You're beautiful, Victoria." His thumb traced her cheekbone as if he couldn't help himself.

Her gaze slashed up to him. "Would you care to explain why you're touching me?" She tried to sound authoritative.

He paused and straightened, his hand dropping. "I, ah, don't know." His gaze darkened. "I apologize."

Yeah. That sounded right. Most people in her life would've muttered *sorry*. Not a classy *I apologize*. She drew on strength and met his gaze. "What about the CE9 tattoo? What does that mean?"

"I'm an Enforcer for the Coven Nine," he said, his voice low and rough.

She shivered. "How old are you, anyway?"

"Over four centuries." He moved into the bedroom.

Her knees wobbled. She let out the breath she'd been holding. He'd lived for so long. What did his scent remind her of? She used to go camping in the mountains by the river with a bunch of friends, often during the fall. His scent was like the air in a forest right before a raging storm broke. Was there a name for that smell? If so, he probably knew it. He most likely knew all the words out there. Her two years of community college, where she'd studied music, probably didn't come close to his education. Of course, if she had four centuries to study, she might go for a couple more years. Or maybe not.

School hadn't been her thing.

She rubbed her still-tingling face. Why *had* he touched her? More important, why did her entire body feel electrified? She had to get herself under control before she looked like a complete idiot. Plus, she had a job to do, one that definitely would piss Adam right off— as the very best scenario. At the worst . . . he'd want her dead.

She had a feeling that if Adam wanted somebody dead, they ended up underground.

Clearing her throat, she hustled into the kitchen and took another quick shot of the expensive whiskey. The potent brew exploded in her stomach, spiraling out, heating every nerve. Okay. Maybe not the best plan for dealing with her attraction to the witch. She poured another glass and wandered into the living room, studying the screens.

She had to get to a phone. This place was so well set up, there had to be a phone somewhere. She scrambled through the cupboards inset beneath the screens. Computer towers and a bunch of electronics were in the first. The second held guns. She felt one, tugging it free. Green and rather heavy. She didn't have anywhere to put it, so she placed it back in the cupboard. She could get to it easily if needed.

The third cupboard held a box of phones. She knew it. Taking one out, she studied it. No brand name . . . and a larger screen than she'd seen before. It figured the witches would have advanced technology, right? Where was the on button? She twirled the black device in her hand, running her finger along the side. Nothing. Squinting, she held it to the light.

Come on, damn it.

She pressed along the screen, and it lit up, bright blue and glowing. A series of squiggly lines took form right before a keypad came up. Relief rushed through her.

"Put the phone down, Victoria."

She gasped and looked up. Adam stood in the bedroom doorway wearing nothing but a pair of black shorts, his hair wet, irritation sizzling in his eyes. The swords danced across his torso as he moved.

"Um, no." She straightened up, clutching the phone. "There are people I need to check in with."

One of his dark eyebrows lifted. "Your sister knows where you are, and she has reassured Junie, who's still on her cruise."

"Jennie," Tori corrected automatically.

"Huh?" he asked.

She cleared her throat. "Our mom's name is Jennie Juniper, or Jennie Junie. Some people call her Junie, but her name is really Jennie."

"Oh." He frowned. "My dossier on her said Junie. Interesting."

"She goes by both," Tori said, wondering why the hell they

weren't fighting about the phone. This was just weird. "I have other people to call besides my family."

He shook his head. "No phone calls out right now. Sorry."

The man didn't sound sorry. She held the phone, not sure what to do. Oh, she had to call in to the DEA, but she couldn't let him hear the conversation anyway. "Fine." At least she knew how to find a phone. She put it back into the box and shut the door. "Happy now?"

His head lifted just enough to look threatening. "Yes. We need to get a few hours of sleep before moving tomorrow. You can take the bed."

She glanced at the settees. "You won't fit on either of those."

"I barely fit in the bed." He sighed. "I'll sleep well enough. Don't worry."

His high-handed manner annoyed the crap out of her. Oh, it probably wasn't proper for them to share a bed, since they weren't married. Or mated. But if they were going to outrun the bad guys tomorrow, she needed Adam at full speed. "We can share the bed."

A light flared into his eyes. One that sent tingles through her abdomen. "I don't think so."

Her temper ignited. She wasn't some dumb mutt trying to get laid by a purebred, for Pete's sake. There was no doubt they came from different worlds, and she wasn't even considering the difference in species. "I'm not propositioning you, dumbass."

His chin lifted now. "Name calling?" he murmured softly. Way too softly.

Her breath hitched. "Yes. You're a prissy snob from Fifth Avenue, and I just want you in fighting shape, believe me. Other than that, I don't want anything to do with you."

He moved fast.

She found her arms restrained and her butt against the wall. Her ass had already hit before she could even get out a shocked breath. "Wh-what are you doing?"

He leaned into her face, tension sizzling along his hard jaw. His strength in holding her only matched his speed in grabbing her. "Lying is not nice."

"I'm not lying," she spat. "Not at all. Apparently you have a colossal ego, classy boy. But let me tell you, I don't want you. Not even in the slightest."

His face lowered until his nose nearly touched hers.

All the air left her lungs. Heat washed over her, through her. If she moved forward millimeters, her mouth would be on his. What would his kiss taste like? She couldn't even imagine.

He breathed her in. "See, that's the problem, Victoria."

She blinked. "Problem?" she whispered, her focus captured more solidly than ever before.

"Aye." His gaze dropped to her lips. "Because . . . I do want you."

Chapter 4

Adam finished surveying the wall screens, a kink in his neck, and a low-grade headache pulsing against his temples. Morning light cascaded through the alleyways, and most of the Guard had disappeared from the neighborhood. They'd lost him, and they knew it. He wondered if any of them suspected his identity. Even if they did, they had no proof—not at this point, anyway.

He turned and glared at the settee where he'd slept a short while after sending Victoria to bed. He'd rested sitting up, his boots on the table, his chin on his chest.

Her kindness in offering him the bed warmed him, but unlike Victoria, he could be brutally honest with himself. If they shared a bed, he'd have her naked within minutes. The attraction, although crazy, was definitely there. For both of them. The woman didn't hide her interest or arousal in the slightest.

She was exactly wrong for him, and he knew it. Young and wild . . . definitely undisciplined and carefree.

While those traits should turn him off, *way* off, they drew him like never before. Which was exactly why he had to keep a distance between them. That, and the fact that her older sister was pretty much his new sister-in-law. If he started something up, it would have to end at some point, and that would cause family problems. He wouldn't allow family problems.

Someday he'd find his mate, and then he wouldn't have to deal with attractions like this. Not that he'd had one like this in, well, ever. Even so, his mate would be immortal already; experienced and strong. He wouldn't go through the agony his brother Kell did every day, being mated to a fragile human. Oh, a mated human gained immortality, but no extra strength or speed . . . and immortality wasn't absolute. A good beheading killed an immortal, as did a burning.

So he needed to keep his distance from Victoria.

Good talk. His mind cleared, he started switching off the screens.

"Are we safe to go?" Victoria asked from the doorway.

He turned, surprised to see her in the athletic outfit still. Then he remembered. He'd torn her pants from her. All the blood in his head rushed to his cock. Damn it. "Yes. Now is a good time to go. I'll, ah, have clothes waiting for you at the airport." He already had the transport arranged.

She smiled sweetly. "Thank you."

Awareness crawled up his back. He narrowed his focus. Sweetly? Oh, hell no. "What are you up to?" he rumbled.

Her stunning blue eyes widened. With her purple-streaked blond hair tumbling around her shoulders, she looked like a wild child on the way to a concert. "Nothing. Why?"

His patience frayed. "I don't have time for games, Victoria. Whatever you're planning, stop. Now." He crossed his arms.

She rolled her pretty eyes. "You're paranoid." One purple nail tapped against her lips. "I guess at your age, I mean, after so long on earth, paranoia probably sets in, right?" Her voice couldn't be any softer.

He eyed the purple nail, wanting his mouth on those lips. "You'd do well not to cross me."

"Cross you?" Her eyebrows rose, laughter in her eyes. "How old-fashioned. Cross you." She chuckled, the sound low and throaty.

Oh, the hellion was asking for it. "Victoria." He allowed his voice to deepen to a threat most animals instinctively would catch. "I already spanked you once. Do you want another for good measure?" He hated threatening her, but there wasn't time for this nonsense.

She lost her smile. Her head tilted to the side. "Well now, I'm not sure. Do you know how to properly spank a woman?"

His mouth dropped open. What the holy hell? "Excuse me?"

She smiled again, flashing her teeth. "I love a good spanking as much as the next woman, but only from somebody who knows what he's doing, you know? Relieves the tension." Her gaze swept him, head to toe. "You're kind of uptight and probably way too rigid. So

I guess I'll have to pass. It's kind of you to offer, though." She clasped her hands together.

"Oh baby," he murmured, truly enjoying the challenge she'd hurled. Victoria Monzelle was one of a kind, without question. She met his gaze, amusement and a glittering triumph in her eyes. He smiled, wishing they had all day to explore just how *rigid* he could be. But the second he put his hands on her, it was over. He knew it. By the curve of her mouth, she knew it, too. For some reason, she wanted to goad him. She'd misread him if she thought he'd back down. "You really do like playing with fire, don't you?" The irony, considering he could create fire, only amused him more.

"I truly do." She moved his way, no fear anywhere in her. "But we both know you're all talk, don't we?"

"The second I stop talking, we're both in trouble," he said honestly. "Yet trouble is something you seek."

She moved into his space, and the scent of wild orchids, the kind growing abundantly around his childhood home, washed over him. "I love trouble."

Aye. He got that. What he didn't understand was why he was fair game all of a sudden. Did she truly think he had that strong a grip on his control? The idea was a bit flattering and immensely disconcerting. A part of him, one he didn't much like, wanted to forget the control and teach her a lesson. Yet that was exactly what she wanted, now wasn't it? The very second he lost control, she gained it.

And she knew it.

"Off screens," he ordered, keeping her gaze. The computers, unlike the woman, obeyed him instantly. "The second we leave here, you stay on my six. If I tell you to move, you do it. Got that?"

Her smile was cheeky. "Of course."

His chin lifted. The animal inside him, the one he kept tightly tethered, stretched awake. He was a Coven Nine Enforcer, a primal male, and turning away from a challenge didn't sit well. He'd been as noble as he could be, and he was done. Finished. "All right, Victoria. Here it is."

Her head tilted. "Here what is?"

"The truth." He slid his hands casually into his jeans to keep from grabbing her and taking her down. "You've played little domination games? A fun slap and tickle once in a while?"

A light pink tinged her cheeks, and her chin firmed with pure stubbornness. "Who hasn't?" she asked flippantly.

Yeah. That's what he'd thought. "You like games. I get it. Games are fun."

Her smile wavered.

"But I don't play games." He leaned in, gratified when her breath caught. "If I dominate you . . . you will submit. Not out of fun or play. Truly submit."

Her pupils dilated.

He didn't release her gaze, noting she hadn't twitched a muscle. "I bet you never have, have you?"

She blinked.

"That's what I thought." He let his fangs show. "You challenge me again, and I'll meet it. I won't stop until you're begging."

A rosy flush wound down her neck. Her nostrils flared just enough to prove her interest. "Begging for what?"

He retracted the fangs. Did that flush reach her full breasts? "For whatever I want you to beg for."

Defiance played across her face.

He shook his head. "You have a plane to catch. Do you want to go home, or do you want to challenge me again? Right now and right here." He jerked his head toward the bedroom, allowing no expression on his face. His body heated. His cock pounded. "If we stay, we're staying for quite some time." His lungs compressed like he was standing on a cliff, ready to dive. "Home or bed, Victoria? Your choice." He meant every damn word.

Her gaze flickered to where the door should be and then back to him. Indecision and frustration all but rolled off her. Along with need. She swallowed. "Home."

He nodded, disappointment flashing through him with relief on its heels. "Wise choice."

Victoria leaned against the metal wall of the hangar after having changed into jeans and a soft blue sweater. Once they left the safe house, Adam had her in a car and at the private airport within half an hour. The drive had been made in silence. Her mind still spun, and her body continued to riot. She couldn't grab a thought. Worse yet, Adam Dunne had made her back down.

Nobody in her entire life had made her back down.

She watched him from beneath her lashes as he finished speaking to the pilot of a small airplane. The pilot was a thirty-something guy with a crew cut and pressed clothes, and next to Adam he faded into nothingness. It was futile to explain to either of them that no way in hell was she flying anywhere. So she waited for her chance.

Adam, still in his worn jeans and wrinkled T-shirt, somehow looked more put together than Tori ever would. He nodded at the pilot and jogged around the plane, taking inventory of the machine. He ran his hand along the nearest wing, and she fought a moan.

If she had met his challenge, she would've had that hand on her. Her nipples pebbled, and her abdomen heated.

She'd enjoyed goading him, sure he wouldn't follow through. She'd been wrong.

He looked up, his dark gaze catching her. She swallowed. Why the hell she always felt like a naughty kid caught in the principal's office around him she'd never understand. Which was why she'd tried to take him down. She'd mistakenly thought she could mess with him, embarrass him, and stop feeling like that.

Again. Wrong.

He straightened and moved toward her, his steps graceful and smooth. As a child on a field trip, she'd seen a jaguar in a zoo, and it had moved the same way, as if casual was just temporary until it decided when and how to pounce.

Adam reached her. "I have a meeting across town and need to go to avoid an internal witch war. The pilot is finishing up the paperwork, and then he'll fly you to Paris. You'll catch another private plane there to Miami, and from there, to Seattle. Kellach and your sister will be waiting in Seattle to get you underground." He rubbed a hand through his short hair. "I expect you to cooperate all the way home, Victoria."

Wasn't he a bossy pants all of a sudden? Give the guy one good victory and he thought he had her. A girl had to have some pride, and she really didn't like the rein of control he'd drawn tight since they'd left the safe house. Time to play with fire again. It was safe in the small hangar. She leaned up into his face, her lips hovering less than an inch from his. "I understand, oh dominant one."

His eyes glittered. Warning gleamed, hot and bright. "I don't think you do." His brogue rolled out with the words.

Oh, man. She couldn't help it. Her lips tickled into a small smile, and she flattened both hands across his wide chest. Raw power shifted beneath her palms. At the first touch, her knees went weak. He just felt so damn *good*. She went up on her tiptoes and pressed her mouth against his. "Thank you for rescuing me yesterday," she whispered, teasing them both.

His lids half lowered.

The devil had her. That had to be it, because she slowly sank her teeth into Adam's bottom lip. She just couldn't help herself.

The muscles in his chest contracted and swelled, vibrating against her. He growled, and the sound dug deep into her abdomen. She blinked, reality brightening the day. What in the hell had she just done? She dropped to her feet and yanked her hands away as if burned. Had she been? She wasn't sure. "Um."

"Um what?" he asked, his voice darker than chocolate and rougher than rock salt.

"Oh." God. *Get out of there. Run. Retreat. Drop dead in a faint.* But her knees wouldn't move. "So. Well. Bye." She moved to go past him.

He moved with her, blocking her way.

She stopped breathing, her gaze lifting to his.

Hunger. Raw and feral, it glowed in those dark eyes. Her legs stopped. She tried to hitch around his other side. He easily moved with her in an odd dance that she definitely was not leading. She took a step back. He matched her step. Mad. That should make her mad. She dug deep for some anger, but only awareness filtered through her, setting her nerves on fire. "I should go," she whispered.

"Think so?" he asked silkily.

She winced.

"I warned you, Victoria," he rumbled.

Yeah, he had. She shook her head. "No committing battery here in public. Sorry, buddy." Her butt clenched.

His low chuckle echoed against her, surrounding her with the sense of male. "You think I need my hand on your ass to get submission? That's my least favorite way, baby."

Oh man. Way out of her depth. Why couldn't she breathe? Her damn lungs weren't working. So she lifted her head, forcing bravado. "Eh. Gotta go. Sorry." Did she wheeze that sentence? Hell. She had wheezed. Wheezing wasn't tough. No. A brogue was tough. Yeah. She needed a brogue like he had.

He moved into her, not fast, not slow, just deliberately.

She tried to back up, but the metal side of the building stopped her. "Adam."

"Aye." One knuckle lifted her chin.

Her legs trembled.

He leaned down and pressed his heated mouth against hers. His hand speared through her hair, holding her in place, and he kissed her. Liquid heat poured from him to her, swirling and catching her on fire. He didn't touch her anywhere else, keeping her captive with his mouth, with his tongue. He took everything she had, and she wanted to give him more. Gladly.

He was gentle and firm, fire and lava. All male, all-consuming. It was seduction in the smoothest sense, and he used not one ounce of his superior strength to subdue her. His kiss, alone, did that.

She may have whimpered in denial when he released her.

He gazed deep into her eyes. "There it is." Releasing her hair, he ducked and tossed her over his shoulder.

The world spun, and she still couldn't speak. Couldn't even think. Within seconds, he deposited her inside the plane. Turning her gently, he patted her on the ass until she continued inside. "Have a nice trip, Victoria." Whistling, he turned to go.

She blinked and all but fell into a leather seat. What the hell had just happened? Her mind cleared, and fury swirled through. Oh, she'd kill him. Leaning toward the nearest window, she saw him stretch into his car and drive away from the airport.

The pilot jogged up the stairs, a smile on his broad face. "Are you ready to go?"

"Only if you want to die." Her survival instincts kicked in. Finally. She stood and moved to leave the plane.

He grasped her arm. "My orders are clear."

She nodded, turned, and kneed him hard in the balls. He cried out and dropped to one knee, falling forward on the carpet. "You'll thank me later," she muttered, running down the steps and toward the parking lot. She had probably five minutes until the guy called Adam. Time to move.

Chapter 5

Wrong side of the road, damn it. Tori ignored the blaring horn and jerked the steering wheel to the left. Why did they drive on the left here? She gulped. Okay. No wrecks. She couldn't get pulled over, either. What was the penalty for hot-wiring and stealing a car in Ireland? Her brow creased. Probably jail in one of their castle dungeons somewhere.

So far, her odd curse hadn't caused the engine to turn off. That was good. Rare, but not unheard of. Sometimes a car worked all day for her.

The drive took almost thirty minutes, but she reached Dublin and abandoned the stolen car near a park. There were tons of parks in Dublin, so it seemed like a good place to leave a car so it'd be found eventually. Who the heck knew?

A light rain started to fall, dotting her sweater. She ducked her head and hustled around a wrought-iron fence, moving into a small store. She paid for a green knit cap with money she'd found in the stolen car. Man, she was messing all over with Karma today. Tucking her hair up, she grabbed a pair of wire-rimmed glasses and perched them on her face on the way out.

Okay. Just a phone place. That's all she needed.

She wandered the busy streets of central Dublin, crossing several times to avoid construction. Apparently, they were putting in a new public transport system. For now, she used the barricades and walls to her advantage. Finally, she came across a small electronics store. Dodging inside, she made her way to the back. "I need a temporary phone with minutes," she told the proprietor, an elderly man with grizzly white hair and multiple age spots across his weathered face.

He reached for a box and shoved it toward her. "Take your pick."

She grabbed one still in the plastic that had two hours and handed over the rest of her money. Giving him a nod, she ripped it open and left the plastic on the counter before hurrying back into the rain. Keeping her head down, she plowed through crowds toward a series of alleys, trying to stay away from any cameras. Finally, she leaned against the ancient rock of a building, her gaze on a deserted park on the other side. She rapidly punched in numbers.

"Agent Franks," came a low female voice.

"Franks. It's Victoria Monzelle." She clutched the phone to her ear, her fingers going numb.

Franks was silent for a moment. "Where the fuck have you been?" she snapped. "I'm one day from putting a BOLO out on you."

Yeah, right. Like the agent cared about her safety. "Yet you didn't," she snapped right back. "I'm in trouble."

"You've been in trouble for months," Franks returned. "I'll send a car to get you."

Tori rubbed rain off her face. "That might be a problem. I'm in Dublin."

"Bullshit. You have an hour to get your ass in here or I'm going to pull the plug. On everything. Say good-bye to your sister." Rustling paper came over the line.

Nausea slammed into Tori's stomach. "I'm not joking, you twit. It's a long story, but I'm in Dublin, and you have to get me out of here. Preferably by boat. There are cruises that leave Dublin, right?" It'd take time, but it was the safest way for her to go.

Pounding boot steps filled the day. Oh God.

"Monzelle? Stop fucking with me," Franks bellowed.

Movement showed around the corner. A shadow. "I have to go," she whispered. "I'll call back as soon as I can. Find a boat for me." She clicked off and threw the phone on top of the roof, turning to run. More rain slapped down and she hustled, winding crazily through alleys until finally coming out to a busy street. She looked frantically for a bus to jump onto.

A gloved hand wrapped around her arm. She partially turned to see a man in black combat gear, his face carefully blank. Shit. She opened her mouth to scream, and he plunged something into her arm.

Then . . . she couldn't move. He picked her up as if she were fainting and walked easily toward a car waiting at the curb. Her eyes were open, but her mouth stayed shut. She couldn't move her hands. What the hell had he given her? Terror filled her. He sat in the rear of the black vehicle, holding her on his lap, looking straight ahead. As they left the city, he moved slightly, and a blindfold dropped over her head. She tried to scream, but only a mewling came out.

"You're safe for now," he said, his brogue deep. "The location of our headquarters is confidential. That's the only reason you're blind-folded."

So he didn't want to hurt her. For now. Yeah. She'd caught that. Her eyelids fluttered shut. Good. She breathed deep, trying to shove whatever drug he'd given her right out of her system. Soon her fingers began to tingle. Then her toes and legs. Then her arms started to move. The car stopped, and the man lifted her out of the vehicle, carrying her through the rain and inside an extremely quiet building. A few more twists and turns, and he set her down on what felt like a soft sofa. He removed the blindfold and quickly exited the room.

Fifteen minutes later, she stumbled to her feet, shaking out her arms. "Thank God." She said the words out loud, just to make sure she could speak. The drug wore off quickly, at least.

She moved forward and patted down the plain stone wall that had been a doorway a few minutes ago. Nothing. No grooves, no dents, no rough patches. Smooth rock. The damn kidnappers had found her again.

How?

She turned and viewed the cell, if the opulent room could be called a cell. A purple velvet divan took up one entire wall, complete with brocade pillows. It was a divan and not a couch. Wealthy people called them divans. An oil painting, stunning in its vibrant colors of a sunset over a stormy ocean, hung above the furniture. She squinted and moved to read the signature. Brenna Dunne.

She liked Brenna, who was Simone's cousin.

A bathroom, complete with marble and gold accents, lay at the other end of the room that no longer had a door.

Tori had to get out of there. Could she use her odd gift against fake walls? She pushed against the wall. Nothing. Taking several deep breaths, she centered herself and rubbed her hands together

quickly until her skin hurt. Then she placed her hands on the wall
again.

The rock rumbled, a crack appeared, and then it began to open. It
stopped when there was only an inch-wide opening.

Awesome.

She rubbed her hands together again. While she'd never understood her weird problem with machinery, apparently she could affect
the door.

It slid wide open on its own, and she dropped into a fighting
stance before she could stop herself.

Brenna Dunne-Kayrs stood on the other side, her head tilting.
"You okay?"

"No." Tori stood and pretended to fumble a bit as she did so. It
wouldn't do for anybody to know that she'd received a little training,
now would it? "You people have kidnapped me again." Brenna was
Simone's cousin and yet another witch. Hopefully Tori's friendship
with Simone would extend to Brenna. She needed a friend in this
place. "Where's Adam?"

Brenna sighed and swept inside the cell, her clothes perfectly
enhancing her gray eyes and brunette hair. Her belly protruded
slightly, showing an early pregnancy. "He's out looking for you, and
I just texted him that you're here."

"Where is *here*?" Tori spat.

Brenna winced. A hulking guy leaning against a far wall pushed
away from the stone. He had light brown eyes and hair, and a scar
on his face. Tall and broad, dressed all in black, the guy looked like
pure danger. "Should we get going?"

Brenna nodded. "That's Jase, who's my mate. He's a vampire."

A real vampire. He looked like he could deliver death if the mood
so struck him.

"What's the plan here?" Tori bit out.

"You know about immortals, and that puts a bull's-eye on your
head." Brenna's eyes swirled with fear. "We need to face the Council,
our ruling body, and you have to promise not to tell anybody."

Tori's mind reeled. "Like anybody would believe me anyway."

"True, but you're in danger, so take this seriously." Tension lines
creased the edge of Brenna's full mouth. She ushered Tori out the
door and down a long hallway, where the vampire waited.

Tori cleared her throat. "What's the Council?"

"Council of the Coven Nine, which leads the witch nation," Brenna whispered. "I'm a member, but because of my ties to Simone I've been relieved of duties, as she faces treason charges. Or rather, the conviction." Brenna reached another blank wall, tapped in the middle of nothing, and the rock slid open.

"What the heck is up with all the invisible rock doors?" Tori muttered.

"Amen, sister," the vampire said from behind her, his voice hoarse in a totally inappropriate and too-sexy way.

A cold breeze swept through the hallway. Tori shivered. Another wall, another doorway, and she entered what could only be called chambers that looked like a modern courtroom, save for the stone everywhere. "Where's Harry Potter?" she murmured.

The vampire burst out laughing behind her.

Brenna elbowed her. "Try to take this seriously. These people have the power to cut off your head and will do so without losing a second of sleep."

The humor had been an attempt to keep Tori from screaming in a total panic attack. Gut instinct told her this was deadly serious, but she couldn't just drop to her knees and freak out, now could she? She'd been so damn close to escaping them earlier, she'd surely get another chance soon. So she took her place behind a stone table.

"I'll be up over to the side just to watch the proceedings." Brenna sounded rather peeved as she nodded to the stone bench. The room was kind of similar to the chambers of the Supreme Court of the United States, which Tori had seen on a tour a year or so previous.

Tori nodded.

Brenna glided across the room and up some steps to sit in a chair over to the side. Another freakin' invisible door opened, and three people walked in and seated themselves on the dais like judges in a courtroom. Two men and one woman.

"Why are there six empty seats, um, Mr. Vampire?" Tori whispered to the guy remaining at her side.

"Call me Jase." He stood next to her, big and dangerous, and she was very glad he seemed to be on her side. "This is all that's left of the Council right now."

She'd heard that before, but it seemed more ominous now. "I'm an American citizen, and my country won't like this."

"Aye." Brenna gave her a look. The one that said *Shut the fuck up, you're in enough trouble*. Tori had seen it her entire life and could read that one easily. So she gave a look back that said *You are so going to explain everything after this if I don't die*.

Brenna nodded, in perfect sync.

The judge in the middle, a guy handsome in a too-smooth way, banged down a gavel. "I'm Peter Gallagher, and we seem to have a problem with your knowing about our people, Miss Monzelle."

Jase angled his body in a subtle way that somehow put Tori a little bit behind him. "I vouch for her honor and that she won't speak a word. In addition, her sister is mated to an Enforcer, which makes her family."

Peter's eyes flashed dark and deep. "I don't appreciate a vampire being her representation here. It's as if the vampire nation is taking a stance in a matter that does not concern it, especially since some think we're now at war."

"Yeppers." Jase settled his stance.

Tori fought an incredibly inopportune giggle. The vampire had said *yeppers*. It was nice to be with another total smart-ass. A good guy, that vampire.

Another man with slicked-back dark hair and intelligent eyes came in from the side wall, holding a stack of papers. "Sorry to be late. We have an issue with the bear nation, as you can imagine." He read through the file, looking just like a human prosecutor. "The human knows too much, and I've prepared the proper confidentiality papers for her to sign."

Not a problem. Tori smiled at him.

Peter cleared his throat. "We're under attack and most likely going to war. Papers won't do it. We must eliminate all threats right now."

Jase jerked next to her.

Tori reared back. The guy was so matter-of-fact about killing her. "I object."

Peter's lips tightened into a white line. "This isn't a US courtroom. No objections."

Tori slammed her hands on her hips. "I disagree. If everyone wants to eliminate me, I definitely object."

Jase coughed. "I get that. Don't you all get that?"

She tried to find the exit.

Peter banged the gavel. "I don't think you two are taking this seriously enough. Miss Monzelle, we can't have you telling people about us."

Tori nodded. "I understand, but come on. Nobody would believe me, so you have nothing to worry about." She gestured around. "Plus, you're witches and are immortal. How scared could you be?"

"Very," Peter said. "Humans outnumber us by a ridiculous amount, and while we're more powerful, it would be a disaster if they came after us."

"Why not just get rid of humans?" Tori asked, her curiosity taking over.

"Vampires are male only, demons have few females, and immortal species often find mates within the human population," Peter answered.

Mates? Her mind flashed right to Adam, and her face heated. *Concentrate, damn it.* While she might be able to use her oddity to open one of the secret doors, there had to be guards with guns and fire on the other side. Her only allies were Jase and Brenna . . . and her enemies outnumbered them.

Adrenaline flowed through her. Her palms grew slick with sweat. These people could actually kill her, and nobody would ever know what had happened to her. Sure, her sister would search far and wide, but even she probably didn't know about this odd council chamber. "I promise I won't tell anybody about you."

The man who seemed to be a prosecutor cleared his throat. "I understand we're in difficult times, but it's not our way to put a human to death simply for knowing too much. These papers should suffice."

The lone woman on the council, a pretty one with dark hair, slowly nodded. "I concur. We don't just murder people."

The third guy simply watched the proceedings, his eyes almost bored.

Peter straightened his tie. "I'm sorry, but we're basically at war right now, with more enemies than we know." He gave Jase a hard glare. "Including the Realm, as well as the bear and dragon nations."

Bears and dragons were nations. Tori shook her head. She'd taken an acid trip once that wasn't this interesting. "I give you my word."

"Unfortunately, we can't take the risk," Peter said. "I'm recommending death."

Jase shook his head. "This is unprecedented. What's your game, Pete?"

There were way too many undercurrents going on. Tori tried to clear her mind. "You can't just put me to death."

The side door opened again, and Adam Dunne stalked into the room, raw fury across his rugged face. "There will be no death."

Tori nearly leaped into his arms. Thank God. Adam could handle anything. "Adam," she whispered.

He didn't spare her a glance. "This atrocity stops right damn now." He faced the Council, not one ounce of fear in his posture. In fact, he kind of looked like he was about to throw fire at the lot of them.

Peter reared up, his face turning a motley shade of red. "Adam Dunne, you are an Enforcer for the Coven Nine, currently our *only* Enforcer, and you will damn well behave like one."

Adam put his hands on his very fit hips. "I don't give one fuck what my job is. You will not kill this human. She's sister to my brother's mate, and thus she's protected."

Tori shuffled her feet. "They're all kind of inbred, aren't they?" she whispered to Jase.

He barked out another laugh.

Adam cut a hard look her way that instantly shot awareness through her. "Not another word."

Once again, she could see the predator beneath Adam's intelligence and arrogance. Crossing him was dangerous—she knew that firsthand. But still. "You people are crazy," she muttered, loud enough for just him to hear. A girl had her pride, after all.

He pinned her with a hard stare, apparently not giving one shit about anybody else in the room.

Heat climbed into her face, and her knees wobbled, but she didn't lower her gaze. Her eyes started to water, but she couldn't give in.

The gavel banged down, and Tori jumped, facing Peter.

Adam turned toward the Council. "I'll vouch for the human."

"Good," the female councilwoman said.

"No, Nessa." Peter shook his head. "Not good enough, I'm afraid."

Adam straightened his shoulders, looking even bigger than usual. "You are not serious."

Peter shrugged. "I am. At this difficult time, we need assurances, especially since you're the only Enforcer who isn't currently wanted for arrest by the Guard."

Tori opened her mouth to protest again, and Jase silenced her with a hand on her arm. "Shhh. This is just getting good," he mouthed.

She frowned.

Peter lifted an eyebrow. "I'm glad you think so, Prince Kayrs, because the former Enforcers should be taught they won't be given any leeway, nor will their family members. The human needs to be killed."

Brenna gasped and paled. "That's crazy. What is wrong with you, Peter?"

Jase caught his breath. And Adam Dunne, the silent, thoughtful one, growled low and hard.

The sound vibrated right through Tori to land hard in her abdomen. What in the world?

Adam was somehow at Tori's side without seeming to move. He manacled Tori's arm. "I'll mate the human."

Brenna stood, her pretty face flushed. "Adam. That's sweet of you, but you can't tie yourself to somebody because of blackmail." She nodded at Tori. "Same with Tori. Nobody should be forced into mating."

Tori tried to jerk free, with absolutely no success. "The human says no mating." Why was everybody actually using a world like *mating*? It wasn't like they were baboons, for goodness' sake.

"Then the human dies," Peter said gently.

Adam tugged Tori into his side. "I, Adam Dunne, Enforcer for the Council of the Coven Nine, give you my solemn vow I will mate this human and thus negate her threat."

"So be it." Peter crashed the gavel down. "You have twenty-four hours to mate, or you've committed treason—much like the rest of your family."

Tori shoved against Adam. "Oh, hell no."

Adam pivoted, ducked, and tossed her over his shoulder. Again. The position was actually becoming familiar, and that ticked her right off. The air blew out of her lungs, and she gasped. Without another word, he strode toward the wall, which of course opened.

Tori kicked hard, struggling. How in the world had her life ended up in chaos like this? "Put me down."

He didn't say a word and completely failed to comply.

They maneuvered through tunnels, and the air turned first chilly and then warmer. Finally, after moving through another wall, they ended up at the back of a stone building, where a motorcycle waited on the curb.

Adam flipped her over so she could stand.

She hissed and pressed both hands to her hips. "I am not mating you."

He straightened up and gave her another one of those hard looks. "I'm afraid you are, darlin'."

Chapter 6

Adam engaged in a small struggle with the hellion that ended with him forcibly plunking her ass on the motorcycle seat. The door to headquarters opened, and Brenna rushed out with Jase on her heels.

"Are you crazy?" Brenna snapped.

Aye. He was getting crazier by the minute. Adam ignored his furious cousin and focused on the quiet vampire behind her. "What's the Realm's position in regard to the Council right now?"

Jase's older brother was the king of the Realm, which was a coalition of vampires, demons, witches, and shifters. "We're mulling it over," Jase said, his eyes a dark copper. "If the witch nation withdraws from the Realm, they'll be fair game for every enemy you have lying in wait."

"We can't face another war so soon," Brenna murmured, smoothing her hands down her skirt.

"Agreed," Adam said. Sun glinted off the wet cobblestones, while clouds gathered above them. He had about an hour before rain struck again. "What's your plan, Kayrs?"

Jase scrubbed a hand through his thick hair. "We have a plane waiting to take us to the States."

Brenna turned a look on him. "The Council is fracturing, and I need to be here."

"No. You're nearly four months pregnant, and I want you safe." Jase's tone was gentle, but his expression impenetrable. "Peter Gallagher is taking great pains to restructure the Council without any of your family involved."

"I agree," Adam said, before Bren could reply. "This death threat to Victoria is bizarre."

"We don't know how far he'll go," Jase said.

"I know." Adam's shoulders stiffened. "He's trying to draw out my family. To bring my brothers out of safety."

Brenna nodded. "Probably."

"Okay." Adam breathed out. "We're all regrouping in the States, Bren. Together we'll figure out how to take out Gallagher as well as the people trying to kill us." He'd been away from the investigation into the deadly drug Apollo for too long. The key to the case was in Seattle, and he needed to get back to work. "We're stronger together as we form a plan. Besides, you're with child and need to remain safely under the radar." No way would he allow his pregnant cousin, one of the kindest women in the world, to remain here in danger.

"Stop being such an ass," the sweetheart snapped. "I don't need to be safe. I need to retake my damn place on the fucking Council."

Adam sighed. "Jase. She was so much more reasonable *before* she mated you."

Jase kneaded Bren's neck. "She's brilliant and reasonable. If anybody can think of a nonviolent way out of this mess, it's my Brenna."

Bren flushed a pretty pink. "Pooling our resources is a good idea. Adam's right—except for the part about me staying out of it. If most of our family and allies are in the States right now, we should plan from there." She turned and pressed a kiss to Jase's jaw. "But if I need to come back here to retake my seat, I will come back here."

Tori cleared her throat. "Sounds like you all have a lot going on. How about the little human here takes off and gets out of the way?" She moved to jump off the bike.

Adam stopped her with a hand on her thigh. The second he touched her, his body flared wide awake.

Brenna shook her head. "Tori, they're not messing around. You have to get out of Ireland before Peter talks the rest of the Council into killing you. He seems to be on some weird mission right now."

Adam nodded. "Agreed." He slid onto the bike in front of Victoria. "We'll see you in the States."

Brenna's eyes widened. "Why don't you catch the plane with us?"

"No. Too many of us in one plane—too tempting to take out," Adam countered, strategizing the next week in his mind. "Plus, Victoria and I need to have a little discussion." If he had to guess, it wasn't going to be a quiet one.

Brenna looked from Victoria to him. "You can't seriously be planning to mate just because the Council ordered you to."

That might be the only choice for either of them. Oh, he'd try to find a way out of the mess, but so far, his hands were tied.

"We could take out the three council members," Jase said quietly.

Adam met his gaze evenly. The idea went against everything he was inside, everything he'd vowed to give his life to protect. Fate only knew what kind of strife and fury that would create in the witch nation. Not to mention fear. He started the bike, gratified when the engine roared to life. "I'll be in touch." Forcing a smile to combat Brenna's worried gaze, he turned the bike and sped out of the parking area.

Victoria wrapped her arms around his waist and settled her face against the back of his shirt. Trusting little thing when he gave her no choice, now wasn't she?

He could almost hear her turmoil-filled thoughts. So he opened the throttle and let the beast go. The second her worry turned to enjoyment, he smiled. Figured she'd like it fast and dangerous.

The cobblestones tried to grab the tires, but he drove evenly, allowing the world to flash by. The first hiccup came in the form of a rapid decrease in speed. Then increase. Then decrease. "What the hell?" he muttered.

Victoria shook her head against him.

The bike slowly petered out and then stopped. Trees lined one side of the road, while the river lined the other. He jumped off and crouched down, holding the bike with one hand.

Victoria gingerly slid from the seat. Her hair was a wild mass around her pretty pink face, and her eyes sparkled the deep blue of the center of the ocean.

His groin hardened.

She swallowed. "The bike won't start."

What was wrong with his bikes lately? He reached for a cell phone in his back pocket. "I'll have somebody come get us and take us to the airport."

She paled. "I can't fly. Can't be anywhere near a death contraption in the sky."

Oh, the sweetheart. She was afraid of flying. He stood and secured the bike. "Our pilots are the best, and the planes very safe. I won't let anything happen to you."

She fisted her hands. "Adam. You are not listening to me—I just said that I *can't* fly."

He paused and focused, his phone silent in his hand. Her eyes blazed, and her shoulders had gone rock hard. "Okay. Talk."

She gestured toward the bike. "Dead bike. Again."

He frowned and studied his perfectly maintained motorcycle. Interesting. "True. Go on."

She huffed out a breath. "There's something wrong with me." Both hands scrubbed through her curly hair. "I can't explain it. Anything with a motor or electricity . . . I can make it go dead. Not on purpose. Even the automatic doors at a grocery store. Half the time, they won't open for me." Her eyes widened, the look a little wild. "And cash registers. Geez. Many times, they stop working when I get near."

He gaped at her. Fascinating. "So, your enhancement as a human is . . . what? You affect machinery?"

She shrugged. "I don't know. It's weird, but I've gotten used to it. Sometimes a car will stop. Not all the time, but I can't control when or how. I try to stay away from engines, but sometimes that's not possible. No way am I getting on an airplane. No way."

He wanted to banish the fear crossing her stunning face. "You flew to get here."

"I know," she breathed, shaking her head. "They kidnapped me, and I was unconscious the whole way here. Maybe that helped? I'm not sure."

Fury slashed through him that somebody had knocked her out. "Who hurt you?"

She took a step back. "I have no clue."

Oh, he'd find out, and that bastard would bleed. "Okay." He rapidly clicked thoughts into place. "Can you affect machinery on purpose?"

"I've tried," she admitted, kicking a pebble. "Sometimes I can, but often not so much." She wrinkled her nose. "It's weird, right?"

"No," he said. "Not really. I mean, waves are all around us. Light waves, sound waves, thought waves, microwaves . . . your waves just mess with machinery. There's plenty of logic to it."

She blinked. A slow smile lifted her lips. "Logic? Me?"

He coughed. "Good point." Then he grinned. Man, she was cute.

"So." She hunched her shoulders just as a light rain began to fall. "Do you have a boat?"

"Better." He quickly dialed a number and pressed the phone to his ear. "Much better."

"Kayrs," came a low voice.

Adam smiled. "King? I need a favor."

Tori wiped rain off her cheeks, her heart thrumming. She'd confessed her oddity to Adam, and he hadn't blinked. In fact, he'd figured it out. Maybe. Who knew? She watched him on the phone with somebody named King.

"I need a ride, and I'll owe you one. Lock on to my cell phone, would you?" Adam sent her a reassuring smile. "King?" he said into the phone.

A man appeared on the road. Out of nowhere. "What?" he asked.

Tori gasped and backpedaled three feet. Her heart slammed against her rib cage, and her legs twitched with the urge to flee. What the hell?

Adam slid his phone into his back pocket and turned to face the guy. "Have to make an entrance, don't you?"

The man grinned. He wore dark jeans and a black button-down shirt that looked expensive. Comfortable and expensive. "I was in a meeting with Kane and Conn. They hate it when I just disappear."

Tori's mouth opened, and she snapped it shut.

"Hello," the guy said.

She shook her head slowly. The man was as tall as Adam and very broad across the chest. His eyes looked kind of silver in the misty day, and his dark hair reached his shoulders. An odd gray patch ran through the thick mass, but he couldn't be more than thirty years old. Tension rolled off him . . . charisma? No. Power. Yeah. That was it.

Adam moved toward her and took her arm, his bulk and warmth providing comfort. "Don't bolt, little rabbit. Dage is a friend."

Dage. Yeah. The name fit. She lifted her chin. "Hello."

Adam smiled. "Victoria, this is Dage Kayrs, King of the Realm. Dage, this is—"

"Victoria Monzelle," Dage said smoothly, seeming content in the center of the quiet road. "Sister to Detective Alexandra Monzelle, who is mated to Kellach Dunne, the former Coven Nine Enforcer currently wanted for treason."

Adam sighed. "Show-off."

"Not even close," Dage said. "Known as Tori to those close to you. You're a singer in a band, have a two-year degree in music, and you supplement your income by selling lyrics to bigger names in the business. You're underpaid, by the way."

Tori blinked. Nobody knew about that. Hadn't they told her that the king of the Realm was a vampire? A real freakin' vampire. "You have good sources." What else did the king know?

He lifted a massive shoulder. "I'm the king. Everyone forgets that sometimes."

How the hell would anybody ever forget that fact? There was no doubt he was something . . . *more*. If he knew any of her other secrets, he chose not to tell. At this moment in time, anyway.

His eyes sparkled. "It's very nice to make your acquaintance."

Adam released her arm. "We need a ride."

Dage cocked his head, his gaze darkening. "You're a Coven Nine Enforcer, and I believe the witch nation is about to withdraw from the Realm. War might be imminent. Thus, we would no longer be allies."

Tori shivered.

"I'm asking as a friend," Adam said simply.

The king brightened. "Well then. Of course."

Who were these people? "Um, ride?" Tori asked, her voice wavering slightly. "You appeared out of nowhere." She didn't want a ride on his magic carpet, or whatever it was. Who knew how much she could screw that up? "This is a bad idea." One she didn't even understand.

A small smile played on the king's face. "Out of curiosity, why not take a plane?"

"She's enhanced with an ability that somehow jams engines, motors, and some electrical devices," Adam said simply.

The king studied her. "Cool."

Cool? Huh. She'd always thought it aggravating.

"But she can't control it. Yet." Adam glanced down the empty roadway. "It's imperative we get out of Dublin."

"Ah, yes." Dage studied the tumultuous sky. "I heard you offered to mate Miss Monzelle."

Adam glowered. "How the hell—"

"I'm the king," Dage said wearily. "Geez. The. King."

Tori tried to retreat another step, and Adam grasped her hand, completely enfolding it. "I'm not riding with him." She forced a smile. "Sorry, king."

"Dage. Please call me Dage." Amusement brought one dimple into play in his rugged face. "I can teleport, Victoria. It's a matter of moving between dimensions with the application of string theory and a bunch of other boring science stuff. No motors. No engines. No electricity." His hands opened and spread wide. "In fact, metal can't even come with us, so no weapons. Or phones."

Okay. Life was so much different from what she'd thought. She couldn't even imagine this craziness. "Um, no."

Adam moved toward the middle of the road, forcing her to follow. She tried to pull back and free her hand, but he held tight.

Dage watched the struggle, his dimple winking again. "I promise it does not hurt. You'll be fine." He waited until they'd reached him, and the atmosphere grew heavy in his vicinity. "Where are we going?" he asked mildly.

"My penthouse in Seattle," Adam said tersely. "Trust me, Victoria. I wouldn't allow anything to harm you."

Well, that seemed to be true. She stopped fighting him. "I, ah, I don't know about this."

Dage nodded. "Understandable. I assume your world has been rocked by quite a few revelations lately. Incidentally, if you'd like, I could have the man who stole your last song from you beheaded. Or tortured for a few weeks."

The saliva in her mouth dried up.

"Somebody stole one of your songs?" Adam asked, his eyes flashing.

She tried to swallow, but her throat ached. "Well, yeah. He's an old friend, or I thought he was, and I showed him a song. He basically stole it and sold it for a decent amount, and there was nothing I could do." Her gaze remained on the king. He sure knew pretty much everything. Why wasn't he telling Adam about her working for the DEA and investigating him? As she watched, Dage slowly winked. Man. He was just messing around. "I appreciate the offer, but I've made peace with it. Please don't, ah, behead anybody," she whispered.

"Your call," Dage said cheerfully. "Everybody ready to go?"

"Wait." Adam pulled out his cell phone and ripped it apart easily, crushing the chip with his bare hands. He dusted the pieces to the ground. "All right."

"I don't—" Tori started to say, just as Dage moved forward, sliding an arm around her waist and one around Adam's.

Then . . . nothing. No sights, no sounds, no feelings. Just nothing.

Light slammed into her, along with gravity. She blinked. An opulent hallway slowly came into focus. She blinked again . . . right into the barrel of a gun.

Chapter 7

Adam reacted instantly, kicking the nearest gun and sending it spinning. Dage pivoted to take out a guy to the right, while Adam shoved Victoria behind him. A bullet whizzed by his head. He went into battle mode, sizing up his opponents.

Four-man attack team, armed, and shocked as hell to see them appear out of thin air in his own Seattle penthouse vestibule. The first guy reached for a knife in his pocket, and Adam tackled him into the wall. A couple of hard punches to the gut, one to the jaw, and the guy went down.

Cold metal pressed against Adam's ear. He stilled, slowly turning around, grabbed the gun and punched for the temple. The guy dropped like a rock.

Dage stood to the side with an attacker in a headlock, while the fourth man held Victoria easily before him, his gun against her rib cage.

Fury swept through Adam, and he stilled, forcing control through his limbs. "Get that gun away from her, or I'll rip off your fucking head." His fangs dropped low. Witches had fangs just like vampires, but they rarely used them.

The attacker eyed him and then looked at the king.

Adam concentrated on the team, noting their signatures. The guys were witches. "Were you sent to attack us?" he snapped.

"No," the guy in the headlock croaked.

Oh. "I'm still an Enforcer with the Coven Nine. Want to explain why you just attacked us . . . as well as making a move on the king of the Realm?" Adam demanded.

The guy holding Victoria slowly lowered his weapon and then released her. He paled. Yeah. Nobody messed with the king.

Victoria stumbled over the prone body, headed straight for Adam, her eyes wide, panic across her features. He held out an arm, and she ran right into it, snuggling into his side. Damn, if that didn't feel good.

Adam nodded at the king, who had apparently tightened his hold, because his hostage was turning purple and kind of flopping while standing up. "Dage? I think you can let him go."

Dage's mouth turned down. "Oh, all right." He shoved the guy toward his buddy.

"Explain," Adam ordered.

"We were sent to investigate the penthouses and look for the traitors, Simone Brightston, Kellach Dunne, and Daire Dunne," the first guy said slowly. "Then you appeared out of nowhere."

"Those people aren't traitors, you dumbass," Adam shot back.

The guy lowered his chin. "According to the Council, they are, and they'll be treated as such. If you have information pertaining to their locations, you must divulge that now or face your own treason charges."

Adam pinned the guy with a hard look. "We've just arrived from Dublin, as you can see. I have no information." He tightened his hold on Victoria. "And if you ever threaten me again, you'll be eating through a straw for centuries."

Dage looked around the foyer, pausing at one demolished and boarded-up door. "This must be where Daire lived? I heard your brother's penthouse was attacked last week."

"Aye," Adam said, keeping his gaze on the two still-standing attackers. "Take your team and get out. Now."

The men each lifted an unconscious witch over his shoulder and headed down the stairs.

Dage whistled, glancing at the scorch marks on the damaged walls before looking up at the cracked ceiling tiles. "This place looks like it was bombed. It's shocking nobody got injured."

"Everyone got injured," Adam returned. "But we all lived." A rogue demon had bombed his brother's penthouse a couple of weeks previous.

Dage nodded. "Even so, you shouldn't stay here. I have a couple of safe houses."

"We're covered. Just want to grab some things," Adam said, his shoulder blades itching. "Thank you for the ride, Dage."

"No problem." Dage smiled at Victoria. "It was truly a pleasure." With that, the king zipped out of the foyer.

"Wow," Victoria murmured. She shook her head and pushed away from Adam. "That was exciting."

Talk about an understatement. Adam ignored the shattered tile beneath his feet and moved toward his door, unlocking it by using the keypad.

Victoria followed behind him. "What happened to this place?"

"Bombing." Adam stepped inside, closing his eyes to listen for threats. Nothing. He turned and gestured Victoria inside, locking the door after her.

She looked around the spacious main room. Only one of his walls showed damage. "You sure have an exciting life."

"Not usually," he said. Hell. That wasn't true. Being an Enforcer, even during peacetime, rarely offered a peaceful moment. "I'll keep you safe from the dangers of my job, Victoria."

She hovered in the surroundings, seeming uncomfortable for the first time since he'd met her. "I'm not staying in your life. Surely you know that."

"Considering your sister mated my brother, you are always going to be in my life." How did she not understand the concept of family?

She cleared her throat and gingerly strode down the two steps to the plush living room. "We're not mating. You get that, right?"

He scrubbed both hands down his face, his whiskers burning his palms. "Listen, I'll try to figure something out. Right now, the entire witch nation is in flux, and I promise we won't do anything without pursuing all avenues." Yet, he had to tell her the truth. "But the Coven Nine, even fractured, is extremely dangerous. While the Enforcers are on our side, the Guard follows Coven dictates, and I've trained some of those soldiers. If the existing council members order our deaths, we'll be running forever."

She crossed her arms, looking small and fragile in the large room. "I am not mating you, damn it."

"Some people think I'm a catch," he murmured, gratified when her lips twitched. Oh, her smile was unwilling, but still. Making her smile spread pleasure through him. He nodded toward the kitchen. "I'm sure there's something to eat in the kitchen. Why don't you go rummage through the cupboards while I take a quick shower and change clothing?" He glanced down at the tattered remains of his outfit.

She swallowed and looked toward the wide expanse of windows. "I, ah, like you in casual wear."

His attention was caught. "You do?"

She shuffled her feet. "Yes. You're more approachable when you're not dressed like a lawyer."

A lawyer? She thought his dress pants and shirts made him look like a barrister? He frowned.

She shrugged. "I'll go find food. Take your time with the shower. I may cook something." Dodging him, she picked her way to the open kitchen, going right for the refrigerator.

Tori looked into a refrigerator bigger than her first apartment. Every once in a while, she forgot that Adam was completely loaded. How much did a penthouse in downtown Seattle go for, anyway? Probably for more money than she'd ever see. Ever.

The fridge was mainly empty save for a beer, a shrunken orange, and some ketchup. At least he was a normal bachelor.

She shut the fridge and returned to the great room. The apartment was silent. Was he in the shower yet? Probably. It was sweet that he hadn't even questioned her willingness to stay in place, considering she'd already run from him once. Of course, he probably thought she'd been afraid of the plane crashing because of her motor issues.

She had more problems than her curse.

Glancing down at her borrowed clothing, she had to admit the witches had style. The long pants were top quality, as was the silk blouse. The boots were like butter against her skin. Good enough to meet with DEA Agent Franks.

She reached the door and took one last look around. "I'm sorry," she whispered. "Duty calls." Dodging outside the penthouse, she quickly reached the elevator and headed down.

The first floor of the building held a gathering area, sofas, and a long counter complete with a doorman. She nodded and kept walking, hurrying outside to a gray Seattle day. There were probably cameras everywhere, but she didn't have time to change her clothing or find a hat. So she walked several blocks to a coffee shop. A cute kid of about eighteen sat in a corner, typing on his laptop. She approached him and smiled.

He looked up, his jaw going slack.

"Hi."

"Um, hi." He squinted from behind trendy glasses.

"You look like a decent guy. My phone was stolen while I was in Nordy's, and I wondered if I could borrow yours. Just to call a friend of mine. She's a cop." She slid her smoothest smile into place. "She's local. I promise."

The kid fumbled to hand over his phone. "Of course."

"Thanks." She smiled again and quickly dialed.

"Franks," the agent snapped, her voice ticked.

"Hi. It's Tori."

Franks huffed out air. "You still in Ireland?"

Tori rolled her eyes. "No. I'm in Seattle but lost my phone and purse. Let's meet at Georgie's, and I'll give you a full report."

"Ten minutes. If you're not there, the deal is off." Franks disconnected.

Tori kept her smile in place and handed the phone back to the kid just as it started to smoke. "Thank you. I really appreciate it."

"How about I buy you a latte for the road since you lost your purse." The kid stood. "I insist."

Her stomach clenched it was so hungry. "No, I really couldn't impose. Thank you, though." She turned and hustled into the rain, careful in her nice boots. It took her nearly ten minutes to reach the small diner, and the second she walked inside, the smell of cooked everything slammed into her. She nearly gasped.

DEA Agent Brenda Franks was a sleek tigress who favored silk clothing and stood to about five foot ten. Her eyes were blue, her hair brown, and her face always set in a pout with very red lipstick. She waited in a back booth, stirring a pound of sugar into her coffee. Her eyebrows lifted as Tori approached. "That's a fancy outfit."

"You have no idea." Tori sat and grabbed a menu. "You're buying me food, Franks. I'm starving."

"Well, I figure zipping through time and space from Dublin to Seattle would make a gal hungry," the agent said dryly.

Tori's mouth dropped open. "What? How? Wait." Then it hit her. Franks was joking. "You have no damn idea." She returned to the menu. A waitress approached, and Tori looked up. "I'll take number nine with bacon, eggs over easy, and wheat toast. And a Pepsi." The waitress, an elderly woman with bright blue eyes, nodded and turned for the kitchen.

"You'd better have info for me," Franks muttered over her coffee cup.

Well, not really. She scrambled to think of something. Anything. "I still have my ear to the ground."

Franks lowered her cup. "That's not promising."

Tori cleared her throat. "I've been spending time with one of the Titans of Fire Enforcers. Adam Dunne? Well, we're getting close. So far, I'm not sure Fire is really involved in the drug trade." For some reason, Adam and his brothers had joined the motorcycle club about three months ago, right when Apollo was hitting the streets.

The drug had earned its name because it gave the taker a sense of being a god . . . powerful and strong. Well, until it burned the victim from the inside out. It was a killer, as were the people making and selling it. "Adam isn't the type. I just know it." Yet did she? His smoothness. All that money. Could it be from drugs?

"The Dunne boys were part of an MC club in Ireland that joined forces with Fire. They're trading guns for drugs." Franks snorted. "Titans of Fire is instrumental in the distribution of Apollo. We know that for sure. What we don't know, what you're supposed to be finding out, is who the damn manufacturer of the drug is. That's why your friend isn't in jail, and that's why we haven't brought Internal Affairs down on your sister."

Tori met the agent's gaze without flinching. She'd been recruited as an informant by the DEA when her good friend Malanie had been caught with Apollo. Tori was an ideal target because of her ties both to motorcycle clubs and to her sister. Franks was a bully, but her job definitely drove her. "Listen, Franks. My sister is a good cop. She can withstand any investigation."

Franks sat back, her long fingers drumming the scarred table. "Your sister is dating an Enforcer for the Titans of Fire. They're criminals, without question. Either give me something, or I'm taking her down. Now."

Tori scrambled for something. Anything. "Fine. I may have something. Do you know about Bear? The leader of the Grizzly Motorcycle Club?" Oh, telling Franks this was a mistake.

Franks's gaze sharpened. "Yeah. What about Bear?"

"Ah, well, he and the Dunnes are friends." Kind of. Really, Bear had been kidnapped at the same time Tori had been. But still. He had met with the Dunnes in Ireland, right? And they'd allowed him to return to the States, unlike her.

Franks shook her head. "That's crazy. The Grizzlies and Titans of Fire are enemies—rival motorcycle gangs. They barely tolerate each other." She leaned back, her gaze turning thoughtful. "Although . . . I had heard the Grizzlies were looking to get into the drug trade." She reached for her cup again. "One of our sources let us know that there is a party tonight at Grizzly headquarters. Are you still dating Lucas Bryant?"

"Clarke. He goes by Lucas Clarke now," Tori said. "Something about dodging his past. Um, we haven't talked in a while." She'd been investigating him, not dating him. Lucas was Bear's right-hand man, and if the Grizzlies were selling drugs, he'd be in the thick of things. "It's complicated."

"Good." Franks smiled, looking more like a model than an ambitious DEA agent. "Then you won't mind attending the party."

Chapter 8

Adam shoved his backpack on and straddled his Ducati, swearing the entire time to himself. He'd trusted her. Why in the fuck had he bothered to trust her? Oh yeah. They'd reached an agreement, and he'd saved her life. One would consider that a trust-building scenario.

The pipes ignited, and he zoomed out of the parking lot, his earbud attached to his ear. The second he'd discovered Victoria had taken off, the brat, he'd set the Realm computer gurus to finding her. He'd searched nearly the entire city by the time they called him with some actual news. They fed him locations from hacking into cameras, and he followed the directions, his temper frayed. Finally, he reached a diner off of Sixth Street and parked, striding inside to look around.

No Victoria. He tapped the bud. "She's not here."

Keys clacked. "She went out back, got a taxi, and headed into traffic about four hours ago. This will take some time," the tech said. "I'll call you back."

When he got his hands on her, she'd regret it. Why had she left? He'd thought they were getting along fine and she was starting to trust him. He reached in his pocket for his secondary phone, just to make sure she hadn't called. Did she even have his number? Probably not.

He quickly texted his brother to see if she had checked in with her sister. His brother texted back in the negative. Damn it.

He got back on his bike and opened the throttle, heading out of town. The fifty-minute ride calmed him, and he started to plan. Soon pine trees dotted the way, and the streets narrowed. Finally, he turned down a barely there road, followed the river for a while, and then parked in front of a small cabin. Tori would like this place once he found her ass and tied her to the bed inside.

His cock perked up.

Not the bed. The sofa. He'd tie her to the sofa.

He parked the bike and strode up the steps, pushing inside the two-room cabin to see his brothers at the table eating cheeseburgers in the small kitchen next to the living area. Daire, the oldest, had longish black hair and sizzling green eyes. Kellach, the youngest, had lighter green eyes and longer black hair. They were both big and muscled . . . and looking at him oddly.

"What's up with the T-shirt and jeans?" Daire asked, reaching for a mountain of french fries.

"I rode the bike out here." Adam's stomach growled, and he moved instantly to take two burgers from the bag.

Kell passed over a beer. "So? You still usually ride in nice jeans at the least. I didn't even know you had jeans that weren't almost black."

Adam's ears burned. Maybe Victoria had mentioned something to him about his uptight clothes. Either way, who cared? "You two are wanted for treason against the Coven Nine, and you're concerned about my wardrobe?" He pulled out a chair, his muscles going stiff with the truth of his statement. How was he going to protect his brothers and still remain true to his beliefs? To his vows? "What's wrong with you?"

Daire shrugged and took a swig of his beer. "I'm not worried about treason."

"You should be," Adam shot back. He glanced at the closed door leading to the bedroom. "Where are your mates?"

"Mine is safely at Realm headquarters in Idaho," Daire said, taking another burger. "Kell's is at the local police station."

Alexandra, Victoria's sister, was a cop in Seattle—a good one. Adam searched carefully for the right words. "Your mate needs to take a leave of absence." He held up a hand when Kellach started to speak. "Just listen. The Nine and the Guard will come after you through her, and you know it. They won't care that she's a cop with a human agency." He took a bite of the burger and almost moaned out loud. When was the last time he'd eaten? "Also, she's a new mate, and the Apollo darts would still kill her. What's she doing at the station, anyway?"

"Turning in papers for a leave of absence," Kellach said mildly.

"Oh." Adam finished off the burger. "Well, good. I bet she wasn't happy about that."

"She was fine, considering we're facing treason charges and probably need all hands on deck to work the case." Kell leaned forward. "My mate is expecting to see her sister when she gets here. Do you want to explain why Tori isn't here?"

Adam ignored the frustration ripping into him. "I'm having her tracked down as we speak."

Daire frowned. "You lost the human?"

"Yes, Daire. I lost the human. She's irresponsible, disobedient, and a pain in my ass," Adam returned. "I took a shower, and she took off."

Kellach sat back, studying him. "Is it just me, or has somebody finally gotten under his skin?"

"Yep. I believe it's true," Daire said, taking another drink of his beer. "Of course, since he vowed to mate her, maybe he's let her in."

"Would you stop talking about me in the third person?" Adam groused, reaching for a basket of Tater Tots. "I have enough on my mind."

Kellach flashed a grin. "Apparently. However, considering you haven't mated the human as promised within twenty-four hours, I'm sure the next order from the Council will be to bring you in."

Adam breathed out, his body settling. "Aye, but I'm not ready to go in."

Daire eyed him. "Then you're a sitting duck. If you use your powers, they'll find you."

"I know," Adam said softly. Witch powers, or the manipulation of physics, all but broadcast a signal. If he wanted to remain hidden, he'd have to act nearly human.

"I don't like you having to go dark right now." Kellach sighed. "We've been coming up with a plan, but I'm sure you already have a strategy planned."

"I do." Adam washed down the burger with half of his beer, his mind finally settling as he planned with his brothers. God, he missed them when they weren't in the same town. Peace for their people sure the hell hadn't lasted long. "You guys need to get out of Seattle and work the case from somewhere safe. Anywhere the Guard can't find you."

A phone buzzed. Daire pulled it out to read the screen. He whistled. Tension pricked down Adam's back. "What?"

Daire looked up and slid his phone back into place. "The Council of the Coven Nine has declared Kellach and me dangerous traitors to the nation. There's a kill order on our heads—no need to take peacefully. Kill on sight."

Adam sat back and breathed out, his chest heavy. "A kill order? Seriously?" It was unheard of. What the hell was Peter Gallagher up to? "I can't believe that."

"Aye. Two to one, they voted to have us killed," Daire said quietly. "The ayes were Peter Gallagher and Sal the loser. Nessa voted no."

Adam rubbed a hand over his eyes. He had always liked that young witch. "So. Fuck."

"Yep." Kellach stood and paced to the window. "My mate had better be on her way."

Adam shook his head. "You guys have to get underground. Now."

"Aye," Kellach said.

Daire drummed his fingers on the table. "With the death sentence hanging over Simone's head as well, there are a lot of guns pointed at us." Anger rode his voice, deepening it until he almost sounded like a demon. "We're going to have to make a stance soon."

Adam nodded. Their cousin Simone was pregnant and recently mated to Nick Veis, the strategist for the entire demon nation. "Nick will keep Simone safe." Not that Simone couldn't kick ass on her own. "They're at demon headquarters in Idaho?" Demon and Realm headquarters shared a lake in northern Idaho.

Daire nodded. "I'm heading to Realm headquarters to get my mate next." He glanced up at Kellach. "You should accompany us. At this point, the Council is pissed at both the demon nation and the Realm, so being at Realm headquarters won't cause any more damage to the coalition. In addition, it's a safe place. The Guard won't be able to get to us there, and if we go after the Nine, our mates will be safe."

"That's a plan. So we're thinking of going after the Nine," Kellach said. "I woulda never thought it."

"Maybe. Let's see if we can find another way," Adam said, his body rioting at the very idea of going after the organization he'd vowed to give his life to. The Council's betrayal cut deep, and the tear felt physical. "If there's no choice, I've started formulating an attack plan." One he hoped never to set into motion. "The Council's next move is to declare war on the Realm, the demon nation, and the shifter nation, you know."

"There's nobody left," Daire growled.

Adam's phone dinged, and he lifted it to read the screen. "Bollocks."

"What?" Daire asked.

Adam swallowed. "The Council is requesting proof of my mating, since my time is up." Next they'd probably find an excuse to cut off his head. "The Council is also seeking new Enforcers to take your place."

"That's just fantastic." Daire groaned.

"Aye," Adam said, sighing. "Assuming I've mated, they've given me one week to find the manufacturer of Apollo before I'm to return home."

"A week?" Kellach snapped. "You can't work the Apollo case by yourself—especially without using any power."

"Yes, I can." Adam munched thoughtfully on a fry. "You can still help me from safety. Computer and background work."

"I don't like this, but I'm not seeing an alternative." Daire reached for a red manila folder near the sink. "Here's everything we've compiled on the Titans of Fire Motorcycle Club and their involvement in distributing Apollo onto the streets of Seattle. Mostly humans are the victims here. At some point, whoever is creating Apollo is going to set it free in Dublin—and witches will be harmed. There have been more dart attacks in Seattle, by the way."

Adam growled. The darts were filled with the drug, which was deadly to witches. "Somebody wants witches dead. Who and why, damn it?" He shook his head. It was time to stop fucking around with the human motorcycle club and make them talk and reveal the manufacturer. There truly was no choice any longer.

"What about Victoria and the mating vow?" Kellach asked, his gaze sober as he turned from the window. "My mate will be here soon, and she's not going to like the idea of her younger sister being forced to mate a witch."

"I know," Adam said. "I'm thinking about it. If we don't mate, the Guard will put death orders on both of our heads. She's frail, Kell. She's a human, and I don't see her living well underground for the next sixty years." The woman was all spunk and light. The idea of seeing that wildness scared out of her shot hollowness into his gut. "Like I said, things are going to move swiftly. Step one is getting you guys and your mates to safety."

Daire stood, a powerful man with regret in his deep eyes. "We barely had the chance to enjoy peace. I haven't even had time to relax with my mate." He sighed, scrubbing his fingers through his thick hair. "Neither has Kell. Man, I'm pissed at the Council. Fucking Gallagher. He just wants power."

Adam pushed away from the table. Responsibility slammed into him from all sides. "As the only remaining Enforcer, I need to figure out a way to secure Councilwoman Nessa Lansa as well. She has voted against Gallagher more than once, and she might be in danger." He'd taken an oath to protect, and just because things had gone to shit, he wasn't excused from it.

"She'll be fine for the time being," Kellach said slowly. "After that, we might have to lock her down." His eyes blazed. "I'm not accepting a ruling from two members of the Nine that I'm not an Enforcer any longer. I am, and I'll do my fucking duty."

"Amen," Daire said. "And ditto."

"Aye." Adam nodded.

Daire cleared his throat. "I, ah, wanted to wait until we were together to tell you this. I mean, all three of us."

Adam frowned and stood. "What?" Whatever it was, he'd take care of it.

"Cee Cee is, ah, pregnant." Daire looked a little dazed.

Adam's mouth dropped open. "You've only been mated a couple of weeks."

"I know," Daire whispered. "Believe me, I'm more shocked than you are." He swayed. "A witch-demon baby. It might even be a girl."

Adam chuckled. "A bank-robbing girl." God, things were about to get very interesting.

Daire glowered. "While my mate enjoys robbing the occasional bank, my daughter will not take up the hobby. Ever."

"You have to get to headquarters," Adam said, urgency rushing through him. "Don't worry. I can handle things here." Even without his powers.

Daire nodded. "You have some backup. Bear and the Grizzlies will help if you need them, and the two prospects are in place at Fire, still working the case."

"They need to go home," Adam said. He couldn't be responsible for the two kids currently undercover as prospective members, one a vampire, one a demon, and both related to royalty. They'd been a huge help so far with the case, but things had gotten too dangerous. "I can't cover them, too."

"All right. I'll let the king know," Daire said. The king was basically an uncle to both boys.

Adam's phone rang, and he lifted it upon seeing a familiar name. "Hi Chalton. What did you find?" The guy was the Realm's best computer hacker, without question.

"I tracked Victoria Monzelle through Seattle all day, and she just arrived at the Grizzly Motorcycle Club headquarters for what appears from satellite to be a huge-ass party," Chalton said. "My intel is about fifteen minutes old."

Adam's chest heated until his ribs burned. "Thank you." He clicked off. She'd gone to a party? The world was after her, drugs were being run, and she'd gone to a fucking party? "I am going to kill that woman," he muttered, turning for the doorway. "Tell Alexandra that I found her sister and am about to lock her down for her own safety. You guys be in touch the second you're at Realm headquarters." He paused at the doorway and turned.

His brothers stared at him with different degrees of amusement and concern as they stood and moved away from the table.

"Ah, congrats on the baby, Daire," Adam said, taking another deep breath. "Stay safe, you guys."

They nodded.

"You, too," Daire said, grabbing him for a hard hug.

Adam clapped his back and then moved, hugging Kellach. "We've been through worse." Had they? He wasn't truly sure. "We'll get through this, too."

"Aye," Kellach said, releasing him. "Now go get your woman."

"She's not mine," Adam returned, opening the door. "Not yet, anyway." With that, he jogged into the rainstorm that was kicking up outside.

Chapter 9

Tori swayed through dancing bodies as rock music thumped from speakers set in every corner. The Grizzly headquarters was more like a sports bar, with pool tables, dartboards, and a long bar set into the far wall. The comfortable furniture had been moved out to make room for the dance floor. It was raining, or they probably would've opened up one of the walls to let the party spill outside.

Three bartenders, most likely prospects, were quickly handing out beer and hard drinks.

Tons of people danced around, the women in tight jeans and small tops, many of the men in jeans and their cuts. It wasn't her first party at the Grizzlies, and so far, things seemed fairly mellow.

The music ran through her, and she tapped her fingers along with the piano track. Most people couldn't hear it, but she could feel it. Man, she needed time to practice again.

She smoothed back her hair and made her way to a corner where some tables had been set out.

"Miss Monzelle." Lucas smiled and, with a huge boot, kicked out a chair for her to sit. The VP of the club had longish brown hair, deep brown eyes, and a charming smile. "That's a new outfit."

"Mr. Bryant-Clarke," she said, gratefully taking the seat. "It's not mine. I borrowed it."

Lucas set an elbow on the round metal table, his black T-shirt stretching over his wide chest. "I've dropped the Bryant and am just going by Lucas Clarke. I'm tired of satisfying both sides of my damn family."

"I know. Just messing with you." She smiled and reached for his beer to take a swig, allowing the beat of the music to wash over her.

She missed making music. "About time you made that decision, by the way." His parents were apparently divorced, and his mother had always insisted he go by her last name, while his father demanded the opposite. He'd confided his life story to her during the last party she'd attended with him, after they'd had way too much to drink. "How did they take it?"

"Considering they're both living across the country, I don't care." He motioned for another beer, and a woman brought it over. She leaned over to set it down, revealing an ample set of breasts. Very ample.

"Thanks, darlin'," Lucas said, taking the beer and switching it with Tori's. He waited until she'd left before continuing. "I've been trying to keep tabs on you after you and Bear were taken." He leaned in and caressed the back of her neck. He smelled of after-shave and maybe tequila, but his eyes were clear. "Bear kept me updated, and he said you were safe, or I would've come looking for you. Are you all right?"

She nodded. "I am, now." How the hell was she going to find out if the Grizzlies were running drugs? There was no way to casually ask something like that. She liked Lucas and really didn't want to lie to him any longer. "Where is Bear, anyway?"

She'd looked for him immediately upon entering the clubhouse, but the leader was nowhere to be found. He'd been kidnapped by the witches at the same time as she, and he'd also seen them throw fire. So Bear knew about witches, and yet, they'd let him go free. "I wanted to make sure he was all right."

Lucas took a deep drag of his beer. "He's home, but I'm not sure he's all right."

She blinked. "Oh. Um, why?" Had Bear decided to talk about the witches? He seemed too smart to do that. If he wasn't locked up in a loony bin, the witches would surely have him killed.

Lucas lifted a fit shoulder. "He's been sick for the last week. Pale as milk, shaky, and crankier than shit."

Huh. That was odd. "Maybe he caught the flu?" She leaned back, away from Lucas's touch, the guilt eating at her. Fear dropped into her stomach, turning the beer sour.

His head tilted, and he zeroed in on her. "Are you okay?"

"Yeah." She forced a smile. "Did he say anything about the kidnappers or the trip to Ireland?"

"Bear said that some international force took you both into custody and to Ireland because of Simone Brightston. Apparently she was wanted on some sort of theft charge and has now gone underground. Bear said that our State Department got it all sorted out. It took longer with you than him, for some reason." Lucas kicked back, his gaze not wavering. "Why? Is there something he should've told me?"

"No," she whispered, taking another drink of the beer. Good. Bear hadn't told anybody about the witches. Man, she wanted to talk to him.

"Did something happen between you and Bear in Ireland?" Lucas asked quietly.

She blinked. "Of course not."

Lucas leaned forward again and flattened his large hand on the table. "I'm in the mood to get laid, Tori, and I'm done waiting around for you. Are you comin' home with me tonight or not?"

She tried not to wince. Members of the Grizzly MC didn't date. They hung out, went for rides, and got laid. Oh, there was some romance, and if a guy fell for a woman, he made her his. But so far, she'd been able to enjoy a friendship with Lucas while still investigating the drug issue for the DEA. Being a criminal informant sucked. Now she was supposed to get mated to a freakin' witch, and Lucas wanted her to make a decision. "No," she said, trying to soften the blow with a smile. "I like you, Lucas. You're a good guy."

"But not one you're going to rattle the headboard with." His grin was rueful. "I don't usually just become a buddy with a woman."

"I know. I'm special." She snorted. "I do like being your friend, though."

He tapped his beer bottle with hers. "I could sense it. You act all tough and wild, but really, you're a good girl, Tori. This is a temporary walk on the wild side for you."

"I am not," she burst out.

He chuckled, his gaze knowing. "Sure you are. It's okay. But you're definitely missing out." He looked toward the bodies gyrating on the dance floor, no doubt scoping out talent.

She shook her head. "I'm not so good, really. Well, not always."

He focused back on her. "Then when are you bad?"

She shrugged, and heat climbed into her face. The second she'd turned him down, she'd lost her chance to get him alone. This was her one moment to investigate, and she had to go for it. "I like to get high once in a while. And I've tried a new drug that makes you feel like a god. It's awesome."

His gaze sharpened. "Have you, now? What kind of drug?"

She leaned in to whisper. "A guy in my band got it before we did that concert last month. It was called Apollo. It was amazing, Lucas." She swallowed. God, hopefully she wasn't overplaying her hand. If Lucas had information, she'd feed it to the DEA without getting him in trouble or even using his name. It was the least she could do, but she had to protect her sister as well as the stupid friend who'd gotten caught with the damn drug. "Have you heard of it?"

He studied her for a moment. "No. Why would I have heard of it?"

"Just thought maybe." She settled back in her seat.

He ran his hand down her arm, encircling her wrist. His gaze turned rock hard. "Let me give you a little piece of advice."

The hair pricked at the back of her neck. "Uh, okay."

"Considering your sister is a cop with the Seattle PD, it's probably unwise for you to be asking anybody about drugs." He tightened his hold just enough to show his impressive strength. "Do you understand?"

She opened her eyes wide. "Are you threatening me, Lucas?"

"No, he isn't." A shadow fell across the table. "Tori. How nice to see you back in the States."

Lucas released her.

She looked up to see Bear's inscrutable face. "Same to you," she said, fighting the urge to rub her wrist.

Lucas gave her a look and left the table.

Bear took his seat. The Grizzly leader was at least six foot six, with shaggy brown hair and honey-bourbon eyes. Scruff covered his jaw, and lines fanned out from his full mouth. His chest moved as if it was hard for him to breathe. "If you're here doing undercover work for your sister and the Seattle police department, then I believe you just hurt Lucas's feelings. He had a serious hard-on for you."

She leaned in to whisper. "Why did the Council let you leave

Ireland?" The only way she'd gotten out was because Adam had promised to mate her.

Bear blinked slowly. "What council?"

Huh? "The Council of the Coven Nine. You saw those guys in the fight the same time I did."

He scratched his chin. "The guys fighting with those weird guns that basically threw fire? So what? New weapons are being built all the time."

Was he serious? "You saw them too, Bear." What kind of game was the guy playing?

"Yeah, I saw the firefight, and then I hit my head and was out for about a day." Bear motioned for a drink. "You want anything else?"

"No." She peeled the label off her beer. So Bear was lying. Was it to protect himself? "You can talk to me. Honest."

Two drinks were plunked on the table by a prospect. Bear pushed one toward her. "Really? About what? Apollo?"

Warning ticked down her spine. "I was just curious."

"Drink your beer, Tori." His gaze didn't waver from her face.

For the first time, Tori could see the predator beneath Bear's easygoing attitude. She took a drink of the beer. The liquid burned a little on the way down, to mix with the rapidly growing acid in her stomach.

"Good. Now let's get a couple of things straight," he said slowly.

She wanted to swallow again, but a lump formed in her throat. "What's that?"

"I don't know why you're here asking about Apollo, because I'd bet my last dime you don't do hard drugs." He stretched out long legs and crossed his ankles over size sixteen boots. "If you're here to investigate for your sister, the cop, tell her that wounds me. I thought Alexandra liked me."

The sarcasm was unnecessary. "Bear—"

"If you're working for somebody else, then knock it off right now. That's a dangerous gig, little girl, and you're not up for it." Even pale and a little shaky, Bear was freakin' scary when he wanted to be. "For the record, the Grizzlies don't do drugs, create drugs, or run drugs. Got it?"

She nodded. "I'm not working for anybody."

His eyelids half lowered while he lifted his head. "Some people just can't lie, lady."

"I'm not lying," she lied.

His lip twitched. "Well, I tried to be nice. Get up, Tori."

Her stomach dropped. Was he kicking her out? She'd never get the information then, and her friend would go to jail. And her sister would be in serious trouble as well. "I, ah, I'm fine right here."

His lips peeled back. "Get up and follow me to my office where we're gonna have a little chat." He looked around his domain. "Fight me, and it'll be a waste of energy. Nobody here is going to stop me or help you."

Oh, shit. What the hell had she done? Just one question. One little question was all she'd asked. She sucked as an undercover agent. Or rather, as a CI. "I'll scream, Bear."

He unfolded his legs and stood up. "That's your choice. Either way, you're coming with me." He held out a hand.

She stood on shaking legs, her beer bottle clutched in her hand. His gaze flickered to the bottle, and his twitching lips moved into a full smile that was more hungry than amused. Where was Lucas? Maybe he'd help her. She looked frantically around, only to spot him across the room, kissing the big-chested woman up against a wall.

Bear followed her gaze. "Lucas isn't one to wait around."

Well. Apparently not. Her ego took a small hit. Tori tried to track the way to the front entrance.

"You won't make it."

She breathed deep. "My sister is a cop, Bear. You hurt me and she'll shoot you." Why hadn't she bought a gun before coming here? Oh yeah. No money. Lifting her chin, she swept around the table toward the back door.

Bear chuckled, right on her heels. He opened the door and rain splashed in from thin clouds the moon barely penetrated. He pointed to the next building, which held three huge garage doors and a man-sized door. "My office is in there."

A bunch of bikes and cars were scattered throughout the square-shaped area. Shelter. She bunched her legs to run, and he clamped a hand on her shoulder. Bear's hand was bigger than her shoulder, so he had a nice grip on part of her bicep as well.

"I just want to talk," Bear said.

"Now who's lying?" Would he torture her for information? She'd never been tortured before. How tough was she? Not very, if she had to guess. Time to fight. She swung around and hit him in the arm with the beer bottle. It bounced off and dropped to the ground, shattering on the smooth concrete.

He looked down and sighed. "Glass. Seriously? Glass on my cement? Where my bikes go?"

She gulped and tried to take a step back. His beefy hand kept her in place. "Um, sorry?"

He looked up, his lips pouting. "If you're going to hit a guy with a bottle, you don't hit his arm."

"Oh?" Her voice trembled.

"No," he huffed, looking beyond put out. "You hit him in the face. Preferably the eye."

"Oh. Well, how about I go get another bottle? I'll do better next time."

He began propelling her toward the darkened office. "No."

She struggled, shoving back into him. "Wait a minute. Just wait a minute."

He paused, giving a long-suffering sigh. "What? Let's get out of the rain."

Yeah. It was probably easier to torture somebody without Mother Nature butting in. "What's wrong with you? I mean, you don't look good. I, ah, don't want to catch the flu." Lame. Definitely lame. If he was going to tear her fingernails out one by one, he probably didn't care if he gave her the flu.

"Nothing. Just a little bug. Start moving, Tori." He used his one hand to basically slide her toward the door.

She tried to fight him, but he kept pushing her, finally opening the door and all but shoving her inside. "I'm going to scream, Bear," she threatened.

"I really wish you wouldn't," said a familiar voice from across the room.

The light snapped on, and she squinted. "Adam?"

Chapter 10

Adam leaned against the far wall, crossing his arms to prevent himself from lunging and taking the woman to the ground. She had no idea what the hell she'd just stepped in. "Victoria," he said.

"You're here." Her eyes were wide as she looked around the small office. "This place is a disaster."

"Aye," Adam agreed. Bear had a metal desk and several file cabinets scattered throughout with manila folders, papers, and what looked like playing cards tossed haphazardly all around. There were two old metal chairs for guests, and one looked like it had been set on fire at some point. "What the hell are you doing at a Grizzly party, Victoria?" Adam bit out.

Bear hitched around and flopped into a worn leather chair with a sigh of what sounded like relief. "On first glance, she's here because she and Lucas have been dating."

Adam straightened, heat spiraling down his torso. "That ends right now."

Bear's sharp eyes focused on Adam. "Does it, now?" he asked softly.

Adam rolled his head, reining in his temper. "Considering I told the Council I'd mate her to prevent their removing her head, then yeah, she fucking isn't dating Lucas any longer." The possessive ring to his tone pissed him off even more.

Bear's eyes bugged. "You did what? Why would you promise those asshats anything?"

"Wait a minute." Tori turned on Bear, her wild hair flying. "You know about the Council."

He sighed and rolled his eyes. "Of course I know about the Council. I'm not a moron."

She sucked in air, her pretty skin flushing red. "Wait a fucking minute. You know about *mating*?"

"Uh." Bear bit his lip. "Yes."

"Are you a witch, too?" she spat.

He reared back in the chair. "A witch? You think I'm a witch? Fuck, no. A witch." He shook his head, starting to mutter to himself.

Adam rolled his eyes. Bear was too fucking crazy to be a witch, that was for damn sure.

"Bear, you lied to me," she said, her voice heated.

Bear calmed. A second later, a small smile played on his mouth.

Adam tensed. Oh, he knew that smile on his old friend, and he didn't like it. Not at all. "What?" Adam snapped.

"Lying. It's an interesting concept." Bear seemed to cheer up in front of their eyes. "Tori, would you like to tell Adam why you're really here?" Glee almost cascaded from the Grizzly leader.

Tori's shoulders hunched.

Warning ticked through Adam.

She licked her lips, glared at Bear, and then focused on Adam. So many thoughts scattered across her face, it was impossible to guess at one. Finally, she frowned. "Why are *you* here?" she asked Adam.

His chin lowered. If she was playing at being dense, she wasn't going to like his ultimate response. "Excuse me? I was looking for you."

Her pretty lips pursed. She bit the inside of her cheek, her mind obviously working hard. "Yeah. I get that. Adam, you're an Enforcer for Titans of Fire." She gave Bear a thoughtful look. "You're the leader of the Grizzlies." Her hands swept out. "You're rival motorcycle clubs—even enemies. Not allies."

Bear shook his head and dropped it into his hands, muffling his voice. "Secrets. That's why secrets are so stupid. I don't like secrets. I moved here, to the end of the States, to get away from secrets. Just wanna be left alone. Wanna ride, wanna fuck, wanna eat, wan—"

"Bear," Adam snapped.

Bear lifted his head, his eyes bloodshot and his shoulders weary. "What?"

Adam paused, taking a good look at the leader. "Are you all right?"

"No." Bear shoved away from his desk, swinging his arms out wide. "I'm not all right. Your fucking people kidnapped me, and now my sister is locked down where I can't see her." He growled low, the sound impressive. "You and your brothers are no closer to figuring out your problem, and now it's becoming my fucking problem." He gestured toward Tori.

Adam tried to wade through the outburst. Oh, Bear often didn't make sense unless one knew him, but Adam had been his friend for a long time. "Okay. Did the Council do something to you?" Something that had obviously affected Bear's health.

"No." Bear breathed out, his chest rattling. "They didn't do anything but piss me off. I'm fine. Just a minor cold."

Well, okay. Adam kept a close eye on Bear and moved on to the next concern. "Your sister is fine. Nick has her at demon headquarters, and the Council can't get to her. I promise."

Tori's mouth gaped open. "Are you a demon, Bear?"

Bear rolled his eyes so aggressively his entire head moved. "God, no. Geez."

"Who's your sister?" she asked, her voice almost timid.

Bear looked at Adam, who shrugged. "It's a long story, but Simone Brightston is my half sister." He held up a hand when Tori started to speak. "No, I'm not a witch. We're just half."

Tori shook her head as if life had just become way too confusing. It probably had.

Then Adam turned to the third part of Bear's outburst. "How has Tori made my mission your problem?"

Bear's expression cleared. "Oh yeah." He smiled again and turned toward Victoria. "How about you explain it, chickie?"

She shuffled her feet, eyeing the door to the garage behind Adam.

Adam centered himself, his heart ticking a bit too fast. "Victoria?"

"I wanted to make sure Bear was okay after our kidnapping, and I also wanted to see Lucas and have some fun," she said, her posture straightening.

Some of that was true, but the rest smelled like a lie. He clenched his fingers into a fist, releasing them one by one. He truly didn't like being in the dark, and his temper strained to be free. Now. "The time for lying has passed, woman."

Sparks lightened her blue eyes. Her neck elongated and her chin lifted. "Listen, *man*. My life is none of your concern, and it's time you butted out."

Bear threw back his head and laughed, the sound more subdued than normal. He shook out his arms, skirted the desk, and loped toward Adam, reaching the back door. "Good luck with this. I need to run."

Adam grabbed Bear's arm, noting a loss of muscle mass. "Are you sure?" What the hell was wrong with the guy?

Bear glanced at the hand and then back up to Adam's face. "Yes, Mom. Running helps."

Adam released him, and Bear strode out of the office and into the darkened garage. A far door opened, and then Bear was gone.

"What's wrong with him?" Tori asked.

Adam shook his head. "I really don't know." Perhaps it was just a cold or a touch of the flu. Totally possible, maybe? He wasn't sure. "For now, let's concentrate on you. What the hell are you doing here, and don't even think of lying to me, damn it." He couldn't believe she'd crossed into Bear's territory all by herself, and to know she had an ulterior motive just angered him more. "Are you interested in Bear?"

Her eyebrows lifted. "Bear? God, no. He's nuts."

Adam barked out a laugh. "Yeah. He is." But he was also sick, and Adam would have to figure that out next. For now, he and Victoria needed to come to an agreement. "Why are you really here?"

She edged toward the front door. "I like to party. You should already know that about me."

At the blatant lie, the insult to his intelligence, the shackle holding his temper frayed like an old rope. "Last chance. Tell me the truth, or I get serious."

Tori measured the distance to the door at about three feet. Oh, she could make it there, but could she get it open before Adam pounced? He lounged against the far wall, his body seeming relaxed. But she'd seen him move before. The man was fast.

Plus, if she made it outside, what then? "My life is really none of your business," she said.

Tension rolled from him, swelling through the small room, heating the air. How did he do that?

There had to be a way out of the office. She tilted her head to the side. Bear was gone. If she ran outside with Adam on her heels, other Grizzly members would see a Titans of Fire member chasing a woman who'd been seen with a Grizzly. They'd stop him and probably start whaling on the guy. Yeah. Good plan. "Okay, Adam." She drew a deep breath and slowly exhaled. "This is the full deal." She turned on her heel and leaped for the door, scrambling to open it.

He was on her before she knew it, slamming it shut, his hand over her head. The door vibrated, and the frame cracked down the side. Rough hands flipped her around, and his face lowered to hers. "Nice plan. Run out, yell, and get Grizzly members on my ass?"

She gulped down her suddenly too-dry throat. "Yeah."

His lip curled. "Actually, that was a good plan."

Yeah, but she'd underestimated his speed. Again. "Everything has just gotten too confusing," she whispered.

Heat rolled off the witch, surrounding her, speeding up her pulse. His now familiar scent all but poured inside her, warming the breath in her lungs. Her knees trembled, and for the first time that evening, it wasn't from fear. "Let go of me."

"Not bloody likely."

Boisterous voices and the deepening beat from the loudspeakers cut through the silence.

Adam angled his head to look out the window. "We need to get out of here. So you're going to follow along, meekly, until we reach my bike. At that point, you're going to relax your entire body and clear your mind. Hopefully the bike will work."

She tried to jerk free of his hold. Unsuccessfully. "There's nothing meek about me."

He pressed her against the door, body to body. "I'm done, Victoria. Got me?"

Yeah. She got him. He was one long line of pure muscle against her, and she didn't have a chance in a physical fight. "Fine," she muttered.

"Bear is gone. Lucas is probably not happy you left with Bear. We both need to get the hell out of here so we don't have to deal with a bunch of drunk Grizzlies. Got it?"

That did make a bit of sense. "I said okay. Let's go." Would relaxing her body and clearing her mind actually work?

He gave her one more hard look and reached over her head to open the door. Drawing her out into the light rain, he grasped her wrist. "I swear, it takes near violence to gain your obedience."

The word. The damn O-word nearly shot her head off her neck. Heat flashed through her.

A couple of Grizzly members wandered by from the other garage. Oh yeah? He thought she was obedient? Fuck that. Sucking in air, she opened her mouth to scream.

Adam pivoted and put her back against the building, his mouth crashing down on hers. The first kiss from him, the one in Ireland, had been all seduction and heat. Not this one. No. This one was punishment and fire. He growled low and pressed a knee between her thighs, partially lifting her off the ground. His fingers speared through her hair, and he jerked her head back, giving him deeper access.

She was immobilized, helpless.

A growl rolled from his chest and into her mouth, electrifying her body. Sparks shot through her, zinging out, landing in her erogenous zones. His mouth worked hers, his tongue conquering her mouth. Every inch of it.

Her eyelids fluttered shut as overwhelming sensations claimed her. His hold was sure and hard. Every man she'd ever met, every kiss she'd ever thought she'd had, faded into nothingness, into mere whims in a world of harsh reality. Before she could protest, before she could fight, she found herself kissing him back.

Even so, he didn't relent, his five o'clock shadow rough against her skin, his mouth forceful. She moaned, her body liquefying, leaving her wanting and weak. His thigh muscle tensed against her aching core, sending raw shards of pleasure through her womb. Her legs gave, but he easily held her up with that one leg, forcing her to ride it, making it feel so good she couldn't protest.

Finally, he jerked free.

Her mouth, bruised and aching, opened. She breathed him in, her gaze unable to move from the harsh planes of his angled face. Hunger, ravaged and true, glittered in those dark eyes. His rosy lips looked familiar and dangerous . . . a weapon she hadn't recognized before that moment. His nostrils flared as if catching a scent, and his heart beat against her chest as wildly as if he'd run a marathon.

She couldn't breathe.

Suddenly, sounds came into focus. Rain on concrete. Music pounding. Laughter rolling.

She blinked.

He pressed his leg against her one more time, hard.

She almost dropped from pure need.

Then he released her, allowing her feet to reach the ground, waiting until she stood before stepping back.

There were no words. No words or even thoughts to describe what had just happened. How her body still ached. How her mind had numbed and then fizzled. No words. She couldn't find a one.

So when he took her hand and turned for the parking lot, she followed along silently. Easily. She shook her head, allowing the rain to wash over her face and clear it.

Man, her body hurt. Desire edged with a sharp blade of pain pulsed inside her. Every step forward rubbed her aching clit against her jeans. She bit back a whimper, still moving as if in a daze. What the hell had just happened? How had he done so much damage to her with just one kiss? Oh, she'd underestimated Adam Dunne, but she wouldn't do it again.

"Hey," an unfamiliar voice called.

She lifted her head to see they'd reached the far side of the parking area. Three tough-looking guys leaned against a classic car, something red, smoking cigarettes. "Who the hell are you?" the same voice called. The guy was in his late twenties, swaying, and wearing a plain T-shirt, as were the other men. They must either be guests or hopeful Grizzly prospects, or they'd probably be wearing cuts.

Adam set her behind him. "Doesn't matter. We're leaving."

"The fuck you are." The first guy threw down his cigarette. "Titans of Fire isn't welcome here. Prepare to bleed, asshole."

Then he charged.

Chapter 11

Adam pivoted to keep the man from Victoria, swinging out and nailing the younger loudmouth right in the nose. Blood spurted, and the guy fell to the side. His buddy instantly leaped into action.

Thank God. Fury rang through Adam's veins on the heels of a desire so intense he couldn't believe he hadn't formed fire when he'd had his mouth on Victoria's. He morphed the lust into anger, kicked the second guy in the gut, neck, and finally jaw. A combination three-two-five punch, and the kid staggered back. Finally, Adam kicked him directly beneath the chin, snapping his head, and throwing him back into the classic Chevy convertible. He hit with a crunch, denting the pristine metal. Unconscious but still breathing.

Adam winced. He should've protected the car, damn it.

The third guy finished lounging and moved forward, making fists. At the same time, the first guy managed to get to his feet. At least number two was out cold for the duration.

"What are you doing in our territory, anyway?" The first one, a guy with long dark hair, circled him, no doubt looking for an opening.

"We both know this isn't your territory," Adam said easily, keeping both men in his sights. They were in their early twenties and were human, so he'd need to continue pulling his punches. Didn't mean he couldn't hurt them a little, however. "You're not Grizzly members."

"We will be," said the other guy, a blond with amazingly frizzy hair. "Beating the shit out of you will definitely help."

Adam grinned. These guys would never be full Grizzly members, but he couldn't very well explain that to them. He could, however, teach them a lesson. "Grizzly members don't just attack guests in their parking lot."

"You're not a guest," Blondie spat. "You're a Fire member. Are you trying to infiltrate our club?"

What a moron. "No. How do you know I'm part of Fire?" It was a question that required answering.

"We just do," the dark-haired guy answered.

Interesting. Adam feinted back, turned, and grabbed Blondie in a headlock. His buddy tried to help him, but Adam kicked him square in the jaw, and he fell to land hard on his shoulders. Then Adam held tight, despite the blond kid's furious struggles, until they stopped. He dropped the unconscious body to the cement. "He'll be okay," he reassured the guy with black hair, who was rubbing his jaw as he stood, his eyes a furious hazel. "Although he'll have a migraine, I suspect." A quick glance at Victoria confirmed she'd pressed herself against a Ford truck and was watching the altercation with wide eyes. He should probably get her to safety. "Now you talk."

The guy shook out his arms. "Why are you here, damn it?"

Adam sighed. "I came to get my woman." He ignored the not-pleased gasp from Victoria at that.

"Your woman?" The kid glanced at her and then back. "She's with Lucas Bryant-Clarke."

"Just Clarke," Victoria piped up. "He's decided finally to just go with the Clarke part of his name. Too confusing." Her voice stuttered, and her eyes appeared a bit dazed.

The guy gaped at her like she'd lost her mind.

"Now I have to get her out of the rain," Adam said. "She's mine, and Lucas agrees, as does Bear. If you have a problem, ask them."

The guy looked at his two fallen friends. "Um, okay."

Adam's brow furrowed. "I'm afraid we can't leave it at that." He advanced on the guy, noting the widening of the kid's eyes. "I need to hear what you know about me and about Titans of Fire. Why are you guys following us?" Something was seriously off if a couple of hopefuls were watching him, studying him. "I'm having a rough night, and breaking a couple of bones will calm me."

The guy backed up until his ass hit the Chevy. "I don't want any trouble." He held up both hands, and one was bleeding freely.

"Then you shouldn't have attacked me," Adam said reasonably. "The only reason you're still breathing is because you came after me and seemed to take pains to keep my woman out of harm's way." Of course, the guy had thought Victoria belonged to Lucas.

The guy gulped. "I wouldn't harm a woman."

Yet another reason to let him live. "Good," Adam said, standing only a foot away. "Have you been following me?" He would've caught a tail.

"Um, no." The guy wiped blood off his lip. "I've studied files on you and a bunch of the Fire members, and we've conducted, uh, surveillance on their headquarters. I've seen you there."

"Based on whose orders?" Adam asked, the need to punch somebody rushing through him again.

The guy shuffled his feet and looked down at the rain-splattered ground. "I'm not going to say."

"Then I'm going to hurt you."

The kid looked up, his bruised jaw firming. "Yeah. You probably will." He shook out his arms, his hands, and settled his feet.

Damn, but Adam was starting to like this kid. "Just tell me who ordered you to watch us. Watch Titans of Fire." It made sense that Bear was keeping an eye on a rival gang, but he would've left the Enforcers from Ireland out of any surveillance plan. They were old friends, and Bear knew all he wanted to about them. About witches in general, actually.

Voices lifted through the rain, and three Grizzly members came into view, one of them Lucas.

The kid in front of Adam shuddered in what smelled like pure relief.

Lucas looked at the two unconscious men on the ground. "What the hell happened here?"

Fuck. Adam stuck his hands in his pockets, trying to look harmless. Lucas was Bear's second, and he knew Adam was Bear's friend, but he might have to save face here. "There was a bit of a scuffle."

The member behind Lucas growled. "What the fuck is Fire doing here?"

Lucas studied Adam, his gaze intelligent if not fully in the know. "That's a damn good question." Several more Grizzly members came into view around cars and bikes.

Victoria moved forward, tension streaming from her. "It's, ah, my fault." She batted her eyelashes. "When Lucas, ah, dumped me, I called my friend Adam." She sidled closer to Adam as if to protect him from the Grizzlies. "Adam's brother is dating my sister, and well, I just didn't know who else to call."

Smart. Adam slid an arm around her waist. He'd claim a friendship to Bear if he had to, but that would put Bear in a difficult position. It'd also cause hell if the Fire members found out. So the woman had figured out a way to avoid more bloodshed and still give Lucas his pride. "I just want to get her out of the rain."

Lucas slowly nodded. "Don't come back. Next time any member of Fire sets foot in our territory, he eats it."

Adam fought a grin at the descriptive language. "Understood." He moved to his bike and deposited Tori on it. Leaning in, he couldn't help but press a kiss to her upturned nose. "That was brilliant. Thanks for keeping us safe."

Her eyebrows rose. "Us? I was keeping *them* safe. You've hurt enough of them tonight."

He breathed in. The woman was deadly serious. She thought he was that big of a threat. He grinned. He couldn't help it.

Tori wrapped her arms around Adam as the bike flew through the rain. Her body still hummed, and her head still buzzed. Maybe that was why the bike was working and not petering out on the side of the road. She forced thoughts of the bike and her oddity out of her mind. If she didn't think about it, perhaps it wouldn't become a problem.

Her hands spread across his ripped abdomen. Even with the wind and increasing rain, he warmed her. The guy was a heater. Was it something to do with him being a witch and being able to make fire? Or was he just that masculine?

Her mouth still tingled from his kiss. As if what he'd done had been a mere kiss. The bike purred between her legs, sending vibrations up and through her. Not once in her life had she been so close to orgasm after just one kiss. If she moved the right way, she could probably get there from the bike itself. How had he done that to her? The kiss hadn't even been sweet. No. He'd all but eaten her whole.

She turned her face and rested her cheek between his shoulder blades. Muscle shifted along her jaw.

Watching him fight . . . that should've turned her off, right? Yet the brutality, the single-minded sharpness of his blows, excited her. He was deadly and dangerous and breathtaking. There was no doubt he'd fight to the death if he decided to protect her . . . and he'd fucking win. That sped up her breath as much as the kiss that was so much more than a kiss.

The heat beneath her skin pricked, wanting relief. Her entire body needed relief. The rain and wind weren't even coming close to cooling her libido. She breathed in, allowing the pine scent of the trees surrounding them to fill her. Wasn't pine supposed to be soothing? If anything, the wildness of the land on each side of them spurred her own.

Adam turned off the main road onto a barely there trail.

Soon a river rushed alongside them.

God, she hurt. Her breasts rubbed against his back, and she stifled a moan.

He stiffened.

Oh, man. It was too late. Way too late to turn back. She'd learned young, very young, to take the pleasure life offered before it went away. Well, he'd created this problem, and he'd damn well solve it.

Gathering courage she'd never doubted, she clasped his rib cage with her left hand. Her right flattened over his abs, slowly sliding down.

He stiffened against her.

She reached the hard—very hard—ridge beneath his jeans.

He jerked the bike to the side and toward the river. She yelled and tightened her hold on his dick.

He frantically pulled the handlebars, getting them back on the trail. His cock pounded against her hand, even through the jeans, a fierce cadence of rapid pulse. His head lifted, and his entire body seemed to swell somehow. Reaching a small clearing, he swung the bike in an arc, stopping at the steps to a quaint little cabin. A second later and he was off the bike. "What in holy hell are you fucking doing?" he bellowed.

Finally. She'd finally made badass Adam Dunne lose his control.

She swung her leg and dismounted from the bike. "You started it," she yelled back, pushing rain-soaked hair away from her eyes.

"Two seconds more and I woulda finished it," he rumbled.

She swallowed. Shit. They were back at the cabin. The one where her friend had died after taking Apollo weeks ago. She'd rushed him there, thinking the Dunnes could help him. He'd burned in front of her eyes, and she'd been helpless to stop it. Even Adam and his brothers couldn't stop it.

"Victoria?" Adam asked.

She shook herself away from bad memories, determined to make good ones. Excellent hot and sweaty ones, with the bad boy facing her. He was the epitome of male, standing in the rain and wind, a romantic cabin behind him. His eyes had turned to dark emerald, his lips to a fine line, his body to one long tense masterpiece. All sculpted and hot and waiting for her. She took a step forward.

He stepped back.

Power flushed through her, heated and sharp. Feminine and dangerous, it went to her head and narrowed her focus. She stepped again, avoiding rocks and downed pine needles, her gaze on the man. On the male. Yeah. Witches weren't men, but he was all male. "Adam," she said, her voice lowering to a siren's purr.

His head tilted just a bit, his nostrils flaring. "Watch yourself, Victoria."

Ah, that voice. Dark and low . . . gravelly and so harsh. It kissed across her, licking and biting, and she wasn't even touching him. If she was bewitched, she didn't care. Not now. Probably not ever. So she reached him, sliding her hands beneath his wet shirt. Her eyelashes swept down as the heat from his skin, the hard muscles beneath her hand, forced even more lust through her body. It was too much to keep her eyes open, but she forced them open anyway. "You can't break a promise."

His gaze dropped to her lips. "A promise?" he asked, his arms visibly vibrating with the effort of keeping his hands to himself.

"Yes." She rose up on her tiptoes and licked beneath his jaw. Whiskers tickled her tongue, and she kissed down the hard cords in his neck. "Back at the Grizzlies. The kiss you gave me, that was a promise."

"Victoria," he whispered, his voice now tortured.

She had him. She could feel it. So she stepped fully into him, body to body, her breasts hard against his even harder chest.

Fire, blue and fierce, flashed down his arms as his control snapped.

He growled and lifted her up, his mouth on hers before she could draw a surprised breath. His hands clutched her butt, and he turned, gracefully carrying her up the steps and kissing her until his mouth, his brutal body, were all that existed.

A door closed.

Warmer air brushed her.

His kiss deepened, the heat from his mouth nearly scalding her. He released her, twisting his head.

No. She reached for him, her nails digging into his wet shirt.

His gaze met hers, and he gave her a small shake. "Say you're sure."

Oh God. "I'm sure," she whispered. So, so, so sure.

He ripped her shirt down the front. She gasped, her hands growing still. The look in his eyes. She'd seen it in wild animals on television. Hot and feral . . . absolute. Planting a hand on her chest, he flicked her bra open.

She jerked and looked around, seeing a small living area next to a kitchen. "Ah, bedroom?"

His smile transformed his handsome face into stark beauty. Wild and primal. "We're not garna make it to the bedroom."

Chapter 12

Adam's fangs dropped for the briefest of moments.

Victoria's eyes widened, and she craned her neck to see better. "Witches have fangs? Like vampires?" she whispered.

"Aye." All immortals had fangs. He retracted his, flattening his hand over her upper chest. Small. Delicate. His body rioted as he slid down and cupped one breast.

Her eyelashes closed and then swept open. A pretty pink spread across her face. Ah, the woman was so responsive.

Grasping her hips, he lifted her to the back of the sofa, stepping in so she had to open her legs. His fingers snagged the strap of her bra, and he drew it down her arm, prolonging the sensation.

She trembled.

The hunter inside him, the one he'd banished in favor of cold logic and strategy, stretched awake. "You're beautiful, Victoria," he murmured, tossing the bra to the ground. Her breasts were heavy and full, her nipples the light pink of a true blonde. He trailed his fingers across one, and the trembling of her body warmed him. "Stunning."

She leaned into his touch and reached for his shirt. "You're overdressed." Her nails scraped his abdomen as she yanked the material up.

He ducked his head so she could pull off the wet mess.

"Oh, Adam." She stroked down his torso, her nails light. Fire streaked through him to land in his groin, which already pounded like he'd never had sex before. "I could touch you all day," she murmured.

Aye. He could get on board with that plan. Moving in to her again, he gripped her chin and lifted her face, kissing her deep. She tasted like ginger and something temptingly sweet, all Victoria, wild and succulent . . . and, for the moment, his. Oh, this was a mistake, and he should back away. Instead, he leaned forward and nibbled along her lips, winding across her jaw to sink a fang into her earlobe. The second she'd grasped him on the bike, the moment had become inevitable.

She grabbed onto his ribs, the smoothness of her skin against his a reminder to go slow.

Then, even with his mouth working hers, she reached between them and found his cock, stroking him from base to tip over his jeans. He jerked against her, and his head swam. A second later, she unzipped his jeans, freeing him.

He slid his hand around, grasping her neck. Then he released her lips, tilting his head to study her eyes.

Need and want . . . along with triumph. Yeah. Interesting.

She stroked him, and pleasure streaked through him, making him swell in her palm. His lids half lowered. "You're used to being in control," he said. It was made as a statement—no need to question.

She smiled then, a woman secure in her place. In her curvy body.

Fuck, if that wasn't the hottest thing he'd ever seen.

"Control is an illusion," she murmured. Her nails scraped his balls.

Fire shot through him. He growled low.

"I guess I just like your body." Her hand tightened around the base of his shaft.

He let her stroke him, enjoying her soft touch, trying to see more than she'd let him. Oh, what would it be like to get this woman out of her head, to really find all of her? For the first time, he could see the complexity that was Victoria Monzelle. The wild child, the hot singer, the secret-keeping woman—they were all facets of her. The core of her, who she truly was . . . remained hidden.

Not for long.

He ran his thumb down the delicate skin on her neck, felt her racing pulse, and tightened his hold.

Intrigue and desire leaped into her eyes.

Aye. A wild woman, to be sure.

His free hand snapped her pants open, ripping the zipper away.

She gasped and then chuckled. "Nice."

Yeah. That was him. Nice.

Challenge curved her lips. "There's not much you can do with me sitting here." Her chin lifted just as her nails scraped his entire length.

He sucked in air as electricity burned him from within. Though he didn't know her, not really, one thing was abundantly clear. No way could she win this one. "You sure about that?" he asked, his hand remaining around her throat.

She smiled, the mystery of feminine power all but rolling from her.

Blast but she was incredible.

"Kick off your boots, lass," he whispered, his brogue breaking free.

Her breath hitched. Ah, she liked the brogue. 'Twas good, that. Then she toed off the boots, and they clunked on the floor. Still feeling pretty safe, now wasn't she? He hadn't spent centuries studying quantum physics and the rest of the physical sciences for nothing. If he was careful, since they were in the middle of nowhere, he could use a whiff of his powers without getting caught. With a wave of his free hand, blue fire enveloped her jeans, burning them away and then dying out.

Her mouth gaped open, and she looked down at her bare legs. "You, how, what?" Then her head snapped up, the challenge brighter than ever. "My panties survived the burning by Adam."

He swirled one finger in the air, creating a flame, twisting it around and around.

Her eyes widened, and she tried to shove herself away from him and over the back of the sofa. Ah, she'd forgotten about the hand around her throat. He held her in place, almost easily, and moved the finger toward those pretty mint green panties.

She stopped breathing and watched, her gaze fascinated and wary. The combination almost made him come right then, even though she'd finally released his cock.

"Adam?" she asked, sucking in her stomach.

"Aye?" he answered, flicking the flame across the thin material. The green turned to white and then burned away.

She coughed and then laughed, joy in the sound. "That was

awesome." The flame continued on, controlled by his index finger. She tried to inch away. "Um—"

He ran it along her labia, keeping it hot but not burning. She gasped, and her legs trembled. He dropped to his knees and kissed her clit, forcing the flame along her thigh and controlling it to keep from burning any part of her.

She moaned, and trembles shook her thighs.

He tasted her then, running his tongue where his finger had blazed. Woman and spice . . . with a hint of sweetness. Everything he could imagine, even better, right there for the taking.

She gasped and pushed against him. For answer, he flattened his hands on her thighs, forcing them wider. Then he set in to torture her. Using his fingers, his flame, his tongue—he nipped, licked, and sucked. Within minutes, she gyrated against him, muttering and pleading off and on. He could feel the tension in her beating against him. The desperate need to come. His legs tangled in his jeans, and his cock pounded with pain.

She grabbed his hair and pulled before shoving him closer to her.

He chuckled, and she moaned. Then he increased the pressure of his tongue right on her clit, lashing until she broke. Her entire body jerked and stiffened, and her thighs clamped hard on his shoulders. He prolonged her ecstasy until she came down with a muffled whimper. Then he stood and kicked his jeans across the room.

Her eyelids partially closed, and a small smile lifted her pouty lips. Her gaze dropped to his erect cock. "I don't suppose you can create fire with that, can you?"

Tori couldn't think, much less move. Her body was partially satisfied, with a huge hint of needing more. Adam was even more spectacular nude than he was in faded jeans and a badass T-shirt. His dick was long and thick . . . and harder than rock. He had no shyness about his nudity. Why would he? Seriously. He had muscles, hard and roped, where she hadn't realized muscles could be. But he wasn't all bumpy or out of proportion like guys she'd seen on television. Instead, he was long and lean with a natural physique. Like a wild animal.

He swept her up, easily holding her against his chest before turning toward a door next to the massive stone fireplace.

She traced the hard cord in his neck, marveling at his sheer maleness. Reaching up, she licked along his jugular. "I think your neck is my most favorite thing in the world."

"We'll have to change your mind about that," he said dryly, tension in his tone.

She chuckled. Adam was funny. Who knew?

He carried her into a quaint bedroom with a huge bed covered by a wedding ring quilt. Oak tables with gas lanterns sat beside the bed. The room smelled like wood polish and cleansers. A window opposite the bed was open, letting in the breeze and the rhythmic drumming of rain. He set her down gently, as if he was afraid of harming her.

"You can't break me," she murmured, sliding her hands down the outside of his thighs.

A knuckle under her chin lifted her face. "Ah, baby. I *won't* break you. Don't assume I couldn't." He pressed a kiss to her nose and pushed her down on her back.

Not for a second did she think he meant physically. He was smart, and classy, and even fun with the whole fire thing, but she'd never let any man get close enough to hurt her. Not ever again. But she'd sure enjoy every second she had with Adam. She reached for him, and he covered her. The second all that hard muscled warmth rested against her, desire spiraled even hotter than before. She widened her legs.

He rolled then, flipped her on top of him. She yelped, clutching his pecs to stay on him, her hair flying in every direction.

"Figured you'd want to play a bit," he said, his voice rough. Both hands wrapped around her breasts and slid, tugging her nipples toward him. Pleasure streaked straight from his fingers to her clit, and she pressed down on the hard length of his erection. Were all witches like him? Something told her Adam was gifted, something special, even among his own people.

She stilled. "Wait a minute. You can't mate me, right?"

"No." He reached up and pulled her head down, hissing out a breath when her pebbled nipples moved along his chest. "To mate, I need to bite you and brand you. I won't do either."

Curiosity swirled through her. "Brand me? With a branding iron?"

He frowned. "No. Long story. A brand from my hand transfers to you." He held up his smooth palm. "It's not here. No worries."

What the heck? "Why isn't it there?"

He apparently got bored with the conversation, because he rolled her nipples again, his gaze caught by his own action. "It just appears when a mate is near. Or rather, a potential mate. Fate somehow plays a part." He pulled harder, and she gasped, moving with his hands this time. "Or it's biology. Probably biology. Some sort of recognition on a genetic level." Fire flashed from his fingers and captured her nipples.

She moaned from the delicious snap of pain that turned to pleasure. Wait. She needed to think. Wetness spilled from her to cover him, and she couldn't keep from rubbing against his cock. "Ah, can you, um, bite me without mating me?"

His eyes flashed.

She blinked.

"Aye. Want me to bite you?" Gravel roughened his low voice.

She nodded. "I think so." Tossing her head to the side, she bared her neck to him. "Will it hurt?"

He slid his hand in her hair and tugged her to the side. "You like a little pain, baby." His other hand clamped on her hip, and he rolled them until he lay on top of her again. "If I'm biting you, I'm on top."

Her eyes nearly rolled back in her head from the feeling of his hard penis resting on her clit. God, he felt too good.

His fingers twisted, and he turned her neck, holding her in place. She looked at the far wall, tingles exploding through her abdomen. She couldn't breathe. Was this a mistake? She panted, trying to fill her lungs.

A fang scraped her neck, and she jumped.

He licked her, taking his time. If she asked him to stop, would he? She tried to turn her head back toward him, but he didn't let her. More tingles . . . harder explosions. She gave up breathing and just held her breath.

His fangs slid in, so sharp it didn't hurt. She felt the movement of his mouth, of her skin, but no pain. Then he was licking her, hurtling streaks of raw pleasure from his mouth through her entire body. Then he levered himself up and pressed against her, pushing inside her with long, sure strokes.

More pain combined with pleasure as he took his time, worked her body, allowed her to grow accustomed to his size.

She stilled. "Wait. Protection?"

He chuckled and pressed his forehead to hers. "I'm a witch with no diseases. We can't get any. Protection would just burn off, anyway."

She blinked, her body overtaken.

"Widen your thighs more, baby. I need more room," he whispered, laying gentle kisses on her eyelids, nose, and mouth.

She obeyed, thrilling at the feeling of his strong body pinning her to the bed. "Wh-what about pregnancy?" she asked, her mind already drifting away.

"Have to be mated," he said, pushing hard to embed himself fully inside her.

The word *mated* softened everything inside her. Why, she'd have to figure out later. Her thighs ached from being so far apart, but the pain inside her, the need for him to move, was even stronger. She ran her nails down his back, no doubt drawing blood.

His lips drew back at the rough treatment.

She nipped his lip. "Start moving. Now."

"Yes, ma'am." He held her hip down with one strong hand and pulled out, pushing back in.

It was too good. Way beyond good. He stroked nerves inside her that had to be new. Had to have just arrived because of him. They weren't there before. She lifted her knees to take more of him.

He growled. An actual, animalistic, growl.

Everything inside her shuddered and swelled. More. She needed more.

As if hearing her unspoken plea, he started to pound. Hard and strong, he stroked inside her, giving her more than she'd ever imagined. Lights flashed behind her eyes. She scooted her butt down an inch, and his shaft caressed her clit on the way in. Oh God. He moved faster, angling more, hitting a spot inside her she'd never known before.

The room sheeted white and then went dark. Sparks flew behind her eyes, slashing through her with sharp claws of devastating ecstasy. She cried out, arching against him, her nails digging in enough she could feel his flesh give. The orgasm wrung her out, taking everything. She finally gave, her body going limp against the bed.

He bit her again, this time harder, so she could feel the burn.

With a shudder, he came with her name on his lips.

Her heart beat wildly, and her neck hurt. Her whole body felt like it had tumbled down stairs and then taken the best drug ever made. She was satisfied beyond measure. Yet her mind rioted. It spun and twirled . . . throwing warning down her spine. She had to be careful. Adam Dunne was more than she'd imagined a man could be. Maybe because he wasn't a man.

He lifted up and placed a soft kiss on her nose. "That was a nice start."

Chapter 13

Adam piled wood in the fireplace, his unbuttoned jeans hanging off his hips. Morning light peeked through the rolling clouds, and in the distance, thunder growled. Victoria slept in the room still, mumbling, tossing and turning. The woman talked in her sleep all night, which was beyond adorable. Unfortunately, it sounded like she was speaking in Klingon.

He'd have to get a dictionary.

His body had calmed after the third time with her last night, but it had been hours, and now he was primed and ready again. Never in his life had a woman affected him so. He'd bitten her, damn it. What had he been thinking?

He had not been thinking. Period.

He scrubbed a rough hand through his tousled hair. Worse yet, he had failed to get the truth from her about why she'd gone into Grizzly territory. Bear had all but shouted she had an ulterior motive, and Adam was an expert at finding hidden motives in both friends and enemies. Not in Victoria, however. It had been an entire night, and he hadn't discovered the truth.

In fact, he'd barely even asked.

A phone buzzed. He loped for the kitchen sink and drew out a box of phones, taking the one that was buzzing. He read the screen and sighed. The caller was Pyro, the president of the Titans of Fire Motorcycle Club.

"What?" Adam asked.

"Who is this?" Pyro snapped.

"This is Adam."

Pyro swore something. "We have a meeting at noon, and I want all three of you fucking Irish Enforcers here. Period. You'd better have news about my fucking guns, too."

Adam fought his temper, waiting until he could speak clearly before answering. "Our supplier wants to know more about the drugs. You give a little, and we'll give a lot." He was done waiting for news about Apollo. "I know in this little part of the world you're a tough guy, Pyro. But my people were inventing interesting ways to torture people long before this continent was even settled."

"Yeah. I'm scared of a bunch of Irish leprechauns."

For the love of the motherland. Leprechauns didn't exist. Adam couldn't very well tell Pyro that witches did, however. The agreement had been that Adam would trade guns from Ireland for the Apollo drug, and Pyro apparently was getting tired of waiting for the shipment. "I'll be there." Adam clicked off.

"Who was that?" Victoria asked from the bedroom doorway.

He turned. Her hair was wild around her shoulders, a sparkling blond with defiant purple streaks. Her blue eyes were full of slumber, and she'd tugged on an old Metallica T-shirt she'd apparently found in a drawer. The material reached her knees, leaving her defined calves visible. He'd never considered calves sexy until right that second. Then his gaze reached her bright purple toenails, and his heart kicked hard against his ribs.

"Adam?" she asked, her head tilting.

He shook himself out of his thoughts. "It was Pyro, the president of Titans of Fire."

"Oh." She blinked. "Oh yeah. Care to explain why a Fire member dared infiltrate Grizzly territory? I know you're an Enforcer for that club. How are you and Bear friends? And how are Bear and Simone siblings?" Victoria pushed away from the door and padded barefoot toward him, lines creasing her forehead. "You have a lot to explain."

When the woman foolishly came into arm's reach, he grabbed her, hauling her up against his chest. She gave a muffled *oof* as her breasts pressed against him. "Good morning," he murmured, bending down and kissing her. She mumbled something and in seconds was kissing him back, her hands folding over his shoulders.

Desire streaked through him, and he settled himself. For some reason, he couldn't seem to hold tight to his control with her near.

"Are you all right?" he asked quietly. There was no doubt he'd been rough with her during the night.

She lifted an eyebrow. "Yeah. Why wouldn't I be?"

Brave, wasn't she? A little defiant as well. He brushed the hair off her shoulder and ran his thumb along the twin bite marks in her neck. Her body trembled against him, and her eyes widened. Aye. He hadn't explained that little tidbit, now had he? He released her and moved to the kitchen, taking out pots and pans. "I have eggs and bacon. There might be some sort of fruit in the fridge."

"Answer my questions, Adam," she said, her voice a little breathless.

He opened the fridge and took out the breakfast ingredients. "I plan on answering your questions, Victoria. But first, you're going to tell me why you went into Grizzly territory. Right now works for me." He placed the ingredients on the counter and then faced her, crossing his arms over his bare chest.

Her gaze caught on his chest. "I wanted to check on Bear."

Truth. He could smell a lie, and she was telling the truth. "Why else?" he asked calmly.

She swallowed. "Figured I should set things straight with Lucas." Her throat cleared. "We were kind of dating. Not really, but I do value him as a friend."

"Did you sleep with him?" Adam asked. He had no right to ask the question, and if he had to guess, he'd say no. Lucas had let her go way too easily. No way had the shifter tasted her.

"That's none of your business," she said, meeting his gaze levelly.

"You're right." He didn't twitch. "I'd still like to have confirmation. I don't think you did, but if you did, then it's no concern of mine. It'd be nice to know just for future dealings with Lucas."

"How are you and Bear friends?" she asked, her chin up.

He nodded. She had every right to make the questioning two way. "All right. It's like this. Simone is my cousin, and turns out, she's half-sibling to Bear. So in this crazy immortal world, that makes us all allies. For the moment, anyway."

"But Bear isn't a witch."

"No." Adam rubbed his scruffy chin. He had no right to reveal Bear's history, but he was asking Victoria to go a long way on faith here. "I really can't go into Bear's life, but he's not a witch. He and

Simone shared a father, who also wasn't a witch. Simone's mama is a witch, who led the Council until recently."

"Until Peter Gallagher took over, and now he's trying to force your family out or kill you all."

"Aye." Adam's shoulders tensed. "This is a bad time to bring you into our world, and I'm sorry for that."

She moved to the cupboards and started opening them, taking out plates and glasses. "I'm not scared, but I'd really like to talk to my sister. I need to touch base with her."

Adam's brow creased. "I know, and I'm sorry about that, too. Alexandra and Kell are locked down, which means no communications in or out for right now. Kellach has a kill order on his head, and the Guard won't care much if they take her out at the same time. I assure you, she's safe."

"Yeah, but she'll be seriously pissed if she can't get hold of me." Victoria shook her head.

"She is, I'm sure. Your mother is also safe on the cruise. We have full twenty-four-hour bodyguards on her, and they're well trained." Though if things heated up any more, they'd have to secure the woman somewhere she couldn't be found. Right now, it was better to leave her in the dark.

Victoria set the dishes on the table. "Why are you here, Adam?" She breathed out and spread her hands wide. "Why Seattle? Why Titans of Fire? I just don't get it."

Fuck. He didn't blame her. It was confusing. "The drug Apollo is why we're all here. It's made from a mineral called PK, or planekite, or phenakite, that comes from Russia and kills witches. It also makes humans feel invincible before it burns them from the inside out."

"I know," she whispered, her face paling. "One of my friends died, remember?"

"Aye." He studied her. She'd brought her burning friend to the cabin, and he'd died there. "I know. He was young and in your band."

She swallowed, tears hazing her eyes. "Another band member gave him the drugs. Afterward, the DEA approached me to be a, well, a confidential informant. They said they wouldn't arrest Malanie, and they also said they'd protect my sister. She's in trouble for dating your brother, a Fire member."

Ah, shit. Anger stirred inside him, throughout him, tingling fire inside his hands. "The DEA is blackmailing you?" Even his breath felt hot.

She drew back at the description, frowned, and then nodded. "Yeah. I guess they are."

"Why didn't you tell Alexandra?" he asked.

She shrugged. "At first, I was trying to protect her, and then we haven't been in the same place. Seriously. It's been forever."

That was true. He relaxed and then stiffened all over again. "Wait a minute. You were at the Grizzly club to investigate them. Rumors abound that they run Apollo."

"Yeah," she said, a cute pout forming on her lips. "But I wasn't very good at it."

Jesus. If she'd been anybody else, Bear would've probably just eviscerated her and left her body in the woods.

"Your undercover work stops right now," Adam said, shoving his hands in his pockets to keep from shaking her. What had she been thinking? What had the fucking DEA been thinking to put her in the middle of a drug war? Oh, he was going to burn some federal assholes the first chance he got.

She shook her head. "No, I—"

"We'll protect your sister," he bit out. "I guarantee Alexandra will be protected."

"What about Malanie?" Victoria asked, her lip trembling until she bit it. "She's only twenty, and she made a mistake. A huge one that she's already living with. Agent Franks said she'd have Malanie charged with not only drug dealing but murder."

"They don't have a body," Adam said quietly. He knew, because Kellach had buried the dead kid in the woods far away from the river.

Victoria swiped her eyes. "They don't need one to make a case. Enough people saw him begin to burn, and plenty of people saw me take him out of the bar."

Adam reared back. "They're threatening you with prosecution?"

She nodded numbly, fear in her eyes.

He fucking lost it. Fire shot from all five fingers on his right hand and sizzled against the sofa, burning a large round hole. His mouth gaped open.

Victoria yelped and jumped away from the sparking material.

Damn it. Adam filled a pitcher with water and flung it over the flames, extinguishing them immediately.

She swung her gaze to him, her eyes wide and a deep blue.

"I'm okay." He tried to sound much calmer than he felt. His fists clenched. "You no longer have a problem with the DEA. I promise you I will take care of the matter."

"How?" she asked.

He gave her the easiest answer. "I'm undercover for the Council and it has powerful ties with Interpol. Don't worry." In truth, he was going to bust heads. But she didn't need to know about that.

She eyed the couch and then the innocent breakfast foods. "So you're undercover at Titans of Fire just to find out about the Apollo drug. But if the mineral hurts witches, why Seattle and not in Ireland?"

He nodded. "We think it's a testing ground before it hits Dublin. There are a lot of witches in Seattle, and there's an established human drug pipeline here." He pressed his lips together, wanting to keep her out of the rest of it, but knowing she needed the full truth. "And your father is incarcerated here." Her dad had been a major drug dealer in his time, and all sources confirmed that Parker Monzelle was still involved in the trade, even from prison. "My people know he's involved somehow."

Tori's mouth firmed. Hurt swirled in her pretty eyes. "That doesn't surprise me. At least, he only lasted a day on parole before getting in trouble last month."

No, the asshole had actually shot Victoria's sister while on parole, but Alexandra had decided to keep that fact from Victoria. A mistake, Adam thought. But it wasn't his mistake. "That's pretty much the whole story. As much as I can tell you right now, anyway."

"Oh. Okay." She took a breath and released it, moving her breasts nicely beneath the T-shirt. "All right, then. So. I did not sleep with Lucas." One of her small shoulders tilted. "If you still wanted to know that."

Adam grinned.

Chapter 14

His smile flayed her every time. Tori pushed unruly hair back from her face and moved to help Adam make breakfast. The sheer domesticity of the moment caught her in the chest and sent warning throughout her body. Her entire life she'd been able to keep men at a distance, where they should be. Always.

Adam didn't like distances. He hadn't told her that, but it was clear from the way he acted.

She cracked eggs in a bowl. "How much danger am I in from the Council?" she asked.

He placed bacon in a pan. "I'm not sure. We don't kill humans. But with Peter in charge, if we don't mate, there might be a death sentence over your head."

The guy didn't pull any punches, now did he? She tried not to rub the bite marks in her neck. Every time she touched them, a small electrical zap wound through her body. When Adam had touched them, she'd nearly dropped to her knees. Even now, her sex felt uncomfortably swollen and needy.

Which seemed impossible after the night they'd shared.

"So, ah, is there an out from the mating?" she asked, starting to whisk the eggs, curious about this huge world she hadn't realized existed. "I mean, say we mate. Then can we unmate?" The idea blazed a high voltage inside her, and she tried to cover the reaction, to hide her need, by focusing on the eggs.

"No. Mating is for life," he said, turning bacon over. The delicious smell filled the small cabin. "Not only that, but a mated person can't be sexual with anybody else. There's an allergy, a horrendous one, that instantly pops up."

Man. If fate landed you with someone against your will, what a bitch. Forever with Adam? He wouldn't accept less than all of her, and she didn't know how to do that. Worse yet, she didn't know if she could. After her father had betrayed his two girls by being an asshole drug dealer, she'd never looked at men the same. Being well aware of her own issues didn't make them any easier to overcome. "It seems like you immortals, considering you've had forever, would've figured out a way to negate a mating," she mused.

He sighed, his impressive back muscles moving. "Supposedly there's a virus that negates mating, but it has never been used when both halves of a couple are still living. It has only been employed with widows or widowers who have been bereaved for quite a long time. So if we mate, it will be forever, Victoria. Don't even consider otherwise."

Her breath felt funny. Too hot. "Are you thinking about mating me?" She shook her head. "You're not, right? I mean, you can't be."

He turned, his lips twitching. "Don't look so terrified."

"I'm not," she burst out, panicked, maybe. There was a moment during the night, when she was orgasming so hard she might've gone blind, when she would've let him mate her. "It's just, how can you be considering it? While I don't know you very well, you don't seem like the type of guy to let anybody push him around."

He finished cooking the bacon and reached for the whisked eggs to pour into the pan. "I don't do very well with orders, that's true." He started scrambling the eggs. "Yet, I've been thinking."

Her gaze was caught by the interesting play of muscle in his back, in his shoulders, as he cooked. "That can't be good," she murmured.

He barked out a laugh. "Well, maybe not. But here it is. I don't want a death sentence on your head. Or mine, for that matter."

"I thought you were thinking of taking out the Council," she countered, warning whispering over her skin.

"Aye. Even so, there will be members of our nation who won't like that. Maybe even part of the Guard. We'd still be in danger." He scooped eggs onto a platter and turned back to the table. "Plus, there are other considerations."

Her head dropped, her eyes opening. "Such as?" Had her voice trembled on that?

"We're good in bed. I like that. You're smart, spunky, and holding a shitload of issues." He frowned. "I don't like that last part."

She shook her head, seeking reality. "Excuse me?"

"I can deal with it, however," he mused, almost to himself. "Your sister is immortal, and I'm sure she'd like you with her. Honestly, it isn't the worst idea I've ever heard."

"Uh." She couldn't find words. Drawing out a chair, she flopped into it. "You're crazy."

"No. Think about it."

Her head spun. Or maybe the world was spinning too fast. Yeah, that could be it. "Listen, Adam. What about marriage? Heart strings? You know, love."

He pinned her with a sharp look. "You'd let yourself love somebody?"

She blinked. "Maybe. Someday." Yeah. She figured she'd love somebody someday. And she definitely wanted kids. So far, her rioting feelings for Adam Dunne, even outside of the bedroom, were the closest she'd come to exploring her heart. Her gaze narrowed. Oh, he was dangerous. There was no doubt. "What about you? No love?"

He dished out the food. "Well, I believe in the concept. But among my people, until very recently, most matings were arranged. You know. Alliances and such."

"Lexi and Kellach weren't arranged," Victoria protested.

"I said until recently," Adam said, pouring orange juice for them both. "We've entered an era where passion and love seem to be taking over. It's just temporary, I'm sure."

Whoa. Here she'd thought *she* was a little clueless. "Let me get this straight." She took a deep drink of the orange juice, pleased there was no pulp. "You're considering mating me for convenience because my sister is immortal, you don't want to die, and I'm a good fuck?"

He blinked slowly and set down his drink. His eyes glinted with raw intelligence, and his lip curled. "I don't believe I like the description you just gave."

"It might not be all classy and sophisticated like your fucking vocabulary, but it's an accurate rephrasing," she snapped.

He took a bite of bacon, chewing thoughtfully and watching her. "What's your problem with class and money?"

"Most people with money are assholes," she retorted.

"Interesting." He drank more orange juice.

She kept hold of her temper, more confused than angry, which just pissed her off more. "Answer me. You're considering mating me for eternity to avoid a death sentence, keep my sister happy, and because you like fucking me."

He leaned toward her, all male, all determination. "In a word? Yes."

Adam rode his brother's Harley down the long drive toward Titans of Fire headquarters, noting the scattering of pine needles across the road. Wet pine needles. The autumn had been brutal, and if this was a sign of the winter to come, he wanted to be out of Seattle by that point. The question was, would he be taking Victoria with him?

He still had doubts, but oddly enough, he wasn't as concerned as he'd been earlier. At first glance, Victoria was young and reckless with a side of immaturity. But getting to know her, just a little, had shown him the woman held depths he might never truly plumb. She wore her wildness like a shield and her defiance like a sword. He'd read a complete dossier on her the second Kellach had become interested in her sister, and he knew all about her past with a drug-dealing father who'd abandoned her.

What the file had neglected to show him was the softness of her skin or the sweetness of her taste.

Yet he could not allow anybody to force him into a mating.

He swallowed and pulled his bike up next to a large building. Titans of Fire holdings consisted of buildings forming a square that included two large garages and a sprawling clubhouse complete with a myriad of bedrooms. He parked the bike and strode through the rec room, wincing at the smell of beer and puke . . . and possibly piss. What a shithole.

Through his years, he'd visited many a motorcycle club, and most were fairly clean. Not this one. Not even close. A member wearing a cut was passed out in the corner, black permanent marker all over his face in a design that looked like a fish. A couple of bras hung from lights in the ceiling, and one was big enough to hold watermelons. Frowning, he stepped over a pile of glass, a baggie of pot, and several mismatched boots of different sizes. What kind of a party had recently gone on, anyway?

Shaking his head, he wound through the hallway to the only conference room. Inside, three men were already seated. Pyro sat at the head, his beer belly protruding over his too-tight jeans. Jamm, another middle-aged man and a recently paroled felon, sat next to him smoking a cigarette. The third man, this one with a long white beard, sat on the other side of Pyro. Ziggy. His name was Ziggy.

Adam closed the door and leaned back against it. For the meeting, he'd worn an old Grateful Dead shirt, even older jeans, and his leather jacket complete with Fire cut. He couldn't wait to burn the damn thing.

"Where the hell are your brothers?" Pyro snapped. He'd earned the name because he loved fire.

"Unavailable," Adam said easily, trying to banish the smell of tequila and sweat from his nostrils. "Where are your Enforcers?" Fire had two of its own Enforcers, but last time he'd seen one of them, the man had been facedown in a pile of coke.

Pyro snarled, flashing his cracked gold tooth. "They're out on assignment."

Sure they were. "All right. Is it time to elect a new VP?" Adam asked, keeping his expression stoic.

Jamm's head jerked up and swung toward Adam. "Excuse me?"

Adam shrugged, measuring the temperature in the room. Heated, hungover, and pissy. Yep. Just what he'd expected. "We all miss Duck, but we need a full Board." Nobody missed Duck. The guy had been a colossal asshole as well as Pyro's nephew. He was dead, and the club really did need a VP. "I meant no disrespect." Had he? Aye. Definitely.

"We'll get to that later," Pyro sneered. "For now, I want to know where your brothers are."

"Underground," Adam said easily. Oddly enough, truthfully as well. "They're wanted by the authorities in Dublin, and it got too hot, even here. So they're gone. Not coming back."

"You're not wanted?" Ziggy asked, his tone nasal.

"Not yet," Adam said.

Pyro studied him for a moment with bloodshot eyes. "Looks like we'll need more Enforcers. However, you can now tell me when my guns will be here."

Adam held his gaze. At some point, they might have to actually give the jackass some guns. "The guns are ready. The minute you deliver Apollo to us, we'll hand them over." It was the initial deal. "Where are the drugs?"

"I've ordered the quantity you want. Friday is the date," Pyro said easily. "Are you up to it?"

"Aye," Adam said. He had to figure out where the damn drugs were coming from by Friday. "Who's the manufacturer?"

Pyro shook his head. "Not something we're sharing. The name is irrelevant."

Ah hell. Fucking Pyro didn't even know the guy. Or rather, he didn't have a clue who he was dealing with. It figured the mastermind of the whole disaster wouldn't just give his name to Pyro. "This meeting is irrelevant." Adam pushed away from the door. His whole undercover op with Fire was irrelevant, damn it.

Pyro halted him with a hand. "Adam, we have good intel that the Grizzlies are starting to run Apollo and compete with us."

"No, they're not," Adam said, holding on to his temper with both hands. There were many things in life that irritated the shit out of him, and having somebody else waste his time was at the top of the fucking list. "You've had a hard-on for the Grizzlies for too long, and each time we go to fight them, something goes seriously wrong." Usually Alexandra and the cops showed up, which was fine with Adam. "The Grizzlies aren't into running drugs."

"They are now," Jamm said, flicking cigarette ash on the tiled floor. "One of our skanks bought from a Grizzly member two nights ago. Said the guy's name was Chuck."

Who the hell was Chuck? "How does she know he's Grizzly?" Adam asked.

"Wore a cut at Mondo's bar in Grizzly territory," Jamm said, his voice hoarse. He took a deep drag on his cigarette, turning the tip bright red.

Adam eyed the man from beneath heavy lids. "What was one of our women doing in Grizzly territory?" he asked softly. He just couldn't use the word skank.

"Trying to score Apollo," Pyro snapped. "Shit, you're dumb. We've had skanks all over town trying to see if anybody was horning in, and guess what? They are."

How the hell was that possible? No way was Bear selling Apollo. "I'll investigate the issue," Adam said tersely.

Pyro's eyes gleamed. "That should be easy for you to do, right?"

Warning ticked down Adam's back. "What do you mean?"

"You were at a party there last night." Pyro's gold tooth gleamed.

Adam straightened away from the wall just as Jamm pulled a gun, leveling the barrel at his chest. A bullet from the Ruger SR9 wouldn't kill him, but fuck, it would hurt. And if Jamm aimed for the head, it'd take months for Adam to repair his brain. "What in holy hell are you doing?" he snapped.

Pyro drummed his beefy fingers on the scratched wooden table. "Waiting for an explanation. What were you doing at a Grizzly party last night?"

"Are you having me followed?" Adam growled, going on the offensive out of instinct.

"No, dipshit. We were watching the Grizzlies," Pyro said, his chest puffing out. "You have two seconds to explain, or Jamm is going to blow your head off."

Wonderful. A head shot. "Fine," Adam said, keeping his gaze hard. "I was in Grizzly territory getting my old lady."

Jamm kept his aim steady. "He did leave with a bitch."

"She's mine," Adam growled, measuring the distance between them. Even if he jumped, he'd most likely get shot at least once.

Chapter 15

Tori finished cleaning up the breakfast dishes, her body tingling and kind of aching. The night had been wild, and for a short time, she'd lost herself. Worse yet, at breakfast, when Adam had so calmly said that he'd consider mating as a last resort since he pretty much didn't believe in love, every competitive impulse she'd ever had rose hard and fast to the surface.

He didn't believe in love?

Oh yeah? She'd show him. A part of her, one deep down, wanted him to love her. She wanted to show him that love existed. How screwed up was that?

She set the towel beneath the kitchen sink, and a basket caught her eye. Taking it out, she counted eight cell phones. Were they burner phones? They would have to be, right?

Grabbing one, she gently dialed her sister's number. Four rings, and Lexi's voice mail came on. Tori left a quick message for Lexi to call her, just as the phone started smoking. Her palm burned and she yelped, dropping it to the floor.

Okay. Deep breaths. She focused her energy, trying to calm herself. Then she tried another phone. This time, she only made it five numbers before it shorted out.

That one clunked on the polished wooden floor and bounced three times.

She could do this. Adam's words in his low voice filtered through her mind. Relax her body, clear her mind. Think nothing. She sucked in air and shut her eyes. Her muscles relaxed, one by one. She took a third phone and lightly pressed the screen.

"Agent Franks," came a low voice.

"Agent. It's Tori Monzelle," she breathed, trying to gingerly hold the phone just an inch from her ear.

Papers rustled. "Where the hell are you?"

"Somewhere safe," she said quietly. "Things heated up at Grizzly territory last night."

"How so? Did you get proof?" Franks asked, her voice rising.

Tori leaned against the counter. "Yeah. I got proof. There are no drugs going through the Grizzlies. Those guys don't even do drugs."

Quiet reigned for a second. "You were seen leaving with a Fire member, Tori. Say good-bye to your friend Malanie. She's going to jail."

"No, wait." Tori thought rapidly. The phone zapped against her ear, and she winced. "I'll call you back." But it was already dead. Shit, shit, shit. Okay. She grabbed another phone and dialed.

"What the hell?" Franks hissed.

"Sorry. Bad phones," Tori rushed out. "Listen. I'm dating a Titans of Fire member now, and I can get you intel." She just needed Agent Franks to back off for a while and she'd figure something out. Maybe Adam could help her, considering he was undercover, too. Not for one second did she consider telling Franks the full truth about him. "Fire is known to run Apollo, right?"

"Yes." Now Franks's voice turned calculating. Thoughtful. Calm.

Tori fought the urge to throw up. "Hey. How did you know I left with Adam?"

"You're not our only CI, Monzelle," Franks muttered. "Not even close. You told me you were hanging out with Adam Dunne yesterday. How long have you been dating him?"

Tori closed her eyes as dizziness slapped her. "Um, yeah. Since my sister is dating his brother, I, ah, got to know him a little bit. So he came to the Grizzly party last night and got in a fight taking me away." If a CI had been watching, that's what he or she would've seen.

"Good." Franks's tone turned conciliatory. "You did a good job. We think Fire has been involved with the Apollo trade much longer than the Grizzlies. Now you're on the inside. This will protect your sister and your friend better than the other plan. Excellent thinking. So, what do you know so far?" More papers rustled.

"Nothing," Tori whispered. "I just got in, Franks. I need time."

"Time is running out. Did you know your sister has disappeared?"

Tori clutched the phone. "I think she and Kell took a vacation, but I don't know where."

"We both know she's running from the law. It's up to you to save her. Get me information about Apollo and Titans of Fire. You have three days." Franks clicked off.

The phone burst into flames, and Tori yelled, dropping it and stomping it with her foot. Her sock was singed. Tears pricked her eyes and she batted them back. Okay. This was all right. Lexi was safe somewhere in Idaho, and now all Tori had to do was save Malanie.

Maybe she should have Adam get her friend underground as well. Malanie didn't have family in the area. It wasn't a bad idea. Not really.

The sound of motorcycle pipes echoed through the lightly falling rain. Her heart sped up. Adam was coming back so soon? She hurriedly smoothed back her hair and ran to the bathroom, rifling through a drawer to find one bright red lipstick. No eye shadow, damn it. The high-end lipstick had to be Simone's. Tori brushed the expensive cream across her lips and then quickly wiped most of the color away, leaving a muted red that was almost pink. Better.

Then she rapidly brushed her hair into a ponytail, using a band she found in another drawer. A couple of pinches to her pale cheeks and she was good to go.

The pipes came closer. A loud rumble of pipes. A couple of bikes? Who would Adam bring back to the cabin? That was odd. She stilled and then sprang into motion, hustling for the bedroom to look out the window. Soon three bikes came into view with a lifted black truck behind them. She squinted. The riders wore Titans of Fire cuts.

The biker in front had a silver gun half in his pants and against his belly.

The bikes stopped, and the men parked just as the truck rolled up. A man jumped out. She recognized him as a member of Fire but didn't remember his name. None of the men smiled.

Her skin iced over.

One by one, they dismounted from the bikes. The first guy pulled out his gun and checked the clip.

Her stomach knotted. Oh, God. Why were they here? For Adam or her? Either way, the guns didn't promise a conversation. She looked toward the bedroom door. There was nowhere to go. The men nodded at each other and then turned the corner of the cabin, headed for the front steps.

Holding her breath, she lifted the window as quietly as she could. The front door banged open. Panicking, she scrambled out the window and landed hard on the wet weeds below. Pain lanced up her arm. She shoved herself to her feet and ran for the forest.

Loud bootsteps pounded in the house, and another door slammed against a wall. Men shouted. She reached the trees and skidded around a small pine, her socks catching sticks. Panting, she crashed like a wild animal through trees and bushes, her arms pumping, her legs furiously kicking. She heard more male voices shouting behind her, along with the sound of men barreling through the trees.

Branches scraped her cheek, and she ducked, trying to keep going. *Don't stop. Don't stop. Don't stop.*

She looked frantically for any shelter. If she tried to reach the river, she'd be exposed.

Silence settled.

God. They were listening for her. She tried to make less noise, but branches broke beneath her aching feet. Sharp rocks cut into her, yet she kept going. Rain slashed her, branches snapped her, and the wind slapped her. The knot in her stomach spread out, filling her chest, making it hard to breathe.

The terrifying feeling of the forest closing in on her made her pulse race and her gaze swing wildly around. Were they trying to surround her?

A shot rang out, plugging a tree above her head. She screamed, and bark flew. Trying to hunch and make herself smaller, she kept going, twisting and turning around trees and scratchy bushes.

"There she is," a man yelled out.

She whimpered and increased her speed, almost running into a group of rocks. She cleared them, her socks slipping on the last one and sending her sprawling. Her stomach hit first, followed by her chest and then her cheek. Sparks exploded in her mind. She lay, panting, her body paralyzed as she regained her breath. Tears filled her eyes, making it impossible to see.

Hands clamped on her arms and yanked her up.

The guy shook her. Hard.

Her teeth rattled in her head, and pain bloomed in her skull. He turned her and shoved her toward his buddy. The barrel of a gun pressed right against her nape.

"Move," he said.

Her legs trembled, and blood dripped from a cut on her cheek. She brushed it away, slipping again on the rocks. "Wh-what do you want?" she whispered, her body shaking.

"You'll see when we get there." He pushed her harder with the gun.

Adam kept his stance casual when his temper was anything but. It was entirely possible that Jamm might shoot him. "If it were your old lady, you would've gotten her, too," Adam said, his gaze returning to Pyro.

Pyro glared at him. "If it was my fuckin' old lady, she wouldn't have been at the Grizzlies."

Now that was probably a fair statement. "She might not have known she was my old lady yet," Adam said, looking for any sort of common ground. "I took her from Lucas Clarke."

Pyro sat back. "You stole his old lady?"

"Sure did." Well, she hadn't really been Clarke's. But Pyro sure as hell didn't know that fact. "I took her, beat the shit out of a few of them, and that's the end of it."

"You were in Bear's office for quite a while," Jamm said, looking like he wanted nothing more than to put a bullet in Adam's head.

Adam kept his concentration on the leader. "Bear was threatening to kill me for entering his territory, and I threatened to bring down the entire hammer of Fire on his ass, and we scuffled a bit. Broke several of his ribs." Adam smiled at the blatant lie as if remembering the moment fondly. If anybody had seen Bear afterward, he really hadn't looked healthy. Broken ribs could account for that.

"You fought Bear and then a couple of other members?" Pyro asked.

"Sure," Adam said calmly. "That's what you would've done, right?" Pyro was definitely a waste of space. It was probably time to burn Fire to the ground and investigate the case from a different angle. It had been a miscalculation to work with the club for so long. Pyro couldn't give him the information he needed.

Pyro steepled his stained fingers beneath his chin. "I do like the thought of you beating on Bear." He gestured toward the seat next to

Ziggy and across from Jamm. "Please take a seat so we can discuss your place here."

Jamm gestured with the gun, not giving Adam much choice.

Even so, awareness filtered through Adam and tensed his muscles. He was missing something. "What would you like to discuss?"

The sound of an altered truck engine roared through the rain outside along with several motorcycle pipes. Adam stiffened. "Did I miss a ride?"

Jamm snorted. "You could say that."

Adam half rose, and Jamm gestured with the gun. Adam sat and turned toward Pyro, letting the predator he really was show. "What's going on?"

Pyro blinked and sat back in his chair. Then he shook his head. "Just wait."

Ziggy's phone squealed like a stuck pig, and he lifted it to his ear. He gave one short nod. "Shipment is in."

Pyro nodded. "Go take care of it. I'll be in touch in about an hour."

Adam crossed his arms. "Apollo shipment?"

"One thing at a time," Pyro said, anticipation lighting his eyes. Ziggy sauntered out of the room, and it was all Adam could do to let him go.

Five minutes passed. All right, that was enough. Adam tensed to jump for the gun when footsteps echoed outside. Then a knock on the door.

"Ah. They're here." Pyro moved around the other side of the table and opened the door.

The door opened, and a member named Tinker shoved Victoria inside in front of him.

Everything in Adam went deadly silent. "Victoria?" he asked.

She looked at him, dazed. Just like that, relief filled her pretty eyes.

Scratches marred her neck and face, while pine needles stuck out of her wet hair. Blood flowed down her arm from a cut he couldn't quite see. Bruises were already turning dark along her neck, and mud covered most of her.

Adam pushed back his chair and stood.

"Sit the fuck down," Jamm ordered.

"What did you do?" Adam asked Pyro, his voice sharper than cut glass.

Pyro nodded at Tinker. "Do you have men watching Grizzly territory? We're taking them out soon." When Tinker nodded, Pyro gestured toward Ziggy's empty seat. "Watch how things happen. I need a VP, and I'm thinking you're a candidate."

Tinker's eyes widened, showing his dilated pupils. The guy definitely tried the products. At about forty, he had a large beer belly and a sunken chest. He took his seat with definite pride.

Pyro faced Adam squarely. "I wanted answers and figured your bitch would be able to motivate you. Finally."

The beast inside Adam, the one that had tasted Victoria the other night, bunched and tried to spring free. He held it at bay for the moment, focusing on Victoria's battered face. "Are you all right?"

She swallowed and tears filled her stunning blue eyes. "I think so." Her soft voice trembled, and the bewilderment in it threatened to send him over the edge.

The motorcycles roared into action outside and zoomed away.

"Shoot her in the leg, Jamm," Tinker said. "That'll motivate the bastard. We'll know where the guns are within seconds."

Fire and rage mingled in Adam's chest. "You're gonna die second, Tinker," he said.

Tinker snorted. "Right, big guy. Jamm has a gun on you."

Pyro grabbed Victoria and yanked her back to his chest, his gun already out and pointed at her neck. "I'm done dickin' around. I have no problem putting a nice hole in your bitch. Give me the location of my guns, and do it now."

"You're going to die first, Pyro." Adam finally let his beast off the chain.

Chapter 16

Tori tried to use her powers, such as they were, to jam the gun pushing against her neck. Her mind fuzzed, and her body shook from cold and fear, but she needed to focus. The gun hurt her already damaged throat. But seeing the gun pointed at Adam filled her with an all-new terror. One that made it nearly impossible to move.

No expression sat on Adam's angled face, but fire burned in his eyes. Hot and dark, it glittered with fury. He was absolutely more than a man, and it was shocking the other people in the room couldn't see the predator preparing to attack. She watched him, waiting for a signal.

Then he moved.

Somehow, he launched himself across the table toward Jamm. The gun went off, but it didn't stop Adam's momentum. He plowed a fist into Jamm's face the same second he wrenched the gun free, pivoted, and shot Pyro in the head.

Blood sprayed across Tori's face, and she screamed, falling against the door as Pyro plunged to the floor. Adam didn't pause. He turned again and shot Tinker between the eyes. Then, doing a full turn, he pivoted and shot Jamm, whose head jerked back, hit the wall, and then dropped forward. His body slumped in death.

Tori opened her mouth, but another scream wouldn't come out. Her body shook, adrenaline flooding it.

Adam turned toward her, his fangs out, raw rage in his glittering eyes. "Are you okay?" His voice sounded more animalistic than human.

She slowly shook her head, spraying tears. "N-no."

"I'm sorry you saw that." He pounded the gun against the table, shattering the wood. Then he moved toward her, and she recoiled instinctively. Pain flared in his eyes, but he kept coming, his movements calm and deliberate, as if he hadn't just killed three men. "It's okay, sweetheart." Taking her hand, he led her from the room and away from death.

What had just happened? The smell of blood filled the world. She followed woodenly behind him, her movements stiff and jerky. "You're bleeding," she whispered.

He looked down at the bullet hole in his left shoulder. Blood flowed down to his wrist. "It's okay. I'll heal." His voice remained low, almost soothing, as he helped her through the clubhouse and out into the rain. Away from the macabre scene.

She lifted her face, taking a deep breath. The smell of blood and death continued to linger, but the punishing rain helped wash away some of the terror. Her legs trembled.

Glancing around, he took her over to one of the garages, leaning her against the door under an awning. The wind burst against her, but she was out of the rain. "I need you to stay here for just a couple of minutes, okay?"

She nodded, the entire world fuzzy. Shudders wracked her body, but she didn't really feel the cold. She wasn't feeling anything.

He shook out of his jacket and pressed it around her, zipping it up. "You're going into shock. Just give me a second. Stay here."

Her head lolled on her neck, and she pushed against the building, forcing it to hold her up. Adam disappeared inside the garage. Her knees shook so hard she just gave up and slid to the wet ground. Her arms instinctively wrapped around her calves, and she hugged her knees to her chest inside his jacket. So much blood and death.

The smell of him surrounding her helped her to find a shaky center. She breathed deep his scent of wildness and the forest before a storm.

Adam had just killed three men. Oh, they were bad men, and they probably would've killed both Tori and Adam. But he'd moved so quickly and shot so rapidly without even thinking it through. And he hadn't used any fire or witch abilities. Just sheer male power.

Except for the speed. Maybe the speed was witch born. It was as if he'd flipped a switch to go from Adam to somebody else. To some*thing* else. Was that him in true Enforcer mode? Was it a mode? Or was it the true being at his core? She bit back a sob.

Even so, his scent offered comfort. Protection. Safety. No matter what he'd done or how easily he'd done it . . . he'd saved her.

She lost track of how long he was gone.

Rain continued to pelt all around her, hitting the concrete and bouncing up. Her body ached but the pain seemed to come from a distance. Nothing touched her. Not right now. Maybe not ever. Somewhere deep down, she realized it was shock. Closer to the surface, she just couldn't find the energy to care. The numbness helped, and she let it hold her.

Adam finally came striding out with a backpack over one shoulder, a hard angle to his jaw. Concern lit his eyes when he saw her on the ground. "The clubhouse is empty right now, baby. We have to go."

His words kind of made sense, but she couldn't make herself move.

He curved a hand around her elbow and gently lifted her. She wavered. "It's okay, Victoria. I'm getting you out of here and to somewhere warm." Sliding an arm around her shoulder, he led her to his bike. Without waiting for her to get on, he lifted her by the waist. Her hands flattened on the leather seat to keep herself from falling off.

He lifted one leg in front of her and straddled the bike with the pack still over his uninjured shoulder. "Can you hold on?"

She looked numbly toward the trees down the lane.

"Victoria." His voice sharpened.

She jerked. Rain slashed across her face. She shivered.

"Hold on. Now." His voice held a frightening command, and she obeyed instantly, holding him and settling her face against his back. The rain had already drenched his thin T-shirt, but his warmth radiated beneath. She tried to lean into him, to borrow some of that warmth, but nothing penetrated her haze.

He gunned the motor and the bike jumped forward. They'd gone nearly half a mile down the drive when he swung the bike in a wide arc, facing the clubhouse.

She lifted her head, blinking rapidly against the storm.

Adam held the handlebars, tension rolling from him. "They hurt you, Victoria."

She gulped in air.

"This is what happens because of that."

The world went silent for the briefest of moments. Then the ground shook. The clubhouse exploded, throwing fire, barstools, and debris high into the air. A second later the first garage went, and then the next. The hood from a cherry red muscle car crashed onto the road and tumbled end over end, fire consuming it, the metal burning with a shriek.

She gasped and went rigid but couldn't scream.

Several smaller explosions rocked through the structures, blowing out every wall and window. Glass shattered out, scattering through the forest. Even the cement of the square cracked and gave, pebbles of concrete careening in every direction. The pool table imploded on itself, spraying burning billiard balls in every direction. An eight ball impacted with a nearby pine tree, sticking hard in the bark. Bottles of alcohol blew up, sending glass and liquid flying, increasing the spitting of the fire.

She couldn't move. Not one part of her could move. He'd done this because they'd hurt her.

The flames rose high in the air, combating the rain, more powerful than the storm.

Any remaining interior walls crumbled and gave. The fire continued, somehow not reaching the surrounding trees. It was as if its hunger remained with the walls, targeting anything having to do with Titans of Fire.

He had ended them. The entire place. It was over.

Tori shivered again. He'd done this while protecting her—as her protector and possibly her lover. What would he do for a mate? The heavy mantle of responsibility slammed down on her shoulders. Belonging to a male like Adam held power . . . and duty.

She could see it so clearly in the glowering flames. Was she strong enough to even consider it?

Adam lifted a phone to his ear and dialed. "Detective Bernie Phillips, please." He waited several beats before speaking again, his voice rising three octaves and gaining a Russian accent. "There's been an explosion at Titans of Fire, and I don't know how it happened. For now, I have files I'm e-mailing to you that will help you bring down the entire club. Hard copies and other documents are coming as well. You're welcome." He clicked off and watched the fire burn a little bit longer.

She shivered and pressed more closely against him.

He dialed another number. "King? Titans of Fire just exploded and the cops are going to raid all the members. Get your boys home." He paused. "They're at headquarters already? Good. Keep them there." He slipped the phone into his jeans pocket.

"Boys?" Tori mumbled, her gaze caught on debris drifting slowly down.

"A couple of prospects who'd gone undercover with us. They're young and they need to be away from here." Then he slowly swung the bike around. "Can you hold on?" he asked quietly.

"You killed them," she whispered, trying to get a hold on her emotions as well as on the reality of the moment.

"They signed their death warrants when they put you in harm's way. The very second Pyro held that gun to your neck, he was a dead man." No give, no regret, no real emotion rode on Adam's words. "I get that you might not understand that. But it's absolute." He gunned the engine, driving rapidly away from what used to be Titans of Fire.

Adam reached the cabin, making sure Victoria kept a good hold on his waist. By the time he stopped the bike, he'd already healed his shoulder, although a residual ache remained. It had taken a minimal use of his powers, so hopefully he hadn't sent out a signal.

He focused on the most immediate need—Victoria. She had certainly gone into shock, and he had to warm her up. Now. Turning, he swept her up and strode through the cabin, dropping the backpack on the way. In seconds, he had her in a warm shower and was shampooing the dirt and twigs out of her thick hair.

She stood mainly still, allowing him to tend to her, her blue eyes wide and unfocused.

So many emotions bombarded him he shut them all down, focusing on her. As an Enforcer, he knew well how to do what needed to be done.

It had been necessary to end Titans of Fire. Yet the precision and absoluteness with which he'd done the job had been because of

Victoria. Because they'd hurt her. He might be a real bastard, but he was painfully self-aware.

Her skin was like silk, and her bones frighteningly delicate. Fragile and so breakable. He fanned his palms down her soft arms.

He'd taken Fire out without Coven Nine orders, outside the framework of his job. The betrayal of the Council, of the remaining members, left him lost and adrift. Yet even more determined.

"I'm all right," she whispered, reaching out to cup his jaw.

He swallowed and finished washing a scrape on her wrist to keep it from infection.

"You're all right, too." She tugged his earlobe.

He blinked, focusing on her gaze. "I know."

Her expression softened. "It's okay to be angry, Adam."

He paused. "Angry?" No. Emotion had never ruled him.

"Sure. Titans of Fire threatened us. Hurt us. But that's not why you're looking so lost." Her voice was throaty, as if her neck ached.

He turned off the water. "I'm not lost." Yet the words tasted like a lie.

"I understand betrayal." She let him dry her, head to toe, standing there with acceptance in her eyes. "Believe me. My father has done nothing but betray us his whole life. My loyalty is still to my family, even though he was once part of that."

Adam finished gently rubbing her skin to a pretty pink glow, his chest heating. Could he stay true to his values, to his vows, and not protect the sitting council members? His head began to ache as he lifted her against his chest and moved toward the bed. Now wasn't the time for him to figure out his messed-up life. She needed rest. "Get some sleep. We can talk later."

She nodded and snuggled under the covers.

Barely thinking about it, he leaned over and kissed her forehead. Then he grabbed clean jeans and a shirt to yank on before heading into the living room, where he built a roaring fire.

The flames crackled, and he straightened, his muscles tensing. Had there been a way to finish off Titans of Fire without putting Victoria through the ordeal of watching it? Or had he, perhaps, wanted to let her see the real him?

If they mated, and he was truly considering the possibility, then she needed to know him. *Him.*

He examined the situation from several angles and couldn't find another way he could've handled the evening. Pyro had held a gun to the woman's neck. Speed had been of paramount importance.

Closing his eyes, he calmed his body and then his mind. Control was his.

He made coffee and took a steaming mug over to the table, spreading out all the documents he'd taken from the motorcycle club. If there were any pertaining to him or his brothers or even Dublin, he needed to destroy them before sending the rest on to Alexandra's partner at the police station. Bernie Phillips was a smart guy, and it wouldn't do to give him any threads to pull.

Several future plans caught Adam's eye, including one that involved Pyro kidnapping a bunch of kids from the local elementary school for ransom. His stomach rolled. Adam had already known that at least one of the assholes was a pedophile. Good thing he'd taken them out.

The door opened, and Victoria walked out, her feet bare and her damp hair curling crazily around her shoulders. The paleness of her face only emphasized the cuts and bruises.

Just seeing one scratch on her fragile face made him want to kill again.

She reached him and flopped into his lap.

He stiffened, surprised, and then slid both arms around her. "I told you to go to sleep," he murmured, feeling the hard-won control over himself spin away into nothingness.

She set her cheek against his chest with a soft sigh. "I wanted to check on you."

He inhaled the fresh scent of her hair and allowed himself to settle. Finally. "I'm still here. Not leaving for a while."

"That's not what I meant." She played with a loose string on his collar. "Are you all right? I mean, after what you had to do."

He frowned. It took him a minute to catch her meaning. "At Fire?"

"Yeah," she said softly. "Taking those guys out and then blowing the place up. That has to weigh on you. I wanted to make sure you were coping okay."

He closed his eyes, holding her tighter. Everything in him warmed, spiraling out from his chest. When was the last time any-body had been concerned about his feelings? His soul? "Ah, baby.

You're a sweetheart." He kissed her forehead. "Pyro was a criminal selling drugs to kids. Tinker was a creep who liked little girls, and he was dead the second I discovered that. And Jamm was a twice-convicted rapist, and no way had he reformed." All three had needed to be wiped from the earth.

She nodded against his chest. "I understand. They were bad guys, and they kidnapped me. I get it." She leaned back to study his eyes, hers a luminous blue that nature could never duplicate. "But are you okay with it, anyway?"

He swallowed, wanting nothing more than to hold her like that forever. "Aye," he murmured. His life was black and white, cut and dried, and he'd never searched for flowery words. Offering comfort was foreign to him, yet it was in her very nature. So he just went with the truth. "Part of my job is to get difficult things done. But I am truly sorry, more than you can know, that you had to see me doing it." If there had been any way to protect her, he would've done it. Without question.

She cleared her throat. "I know, Adam." Leaning in, she pressed a comforting kiss on his neck. "I was thinking about, well, the bodies." She stiffened.

He rubbed her back. "Don't think about it. Just let it go."

"No." She frowned and shook her head. "I mean, bones don't burn completely. There will be three bodies found, and there will be bullet holes in them. You're a known Fire member. We should probably get out of town."

Ah, the sweet woman. She truly was worried about him, and it was impressive how her mind worked despite the shock she'd had. He couldn't help but lean in and press a kiss against her full lips. "I used more than regular fire."

"Oh." Her face brightened. "Hotter than regular?"

"As hot as an incinerator," he confirmed. If this wasn't the oddest conversation he'd ever had with a woman he'd slept with, he wasn't sure what had been. "Stop worrying about the logistics and my getting caught. I know what I'm doing." He nearly winced as he said the words. "Though I'm not usually a killer. I've killed, but only when necessary." He didn't want her thinking he was some sort of serial killer.

A slight smile hovered on her lips. "I know. Don't worry about that." Then she sobered. "Wait a minute. I thought it was too dangerous for you to use your powers."

He held her tighter. "I barely upped the heat for the fire. Unless somebody was in the immediate vicinity, I should be all right." Yet he couldn't do it again. His powers were significant, and if another witch had been in the area, he would've been felt. Without question.

She fingered his wet hair, and her eyelids fluttered. "Would you come back to bed with me? Just to sleep?"

The moment caught him around the throat and clenched. He had no doubt Victoria Monzelle had never trusted a man enough to ask for comfort and shelter. His heart warmed and turned over as he stood. "Of course, darlin'."

Chapter 17

Tori stretched awake the following morning, her brain rapidly catching up to her body. Her face ached, as did her legs, but considering she'd run through a forest away from three psychos who'd wanted to harm her, she wasn't feeling too bad. She rolled over, pressing her face to the pillow that still held an indent from Adam's head. His scent, the wild one, filtered through her.

How did she really feel about what he'd done?

There had been no passion, no fury, when he'd killed. As with everything else he did in life, he'd been precise and deliberate.

Just who was the witch Enforcer? What would it take to get under his skin? For the first time ever, she wondered what it'd be like to truly belong with a man. His sheer focus and dedication proved he'd never stray. He'd never betray somebody he cared about, and she wanted to be that person. Well, maybe.

He had plenty of faults, too. He was bossy, arrogant, and that precision was a rock wall. It was his way or . . . there was no *or*. Adam lived life his way.

She wasn't exactly the type to fall in line. Never had been, and never would be.

Yet there was something between them. She could feel it in the air, could taste it on his skin.

She rolled her eyes. Enough. A new lyric ran through her mind— a song about power and fire. She'd have to write it down later.

Throwing the covers off, she wandered around and tugged open drawers in the heavy oak chest in the corner. A pair of neatly folded capris caught her eye, along with a deep blue sweater. Perfect. She tugged the clothes on. The sweater fit like it was made for her, while the capris looked more like jeans on her. Must be Simone's. The witch was much taller than Victoria.

Taking a deep breath, she moved into the main room of the cabin, stopping short when she found it empty.

A hearty fire crackled in the hearth, and a note lay on the table. She grabbed it up, reading quickly.

Victoria,

I've gone to deliver the materials to the police. You're safe now. All the Fire members have been rounded up or have fled town. The Guard won't make a move on foreign soil for at least a couple more days. So relax and take a moment just to heal those bruises. I'd prefer you stayed at the cabin for the time being. If you need me to bring anything back with me, there are phones under the sink. Try not to destroy all of them.

Yours,
Adam

She swallowed and moved to the fridge to find a soda. Tipping back her head, she took in the sugar and caffeine. Okay. That was good. She could use some alone time. Then she looked around, noted it had stopped raining, and bit her lip. Alone time? Screw that. She had stuff to do.

Retrieving the basket of phones, she placed it on the table. Lately, she'd been able to ride on Adam's bike without stopping it. Perhaps she was finally learning to control her oddity. Acknowledging it to him and having him accept it so easily had somehow helped. She took a phone and quickly dialed her friend.

"Hello," Malanie murmured, sounding drowsy.

"Mal. I need a ride," Tori said, giving directions. "You okay to drive?" Was the woman still taking drugs?

"I'm fine. We had a set last night. Missed you. When are you coming back?" Mal asked. Rustling sounded, along with the clanking of keys.

Tori rubbed a bruise on her neck. "Soon, I hope." Though did she?

Oh, she loved music, but the bar scene had gotten old about a year ago. But what else would she do with her life? She sucked as a CI and undercover operative. Maybe it was time to truly start writing and creating music again. "How soon can you get here?"

"On my way now," Mal replied, a car engine igniting. "Oh my gosh. Did you hear about Mike Bray?"

Tori stiffened. Bray was the dickhead who'd stolen her song. Her stomach rolled. "Please don't tell me he's dead."

"Dead? No, of course not. But his place was raided, and a bunch of drugs were found. As well as evidence that he'd stolen songs from a bunch of people. Not just you." A horn honked in the distance. "Supposedly, the studios involved are contacting the real song-writers. Let me know if you get a call."

"Okay," Tori said weakly. Something told her she'd be getting that call. Had Adam taken care of the matter? Or had it been the mysterious king? Somehow, her new allies seemed hell-bent on taking care of her, whether she wanted it or not. However, seeing Bray get what he deserved held definite appeal. "Drive carefully, and I'll see you soon." The phone heated in her hand but didn't burst into flames, so she set it down. That was an improvement, right?

She scoured the cupboards and found a box of granola bars. Munching on one, she viewed the dewy forest outside. One of the phones in the basket rang an old Bon Jovi song, and she took a moment to appreciate the melody. She could see the chords in her mind. Finally, she answered. "Ah, hello?"

"Tori," Simone burst out. "I'm so glad I found somebody. I tried to call Adam, but he's not answering."

Tori leaned against the counter, her pulse picking up. She'd missed her friend. "It's so good to hear your voice. It's crazy that you're a witch. I'm here. Are you okay? What's going on?"

"I'm fine——and sorry about not telling you I'm a witch. We're not supposed to tell." Simone chuckled. "Other than that, I'm knocked up and locked down, but fine."

Tori's mouth gaped. "You're pregnant?" Geez. Adam could've mentioned that tidbit. "Um. By whom?"

"Oh, I mated a demon. Nick Veis. You met him in Dublin." Simone's words rushed together. "Right now, I need help."

Tori stood up straight. She'd love a mission—something to do.

Anything to do. If she just sat around, she'd start worrying about the DEA. And her sister. And her mother. And her dead friend. And the Guard. And Adam. Yeah, definitely Adam and the whole mating issue. "I would love to help," she said, meaning every word.

"Rumor has it you're fairly safe now that Titans of Fire has been disbanded," Simone said in a rush. "Is that true?"

"I wouldn't say we're safe, but we're definitely staying under the radar, since we didn't mate like we were supposed to." Tori shook her head. Life had become way too bizarre if that sentence made sense.

"You should mate him," Simone said. "Immortality would look good on you, and I don't have many friends, so that works for me."

Tori grinned. Simone had a kind heart, but she definitely saw life from her own perspective. Someone who didn't adore her might even consider her a little vain and a mite selfish. Good thing Tori adored her. "What can I do for you?"

"Would you please check on Bear for me? He's not answering any of his phones, and I can't find Lucas Bryant-Clarke."

"Just Clarke," Tori said automatically. "He dropped the Bryant." Then the words hit home. "Hey. By the way, you never said you had a brother."

Simone sighed. "Long story. International intrigue. Life-or-death secret."

Tori blew out air. "That seems to be par for the course with you witches."

"It truly is," Simone agreed, obviously not offended. "Anyway, I'm worried about him. Have you seen him lately?"

Tori grimaced. "Yeah. I saw him the other night, and, to be honest, he didn't look good. He was all shaky, pale, and cranky."

"He's always cranky," Simone mused, her voice concerned. "But the shaking and being pale isn't normal. I hate to ask this——"

"Please ask it. I'm your friend, and I'm going a little crazy just looking at cabin walls," Tori said. "Adam isn't using his powers, and he said the Guard won't mobilize to head over here for a couple of days, so we have a reprieve. A short one. Adam wouldn't just give me a platitude to make me feel better."

Simone snorted. "That's a good point. Adam wouldn't know a platitude if it bit his uptight ass."

Tori grinned. It was nice to share tidbits with somebody who also knew the complexity that was Adam Dunne. "The phone is starting to get warm, so you'd better talk fast."

"Huh?"

Oh yeah. She hadn't shared. Maybe everybody held a secret or two. "I have some odd enhancement that ruins electrical devices, motors, engines . . . you name it. The phone I'm using is getting hot." It no longer seemed like an embarrassing secret she had to hide. So she was weird. Who cared?

Simone was silent for a moment. "That's fascinating—and probably something to do with your love of music."

Tori frowned. "What do you mean?"

"I noticed you hear things—patterns in music and dialogue. I've read your lyrics," Simone said thoughtfully. "Perhaps it's related, and you should definitely work on figuring it all out. But don't tell the queen."

Tori lost the smile. "The queen? Dage's wife?"

"Mate. Dage's mate. She's a scientist, and she loves, and I mean *loves*, doing experiments." Fondness coated Simone's words. "She's a doll, but if you tell her, you will find yourself at headquarters in the near future trying to blow everything up with your mind. Or your touch. Or however you do it."

Sounded like an interesting woman. "I'll keep that in mind." A spark from the phone burned Tori's ear, and she winced, pressing the speaker button and setting the device on the counter. "You should probably start talking quickly."

"No problem. Do you mind getting a visual on Bear and slapping a phone into his damn hand? He's avoiding me, I think." Simone sighed. "If he's hurting, I need to know. Depending on what's going on, I may get the queen involved to see if she can assist. The problem is forcing Bear to get help when he thinks he's so damn invincible."

Tori chewed on the inside of her lip. "What's wrong with him?"

"I don't know." Simone cleared her voice. "Just take him a phone and see if he's breathing, and we'll go from there. Thanks." She clicked off.

Tori frowned at the slightly smoldering device. What was the deal with Bear? Apparently, she'd have to go to the source to find out. Plus, it was the least she could do for Simone, and it would get her out of the cabin. She grabbed a couple more phones from the basket, making a mental note to buy more. Where did one find disposable phones in town? Probably at an electronics store.

A car pulled up outside. She ran out and jumped into Malanie's faded blue Pinto, turning to study her friend. Clear eyes, smooth skin, steady hands on the wheel. Excellent. She'd stopped using.

Mal looked at the cabin, her dark brown eyes sparkling. "Nice place."

Tori nodded. "Yeah. My, ah, new boyfriend owns it." Calling Adam a boyfriend was like calling a wolf a puppy, but it would have to do.

"Boyfriend?" Mal asked, her grin widening as she turned the car around. Her long dreadlocks were tied with metal beads stamped with cool designs. "Lucas owns this place?"

Oh yeah. Lucas had come to one of their concerts at a Grizzly bar. "Ah, no. His name is Adam. Lucas and I decided to just be friends."

"Figured he wouldn't last long." Malanie pressed down on the gas pedal, fishtailing around a couple of trees. She slowed down. "Two weeks is your limit." Just fact and no judgment filled her tone.

Tori stilled and then settled back in the seat. "This guy might be different."

"Uh huh."

The engine clunked. "Dang it. Not again," Mal said, her dark skin flushing.

Tori shut her eyes and breathed deep, trying to concentrate and keep her waves or whatever from stopping the vehicle. At some point, she should probably try to actually control the oddity instead of just hiding from it. Adam had given her that—the acceptance so she could move forward. Could she accept him the same way? He'd blown an entire compound to bits without even sweating a little. Without a second thought.

If he'd done it out of passion or fury, it would be easier to understand. But he'd been cold and almost matter-of-fact. He'd killed three men—bad men, of course—and then systematically hidden the evidence with plasma fire.

Why didn't that scare the hell out of her? It should, right?

She leaned back in the seat. As her mind worked through the issue, trying to make sense of it, the car continued to run.

"Where am I taking you?" Malanie asked.

"To my place so I can grab my car," Tori said automatically. "I really appreciate this."

Malanie turned wide eyes on her. "Are you kidding me? You've kept me out of jail. If I hadn't bought that Apollo . . ." Her voice trailed off, and her lips trembled. "I feel so bad about Bob. He was so young."

Tori patted her hand. "Bob took the drug on his own. He made his decision."

Mal nodded, blinking rapidly. "Are the DEA people still messing with you? Still forcing you undercover?"

Good question. Considering Titans of Fire no longer existed, what else could she do for the DEA? "I'm not sure. I have a feeling their case is starting to go cold." Tori reached for her friend's arm. "How do you feel about getting out of town for a while? Say, going somewhere warm?"

Mal sighed and turned toward her. "You think that's a good idea? I do have family in—"

Tori held up a hand. "Don't tell me. Just go." If nothing else, she'd protect her friend. She swallowed. At some point in the very near future, she was going to meet up with Agent Franks again. If she didn't know where Mal was, just what exactly could Tori tell her?

Chapter 18

Adam left the police station after having dropped off the rest of the evidence against the Fire members. He walked several blocks before ditching the hat and dark glasses. Another two blocks and he tore off the fake mustache and shrugged out of the plaid jacket, to drop it into a garbage can in front of a fast-food restaurant. The sweatshirt he wore still concealed the gun pressed against his lower back. The air cooled his neck, but finally the rain had ebbed. The sun had yet to make an appearance, however.

He scratched putty off his face, finally getting rid of the rest of his disguise. It was quite amazing what one could find at a dollar discount store.

His mind turned the matter over. He should probably take Victoria to her home so she could get her possessions. When he'd left, she'd been sleeping so peacefully he hadn't had the heart to awaken her. She'd been talking Klingon again, and he'd hated to leave her. But he had work to do, and part of his plan would keep her safe.

Leaning against a brick building, he quickly dialed his contacts at headquarters.

"Yes?" Chalton Reese, the Realm's best computer expert, said calmly.

"Hi. It's Adam. I need everything you have on the DEA's investigation into Apollo, Titans of Fire, and the Grizzlies. Especially anything involving Victoria Monzelle." Adam watched a couple of kids skateboard through the crowd across the street, smoothly missing the pedestrians. Impressive.

"Dage already has me on it," Chalton said. "Give me another hour, and I'll e-mail the info to you."

Of course the king was already investigating. The guy just couldn't keep his nose out of everyone's business. Adam sighed. "Thanks." He clicked off the phone.

Victoria had to be stirring by now. He should grab some takeout for her. Maybe Chinese?

A signature wafted on the slight breeze. Power and tension.

Adam went on full alert, purposely keeping his posture relaxed. He lifted the phone to his ear, pretending to make another call. A scan of the immediate area didn't reveal the threat.

His heart sped up and adrenaline flowed through his veins.

Somebody was near. Somebody holding power.

Not unusual in Seattle, yet he couldn't place the location of the person. No doubt the other immortal sensed him as well—and he couldn't use any powers to pinpoint the guy's location. He kept his ear to the phone and breathed deep, allowing the world to focus to that one signature.

Witch. Not vampire or demon. No chance it was a shifter. Aye. A witch was near.

He studied the people across the street. No. He turned and focused on the nearest stores. No. Whoever it was, they were keeping themselves hidden from him. Finally, he slid the phone into his pocket and moved down the street, his senses on full alert and seeking. Another signature came into play.

Fuck.

Were they trying to surround him? He calculated escape routes, but he wasn't sure which direction they were coming from. Then it hit him. He looked up.

A gun with a long barrel was pointed right at him. He jumped to the side just as a dart embedded itself in the brick behind him, twanging with an odd sound. Shit.

Was it an Apollo dart?

He turned and ducked into a store selling women's lingerie. A full-bodied woman smiled big and hustled up to him, her hands full of bright pink bras. As she started to speak, he spun around her and jogged for the rear of the store.

"Hey—" she called.

He ignored her, bounded over a glass counter, and shoved behind red velvet curtains next to a sign reading STAFF ONLY. He tripped over a box, jumped over three more, and rushed toward the door at the end. The knob was locked. Sucking in, he twisted with more strength, snapping the thing loose. Then he dodged into a back alley.

Garbage cans littered the way, and water-filled potholes dotted the entire length. He glanced up and didn't see anybody. How many were there? More important, who the fuck were they, and how had they found him? He kept to the sides of the buildings and ran hard, avoiding the garbage bins. As he reached the end of the alley, he paused, breathing deep and opening his senses.

It would make sense that they'd been watching the police station for Alexandra, hoping to catch Kellach. And any witch within a few yards would've caught Adam's scent, regardless of the disguise meant to fool surveillance cameras. The idiots knew enough to stake out the police station, but they didn't have anybody inside, or the squad would've known that Alexandra had taken a leave of absence. It was most likely the hitman was from Ireland or taking orders from somebody there. Had the Council decided to take Adam out as well?

Running into the throng of humans bustling around, he kept his senses on full alert and his head ducked. The sun was finally peeking through the clouds, which was probably why so many people filled the area. It was also lunchtime, and briefcases caught his thighs every once in a while as he wound through the crowd.

He scouted the rooftops on either side and didn't see anybody.

Even so, he edged as close to the buildings as he could, often having to skirt wrought iron fences protecting restaurant patrons from the busy crowd using the same sidewalk. The scents of pizza, burgers, and fried rice surrounded him. Even through the smells of food and humans, he could sense the witches growing near.

They were closing in.

A flash from a barrel across the street caught his eye, and he ducked as a dart flew toward his face. It bounced off a steel sign, dropping to the cracked sidewalk. He bent and fetched it, keeping his pace up, looking for the next shooter as the one across the street disappeared. He took a sniff of the dart.

Fury clenched his hand into a fist. Apollo. If they thought they could take him down in broad daylight, they hadn't read his file. Any of his files, actually.

Keeping the poison pointed away from his skin, he stuck the dart in his jeans. He got lost in the center of a group of men in business suits arguing loudly about the Seahawks, and then he took an abrupt turn into a Japanese restaurant. Smiling at the hostess as if he were meeting somebody, he strode between tables and right into the kitchen, passing several chefs and reaching a long hallway.

Perfect.

He walked the distance and then found the stairs. Climbing them three at a time, he kept going up, measuring the building at probably six stories. Once he reached the top, he faced a double-locked steel door. Swinging back, he planted his boot right in the center, blowing it open to bounce against a bunch of stacked bricks.

Then he ran into the sun. Crouching low, he made it over to the edge of the roof and surveyed the crowd below before focusing on the rooftops. Ah ha. One man dressed in dark colors, including cargo pants, came into view across the street a couple of rooftops over.

Adam removed the dart and placed it on the gravel next to him. Then he dropped to his belly, drawing his gun. Stretching out, he set the green laser for its longest distance. The laser would turn to metal the second it hit immortal flesh. He set his wrists on the edge of the roof and lowered his face, shutting one eye.

If he knew these guys were from the Council or part of the Guard, he'd use his powers. If they weren't, manipulating physics to create fire would reveal him to the Council or the Guard. So a human fight it would be.

His target was crouched, his gun sweeping the crowd below. His head jerked, and he tapped his ear. Then his gaze lifted toward Adam.

Shit. Someone behind him had broadcast his location. Adam squeezed the trigger. The green laser shot straight and true, hitting the guy center mass and throwing him back several yards. The dart gun flew up in the air and then over onto a fire escape, where it clattered down the stairs. The witch would live, but he'd be out cold for several hours from the heart shot.

Swinging his legs around, Adam was already firing toward the roof entrance.

A male yelled and jumped behind the bricks. He leaned to the side and fired a series of darts.

One impacted Adam's left thigh, and the other his right arm. His arm went numb. Grabbing his gun with his left hand, he stood and fired repeatedly at the bricks, sending sharp pieces careening through the air. The guy behind the bricks shot another dart.

Adam dipped to the side, and the murderous barb whizzed by his ear.

The guy leaped up and right at him, hitting him in the gut and tackling him to the rooftop. Gravel tore Adam's shirt, cutting along his spine. His left leg shook and went numb. Fury ripped through him, and he clapped both hands against the guy's ears. Something snapped. The attacker screamed in pain, his light blue eyes widening.

He punched Adam in the nose.

Adam punched back with his left hand, getting leverage and rolling them over. The guy fought back, rolling, and soon they were crashing across the roof, scattering gravel in every direction.

The vision in Adam's left eye started to spot. His chest hurt.

Two darts. That wasn't enough to kill him, but he was rapidly losing strength. He punched the guy in the neck. The witch looked somewhat familiar but Adam couldn't place him. Adam flipped him over and grabbed his hair, slamming the guy's face into the roof repeatedly. Blood sprayed, coating the gravel around them.

The guy kicked back but couldn't find purchase.

Adam slipped his good arm around the witch's neck and yanked, using his knees as leverage. "Who ordered the hit?" he growled, digging deep to hold on to his strength, wanting desperately to use his powers.

Fire lanced from the witch's hands, and Adam shifted his knees to the guy's shoulders, using his weight to keep the witch flat. The fire shot out across the roof, bouncing harmlessly. "Who?" Adam snapped, his other eye beginning to twitch.

"Fuck you," the witch hissed, trying to shake his head and dislodge Adam's hold.

"Not my type." Flames poured down Adam's arms without conscious thought. The drug was taking over, and he was losing control. Quickly. The fire burned the witch's neck, and he screamed. "Just tell me," Adam ordered, the world starting to spin around him.

The guy chuckled. "You're going to be out cold in about three minutes." Twisting slightly, he shot an elbow up into Adam's rib cage, throwing him flat on his back.

Adam went into a backward somersault and vaulted to his feet. His left leg gave, and he dropped to his other knee right at the edge of the roof.

The witch advanced, glee lighting his broad face. His training showed him to be in his hundreds, but his fire had seemed unrestrained— definitely not military. He glanced around for his gun and then shrugged. "I'll just kill you the old-fashioned way." He moved forward, cracking his large knuckles as he approached.

Adam's head lolled. He lifted his chin, feeling blood sliding down his neck. "Just tell me. Who ordered the hit?" There was no doubt it was a kill order. This guy wasn't planning on taking him in.

"Private hit not sanctioned by the Council," the guy said, rubbing his hands together. "Not the whole council, anyway." His laugh was grating and his teeth crooked.

Adam swayed, even on his knees.

"Time to die, Enforcer." The witch clasped Adam around the neck.

Adam grabbed the dart he'd dropped earlier and swung up, nailing the witch in the eye.

The witch screamed holy hell and reached for the dart, yanking it out. The second the dart hit the ground, Adam punched him in the balls, grabbed his waistband, and pulled. The witch flew over Adam's head and into the air. His yell as he fell six stories was joined by the screams of people on the sidewalk below. The *thunk* of the witch hitting the sidewalk sounded like somebody had smashed a water- melon.

Adam fell forward, and gravel cut into his chin. Dots blocked his vision, leaving only his peripheral view even a little clear.

He used his good arm to push himself to his knees and proceeded to crawl to the other side of the roof. Using only his good arm, he swung himself over the edge, then all but fell to the fire escape a story below. Grunting, his vision going, he managed to trip and fall all the way down to the alley. God, he had to get out of there.

Sirens sounded in the distance.

Holding his damaged arm to his side, he hurried along the side- walk, his vision gray. A cab was parked up ahead. He struggled to pull open the door and then fell inside. He gave the cabbie the only address he could think of and then promised the guy five hundred dollars if he got Adam there safely. He groaned and made up some dumb lie about having a migraine and needing to rest until they arrived.

Then he passed out cold.

Chapter 19

Tori rolled down the windows of her weathered compact car after having stopped by her apartment, allowing the fresh breeze and meager sunshine in. Her hands remained steady and calm on the steering wheel as the forest sped by on both sides. There was something to inner relaxation that so far seemed to be helping with her impact on devices. She'd even dropped by the grocery store to get supplies, and the automatic door had opened the second time she'd stood on the censor mat. Usually it took five or six times, and last week she'd had to wait until another shopper showed up before the door would open.

This time, once she'd concentrated, she had seen vibrations around the door. Waves?

Her clothes were packed in her bag in the back along with her guitar. It had been a while since she'd written a song, and the cabin would be the perfect place to give it a try.

First she'd drop off her stuff at Adam's cabin, and then she needed to go check on Bear. She'd promised Simone, and besides, Bear seemed like a good guy. If nothing else, maybe he could give her the scoop on Adam. And on himself. Every time somebody talked about Bear, they seemed to be holding something back about him. It was time she figured out what.

She pulled up to Adam's cabin, her back straightening at the sight of the yellow cab waiting next to a long log. Jumping out, she cautiously made her way toward the driver.

The guy, a blond about twenty years old with a long goatee, rolled down his window. "I dropped a man off, and he said he was going inside to get my money, but he hasn't come back. I'm about to call the cops."

Tori looked toward the open doorway and then started digging in her purse. "What does he owe you?"

"He promised five hundred."

Tori stopped rummaging, her head snapping up. "What?"

The man shrugged. "Said he wasn't feeling well and that he'd give me five hundred dollars if I got him here quietly. I did. That's a valid contract."

Why was the door open? "Um, okay. I'll go get the money." She skirted the cab and hustled up the wooden steps.

"Make it fast, or I'm calling the men in blue," the guy yelled.

Her pulse kicked up a notch, and she used two knuckles to edge the door open more. Was it Bear? He really hadn't been looking good the other night. Maybe he'd had to take a cab to get to Adam. She moved inside, seeing a man's legs sticking out of the bedroom. "Bear?" She ran forward. Her heart stuttered. "Adam," she whispered, dropping to her knees.

His eyelids opened. "There's money in the top drawer." Sweat dotted his upper lip and soaked through his T-shirt. "Pay the cabbie." Then he shut his eyes again.

Panic swept her, and she jumped up, rifling through the drawer. A neatly tied stack of hundreds was pressed against the edge. She grabbed five and ran through the living room, leaping off the porch steps to hand the money through the passenger-side door. "Did he say what was wrong?" she asked the guy.

The cabbie nodded. "Yeah. Said it was a migraine. Looked like it hurt like hell." The guy took in the crisp bills and smiled wide. "Call if you all need a ride anywhere else." Tipping an imaginary hat, he rolled up the window and pulled around, zipping down the lane. She watched him go, confusion melding with panic inside her.

Did witches get migraines?

Turning, she ran up the steps and back into the room, seeing Adam now sitting with his back to the side of the fireplace. Maybe the migraine had something to do with the whole throwing fire and plasma. She reached him. "What's wrong?" Her voice trembled.

He closed his eyes and swallowed, shoving himself up with one arm. He climbed to stand by using the wall, the muscles in his bicep bunching. "Got hit with planekite. Apollo darts."

She gasped out, her lungs expelling all the air they held. Her ears rang. "Adam. What should I do?"

"Nothing." He smiled, his lips looking a little blue. "Half of it is already out of my system. They only hit me with two darts, so I'll be fine within an hour." His hands fumbled at the base of his T-shirt. "I'm hot. Fucking hot."

She moved toward him, drawing the shirt over his head. "Come lie down." Taking his arm, she led him inside the cool bedroom. Her heart beat rapidly.

He sat and then stretched out on his back. "Shit burns as it pumps through the blood."

"I figured." She jogged to the bathroom and dampened a washcloth, returning to wipe it across his wide chest. He had to be okay.

He murmured. "Feels good." Reaching out, he snagged her around the waist. "Cuddle."

Cuddle? Did the most dangerous male she'd ever met use the word "cuddle"? She traced her fingers over his abs, and they rippled. "Are you sure you're going to be all right?" she whispered, needing to offer comfort.

"Aye. The second dart just glanced me. My vision is already coming back." He tightened his hold, partially rolling her to lie alongside him. "You feel good."

"So do you." She caressed his chest. He was already cooling. Good. The idea that somebody had harmed him, that he could actually be harmed, shot uneasiness through her. Honestly, from day one, she'd considered him nearly invincible. After discovering his true nature and seeing him fight, there hadn't been any reason to change her mind. "What happened to the person who hurt you?" She slid her hand up and around his neck, her body relaxing at feeling the steadiness of his pulse.

"Shot one guy and threw the other off a roof."

"Of course." She smiled against his shoulder. "I mean, what else would you have done?"

He glanced over at her, his lips creasing into a grin. "That's what I thought. Poked one guy's eye out first."

She laughed. It was a ridiculous statement to laugh at, but she couldn't help it. Life had gotten way too bizarre.

He rolled over, right onto her, flattening her to the bed. "I love your laugh." His eyes twinkled, and his face was only slightly feverish. "Laugh more." The pads of his fingers rubbed along her ribs.

She stared, the oddest sense of wonder taking her. Adam in a playful mood? Well, it had only taken a lethal drug to bring that about. She laughed out loud at her own thoughts.

"That's nice." He lifted to his knees, bracketing her. Then he reached down and tugged her shirt up and over her head.

Her amusement darkened and deepened. "What are you doing?" she whispered, intrigue licking through her.

"Playing." He slid his hand beneath her bra, cupping her breasts.

She arched, sensations torturing her. A throbbing set up between her legs. "You must be feeling better," she gasped.

"I am." He lifted the bra right up and over her head, forcing her arms up. Then he moved quickly, tying them in place. "I heal very quickly. 'Tis a gift, that."

"Hey," she said with a laugh. She struggled, but her wrists remained tied together by the soft silk. So she looked at him, trying to memorize every hard angle.

His bare torso, so strong and wide, made her lick her lips.

"I can't have you disappointed," he murmured, one finger hooking in the bra. He lifted her arms again, moved around a little, and then settled back on his knees.

She laughed and tried to pull her arms down. They didn't move. She stilled. So much fire swept through her, she forgot how to breathe. He'd somehow secured her wrists and arms above her head. She tugged, and there was no give. The helplessness of her position, with him looking down at her, heated the desire inside her to molten lava. "How?" she asked.

One side of his mouth lifted, giving him the look of a pirate. "Let's just say the iron headboard is wearing your bra." He spread out his hands, fingers wide, over her chest. "With your arms attached." Satisfaction lit his eyes a second before blue fire zapped along his palms and between his outstretched fingers.

She gasped, instinctively pressing into the bed, her eyes wide and focused on the fire poised above her very bare and delicate breasts.

"Fire burns, Victoria." He slowly lowered his hands, and the fire sparked.

Her skin twitched, and she tried to hold perfectly still. "Don't," she whispered.

He smiled, his gaze warm on hers. "You don't mean that."

No, she really didn't. The memories of what he could do with fire nearly sent her into an early orgasm. As if reading her mind, he angled his body and slid his knees back, pressing his hard shaft between her legs, over the jeans she still wore.

The feeling of him on top of her, so hard against her clit, was a form of sensual torture she had never imagined. With the fire crackling as a warning so close to her skin, she could do nothing but completely feel every sensation. Warmth from the flames. Softness against his steel hardness. Helplessness compared to his strength.

Relief that he had healed enough to play. To be strong for her again.

He finished lowering his hands, encasing her breasts in full blue fire. An all-consuming zap of heat pinched her nipples. She arched against him, crying out. An orgasm rushed through her out of nowhere, flashing the air to bright and then hazy, forcing her body to jerk against his hard cock.

His head lifted, and his eyes darkened. "That was lovely." Low and guttural, his tone dug down deep inside her and took hold.

The fire sputtered out. He levered up and jerked her jeans off her legs. She may have murmured something, her body still out of her control. Then he stood and quickly removed his jeans.

She pulled against the restraints. "Let me go." More than anything in the world, she wanted to touch his hard chest. Wanted to run her fingers over every angle and hollow. "Now."

He moved back above her, settling against her, his dick against her core. His mouth pressed against hers, forming the word *no*.

She blinked. "Yes."

He smiled, the movement soft against her mouth. "Not a chance." Slowly, he began to penetrate her.

She breathed out, opening her legs, pushing against him to hurry him along.

He wouldn't be rushed.

Instead, in total control, he inched inside her in minuscule increments, taking his time. Beads of sweat dotted his forehead, and his biceps bulged on either side of her shoulders as he held himself in check, torturing them both. "Do you have any idea how lovely you are, bound for my pleasure?" he rumbled, his gaze hotter than the fire he'd already used.

Her fingers curled over the material of the bra. She shook her head slowly, allowing his sweet words to sink in. "I've never seen anything like you," she whispered. He was more masculine than any ideal of a man she could've dreamed up on her best day.

He leaned down and kissed her, his lips firm and his tongue gentle. Sweeping inside her mouth, he took all of her, giving with such gentleness tears nearly pricked her eyes.

With a groan, he finally shoved all the way inside her.

She gasped, her body taken over. The bra secured her hands, and his solid body pinned her to the bed. She couldn't move, even if she had wanted to. Her quick orgasm had just softened her for him, primed her body for what he could do. What he would do. His body, even without the fever, warmed her head to toe with an electrical burn.

He'd been inside her for nearly a minute, not moving, just pulsing. She bit her lip to keep from begging.

One of his hands clamped on top of her head, and he pulled out, shoving back in while holding her immobile. The forced helplessness sent shock waves along her every nerve, and she whimpered, needing more. *Craving* more. His eyes were strong and bright with desire . . . for her.

It hit her then, the realization that Adam Dunne was more than sex. More than just this moment. Somehow, when she hadn't been looking, he'd slid right beneath her skin and into her heart. No matter what happened, she'd always remember him. Always carry a part of him with her. And even if she never saw him again, she'd still have this piece. She smiled at the thought.

His gaze caught. "Now that's a stunning sight."

He pulled out and pounded back in with enough force to push her hands against the bars. Pressure built inside her again, stronger and hotter than before. She lifted her knees to take more of him.

"Next time, I tie your legs, too," he whispered, kissing her deep, taking whatever he wanted.

Her thighs trembled in response, and then her hips started to move, following his lead. The pressure continued to build in a delicious coil that threatened to blow her apart. She didn't care. Only that peak, only that shocking wave of raw pleasure, only Adam's body in hers mattered. Nothing else. No time, no worries, no future. Only right now and the devastating pleasure to be found with him.

He leaned down and pushed one arm beneath her thigh, opening her, showing just how much more helpless he could make her. "Come now, Victoria."

She came apart as the coils inside her detonated, shooting sparks, taking everything. He thrust harder, going deeper, pushing her into a place of sweet agony. Just as she came down, he pressed his forehead to hers, and the spasms of his orgasm took him.

He flicked her wrists free and moved to the side, taking her with him. Tucking the blankets around them, he winced.

She bit her lip. Maybe it had been too soon for him after the darts. "Are you all right?"

His jaw went slack. He held out his arm and twisted his wrist, opening the palm of his hand.

She reached for it to see a stunning Celtic knot, slightly raised with jagged edges, on his palm. That hadn't been there before. She frowned. "What in the world?"

He sighed and flexed his fingers. "It's the brand. The mating brand."

Chapter 20

Morning arrived soft and sweet, climbing over the mountains and finally bringing the sun. Adam finished scouting the area around the cabin, setting a couple of traps, mainly searching for trespassers. So far, the cabin seemed secure. His phone blared *Livin' on a Prayer*, and he looked at the screen. Interesting. "Adam here," he said, accepting the video conference.

Councilman Peter Gallagher came into view, his hair slicked back, his eyes narrowed. "Word reached us that Titans of Fire burned down and the leadership is missing."

"Aye," Adam said easily, noting two wide trout in the river. Did Victoria like trout?

"Don't you think that's information you might've passed on?" Peter hissed.

Adam studied the current leader of the Coven Nine. It was time to stop messing around. "Did you send a hit squad to take me out, Pete?"

Peter drew back, the lines in his neck elongating. "Are you, our only Enforcer, asking the chairperson of the Coven Nine if he illegally and immorally hired mercenaries to perpetrate murder?"

What a dipshit. "Aye. That's exactly what I'm asking. And by the way, referring to yourself in the third person is a sign of lunacy. Just so you know." The breeze picked up but failed to cool Adam's heated flesh.

Peter coughed. "I'm insulted but not surprised. The Dunnes aren't exactly known for class."

Adam leaned into the camera. "What are we known for, Pete?"

Maybe it was time to remind the witch why the Dunne boys were Enforcers.

Peter cleared his throat, his Adam's apple bobbing. "Since Titans of Fire no longer exists, your undercover op is finished there. It's time to come home and train the new crop of Enforcers."

Fuck. Adam wanted to tell the asshole to shove it. The entire thing. The job, the case, the Coven Nine. But he was the only one in the family who still had the inside track, and if they were going to figure out who'd set up Simone, being an Enforcer gave him an edge. "We don't know who the manufacturer of Apollo is," he replied, "but that person will be looking for a new main distributor." There was no question Bear and the Grizzlies would be approached. "I need to be here for that."

"Negative," Peter said.

Adam leaned against a pine tree, his temper pricked. "Did you just use a military term?" Good ole Pete had never served in any branch of the witch military. Of any military. "Really?"

"Dunne, I truly don't appreciate your insubordination," Peter spat.

"Well, hell, Pete." Adam allowed the predator in him to show. "Considering you put a kill order on my brothers and cousin, it's real hard not to reach through the phone and rip out your throat."

Peter smiled then. "I see. In that case, you are hereby given notice that you're required to be in front of the Council of the Coven Nine in three days to pledge your allegiance as well as provide proof of your recent mating. If you have not mated the Monzelle woman, she dies instantly. I have ten Guard squads raring to go, and I'll even offer an incentive for the squad that takes her out."

Adam barely kept the death threat inside his throat. A death threat would instantly be met with termination of his employment, if not his life. "I'll see you in three days," he said, clicking off. Jesus. Three days. He quickly dialed Kellach.

"Kell here." His brother sounded preoccupied and slightly irritated.

"The Council wants me to pledge myself to them after I mate Victoria," Adam burst out, fire lancing down his arms. "I think we need to neutralize Gallagher. I really do." It was the cleanest and smartest way to keep his family alive, but saying the words felt like a sledgehammer to the gut. If Peter died, Sal would fold, and Nessa had always been on their side. Well, maybe not on their side, but she had voted against their being killed. That meant something.

"If we do that, we tear the witch nation down the middle," Kellach said.

"We don't have a choice," Adam snapped.

"Hey. I didn't say it was a bad idea. I just said we'd start an internal war that might destroy us all." Kellach cleared his throat. "I've been thinking about how smoothly Peter Gallagher took over the Council. As if it were planned."

Adam fought his anger and tried to concentrate. "He's an ambitious bastard, but do you really think he set Simone up? He hasn't been in power enough time for the long game."

"I don't know, but what I'm saying is that you're the guy to figure it out," Kell said, his voice calming. "Whatever has you so tied up has to be taken care of. You're the strategist. The smartest one. The guy who'd rather pierce somebody's brain with a good battle plan than punch a guy in the face. Remember?"

"Aye," Adam said as the world pressed in on him. "We know Grace Sadler is somehow involved, and now that we've killed both of her sons, we really need to find her." Grace had been removed from the Council because of treason, and she'd spent decades coming up with her plan for revenge. Her sons had died in separate battles, and a part of Adam regretted that, although there had been no other choice but to kill them.

"Agreed. Also, I know we've left you holding a shitload of garbage, with all of us being charged with treason and going underground. I get that. Plus, you're now the only witch member of Titans of Fire, and I know you hate that place." Kellach sighed.

Adam winced. "Ah, I may have blown up Titans."

Silence ticked for the briefest of moments. "You did what?"

Adam frowned. "How did you not know?"

"Ah, hell. I now owe Daire ten thousand dollars. I hate losing a bet." Kellach turned and yelled over his shoulder. "Adam blew up the Fire compound." He returned to the phone. "I took Alexandra for a night off up at a cabin across the lake. I'm supposed to have a briefing with Dage in an hour."

The king would probably love to impart the information about the explosion. "Pyro kidnapped Victoria, and she was all bruised, and, well . . ."

"You blew the place up," Kellach said simply. "I get it."

Adam rubbed his eyes. What the hell was wrong with him? "I am losing my mind." The brand on his palm brushed his cheek.

A scuffle ensued on the other end of the line, and soon Daire came on the phone. "What the hell is wrong with you?"

Adam grimaced. "I was just asking myself the same question." He couldn't tell his brothers about the mating mark. It only appeared when a potential mate was near, and he didn't want to discuss its significance. Not for a second. "Pyro told us all he could about the manufacturer of Apollo. I don't think he even really knew a name."

"Figures," Daire muttered. "But it does beg the question. Why are you blowing things up instead of following the paper trail to save Simone?"

"Because I'm the only one out here to blow things up." Adam's voice rose, and he rapidly calmed himself. "So you all, who are safely behind walls with no enemies to battle, will have to do the research on this one. Follow the paper yourselves, damn it. Look at all the shipping manifests from Russia, the ones that moved planekite and bore Simone's signature, and figure out who could've doctored them."

Daire chuckled. "That's what we've been doing, I promise you."

"Good. Put Kell back on," Adam said.

Something rustled. "It's Kellach."

"Hey. A hit team was waiting for me outside the police station this morning. Pierced me with two darts, and I put at least one of them in the hospital. Make sure Alexandra doesn't go anywhere near the Seattle PD until we figure this mess out. They're not only looking for you," Adam said.

Silence ticked over the line. "You got shot with Apollo?" Kell asked, the words sounding like he'd shoved them through jagged teeth.

"Aye. I'm fine. Just stay where you are." Adam glanced at the rising sun. "I have to go. I'll call if I get any information from the guy in the hospital." He clicked off before his brother could answer. Now he wanted to check on pretty Victoria before he had to go torture a witch.

He whistled, heading back toward the cabin. The day was finally looking up.

Tori finished a bowl of cereal, twisting Adam's note around with her finger. The guy had a habit of leaving her notes and not waking her up in the morning, now didn't he? This one told her to relax and have a nice morning. The note rather pointedly said that there were hit men in town, and she wasn't to consider leaving the cabin. He'd turned into Mr. Bossy Pants again. But he had ended the note with a promise to bring lunch back, and if she was still in bed, he'd join her.

She grinned. That was an offer she'd accept.

But first, she was definitely remiss in checking up on poor Bear. Rinsing her dish, she loped out to her car. For the trip, she'd put on dark jeans and a light red sweater, leaving her hair down around her shoulders. Considering somebody was shooting Apollo darts in the city, she had no intention of going anywhere but Bear's.

Saying a quick prayer upon starting her car, she gingerly drove away from the cabin. The drive was nice, with the sun shining through the trees and a slight breeze rustling the branches. She kept to the back roads, noting belatedly that the Fire and Grizzly headquarters hadn't really been that far apart. Their respective territories spread out in opposite directions, but the clubhouses were only thirty minutes away from each other. Perhaps they'd wanted to keep an eye on each other.

Singing along with Dierks Bentley, she turned the corner and drove down the long lane to Grizzly headquarters. The place was quiet, almost peaceful.

She parked and stood in the sun, allowing the meager rays to warm her. Fall scented the air, but for now, the sun was making an effort. Tori straightened her sweater and moved toward Bear's office.

A Grizzly member in full cut strode out from around the corner, pushing a sparkling Harley. He paused upon seeing her and then moved her way. About thirty years old, he had a full beard and intelligent brown eyes. His boots were scuffed and his cut looked like it had been around awhile. Finally, he reached her. "Hi, Tori. What are you doing here, sweetheart?" His voice was kind but firm.

He knew her name. The guy looked familiar, so she'd probably met him at some point. "Hi. Um, where is everybody?" The place was usually teeming with bikes.

He grinned and pointed to the sun. "Out for a ride. Finally."

"Oh." She smiled. "That's good."

He sighed. "I'm sorry, but Lucas ain't gonna change his mind. When he dumps a girl, it's for good. You know that, right?"

Oh yeah. She bit her lip and nodded. "I do know that, and I'm not here to cause trouble. I actually need to see Bear."

The guy frowned. "Bear? Why?"

"I, ah, it's personal." Maybe not everyone knew Bear had a sister. He seemed like a man who kept his secrets close and probably wouldn't like Tori spilling the news.

The guy shook his head. "Not a good idea, lady. Bear doesn't like women."

Her eyes widened. "Bear is gay?" If so, she had a friend who would probably love Bear. Her friend played the drums, and he had the worst taste in men. Bear was a little rough, but he'd treat Jonny well. "I have a friend——"

"No. Bear isn't gay," the guy said.

Tori blinked. "But you said——"

"Bear doesn't like men, either. In fact, Bear doesn't like pretty much anybody. That's normal for him, and lately, he's even worse."

Which was exactly why she needed to see him. She took a deep breath and forced her most reassuring smile. "Thank you for the warning, but it really is a personal matter that Bear would like to hear. I wouldn't bother him if I thought it would just piss him off."

The guy pursed his lips, obviously thinking it through. "Well, that does make sense. All right. He's in the office." He hopped on his bike. "Good luck." He ignited the engine and roared away, his hair flying in the breeze.

Tori watched him go and then walked over the smooth concrete toward Bear's office. She knocked, but nobody answered. She knocked again. Finally, she nudged open the door to see Bear behind his desk with a smattering of papers in front of him. A beer in the bottle sat next to his elbow, and a fan rotated with sharp squeaks in the corner. He glared at her.

Her legs wobbled. "Um, hi."

"Did I say come in?" he asked, his honey-brown eyes narrowing. "Did I?"

"No." Her chin snapped up, and she walked inside, shutting the door behind her. "Which was incredibly rude, by the way. When somebody knocks, and you're right inside, then you answer them. Even better, you get off your butt and open the door." He scared the crap out of her, so she had no choice but to babble. "A nice 'come in' would have been acceptable."

He sighed. "Go away."

She turned on him, fully prepared to let him have it. Then she looked. Bear's eyes were bloodshot, and sweat poured down his face, soaking through his shirt. His hand trembled on the desk, and beneath the shaggy hair, his face was stark white. His lips looked blue. "You're not all right. Oh, Bear. You need a doctor."

He chuckled, the sound full of pain. "A doctor can't help me." Then he frowned again. "Why are you here?"

"Your sister wanted me to check on you. I'll call her—"

"No." Bear's bark came out a full growl. "Call her and I'll rip off your arm."

That was a little extreme. Seriously. Tori took a deep breath and circled the desk. "Fine. At the very least, I'm getting you into bed."

He smiled, flashing a dimple in his pale left cheek. "I'm not up to full speed, but I'll give it a shot."

She rolled her eyes and helped him to stand, more than a little surprised when he allowed her to take some of his weight. "Ah, where do you live?"

"There's a cabin out back," he said, his eyes closing.

"Okay." She'd get him to his cabin and then call a doctor. Enough was enough. His sweat rolled down her arm, but she got him out back, and he lifted his face to the sun. "Keep going."

His left leg gave, and he fell, taking her with him.

She landed flat with a muffled *oof.* "Bear." Rolling away, she pushed herself up. She needed help.

He groaned and lifted to all fours before standing and weaving. "Ah, shit." His eyes opened and seemed to darken. "You need to leave, Victoria. Now."

"I'm not leaving you," she said. What a stubborn ass.

Rebecca Zanetti

"Now!"

She crossed her arms. "No."

"Damn it." Bear lowered his chin, and fur sprang up along his arms. Her breath caught. What the hell? She took a step back. Her lungs stopped working.

He growled again. Razor-sharp fangs slid from his mouth. He lifted his head and let loose with snapping growls. His arms spread out, and his soaking-wet shirt ripped down the middle.

She froze in place, her legs refusing to move.

All of his clothes fell from his body. Fur covered him from head to toe, and his face changed shape, becoming elongated. Then he dropped to all fours as a humongous grizzly bear, fur rippling in the breeze.

He opened his mouth wide and roared at her, his canines glistening.

Chapter 21

Adam nodded to yet another nurse as he made his way through the hospital and tried to ignore the scent of antiseptic. Oh, he knew it was necessary to protect human life, but the smell had always burned his nose. His instincts had been humming all morning, and it was time to follow them. Finally, he reached room 545. He entered and shut the door, approaching the man in the bed.

The guy was tubed up everywhere, although he breathed on his own. Tingles cascaded from him as he healed himself, but the humans probably didn't notice the change in the atmosphere.

Adam reached the computer and hacked the system, bringing up the guy's chart. He read several screens. "They think you got shot close to the heart. A through and through." Oh, the bullet had gone through, but it had gone through the center of the heart. "I love humans." He moved closer and casually burned the guy's wrist.

The patient awoke with a start, half sitting up in bed.

Adam grinned. "How's the heart?"

The witch blinked several times, and the beeper connected to his pulse went wild.

Adam sighed. "I don't want to hurt you. Believe me, I understand orders. I do."

The guy's pulse slowed.

"But I need answers." Adam leaned in.

Slowly, the guy nodded, his fear smelling like sulfur.

"Good." Adam patted his arm, and the guy flinched. "You were staking out the police station to watch for my brother or his mate, right?"

"Aye," the witch admitted, color flooding into his face.

Adam tried to show approval. "Good. That's good. You had a kill order?"

The color fled.

"It's okay. I'm a soldier and I've had my share of such orders. Kill order?" Adam asked calmly.

The guy gave one short nod.

"For Kellach and his mate? Or just Kell?" Adam asked.

"B-both," the guy said.

Well now, that would send Kellach around the bend in about two seconds flat. "All right. Where did you get the Apollo darts?" Adam was leading up to the big question, the only one that mattered, and hopefully by then the guy would just keep talking. "Here in Seattle?"

"Yes. We were given directions to a locker near the train station."

Adam patted the guy's arm again. "Do you hate us, or was this just a job?" The answer to that one would determine if the guy lived or died. Well, probably.

"Just a job." Tears filled the guy's eyes.

Adam nodded. "I get it. Really do. And I know the pain you're in. Years ago, I had a heart wound. Hurt like a bitch." True story, that.

The guy eagerly nodded this time.

Adam leaned in. "Who hired you?"

The guy blinked. His monitor went crazy again. He snapped his lips shut.

Adam sighed. "Listen. I don't want to hurt you any more than I already have." He let the truth show in his eyes. "It's not like you shot at one of our mates. If you had, then you'd be dead, right?"

The guy nodded.

"Good. So we get each other. However, the guy who hired you is going to hire somebody else, and I have to find him, you know?" Adam allowed blue fire to flow on his hands for a very brief second. "Have you heard all the rumors about me?"

The guy's eyes widened at the site of the fire. "Are they true?"

"Yep." Adam flattened his hand, and the fire morphed into a disk with razor-sharp edges. "I can cut with fire. It's a nice gift, it is." He only used it to kill, really. Otherwise it didn't make sense. Why just cut off somebody's limb? "Do you have any idea what one of these can do to a neck?"

The guy shook his head on the pillow, his greasy hair sticking to it.

"It can slice a head right off." Adam pushed up gently, and the disk rose in the air by itself. "Want to see?"

"N-no," the guy burst out, trying to push himself back on the pillow.

Adam rotated his finger, and the disk whirled around. "It can also cut off a dick. I've seen it. Fuck, it's grotesque."

The witch in the bed whimpered.

"Now is the time you tell me who hired you to kill my brother," Adam said, narrowing his gaze to daggers. "Or I'm going to cut off your dick and feed it to you."

"Peter Gallagher," the guy burst out. "He hired us. Paid us."

Adam sat back, fury lashing down his back. Even though he'd suspected the truth, to have it confirmed made his blood turn to ice. A killing ice. "How did he pay you?"

"Half up front in cash and then half when the job was done. Double if we got both your brother and his mate." Now that the guy was sharing, he couldn't seem to stop. "I don't know where the money came from, but it was all nicely wrapped with those cool paper holder things."

Adam blew out air, and the disk disappeared. "Were Sal or Nessa involved?" The entire Council wouldn't have done such a thing, would they?

"No. I mean, I don't think so."

"Where's the money?" Adam asked.

"My partner has it. Lars Jensen. I have no clue where he is."

The guy had probably gone way underground after Adam had thrown him off the roof. He did have an eye to heal, after all. They'd have to track him down.

Adam stood, his mind calculating. He walked over and took the guy's wallet out of his pants, memorizing all the identification. "All right. I promised I wouldn't kill you today, and I won't. But if you even think of taking another job to harm any member of my family, I'll disembowel you."

"Okay. I won't. I promise." A tear leaked out the guy's eye.

"Good. But I am going to tell Kellach about your plan to harm his mate, and well, he'll probably hunt you down and make you beg before he kills you," Adam said matter-of-factly.

Another tear slid down the guy's face.

"I know who you are, and now you need to stay where I can find you. Guess what, Walter? You're going to help me nail Peter Gallagher. How much fun will that be?" Adam took out his phone and held up the camera. "Okay. Once more for the camera."

Tori backed away from the massive bear. She frowned, her central nervous system firing like there was a threat near. But the creature didn't seem to want to hurt her. His paws were bigger than platters, and the sharp tips of his claws showed through his fur. Bear was a bear. "Talk about ironic. Or obvious," she murmured.

The bear snorted. He held up a monstrous paw as if to reassure her. The sharp and horribly long claws didn't exactly provide reassurance. But the thing hadn't charged her.

"This is crazy. This is so fucking crazy." Shifters. Oh yeah. She hadn't really figured it out. He was a freakin' bear shifter. She crouched down, her face toward his. If he wanted her dead, it wasn't as if she could outrun him. Maybe Bear was in there somewhere. That was all she could hope for at this point. "Can you understand me?"

The bear nodded its massive head. Then he moved toward her, very slowly, as if trying to keep from spooking her. He moved one paw in front of the other in a primitively graceful lumber. He nudged her hand with his wet snout.

She reared back and frowned. Her heart beat so rapidly her chest hurt. "Seriously?"

He nudged her again.

Her hand shook like crazy, but she held it out and gently scratched between his ears. His fur was thick and surprisingly soft.

His eyes closed and he made a sound like a loud purr. She giggled and scratched harder. This was crazy. Beyond crazy. Had her brain just exploded and left her in a make-believe universe? His eyes opened and he licked her from chin to forehead, leaving her nose sticky. She swatted him away. "Knock it off, Bear. Geez."

This was real. He was real. Man. She needed a drink.

He looked at her, yearning in his big brown eyes. She rolled hers and then petted him again, relief flowing through her. He didn't want to eat her. That had to be good. "You look better. Are you feeling better in this, ah, this form?" she asked.

He nodded again and sniffed her neck, knocking her onto her butt. She yelped and pushed his head. "Stop smelling me. You're even crazier in this form." Probably not true. Bear seemed nuts in human form. At least this way he couldn't yell at her and be mean. She scratched his ears again. "Does your sister know you're a bear?"

He nodded again.

Her eyes widened. The world was so much bigger than she'd imagined. How had she missed all of this? "Is Simone a bear?"

He snorted and shook his head, sending her sprawling back.

She dusted off her hands and just sat on the grass, figuring it was safer that way. So Simone was not a bear. That was good to know. Then it all came clear. "Wait a minute. The Grizzlies. Are you all bears?"

He nodded. The whole time she'd been hanging out with Lucas, he'd been a bear? A real bear? So their name was ironic. Kind of a *screw you* to humans. Yeah, she could see that. And Bear calling himself Bear? What a smart-ass. "Is your real name Bear?"

His shoulders rolled in a bearlike shrug.

"What about Titans of Fire? Were they some sort of tiger shifters or something?" The world was so different than she'd thought.

If a bear could roll his eyes, he did. Then he shook his massive head.

"Just dumb humans?" she guessed.

One nod this time.

"Wow. This is just crazy. I mean, wow."

He lay down and flopped his head in her lap. The force of his heavy head kicked her legs out. She frowned but obediently petted him between the ears, hoping he kept those sharp canines right where they belonged. "Is your illness something to do with being a bear shifter?" she asked.

He huffed out in pleasure, shutting his eyes as she continued to scratch his ears.

"Bear, I'm talking to you."

He flattened a huge paw on her calves, easily covering them both. She shoved at his head, and it didn't move. "We are not going to sit here all day while I pet you."

One eye opened, somehow looking forlorn.

She relaxed and petted him. His eyelid shut and his entire body seemed to flop out in the sun. Hopefully he was somehow healing himself the way Adam had from the bullet wound. Ah, Adam. "You and the Enforcers go way back, as in not just the last few years. You know each other from your super-secret immortal world."

Bear made a snuffling sound of pure contentment.

That finally explained how they could be friends and still belong to different and not-so-friendly motorcycle clubs. "That's also why the Coven Nine let you leave Ireland and kept me. They already knew you, and you were fully aware that witches existed."

He opened both eyes, sighing hard enough he left a wet mark on her jeans.

"Fine. I'll stop talking." She took it back—Bear was every bit as cranky in animal form. "But are you undercover here, like Adam was?"

The animal shook his head.

"Oh. You just like it here in the woods, away from most people." Yeah. That seemed exactly like Bear, from what little she knew about him.

The sound of tires screeching to a stop, many tires, echoed from the front of the buildings. Bear jumped to all fours. A siren trilled once and then cut off. Doors rapidly opened.

The fur stood up on Bear's back. He nudged her toward a barely there trail between two wide-spread pine trees. Her stomach knotted. She turned to run, and a helicopter came into view with a guy half hanging out, gun trained on her. SWAT? The guy was wearing a SWAT vest.

"Run, Bear," she whispered. "Go now."

They'd probably just shoot a bear.

He rose on his hind legs and roared at the helicopter.

She shoved him in the back, but he barely moved. "Get out of here. Now."

With one last furious roar, he dropped to all fours and headed for the woods. For such a massively huge creature, he could seriously move.

Tori lifted her hands in the air.

Chapter 22

A huge guy all decked out in SWAT gear, vest, and guns, rounded the corner. He easily flipped Tori around and zip-tied her hands. Her mind numbed, and she shook her head, stumbling along with him back around the building. Apparently some sort of raid was being conducted on Grizzly headquarters.

When she reached the square area in front, DEA Agent Brenda Franks strode up.

Tori tripped over a rock, and the SWAT guy held her arm until she'd regained her balance. "What in the world are you doing?" Tori asked, the breath heating in her mouth. The blood rushed through her head, making her ears ring. "This is a raid?"

Franks nodded, her full mouth pinched. "We have enough information from other CIs that the Grizzlies are not only selling Apollo but that several of the higher-ranking members blew up the entire Titans of Fire compound the other day."

"They did not," Tori burst out, before she could think.

"Really?" Franks's brown eyes narrowed. "Just how would you know that fact?"

Because she and Adam had been the only living people there. Tori pulled against the zip ties, but they held fast. "I just know Bear and the guys wouldn't blow anything up. Not their style." She glanced at the cops pouring through every door to search all of Grizzly territory. "Could you cut these ties?"

"Not a chance," Franks said, crossing her arms. For the raid, she'd worn another high-end silk pantsuit that somehow looked even cooler with the bulletproof vest covering her full chest. "I'd like to know why you're here at Grizzly headquarters when you told me you had just started dating a Fire member. Especially since Fire just exploded, and at least three of its managing members are missing."

So those bones really had completely disintegrated. How hot could Adam make his fire, anyway? It was impressive in a totally scarier-than-hell way. "I left my favorite sweater here." Tori tugged on the pretty sweater she'd had for years and still loved. "So I thought I'd pop by and retrieve it. That's all."

"You came for a sweater," Franks said, her chin down.

"Yep."

"Right." Franks looked toward the far garage with the door wide open. "See, Miss Monzelle, that's not how it works."

Tori blinked. Franks had no clue how the world really worked. Tori was just finally figuring out that humans were a very small part of it. "Sure it is."

"No." Franks winced when a couch came flying out of the club-house. "Rival motorcycle clubs don't share women. They just don't. So when you left the Grizzlies and took up with a Fire member, you cut off any possible way in hell you could be here. You're stupid, but even you aren't that dumb. Know what I mean?"

Irritation raised goose bumps on Tori's skin. "I'm the friendly sort."

"No, you're really not." Franks zeroed in. "And now that I'm finally putting it together, you're not stupid at all, are you?" Her voice roughened and became calculating. "Holy shit. Holy fucking shit."

Warning caught any reply in Tori's throat.

"You're the key." Franks shook her head as if surprised she hadn't figured it out sooner. Her overly red lips pursed. "You're the tie between the two drug-running clubs, and you're the one with connections. Parker Monzelle's daughter. Why the hell didn't I see it before?"

Tori took a step back. "See what before? What are you talking about?"

"And your sister taking up with a Fire member. Shit. She has probably run interference for you the whole time. The whole damn time."

Tori shook her head. "Wh-what are you saying?"

"I'm saying, you're under arrest for the manufacture of drugs,

for the distribution of drugs, for attempted murder, and for homicide."
Franks grasped Tori's arm above the elbow and pulled her around
toward a black SUV. "I have no doubt we'll be adding more charges
to that, most likely arson to start with."

Tori's feet went numb. "I'm not dealing drugs. I was trying to help
you find out who was putting that stuff on the streets."

"And I made you a confidential informant," Franks snorted,
shaking her head and completely disregarding Tori's words. "I let
you be right in the thick of things so you could do your job, which
was to get that killing drug on the streets. Man, I'm going to get
slapped down for that one." Her fingers tightened on Tori's arm. "My
only consolation is that you'll pay, and pay dearly."

Tori stumbled. "I didn't do anything."

"You'll be charged federally. Did you know that the federal government employs the death penalty for large-scale drug operations?"
Franks seemed to cheer up as they reached the SUV and she opened
the back door. "Then you'll get to feel what it's like to have poison
put into your body. Watch your head."

Tori slid into the backseat, and cool leather brushed against her
skin. Her head spun. The death penalty? But she hadn't done anything. Her sister was out of town, so she couldn't call Lexi for help.
She could call Lexi's police partner, but he was a Seattle cop and
didn't have any sway with a federal agency like the DEA. She didn't
know any lawyers. Would she get a lawyer for a federal drug charge?
She had to. Well, maybe. She didn't know the federal legal system.

They were tying her to her father? God, she hated him. Really
hated him.

What about the witches trying to shoot Apollo at Adam? Would
they try to get her? If the DEA took her into town, she might get
killed anyway. But for now, the witches didn't know where she was.
That was good.

Unless they did know. Did the witches have sources in the DEA?
It made sense, since they were investigating Apollo, too. Thoughts
zinged through her head as quickly as the adrenaline flooded her
body. She had to get out of here. Get to safety. Back to the cabin in
the woods just thirty minutes away.

What about Adam? Tears pricked her eyes. She had to get a call to him somehow. He'd have no idea what had happened.

Shots rang out behind the buildings. "No!" she screamed, scooting to the edge of the seat and pressing her nose against the window. Bear was the only thing back there. Had they shot Bear? She turned her back to the door and tried to open it with her bound hands, but it was locked. Oh God, not Bear.

She muffled a sob and shook herself, trying to think.

Franks jumped into the front seat, and a smaller man with silver hair slipped into the driver's seat.

"Wh-what was that shot?" Tori asked, leaning toward the front seat.

"Some animal," Franks said dismissively. "No Grizzly members. They're out on a ride, it looks like."

Tori choked back another sob. "You haven't found any drugs. Have you?"

Franks turned and looked over the seat. "We've just started searching. Don't worry. We'll find their stash."

"You are so clueless," Tori muttered, shoving herself back in her seat and scouring the area outside the vehicle. Bear had to be okay. "Did they shoot the animal? I mean, did they hit him?"

"Don't know and don't care." Franks turned back around. "You should probably worry about yourself. We'd like to give you a chance to avoid the death penalty, but that means you have to tell us everything."

Tori bit her lip until she tasted blood. She didn't know a damn thing about Apollo or who was creating it. Any knowledge she had, mainly about the crazy immortal world, wasn't going to help her this time. She cleared her throat. "I want to call a lawyer." She'd have to find one in the phone book somewhere.

Franks chuckled. "Let's chat about that when we get to our offices."

That didn't sound good. So much emotion poured through Tori that her hands and feet tingled. "You're making a big mistake."

Franks didn't answer her.

The driver turned the key, and the engine roared to life. He set it in gear, and the SUV rolled forward. The engine clunked once. Twice. The vehicle hitched. Then it went dead.

Tori shut her eyes and leaned her head against the seat. Great. Just fucking great.

Adam stepped into the sunshine outside the hospital just as his phone belted out *King of the Mountain* by Bon Jovi. He lifted it to his ear. "Hi, Dage. What's going on?"

"The Grizzly headquarters was just raided by the DEA, according to a source in Seattle SWAT. They shot some sort of animal and took at least one person into custody." The sound of typing came across the line, and Dage cleared his throat. "I have an emergency with the Alaska shifters, but I'll be there as soon as I can."

"Any idea who it was?" Adam asked, running for his bike.

"No, but I'm having a satellite hacked right now to see if we can get a visual on what happened. Simone doesn't know yet," Dage said.

Adam frowned and lifted his leg over the Harley. "You have to tell her. Keep her there until we know more, but she needs to know that her brother's place was raided." He gunned his engine, his mind settling into the mission. "Don't tell her anybody was shot. Not until we know who it was." There were tons of Grizzly members, and it could've been anybody.

"If her brother was harmed, I won't be able to keep her at headquarters. In fact, I don't think Nick could, either." Dage paused. "Well, okay. Nick could. The demon is a badass."

Adam opened the throttle, making it difficult to hear. "She's pregnant, not weak. I'll secure the area and then let you know." He clicked off. Oh, he'd love to keep Simone safely behind rock walls, but she was a strong witch, a powerful woman, and locking her down would just piss her off. Making Simone truly angry was to be avoided at all costs.

Man, he loved his cousin.

It was no wonder Simone and Victoria had become friends. Both women had strength to spare. Hopefully Victoria was still sleeping at the cabin or, at the very least, taking it easy. Maybe she was even writing a song. He'd love to hear one of her songs.

Lowering his head, he increased his speed, soon leaving downtown in his wake.

A half hour later, he drove into the disaster that was Grizzly headquarters and gave a low whistle. The cops had torn the place apart.

Half of the furniture, including the pool table, was stacked outside in varying degrees of brokenness. The pool table had been slashed and smashed in two, and the sofa was ripped end to end, with cotton sticking out everywhere. White tufts blew in pieces around the square.

Several bikes were parked over to the side.

As Adam dismounted, Lucas Clarke strode out of the largest garage, fury sizzling across his square face.

Adam approached him. "What the hell?"

Lucas shook his head, his body vibrating. "DEA raid. We got here right when they were finishing."

"You weren't arrested, so I take it no contraband?" Adam asked, grimacing at seeing a classic Chevy torn apart in the nearest bay.

"Not here," Lucas said. "The guns are off site, and this is why."

Adam nodded. "Good." It was imperative that humans not get their hands on the guns immortals had created. "Dage has intel that somebody was shot. An animal."

Lucas stilled. "Bear was the only one here." He turned and launched into a run, skirting the far side of the building.

Adam ran with him, his senses tuning in to any sort of vibrations. They reached the back of the buildings, where a rushing stream babbled yards away. Lucas didn't pause but instead turned down a trail littered with pine needles and small rocks. They ran for almost a mile, and Lucas took a sharp left, winding through bushes to reach a small wooden structure set into the rock.

Adam scented blood immediately.

Lucas growled.

They approached the door, flanking it, both on full alert.

Lucas opened the door, and Adam went first, his gun already out.

Bear lay on the floor in human form, buckass naked, blood pouring from his shoulder.

"Bear," Lucas breathed, sliding on his knees to reach his friend. "Bear?"

Adam looked around the one-room cabin and didn't see a towel. He yanked off his shirt and pressed it to the gaping wound.

Bear groaned, and his eyelids fluttered open. His brown eyes were cloudy, and the atmosphere rolled and swelled with his pain. "DEA," he mumbled.

Adam nodded. "We know. Just hold on. Can you send healing cells to the wound?"

"No." Bear shook his head wearily, his shaggy hair moving. Sweat rolled down his face and over his bare chest.

Lucas clamped his hand around Bear's wrist. "You need to shift. It's the only way to heal yourself. This is bad, Bear."

"Yeah," Bear groaned. "I need to shift for good, Luke. For a while, anyway. I'm not getting any better." He spit out each word as if it hurt like hell. "Take care of the Grizzlies, yeah?"

"No problem." Lucas helped him to sit up. "Go do what you need to do. We'll be here."

Adam grabbed his other hand and helped Bear to stand. "I'll be around, too."

Bear hung almost limply between them, sweat and blood mingling down his side. "I stayed hu-human so I could tell you. They, the DEA . . . they took Tori."

Adam shook his head. "What? Victoria? How? When? From here?" What the hell had she been doing in Grizzly territory?

"Yes," Bear whispered, his voice full of pain. "Wanted to tell you." His head lolled. "Tell my sister I love her and not to look for me. I'll be back." He shrugged them both off and limped toward the door, leaving drops of blood and sweat on his way. The moment he cleared the porch, he dropped and turned into a bear.

Seconds later, he was gone.

Adam yanked his phone out and dialed quickly. "Dage? I need a favor. Now."

Chapter 23

Tori sat at a metal table, rubbing her aching wrists. Agent Franks had released the ties and left her sitting in the freezing room for about an hour. The walls were a boring light blue with a couple of black-and-white photographs of the Washington wilderness as decoration. Finally, the agent returned and pushed a steaming cup of coffee toward her.

"Thanks," Tori said automatically, reaching for the fragrant brew. She took a drink, and the bitterness scalded her tongue. She winced.

"Yeah, the coffee sucks." Franks slapped a yellow legal pad on the table and sat across from her. She set her phone next to the files. "I think you're a decent woman who probably never had a real chance, considering who your father is."

Tori lifted an eyebrow and blew on the coffee. "Is that a fact?"

"Yeah. Same with your sister. Oh, I think she was doing all right until she fell for that Titans member, and then I think she got in over her head. Dragged you in with her." Franks reached into a briefcase she'd set on the floor and tugged out several manila file folders. "It's always the men, right? I've seen more than one good woman end up in serious trouble because of a man."

Tori sipped again. That was true about most men, without a doubt. Her father was a real bastard, and Tori had dated more than her fair share of assholes. But Adam? He was different. Oh, he was hard to read, and he'd kept secrets, but there was something about him that inspired trust. Deep down, where it really mattered, she knew he wouldn't let her down. She blinked. What did that mean? That meant something, right? "My sister is a good cop, and she'd never run drugs. Neither would I."

Franks sighed and tapped a closed file folder with one long red nail. "It's time for you to start thinking about yourself. Let me help you."

Tori couldn't stop a small smile from tickling her lips. "Yeah. I can tell. You really want to help me out." Just how dumb did Franks think she was? "Let me ask you: What did you find at the Grizzly compound?"

Franks's bright red lips thinned.

"Yeah. That's what I thought." Tori ignored the anxiety in her stomach and sat back, studying the agent. "You're so desperate to solve this case you actually stink of it. But you're way off base. You have to know that deep down, right?"

"I'm going to be there when they pump you full of poison," Franks snapped.

Tori shook her head. "That's never going to happen. What do you have on me, anyway?" She set down the cup and tilted her head. "I had a friend who bought a drug, and I helped you try to find the drug dealer. That's it. My sister is a cop, and she's dating a motorcycle club member, one without a record. That's it." She leaned forward and let her voice drop even more. "My father is and always was a real bastard who did and probably still does deal drugs, but I'm not in contact with him. Ever. That's. It."

Franks's nostrils flared. "Your friend who bought the drugs gave some to Bob, the poor kid, who disappeared with you that same night, not feeling well. To this day, we haven't found him."

Tori opened her eyes wider. "Bob is a rambler and probably moved on. He was just sitting in with the band as a substitute bass guitarist, and then he left. That's what he has always done." True story, actually. Of course, the poor guy was buried somewhere in the woods around the cabin now. "Have you contacted his family? I mean, if he has any?"

"He doesn't," Franks said. "I think you know that fact. And I think you know where his body is. He's dead, right?"

Tori swallowed and glanced at the stark photograph to the right. "I want a lawyer."

"Wait a minute. You get a lawyer and I have to charge you." Franks *tsk*ed. "How about you tell me who blew up the entire Fire compound? There's one sick crazy person out there, or several, who would do something like that."

Sick? Not even. Adam hadn't acted in passion or anger. He'd blown up the buildings because it was the most expedient way to get rid of the entire motorcycle club as well as hide the bodies. He wasn't cold so much as efficient. Tori twirled the plastic cup around in her hands. "How should I know who blew up the club? Probably Pyro. That means *fire*, right?"

"Where is Pyro? And Jamm and Ziggy?" Franks leaned forward, lines fanning out from her eyes. "We've found most of the Fire members but not those three. Or the three Enforcers whose Irish club merged with Fire. Where are they, Tori? Where's your new boyfriend?"

Man, all the questions were probably driving the agent crazy. But the answers would reveal secrets that Tori couldn't share. "I think the Dunne men went back to Ireland even before the place blew up." She sighed. "Adam said good-bye and told me we were over. Said he missed home and they were all leaving." As lies went, it really wasn't bad. She shrugged. "I guess I can pick 'em, right?"

"I think you're full of shit," Franks said. "Is your sister in Ireland with Kellach Dunne?"

Tori sighed. "All I know is that they took a leave of absence to spend some time together. You know. Explore their love." She faced the agent without blinking. There really wasn't enough to hold her on. "My sister is a good person, and you should know that if you've been investigating her. I hope you're good at your job."

"I'm excellent at my job," Franks said, hard-won confidence on her wide face. "You want to work with me."

"Actually, I want to go home," Tori said, flattening her hands on the table. As a card player, she wasn't bad, especially with bluffing. Her legs wobbled, and her stomach churned, but she kept her expression direct. "So either arrest me, or get out of my way."

"But then you would miss the family reunion," Franks said, flashing her teeth. Against her dark blusher on her cheeks, her teeth were a stark white. Maybe she bleached them.

"Family reunion?" Tori met the agent's smile with her own. "While I'd love to see my sister, she's on vacation. So unless you plan on keeping me here, probably against the law, then I don't think we'll meet up in this place." Her mother was still safely enjoying a sunshine cruise, covered by both witch and vampire soldiers, so Tori wasn't too concerned.

"Oh, not your sister." Franks drew imaginary circles on the file with her finger. "Daddy is coming home."

Tori blinked, the entire world narrowing with a frightening rush of sound. "Excuse me?"

Franks looked up, triumph darkening her expression. "Your father. I've had him moved to one of our interrogation rooms. What do you think? I'm betting he'll give you up in exchange for a carton of cigarettes. Care to put money on that?"

Pain, of the old and childhood kind, rippled through Tori. "I think he'll say anything to hurt us. Doesn't matter if it's true or not."

"Yeah, well, considering he's in serious trouble after shooting your sister while on parole, then maybe you're right." Franks flipped open a file. "Though I'd like to get him on more drug charges."

Tori blinked. "What are you talking about?"

Franks spread out papers. "Drug charges. He violated his parole, within a week by the way, and we have him on attempted murder of a cop and possession of Apollo. I want him on the dealing and manufacturing charges."

Tori shook her head. Her ears burned. "No. What about Lexi? He shot Lexi?"

Franks paused and looked up, a slow smile moving all that red lipstick. "You didn't know?" She threw back her head and laughed. "Oh, that's rich. Big sister gets you involved in the drug trade but doesn't want to screw with your head by telling all the truth? Maybe she wanted you to go on working for daddy." Franks leaned forward, her gaze turning intense. "Maybe she's just like the old man—cold as ice and money is all that matters."

Fury gripped Tori, and her shoulders vibrated with fierce trembling. "My sister doesn't deal drugs, and she hates our father more than I do." Her mind tried to process the new information. "He must have shot her when she had him arrested," Tori said slowly.

"Yep. Aimed right at her. Wasn't just trying to get free." Franks tilted her head and studied Tori. "Why would you protect a man like that? He shot to kill, Tori."

Tori breathed out, her stomach cramping so badly she needed a bathroom. "I would never protect him." Too much information assailed her, and her head swam. Tears pricked the back of her eyes, and she shoved them down, trying to concentrate. How could their own father want Lexi dead? Emotions swamped her.

The agent's phone started to smoke. Ah, shit.

Franks yelped and grabbed the papers. Flames burst from the phone. "What the hell?" She knocked it onto the floor and stomped out the fire.

Tori chewed the inside of her lip. "That was weird." God, she had to get her emotions under control. A speaker in the corner started to buzz.

The buzzing turned into a piercing wail. Tori closed her eyes and dug deep, trying to calm herself. Adam. His face, the feeling of his arms around her, the impressive ripple of his muscles . . . those calmed her.

The wail stopped.

Franks sputtered, "What the hell is going on around here today?"

The door opened, and Tori's head jerked up. What in the world? Adam Dunne and King Dage Kayrs strode in, wearing what looked like million-dollar suits, blazing power ties, and identical irritated expressions.

Her heart exploded, heating her entire torso. She'd known Adam would come. Yeah. She smiled, and then as the facts ticked into place, she lost the grin and her eyes widened. Behind Dage came a rail-thin man with bushy gray hair, a stained tie, and a shabby brown suit. And a frown. He shut the door after they had entered the room.

The area swelled with tension, growing heavy and thick. What was Adam doing there? Agent Franks wanted him locked up, without question.

Adam zeroed in on Tori immediately. "Are you all right?"

She nodded numbly.

The vampire king also looked her over. "If Victoria has more than a scratch on her, I'll shut down your entire organization."

"I'll blow it up," Adam said grimly. "Victoria?"

Agent Franks jumped to her feet. "Adam Dunne, you're going to be held for questioning."

"I don't think so," Adam said, his gaze never leaving Tori's. "I asked you a question."

Her legs wobbled, but she stood, letting her injured wrists fall to her sides. "I'm, ah, I'm fine." Her brows drew down as she focused on Adam. "I don't understand."

The other guy, the one she didn't know, handed a folded piece of paper to Franks. "She's to be released immediately."

Franks drew in a sharp breath. "Not a chance. I have them both now." She slowly unfolded the paper and quickly read. "You have got to be kidding me."

Adam skirted the table and gently took Tori's arm, but his eyes remained hard. Angry. At her? "We've been cleared to leave town, Victoria. Let's get going."

Franks held up a hand. "Wait a minute. Just wait a damn minute here." Her hard gaze swept to Tori. "You're telling me you all work for an international drug-fighting agency in connection with Interpol and Homeland Security?" Her mouth dropped open. "No way."

"And the CIA," Dage said helpfully, looking dangerous in his black suit.

Adam's suit was a dark gray with a fine weave, and he looked like what he was: a furious predator forced to cover himself with the trappings of civilization. How could anybody, especially trained law enforcement people, believe he was human? There was just something too male, too primitive about him. "Are you sure you're all right?" he asked quietly, ignoring everyone else in the room. Anger still threaded through the kind words.

"No." She gave him the truth instinctively. "Did my father really shoot Lexi?"

"Yes," Adam said without hesitation. "I told them they should be honest with you, but your sister wanted to protect you." He rolled his eyes. "Siblings, right?"

She tried to smile at his attempt to soothe her.

A phone buzzed from somewhere on Dage. He sighed. "You're telling me. Siblings."

He was the king, right? Couldn't a king do whatever he wanted? Tori's legs twitched with the need to get the heck out of there. "We can leave now?" she whispered.

"I guess you can," Agent Franks spat, fury in her eyes. "But say good-bye to Malanie Morris. She'll be spending a good amount of time in federal prison."

Panic swept Tori. "But——"

Adam held up a hand. "I forgot to give you this." He reached in his lapel and drew out another piece of paper. "Malanie has also been working for us, and she has been reassigned elsewhere. Here's a directive from your superiors to wipe any mention of her from your case files. She's gone. I assure you."

Tori didn't move. Thank God. Somehow, Adam had secured Malanie's safety. She'd thank him later.

Adam's pants rang out Bon Jovi's *Right Side of Wrong*. He frowned and drew out his phone, pressing it to his ear. "Dunne." He listened for a moment, and then his entire body straightened, making him seem even taller than usual. He clicked off and turned to Franks. "You took Parker Monzelle out of a secure prison."

"Yes." Franks glared and held her own with him. "I don't know what's going on here, but I know you're not an undercover agent for anybody. Monzelle is going to give me the truth."

Anger vibrated down Adam's back. Tori swallowed and resisted the urge to step away from the furious witch. "Adam?" she asked.

"Parker Monzelle escaped the transport van about fifteen minutes ago," Adam said, his words clipped. "He's in the wind. Right now."

Chapter 24

Adam escorted Victoria out of the station, with Dage covering his back. They had snipers on the nearby rooftops as well as undercover operatives milling in the crowds on the busy street. The Realm could mobilize in seconds, which was one of the many reasons the witches had aligned themselves with the superpower. Well, until now. "Are we at war?" he asked absently, opening the door to a long black car for Victoria.

She slid inside and he followed, with Dage on his heels. The car immediately moved away from the curb, with the partition up between them and the driver. From the vibrations, the guy was a vampire. Made sense.

The king sat and smoothed his hands down his pants. "We're not at war. I believe the Coven Nine is meeting shortly to discuss leaving the Realm, but I don't think they'll go so far as to declare war. It'd be suicide." He paused. "For your people. Not mine."

"Withdrawing from the Realm is just as bad," Adam said, swiping a hand over his eyes. "I can't believe this." He turned toward the pale woman watching the two of them. When he'd walked into the interrogation room and seen the fear in her eyes, he'd nearly lost his mind. "What the fuck were you thinking, leaving the cabin?"

She blinked.

"Smooth," Dage muttered, texting rapidly on his phone. "You know part of this deal is that we all have to leave Seattle, right?"

"Aye." Adam kept his focus on the woman, whose eyes were rapidly turning a stormy blue. If she thought to argue with him right now, she was crazier than he'd thought. "There's too much attention on us here now, anyway. But we still haven't figured out the damn manufacturer of Apollo. It's about to be unleashed on my people. I just know it."

Dage sighed and looked up from his phone. "Agreed. Bear is going to have to be our eyes on the ground." He winced. "God help us."

Tori reared up. "Wait a minute. You're all leaving Seattle? What about my sister?"

Adam opened his mouth but didn't have a platitude. So he gave her the truth. "I don't know. Right now, Kellach is wanted by our people, so they can't go to Dublin. But we have to get out of Seattle." So much was up in the air, he didn't have time to be angry with Victoria. Yet his temper would not abate. "You still haven't told me why you left the cabin when I specifically told you to stay there."

Her chin dropped, and her eyebrows lifted, giving her the most smart-ass expression he'd ever seen. "I guess the simplest answer is that I don't fucking take orders from you."

Dage snorted and busied himself with his phone again, not looking at either of them. "You should just mate her and get it over with," he mused.

Adam's head snapped toward his old friend. "Just because you're the king, doesn't mean I won't burn the hell out of you."

Dage's smile widened, and he didn't even look up. "You're as cranky as Bear."

Tori sucked in air. "Bear was shot, right? Is he okay? We have to get out there."

"He's fine," Adam lied. "Well, he will be. He's recuperating."

"As a bear or as a human?" she snapped.

Adam studied her. "You saw him shift?"

"Yeah."

That made sense. "He's in bear form and will be for a while as he heals." Adam frowned toward Dage. "That puts a little crimp in our plans."

"Not necessarily. Lucas can take over for the time being. You really have to get out of town, Adam," Dage said. "I'm thinking you should come visit Idaho."

Tori waved her hand. "Wait a minute. What is wrong with Bear besides getting shot? He was really sick before."

"It's a long story," Adam said.

"So what?" she snapped.

Oh, that defiance needed dealing with. He pinned her with a look. "I don't wish to discuss it."

If looks could burn, he'd be a smoldering ember. She turned toward Dage and gave him her sweetest smile. "King? What's wrong with Bear?"

Dage kept texting. "Shifters have one form, or one animal, at their base, you know? Tigers are tigers, wolves are wolves, cougars are cougars." He frowned and then texted faster. "Family is a pain in the ass."

Tori leaned toward him, and Adam gave a light growl. She ignored him. "And what about Bear?"

"Bear is a bear. His mama was a bear." Dage pressed the screen harder with sharp pokes. "His daddy, on the other hand, was a dragon. A bear can't be a bear and a dragon."

Her mouth went slack. "Dragons exist?"

"Yeah, but they're few and far between," Dage said. "Anyway, to save Simone a couple of weeks ago, Bear made the colossal mistake of shifting into a dragon several times. It harmed him on a cellular level."

Worry darkened Tori's eyes. "A cellular level?"

Dage looked up. "Yes. The closest explanation I can think of is to imagine your soul being shredded with poison-tipped claws until nothing remains but a pile of, well, smoldering agony."

Adam shot him a hard look. "That's a little much."

"But it's accurate." Dage set his phone in his pocket. "Bear will need to embrace his inner animal again and probably run for a month or so just as a bear. He'll be okay. Well, probably."

Tori swallowed. "Simone is half dragon?"

Dage lifted a powerful shoulder. "Eh. Her father was a dragon, but she's all witch. One form only, you know. I don't think she could shift even if she really wanted to. Nope. Simone is a witch."

Tori wiped a hand across her eyes. "I get it." She studied Adam and then the king.

Adam held on to his temper. "What?"

She shrugged. "It's hard to explain. You immortals—with powers. It's like you each have your own tune. I can kind of hear it."

Dage blinked. "You can hear tunes?"

"Yeah," she said, pink flashing across her high cheekbones. "The current of power. Yours is dark and deep. Adam's is streamlined and deadly. Simone . . . well, she was lighter but somehow even more dangerous." Victoria shook her head. "It sounds weird."

Adam breathed out. "Makes sense, really. Your enhancement with motors and engines, and your love of music. It's a gift." To think she'd been in danger. Real danger, because she hadn't listened to him. He bit back a growl.

"Interesting," the king said. "I'll have to tell my mate. I have no doubt she'll want to meet you, Victoria. After this business is concluded." He glanced at a watch on his wrist and then focused on Adam. "I have the supplies and equipment you requested being set up at your cabin. Who knows about the cabin?"

Adam ticked through people in his brain. "Bear knows, and apparently a few of the Fire members were aware of it, considering they took Victoria, but either they're dead or on the run."

Dage nodded. "I think you're safe there for the night, but you really have to get out of Seattle."

"I've been called before the Council in Ireland in two days anyway," Adam said, his plan starting to take shape.

Dage's eyebrows rose. "You're not really considering attending?"

"I am." He held up a hand when Dage started to argue. "I'm an Enforcer for the Council of the Coven Nine, King. That means something to me. I'm going to take the evidence I have and hopefully what else we discover, and I'm going to defend my family in chambers. It's who I am."

"They'll cut off your head," Dage said grimly.

There was enough truth to the statement that Adam's muscles tensed. The car finally reached the cabin and rolled to a stop. "I have people looking for Parker Monzelle and those who helped him to escape, as I'm sure you do as well. Let's coordinate efforts," Adam said.

Dage nodded. "I'm not hiding your suicide plan from your brothers."

Adam sighed. "I didn't think you would." He reached out and

shook his friend's hand. "Thank you for teleporting here so quickly and for the governmental documents. I owe you another one."

The king held his gaze. "Someday I'll collect."

Of that, Adam had no doubt. "I know."

Dage glanced at his watch again. "Any surveillance at the DEA office as well as in the surrounding neighborhoods just experienced a little glitch due to solar activity." The king grinned. "There's no record of us being there."

Adam returned the smile. "Excellent. Thanks." He turned to assist Victoria from the car. "It's time you and I had a little chat."

Thunder cracked across the sky, and Tori jumped. Wind bit into her. She'd been at the DEA office long enough that the weather had turned from nice and sunny to pissed off. Just like the male currently all but dragging her across the wet grass and up the steps of the cabin. The expensive black car turned around and sped down the driveway.

It was too late to ask the king if she could leave with him.

Lightning cracked, and the smell of ozone filled the air. The trees around them swayed violently, throwing pine needles like darts.

Adam shoved open the door and pulled her inside. "Bear owns this cabin, and nobody knows we're renting it from him. It's safe for us until I leave for Ireland." He shut the door, his innocuous words at complete odds with the hard thread of anger in his tone. He left her at the door and strode over to the stone fireplace to set logs in place. Fire crackled down his arms, and he held out his hands, shooting flames to ignite the logs.

Apparently he wasn't worried about anybody sensing his fire. They must truly be alone in the middle of nowhere. She shivered.

Soon a fire crackled, sending soft light across the darkened space.

He turned, a powerful man standing in front of his open fire. The thunder and lightning outside added slashing rain to the mix, pushing energy into the cabin that was no match for the fury pouring off the witch. "You still haven't answered my question," he said.

Her chin lifted, but butterflies zinged inside her abdomen. Her breath came in short bursts. "I believe I did answer your question," she whispered, not backing down. He had no right to be angry with her. Not really. "If you've forgotten, I think I said something about not following orders from you. I also used the F-word, if I remember correctly."

"You are such a smart-ass," he noted, no amusement on his impossibly rugged features.

So she'd heard. More than once, actually. The look he was giving her, all determination and arrogance, pulsed excitement through her entire body. Oh, she wanted to defy him, wanted to put him in his place. But she wanted something else more. Something that was all Adam Dunne. An elusive element of raw power that she'd only just glimpsed. Could she push him to that place?

Did she truly want to?

His nostrils flared, and something wild glimmered in his eyes. "I see. Well, then. Apparently, you need it spelled out for you." He didn't move a muscle, but his very essence rolled through the room, owning it. Owning everything. "When I tell you to stay put, you will do exactly that. When I tell you to move, you move. Until we're cleared by the Council, if I tell you to stop breathing, you fucking hold your lungs still."

She gaped at him. There were words of rebuttal, and she should say them, but her mind blanked. Adam in full temper was a sight to see.

He gave a short nod. "Now, you are to stay here. I'm going to scout around and make sure my alarms are in place." He took a step toward the door.

"No."

He stopped mid-stride. His gaze, lava hot, slashed to her. His lips pressed shut as if he was the one who couldn't find words now. For several long tension-filled seconds, they just looked at each other.

The bite marks on her neck burned and pulsed. An iron fist gripped her lungs. Hunger tormented her along with a warning she didn't know how to heed.

Finally, he spoke. "What did you say?"

There was an out. She could take it and back down. Get a breather from all the tension. "I said no."

He was on her then, faster than she could take that breath. Clamping his hands on her hips, he lifted her onto the table, setting her down none too gently. His face lowered to hers. "What in the hell are you doing?"

"Pushing you," she said, the tingling along her butt spreading inward from the rough treatment.

"Why?" he bit out, his expression fierce.

Now that was the question. Was there an answer? There had to be an answer. Her gaze dropped to his full lips. "Because I can." It struck her then—the truth of that statement. How many people on earth could push Adam Dunne to the edge of his control? Not many, she'd bet. He needed this. He needed to get out of his own head, to step back from the war going on inside him between family and duty, and she was the woman to take him away. She tilted her head to the side, her entire body lighting on fire from within. "What are you going to do about it?" She flattened her palm against the hard ridge of his erection.

He growled.

She shivered, the low timber echoing inside her body. "I like that sound."

His chest moved as if he was fighting something. Himself. So she stroked him, base to tip, squeezing at the end.

He grabbed her shoulders, partially yanking her up to meet his mouth. The noise he made, in the back of his throat, was all male hunger. His fingers curled around her shoulders, holding her in place, his mouth consuming hers. The ice of Adam, the sheer deliberation of the man, merely masked the inferno deep inside.

With only his kiss, he gave her that. Heat and light and raw power. He was hot enough to burn her, and she found herself wanting nothing more than to be surrounded by flames. She could taste a wild edge, almost desperation, in his kiss.

She'd done that. Little Victoria Monzelle, the wild child, the lost one. She'd brought this hunger to such an amazing male.

He set her down, his mouth hot and firm, taking everything she had. Rough hands ripped her shirt open, and he grasped her breasts, pinching hard enough she gasped into his mouth. He twisted his head away and shredded her bra, dropping it to the floor. Grabbing the back of her neck, he pulled her down, laying her flat on the table.

Her jeans joined the bra.

What the hell had she done? His fingers found her and she arched, so much pleasure rippling through her she couldn't breathe.

"You're wet. For me," he murmured, driving her crazy. "You shouldn't push, Victoria."

She lifted up on her elbows, her lids heavy and her body on fire. "Why not?"

"Because." Grasping her thighs, he flipped her over.

She landed on her hands and knees, facing the sink. "Hey."

Fabric rustled. Hard hands clamped on her hips. The wide ridge of his cock pressed at her entrance. She gasped and shut her eyes as streaks of lightning flashed behind her eyelids. "Adam," she gasped, needing more. So much more. How easily he'd grabbed control from her. Or so he thought. She looked over her shoulder, almost stunned by the ferocity on his angled face. "You want me?"

"Aye," he said, his eyes burning.

"Then take me."

Chapter 25

As she looked over her shoulder, the stunning blue of her eyes intrigued him, and the defiance glowing so fully there claimed him. That spirit, that very edge, called to the primitive hunter inside him and drove his hunger to a level that should scare him. But it didn't. He had no choice but to give in to the beast deep down. He gripped her hair, keeping her head turned toward him and her face visible.

Then he pushed inside her, slowly, feeling her body accept him. Her eyelids started to close and he jerked his wrist, tugging her hair. Her eyes opened wide and a little wary.

He smiled, allowing his fangs to drop.

Her sex clenched around him. Yeah. He kept his hold firm and shoved all the way inside her. The sound she made was one of need. Tremors shook her body, cascading around him, claiming him in a way he'd never imagined. His body might be burning, but his heart, maybe deeper, was pulling her in completely. There was no turning back for him now. "You wanted this," he reminded her, his voice hoarse.

"Still do," she said, a siren's dare in her smile.

He reluctantly released her hair, not wanting to hurt her neck. She slowly turned away, shaking the luscious mass down her back. With her skin bare, her ass against him, and the long line of her back revealed, she was pretty much perfection. He reached around and tweaked a nipple. She moaned and pressed into his hand, pushing the globes of her ass against his groin.

The mating brand on his palm burned with a demand that clawed through his entire body. He pressed it against her right buttock, and a rush of power scoured him, stealing his very breath. So long as he kept his fangs in his mouth, she was safe from a mating she had yet to agree to.

For now, it was time to earn her trust. He'd been with many women through his long life. Some had even liked it rough, and he'd been happy to comply. But Victoria was different.

He wanted to take her in every way possible. Burn himself on her, keep his scent on her for the rest of her life. Wanted to strip her down, take everything, make her feel the raw and primitive feelings she brought out in him.

Pulling out, he thrust back in. Hard.

Her ragged moan licked along his balls, landing hard inside him. If she screamed, he wanted it to be his name. Her sex stretched around him, wet and tight, and oh so damn hot. She gasped and writhed against him. He grasped a nipple with unerring accuracy, pinching until she stilled. "You don't get to move," he whispered, leaning over and brushing her ear with his mouth. "Understand?"

She tossed her head like a filly he'd broken to saddle in Ireland a century ago.

Victoria had challenged him in no uncertain terms. But he didn't want to break her. Not in the slightest. However, he saw much deeper than she probably realized.

The little girl raised without a father had turned into a wild woman who didn't trust men. He couldn't blame her. When she'd thrown down the challenge, it had been for much more than a mere orgasm. He plucked harder, and she gasped, her back arching. "I can do this all night, baby." He sank a fang into her earlobe, and her womb convulsed around him. "You just let me know when you're ready to submit."

"Never," she moaned, her head lowering.

Ah, that was the key. Victoria wanted to submit more than any person he'd ever met. She wanted to put her trust in a man more than anything else, but she was going to make him work for it.

He wouldn't have it any other way.

"Never is a long time." He flicked her other nipple, and she sucked in a sharp breath. He sent fire to the tips of his fingers and ran them across both breasts.

She gave a soft cry, both pleasure and frustration in the sound.

"We're just getting started," he whispered, burning a path down her torso. He kept the fire light enough to keep her safe but sharp enough to bite.

"No, Adam, please—"

"Yes," he corrected, reaching her clit. He spread his fingers wide, keeping the flame off her sensitive button, letting the sparks fly close enough for her to feel the crackle.

Her sob was one of the sweetest sounds he'd ever heard. Her forehead rested on the table, even as her body pushed back into his while also reaching for the flames. Her legs trembled against the front of his. Humming softly, he increased the heat level and snapped the fire between her thighs.

She cried out and spread her knees, instinctively trying to avoid being burned.

"Isn't that better?" he murmured, licking along the shell of her ear. "I wanted your legs spread wider, and they're spread wider. See how this works?"

"I'm going to kill you," she ground out, her voice muffled with her mouth on the table.

He flicked a flame up on her clit.

She arched and cried out. Mini-explosions rippled along his cock inside her. That orgasm was hovering just out of her reach. He chuckled. "That was close."

She may have mewled. "You. Are. Such. A. Dick."

God, she was perfect. Just fucking perfect. "Ah, Victoria, you sweet woman. I just wanted to play a little. Make you needy. Now you're going to beg, and it's going to be the way I want. Not the measly little 'please' you gave me the other night." He scraped the late-evening shadow on his jaw down her sensitive neck. "By the end of the night, I'll fucking own you."

Dots gathered across Tori's vision as she tried to focus on his words. What had he said? It was becoming way too hard to defy him, but it was so much damn fun. The lick of fire from his hand left a residual burning sensation, so everywhere he'd touched still tingled.

And he'd touched her *everywhere*.

The wooden table was cool beneath her cheek while the rest of her burned. His cock was hard and pulsing inside her, a constant reminder of his strength and control. She gripped him several times with her internal muscles, and, while he gave a seriously dangerous low growl, he didn't move.

The way he worked her body, her mind, stripped her bare. She should be terrified. Angry. Even embarrassed. But she wasn't. She felt feminine and powerful . . . even though he'd taken control of them both. Not once in her entire life had she given up control to a man. This one had taken it.

His whiskers against her neck made her shiver. One of his hands dropped to the table next to her face, and he licked down her throat, sinking his fangs into the same place he'd bitten her the other night. The dart of pain blended with a raw pleasure.

The sensations streaked through her and made her entire body tremble. She blinked and saw the outline of the mating brand on his palm. Oh. He couldn't touch her and bite her at the same time.

As the thought hit her, his fangs slid deeper, showing no mercy.

She cried out, her body aching, desperately needing to be fulfilled.

"Now, my sweet Victoria, we're going to try something." He slid out and thrust inside her so hard, white spikes of light streaked behind her eyelids. He pulled her back up on her hands and knees. Her body trembled, wanting more. "Good girl."

She blinked. "Adam."

"You do speak." He chuckled, the sound a little menacing. "Good." The palm with the brand caressed down one of her arms, heating her, and then flattened over her hand. He nudged her with his hip, and she gasped. "All right. You don't move now."

Releasing her hand, he grasped her hips and pounded inside her for five hard thrusts. Energy began to uncoil inside her. Then he stopped.

She gasped and hung her head again. Her body vibrated with a tension that held the devastating calm before the storm broke—in her, all around her, on her. The tension tightened to the point of pain. How could he have stopped?

"Did you like that?" he growled, his voice gritty.

"Yes," she gasped, pushing back against him. "Do it again."

He gripped her hair and pulled, yanking her head up. The breath caught in her throat. "You're not giving the orders, love."

Who the hell cared? "Please," she added. At this point, she'd sing it for him. "I said please."

He chuckled again, his fangs scraping along her already sensitive neck. She tilted as much as his hold would allow to give him better access. "Please isn't enough this time." Fire crackled, although she couldn't see it. The second it touched her clit, she cried out at the painful pleasure that didn't quite send her over the edge, her thighs shaking hard enough to vibrate up her back. "Please, Adam."

He kissed beneath her jaw. "Not enough."

She barely had the energy to growl, she was so close to the edge. "Then what do you want?"

He stilled, head to toe, fire and breath—and the world paused with him. "Everything, Victoria. Give it to me."

She blinked. God, she needed. "I don't know how." The words spilled out of her even as she wasn't quite sure what she was saying. He needed to move inside her. Now.

"Tell me the truth. Tell us both the truth." Heat from his hand, from the blue fire, slashed up her body to glow in front of her face.

She eyed the blue on his palm. "The truth?"

"Aye. Tell me who owns you."

Her eyelids snapped open. Her heart and mind rioted at the same time. The blue fire looked back at her. "Wh-what?" He couldn't be asking for so much.

The fire lightened, and he pressed his palm against her neck. Heat flowed through her skin. She whimpered.

He leaned in, his mouth at her ear. "Head to toe." The heat increased, and he moved his hand down to her breasts. She panted, crying out. "Top to bottom." He moved lower, burning along her abdomen. She sucked in her stomach, willing him to go lower. "Heart to mind," he murmured, going lower and skimming heat along her clit to where they were joined.

It was too much. Way too much. "Adam," she moaned.

"Say it." He burned her thigh.

She arched. "You." There. God. She blinked.

"Not enough." Her head jerked against his hold, but he held tight. Tears gathered in her eyes. "Adam."

"Say it. Now."

She closed her eyes as submission flowed through her, sweeter than any release. "You own me."

His sharp intake of breath was her only warning before he manacled her hips and started to thrust, hammering inside her with a brutally strong rhythm that stole every thought she'd ever had. His flesh slapped against hers. The fingers curling into her hips bruised and burned. He drove into her, going deeper than she'd ever thought possible.

Heat flushed through her, uncoiling in a wave of electricity that disintegrated the world and banished all sound. She stiffened and cried out his name, her eyes closing. The orgasm bore down on her, barreling through her with wave upon wave of devastating pleasure. She rode it out, having no choice. Finally, she came down, her breath gasping from her lungs.

He shuddered behind her, his hold tightening.

She leaned down and pressed her cheek to the table again, her body beyond spent. "I'm dead. Just leave me here," she mumbled, her eyes closing.

He pressed a very soft kiss to the middle of her back. "Not a chance. Your taming has just begun."

Chapter 26

Adam finished scouring through the eighth set of documents he'd hacked from the Coven Nine, trying to ignore the table holding his computer. Not the table. The memory of what he'd done to Victoria on that table the night before. He'd taken her to bed and had proceeded to show her she could submit all night, and that he'd be there with her every time.

At one point, he'd submitted, too. He grinned. Or at least she had tried to make him. He had felt the second, the very second, she'd decided she could trust him.

It was a good start.

The woman was still sleeping, and she had certainly earned her rest. It was barely after dawn, so perhaps she'd sleep awhile.

He'd gotten up and had hooked up the computers left by the Realm boys, and now he was systematically figuring out a scheme to take down Peter Gallagher. It was the only way to keep both Victoria and his brothers safe.

The brand burned on his palm from not being used. He'd been very careful to keep either his hand or his fangs off her, no matter how much he'd craved to use both at the same time.

He worked for a while longer, drinking coffee, making meticulous notes. Time was drawing short, and he needed an attack plan that would work. Gallagher was a smart guy. There was nothing in the official documents that even hinted at a problem within the organization, which wasn't much of a surprise.

The door opened, and Victoria walked out, wearing his dress shirt and nothing else. The sleek silver fell to her knees, giving her the look of a delicate temptress.

"Morning," he said, rising.

She hovered in the doorway. "Um, morning."

He reached her in three steps and leaned down to press a kiss to her soft lips. "I thought you'd sleep awhile."

She pushed unruly curls away from her face. "I woke up, and you weren't there." A very pink flush wound up her cheekbones, turning her eyes into sparkling sapphires. "I mean——"

"I like what you said." He kissed her again. "Are you hungry?"

"Not yet." She spotted her guitar in the corner, and her shoulders settled. "Thought I'd play for a bit." Then she viewed the organized piles on the table. "What in the world are you doing?"

"Tugging on threads," he said, turning back to work. "After you play for a while, I thought we could practice your gift."

"My gift?" She frowned, a cute line appearing between her eyebrows. "What gift?"

He grinned. "Your ability to affect electronics. Let's hone that so you can control it." He pushed her toward her guitar, patting her lightly on the ass. "I need to hack into Peter Gallagher's private files now, so take your time."

Her eyebrows rose. "You're a hacker?" She eyed him, head to toe.

His body heated from just her gaze. "Sure. The challenge of hacking into an enemy's accounts has always been a hobby of mine." Yet this was serious and not fun. He was going to take Gallagher down, and hard.

"Oh." She frowned and rubbed her hand down over the Celtic swords and words on his chest.

His abdomen clenched.

"I've been thinking," she murmured.

"Oh?" he asked, his body heating.

"Yes. You're hurting because of your vow and the Council." She looked up, a stunning innocence in her eyes. "Your loyalty isn't just to the three people sitting on the Council. It's to the values of the witch nation. Fairness, security, family, fate, protection . . . you haven't lost that, Adam. No matter what happens next."

His breath stopped. He'd been trying to get inside her mind, inside her heart, and she'd just figured out everything about him. She was trying to find peace for him. "Victoria," he murmured.

She smiled. "I really need to play that guitar. There's a new song filling my head, and I have to get it out. Just think about what I said," she mumbled, disappearing behind the door.

"I will," he said softly, turning back to his work. Could he give her the same type of peace? Only if he secured her safety first. He had to concentrate. Now—where was that spreadsheet? He found it on the bottom of the pile.

"Hey." She appeared at the door again with a green gun in her hand. "There are a bunch of these cool laser guns in the room off the bathroom." The gun looked all wrong in her delicate hand, and she held it as if not quite sure what to do with it. "I take it these are witch guns only?"

"Many species have them. Not humans, however," he said. "Put it back, and later I'll show you how to use it, if you'd like."

She blinked. "Sounds good." Then she disappeared again.

When she emerged twenty minutes later, she'd tied her mass of hair up on her head. Tendrils already escaped. As she passed him, she fingered one of the strands. "I was, ah, thinking of getting rid of the purple streaks."

He sat back. "Why?" They were kind of spunky, just like her.

She shrugged. "I don't know. They're not very, well, classy."

He studied her, his heart warming. "Why not?"

She looked away from him.

"Victoria," he said, waiting until she'd focused back on him before continuing. "I like the purple."

Her gaze darkened. "Oh. The purple. Me. Your walk on the wild side."

He almost burst out laughing until he realized she was serious. Ah. That sure as hell wouldn't do. Why was she so out of sorts? He stood and crossed the room, stopping right in front of her. His knuckle nudged her chin up. "I have a feeling I wouldn't like where your thoughts have gone," he said softly, trying to figure her out.

She shrugged again.

Oh, the little sweetheart. "Feeling a little vulnerable after last night?" he guessed, gliding his thumb along her jawline, over her silky smooth skin.

"No," she said.

He couldn't help the grin. "Be careful, Victoria. I have no problem making you eat those words, and then you wouldn't get to play your guitar until much later."

She blushed, this time a deep rose.

He sighed. "I like you just the way you are. If you ask me, you have more class than any woman I've ever met."

She snorted, still trying to avoid his gaze. "Right."

"As much as I think I'm in your head, I can't read minds. Talk to me." He needed to have her trust all the time, not just when he was balls-deep inside her.

She faced him then, her gaze direct. "You bit me, and your hand has the brand. You could've mated me last night, and you didn't. Don't get me wrong, I'm not saying I want to mate. Definitely not. But it hit me that I'm not the type of woman a guy like you mates."

He frowned, his temper awakening. "Why the hell not?"

"Oh, come on. I barely have an education, and my dad is a major drug dealer." She rolled those pretty eyes. "I'm definitely from the wrong side of the tracks."

He shook his head. "You have it and me all wrong." Who had done such a number on her? "My family is wild and often outcasts. Daire's mate is a crazy-assed demon, a real demon, who robs banks in her spare time."

Victoria's mouth dropped open. "That's not true."

"Sure it is." Adam smiled. "We don't like boring women. You have to know that. I like you." He ran his hands down her arms. "But nobody, especially not Peter Gallagher and the fucking Coven Nine, is going to tell me who to mate or force you into immortality. Period."

She gave a short nod, but her eyes weren't convinced. "I guess that's fair. I mean, not that I want to get mated. But still."

Whoever mated her would have to understand and believe in love. And have a lot of it to give. The idea of anybody else mating her squeezed his throat tight, and he shoved the sensation away. There wasn't time for that. "Are we good?" he asked.

"Yes." She rolled her eyes and moved toward her guitar. "I'll play outside, away from your computer and your hacking plans. If I stay, the laptop might explode."

How interesting. She probably had to have stayed away from

certain technology her entire life. Had that gotten lonely? "You can stay inside," he said.

She gave him a smile. "I spend a lot of time outside away from things I can blow up. I enjoy it."

All right. He turned back to his papers, trying to figure out how to trap Gallagher. Oh, he had the video of the guy in the hospital, but he needed more. He also needed to find Parker Monzelle and take him out before he harmed either of his daughters again.

The question remained as to who had helped Parker Monzelle escape. Something told Adam he really wasn't going to like the answer to that question.

Tori moved out to the front porch and shut the door.

He methodically hacked through Peter's life, going through hidden bank accounts in other countries. Most witches, Adam included, held bank accounts around the world, so that in itself wasn't a problem. But there had to be more.

The strumming of a guitar caught his ear. He paused in the midst of typing. Then she began to sing. A lonely song, a mournful tune. Her voice wrapped around him, wound inside him.

When she finished, the brand on his hand swelled and burned hotter than any fire he'd ever touched.

Tori took a nice shower after a lunch of sandwiches and dressed in jeans and a dark shirt. She pinned her hair back and stepped out of the bedroom to find Adam waiting for her. He'd showered earlier and changed into jeans and a Bon Jovi shirt. She grinned. "You like Bon Jovi. I noticed all your ringtones."

"Aye." Adam moved the computer to the very end of the table.

She cleared her throat. "What's my ringtone?"

He smiled. "If you're a very good girl today, I'll tell you."

Curiosity wandered through her. It was probably something like *Runaway* or *Let It Rock.* She rolled her shoulders. "Okay. What do we do?"

"First, I wanted to tell you how much I enjoyed your singing and playing earlier." Was that pride in his eyes?

She shuffled her feet. "Thanks. I love writing songs."

He cleared his throat. "I've been wondering. Do you miss performing? Is that something that it's hurting you not to do?"

She was touched by the genuine question. He did want to know the real her. "Not really. I prefer writing songs, to be honest. Playing with the band helps pay the bills." She had so many new ideas for songs, and she had to admit, many were from being with Adam. Her feelings lately were complex and deep . . . and made for perfect lyrics, if she could be that honest with herself.

"I see." He studied her, his gaze seeming to see all of her. "I'd love to hear more of your songs tonight, if you don't mind."

She grinned. "If you're a very good boy today, I may play a song for you."

He grinned at her throwing his words back at him. "You are a clever girl, now aren't you?"

"We're about to see." She took another deep breath. What if she could control her oddity? How much fun would that be? "Okay. Where do we start with this risky training?"

"Just relax." He moved to her side and pointed to the microwave. "Let's start small. There are noodles in the microwave, and it's already programmed for three minutes. Concentrate and try to mentally push the start button."

She looked at the glowing start button and blinked.

Nothing.

She nodded and blinked again.

Nothing happened. Adam's grin caught her eye. "What?" she asked.

He tried to press his lips together, but humor danced in his eyes. "You look just like the woman in *I Dream of Jeannie*."

She coughed out a laugh. "I watched a bunch of reruns on the oldie channel a while back. Well, until the television started smoking and sputtering." Okay. That was funny. She lowered her chin and tried to shoot imaginary waves at the start button. No imaginary waves from her. Her shoulders slumped. "I can't do it."

Adam stepped behind her and slid his arm around her waist. His hand pressed between her breasts right at her solar plexus. "Work from here. Lean against me, and work from this part of your body."

She leaned back and let him support her weight. Then she concentrated on his hand, on the pressure and heat where he pressed. A tingle, an odd one, wound down her spine. She caught her breath. Then she squinted and shot out all the energy she could, mentally pushing through the air.

Sparks flew up from the back of the microwave. "Argh," she said, her eyes wide. More sparks, and a fire.

"Shit." Adam released her and ran around the table, reaching to unplug the cord. He grabbed a dishrag and slapped the fire out before shaking his fingers. "Burned me." He stuck his index finger in his mouth.

Tori went blank. What the heck? "You can get burned?" she asked.

He nodded. "Of course."

She looked at the dead microwave. "So. That was a huge bust."

He grinned and released his finger. "That was an excellent start. Don't worry about the microwave. Daire bought it." Adam chuckled. "For the time being, while you're letting your power out, stay away from my computer. Okay?"

"I've spent a lifetime staying away from televisions, radios, and computers. This is nothing new." She edged away from the table. "I've probably read more books than you have. The paper kind—not the e-book kind." Then she noticed Adam gazing at her very thoughtfully. "What?"

"Have you ever tried to jam a gun?" he asked, his intelligent eyes gleaming with ideas.

"Once the other day, but it didn't work," she admitted.

He strode into the bathroom and returned with two guns. "Let's go outside and figure this out. Then we can move on to the motorcycle. You've already affected that before, so perhaps that's the key." His phone rang out *Blood on Blood*, and he lifted it to his ear. "Hey, Daire. Robbed any banks lately?"

Then he sobered instantly.

Tori stilled, unease sweeping through her. Her legs trembled.

Adam's eyes hardened and turned a deeper hue with a hint of fury. "Got it. Keep me informed." He clicked off, his gaze not leaving hers.

She couldn't breathe. Swallowing a lump in her throat, she breathed in and then out. "What? What happened?" He reached her in two strides, and she instinctively backed away, her hand up. "Just tell me." God, was it Alexandra? "Please tell me what just happened."

Adam stopped moving. "We will take care of this, Victoria. Do you understand?"

Numbly, she nodded. "What?"

"Your mother was kidnapped from the cruise ship. The two guards are dead, but she was taken unharmed. Whoever has her wants her alive, and that's good."

His voice trailed off at the end, just as darkness swept in from the edges of her vision. The last thing she saw as she started to fall was Adam reaching to catch her.

Chapter 27

Adam furiously worked the computers as night fell, hacking into spy satellites the US government didn't even know existed. Hell, he wasn't sure the Realm knew about the well-masked satellites owned by the Coven Nine. There were only two, but they were undetectable from the planet.

The codes had been changed when Gallagher had taken office, and they'd been changed by techs who knew what they were doing. They should. Adam had trained most of them.

The fire had died down in the cabin, while Victoria alternated between pacing the porch outside and strumming her guitar. She'd burned up three phones trying to talk to her sister, and finally, he'd had to send her away from the computer equipment on the table. If she demolished it, he was screwed.

She poked her head in the door. "Anything?"

"No, baby." He kept his voice gentle as he continued typing and scrolling through the codes.

She bit her lip, her face too pale. "I've been thinking. It can't be a coincidence that both of my parents are missing, right?" Fear shimmered in her sapphire-colored eyes.

The look punched him in the gut. "There may be more going on here." He tried to think of a gentle way to put his thoughts into words. "I'm guessing your father was sprung because of his potential usefulness." The video from the escape hadn't arrived, so Adam couldn't be sure. "Whoever helped him probably works with him." That was the only thing that made sense.

She swallowed. "Yeah, but when he was out on parole, he took my mom hostage."

Adam frowned. "He talked your mother into meeting him and then used her to secure Alexandra's cooperation." Parker Monzelle needed to die, without question. "It was a calculated move and for business purposes."

Victoria shook her head, and her hair sprang free of the loose knot she had tied. "You don't understand. He may have had business reasons, but his personal ones are even stronger. He wants to hurt us. You don't get it."

Adam sat back, studying her pretty face. How could any man want to hurt somebody as precious as Victoria? "All right. Then here's another reason. Whoever took your mother was well trained and part of the immortal world." He'd been studying the matter from every angle, and there was only one thing that truly made sense. "Why would anybody take her?"

Victoria's gaze darted around as she thought it out. "The vampires have no reason, and neither do the demons."

"True," Adam said. The woman's brain was impressive as she logically connected the dots in a world she hadn't even known existed not too long ago. Her ability to accept the new reality so quickly was unusual. Pride filled him.

She swallowed. "Bear and his shifters wouldn't want anything to do with her." Victoria stopped moving and focused on him. "Why would the witches take her?"

He waited for her to put it together.

Her head went back. "Because of me," she whispered. "You and me."

"I think so," he said, willing her to trust him. "I could make us disappear if I wanted, and they know that. If they have your mother, then we have no choice but to appear before the Council as ordered." He was reaching out to every contact he still had to see if the Coven Nine had Jennie Junie. "The good news is that they won't harm her."

"You don't know that," Victoria burst out, color finally flooding her face.

"Did they hurt you?" he asked calmly.

She faltered. "Well, no. But it was still scary."

He nodded, his body actually aching to get up and offer comfort—but at the moment, he was of much more use in front of the computer. "I'll find her, sweetheart. Just let me keep working."

A wave of energy, one he actually felt, rolled from the woman through the room. His screen blinked and went dark before coming back online. "Outside, Victoria." Man, when they had time to actually harness that gift, she'd be a powerful weapon. "Your emotions are strong. Why don't you go focus them on either the bike or the gun you took outside earlier?" He'd shown her enough to keep her safe. "Just make sure you point the barrel at the trees and not the cabin."

Her smile appeared forced. "All right." The smile slid away. "Yell at me the second you find anything, okay?"

"I promise." Then they could argue about what would happen next. He needed to go to Ireland and rescue her mother, while Victoria would go into lockdown at Realm headquarters. She wasn't going to like that plan.

She cleared her throat. "You, ah, you mentioned getting into satellites."

"Aye?"

"You're really smart," she mused quietly.

Ah. She was needing reassurance. "Aye, Victoria. My brain is fully functional and fast. I'll find your mother."

She nodded. "That's what I thought. Like, your IQ is higher than Einstein's?"

Where was she going with that? "His was clocked only at 160. So yes." Before she could ask, he shook his head. "Can't be measured. So I don't know a number."

"Your IQ is too high to be measured." She said it as a statement, her tone oddly flat.

He blinked. "Well, to be honest, most of us don't think an IQ can really be measured. It's a series of tests created by humans with a number attached. A faulty system, to be sure."

She swallowed, moving the graceful line of her neck. "All right. That makes sense. Call me when you find either of my parents." The door softly closed.

He stared at it for a moment. What was that all about? With a shrug, he turned back to the satellite codes. A button dinged at the bottom of his screen, and he pushed a series of keys to bring up a picture. Kellach took shape with a morphing green screen behind him. Nice. The Realm boys were doing a good job of scrambling locations. "Hi, Kell," Adam said.

"How's Victoria?" Kellach asked, his black eyes sizzling. "Alexandra is about to lose her fuckin' mind."

Adam nodded. "Same here. I've been hacking the Nine but haven't found a location for Jennie Junie yet. Anything on Parker Monzelle?"

"Not yet." Kell scrubbed a hand down his face. "With Titans of Fire blown to hell, he doesn't have allies on the outside like he did. How many of them have been rounded up?"

"I haven't checked," Adam said. "Have more immediate issues. The video from his escape is still being cleared and entered into the Seattle system, so I haven't been able to get it. They should be logging it in today." The damn place still used video recording and not digital.

Kell breathed out. "What about the mating?"

Adam's chin dropped. "Are you serious?"

"Just asking, brother. Last time we talked, you were twisted up about the female." Kell studied him, his gaze seeing everything

Adam enlarged the screen to get a better view of the background. He needed to get something like that once he was back to working as an Enforcer. Well, if he kept his job. "The Nine is not forcing her to mate anybody. I won't allow it."

Kell flashed a grin. "What a nicely logical way to protect her."

"I thought so," Adam said, narrowing his gaze. "What's your point?"

"How do you feel about her?" Kell asked.

Adam blinked. "Shit, man. Being mated has turned you into a girl."

Anger flashed across Kellach's face, hot and bright, to be quickly quashed. "That's not an answer."

"I don't have time to worry about feelings," Adam snapped. The physical attraction between Victoria and him gave him no peace. Even though she was outside right now, he could feel her. All of her. Victoria Monzelle was a complex, highly intelligent woman with a spirit that called to him. But right now, with hell descending on all of them, it was the exact wrong time to even think about forever.

"How about we stick to work? You know? And the kill order hanging over your blasted head?"

Kell rolled his eyes. "I'm just saying. If you like her, and you enjoy her company, it'd be nice for Alexandra to have her sister live for eons, too."

Adam's head heated until he feared it would blow off his neck. "Victoria is full of light and energy. She, of all people in this damn world, deserves a forever mating with love. The real deep, no shit, die-for-each-other type of love." How could Kell not see that? He was blinded by the need to protect his mate, and that was all right. "So butt out."

Kell studied him, his lip quirking. Something glimmered in his eyes for a moment, and then he sat back. "Well, then. I see that. Sorry I interfered."

"It's okay," Adam said, relaxing. "I understand you want to make your mate happy."

"I surely do," Kell said, his expression not changing. "It's a damn good thing you're so smart, Adam."

Adam paused. Was there something in Kellach's voice that sounded a mite, well, sarcastic? "What is your point?"

"Nothing." Kell's smile widened. "It's just nice to see you have things so under control. You know. That you see everything that is right in front of your so-brilliant face."

Okay. That was definitely sarcasm, with a side of amusement. Adam's temper stirred. "Are the Realm boys working on finding Parker and Jennie Junie, or are they not?"

"They are, but we might have better resources." Kell lost his amusement. They both carefully kept from mentioning the two secret satellites. "Daire is at demon headquarters right now, and they have all of their techs working on the same issue. He wants to meet up in person later today and go through all the data."

Adam frowned. "Demon headquarters is just about a mile from Realm headquarters, right?"

"Aye," Kellach said, glancing to the side. "Why?"

Adam shrugged. "Seems like they'd just have one central meeting space." Yet, if witch headquarters moved closer, he'd probably advise against it. Alliances rarely lasted in their world. "Forget it. Speaking of which, has the Coven Nine declared war on anybody yet?"

"No. They've withdrawn from the Realm, but that's as far as it's gone. The Nine aren't strong enough to take on the entire Realm and I think they know it." Kellach shuddered. "I hope. It seems like Gallagher has lost his mind."

"He's not crazy. Just ambitious." Adam glanced toward the quiet day outside. He hadn't heard Tori shoot anything in a while. Maybe she was too upset. He should probably make her some coffee or something. He stood and leaned against the counter just as another screen started to spit information. "Ah, there you are," he muttered.

"What?" Kellach asked.

"I found two more financial accounts linked to Gallagher, and the money doesn't trace back to any of his legitimate or even semi-legitimate investments." The excitement of the chase rushed through Adam. "I'm going to nail this fucker."

Kell nodded, his shoulders straightening. "Perfect. Keep me in the loop." He clicked off.

Adam scrolled through the data, his mind making rapid connections.

Another line beeped, and he hit the button for another video conference.

His brother Daire came into view. "Hey. Just talked to Kell. Are you going to mate Victoria or what?"

Jesus. "Would you knock it off?" Adam snapped.

Daire straightened and then turned to read something off to the side. His jaw hardened.

Adam stiffened. "What?"

Daire focused back on him, his eyes glittering. "It's Parker Monzelle."

Victoria's father? "We've found him?" Adam asked.

"No." A vein pulsed down Daire's neck. "You'd better get Victoria. We have a message from her father. It's not good."

Ah, hell.

Chapter 28

An hour after she left Adam hacking computer systems, Tori was cataloging different species of trees and birds. She'd spent much of her life outdoors, away from electronics, and she could name most of them.

She strode away from the cabin, her tennis shoes leaving imprints in the damp earth. Her nerves felt flayed open and exposed. Oh, she didn't care at the moment about her father being free, mainly because he couldn't get to Lexi or their mom. That is, if the witches had their mom.

The witches *had* to have Jennie.

While the idea didn't thrill Tori, at least the witches wouldn't harm her mother for the next two days. At that point, when it became clear that she and Adam hadn't mated, then all bets were probably off. So they had two days to rescue her mom.

There was no way somebody like Adam wanted somebody like Tori as a mate, even if she wanted to mate him. He was strong and sexy and somehow sweet, and he'd barreled into her life and heart like he belonged there. Her self-esteem was just fine, but the differences between them were pretty huge, even without the whole immortal issue.

Plus, and she felt this in her bones, he'd been very cautious with her. There was a side to Adam, a deep and rumbling side, that he'd kept carefully banked. She'd pushed him the previous night, and she'd gotten a glimpse. But he'd held control to himself, of himself, as usual.

The woman who earned his love, who claimed all of him, would take that part of him as well.

That part didn't belong to Tori. Her chest hurt like she'd been kicked, and her body felt heavy. Okay. So she had a little crush. Like always, she'd get over it. Yet he hadn't left her psyche alone, now had he? He'd stripped her bare, had taken all of her, holding tight and forcing her trust. Worse yet, she'd wanted to give him her trust. In that moment, on the kitchen table, she'd wanted to give all of herself to him.

Damn it.

She aimed at a tree, and the green laser shot out, putting a hole in the pine. It wobbled but didn't fall down. Man, the immortal guns were cool. Who knew? Shooting at things made her feel better. She took aim and destroyed a rock in the center of the stream. Then she squinted, kept her aim true, and tried to hold back the laser as she squeezed the trigger.

Another rock exploded.

She sighed.

A branch cracked behind her. She stilled and then warmed. Was Adam coming out to play? As she started to turn, a tension on the breeze caught her attention. She whirled around to see Adam, his gaze inscrutable. "Hi."

"Hi." He reached out and took her hand, his fingers warm and safe around hers. "I need you to come inside." Without waiting for an answer, he led her around several bushes and trees, right up into the cabin. It was a testament to how off balance she was from the previous night that she quietly allowed it.

She paused by the door, wanting to stay away from his computer equipment. "You're scaring me."

"I'm sorry." He scrubbed both hands down his face. "I was wrong about your mother."

Tori's knees wobbled. "What do you mean?" she breathed.

He started to pull her toward the computers and then paused. "Wait here." Moving forward, he turned a screen that was all fuzz toward her. After he clacked a couple of keys, Parker Monzelle came up on the screen.

Tori's head snapped back at seeing her father.

"It's a recording," Adam said. "He can't see you."

She allowed herself to sag against the door frame. "Play it," she croaked.

Adam pushed a button.

Prison had aged Parker Monzelle. His once-thick black hair had turned a dull gray, and his smooth skin was heavily lined with a map of wrinkles. His chest was still barrel wide, but his gut had gone to fat. His green eyes held the same calculating intelligence, but their vibrant color had faded through the years. He cleared his throat, looking triumphant. "I'm sending this to the last number I had for you, Alexandra, and I hope you share it with your sister."

At the sound of his voice, pricks of pain danced down Tori's back. She tried to breathe from her nose and not get hysterical.

Parker paused. "I enjoyed our meeting last month so much, I'd like a repeat."

Tori made a sound deep in her throat. She swallowed it down. Parker had shot Alexandra, and there was no doubt he wanted to do it again.

Parker's smile revealed a cracked bottom tooth. "As you both probably already know, I'm on the outside again. For good this time." He leaned closer to the camera. Even his nostril hairs had turned gray. "I'm done dealing with the justice system, and I'm never going back."

Adam cut Tori a concerned look, and she kept her gaze centered on the screen. The microwave started to smoke again over on the counter. She looked at it. "You plugged it back in?"

He frowned. "No. It's unplugged." Pressing pause on the video, he strode to the microwave, grabbed it, and chucked it out the front door.

Tori couldn't look away from her father. "Finish it, please."

Adam pressed play again.

Parker smiled. "Here's the deal. I want a nice little family reunion. Both of you girls will meet me at a time and place I've set up, and you'll do it at five tonight in Seattle. You will text me your phone numbers, so I can text you the location with just enough time for you to get there."

Tori glanced toward the bucket that held the phones near the sink. They were down to one phone only.

Parker reached to the side of the camera and yanked Jennie in front of him.

Tori moved toward the computer screen and stopped herself just in time. "Mom," she whispered.

Her mom's eyes were wide with fright, and her pretty hair was mussed around her face. A bruise already showed on her neck. "I'm fine, girls," she whispered.

Parker threw her out of camera range, and something crashed.

Tori bit back a cry of alarm. Tears pricked her eyes. Her fingers clenched, and her nails bit into her palms.

Parker smiled. "I don't need to tell you both to come alone, do I? If I don't see both of you, you'll regret it. Alone. No cops, no boyfriends, no other drug dealers. You two get your asses where I tell you, or I'm going to kill your worthless bitch of a mother." His smile widened. "And I'm going to take my time."

The screen went black.

Adam clicked off the computer and went to Victoria, enveloping her in his arms. She trembled, head to toe, but didn't make a sound. The silence of terror was one of the worst he'd ever felt. "We'll get her back." He tried to keep his voice level, to be reassuring, but the words came out in a thick growl.

Victoria rested her face against his chest.

Fury nearly choked him, so he took several deep breaths. "I was wrong, and I'm sorry."

She lifted her head, and the tears on her lashes nearly snapped his control into pieces. "There was nothing you could do."

No, but he'd still been wrong. Nothing in him could even imagine a man wanting to harm his wife and daughters. Nothing. "We'll make sure he pays."

Victoria's shoulders shook. "I don't care about him. He doesn't exist. But my mom. We have to get her to safety." Panic lit her deep eyes. "Mom has relapsing multiple sclerosis. She has been in remission, but stress like this . . ."

He nodded, trying to provide comfort, but his mind ran through facts too quickly. "I need to know. Your father seems like a methodical man. He'd have to be fairly cold and controlled to be so successful in the drug trade."

She blinked, and a tear slid down her face. "Yeah. Cold as a snake."

So this whole revenge bit didn't make sense. For Parker to put himself out there just to harm his ex-wife or daughters spoke of heat and revenge, not sharp business. There was more going on than Adam could see.

The air shimmered with the hint of a lightning strike. He pivoted, putting Victoria in the corner and covering her with his body.

"What is going on?" she asked, her voice muffled.

The air crackled. Adam leaned back and turned her around to see Dage, Kellach, and Alexandra standing near the fireplace.

"Lexi," Victoria yelped, leaping for her sister.

Alexandra reached her for a hug. Several inches taller than Victoria, she held her tight, her lighter blue eyes closed. "Are you okay?" she asked, leaning back and studying her younger sister with a cop's eyes.

Tears fell down Victoria's smooth cheeks. "I saw the video. He has Mom." She frowned and stepped back, her arms dropping. "And you didn't tell me that he'd shot you. He tried to kill you, Lexi." Now a thread of anger wound through her tearful tone. She took another step back.

Alexandra's shoulders drooped. "You're right. I'm sorry. I should've told you." She shrugged a delicate shoulder beneath a black leather jacket. "I was just so confused. And ashamed."

Victoria's head jerked. "Ashamed?"

"Yeah," Alexandra said quietly, twisting her lip. "It doesn't make sense, but I just felt so bad that my own dad tried to kill me. Like there was something wrong with me. It's stupid. I know."

Victoria's anger melted right before Adam's eyes. She moved in again to hug her sister. "That is stupid," she said quietly. "The problems are his. He's a bastard, and there's no way around that."

Alexandra nodded. She looked over her sister's shoulder, her cop eyes back in place. "Adam."

He barely bit back a grin. "Alexandra." Wasn't sure about him violating her baby sister, now was she? Oh, he had no doubt his gossipy brother had given her the full scoop, even though Adam hadn't told Kellach shit. The drawback of having a brother who'd known you for centuries. Adam studiously avoided looking at the table. "'Tis good to see you again."

Dage cleared his throat. "I have a matter that requires my attendance but will be in touch. Weapons, vehicles, and tactical gear are being delivered within the hour." He nodded at Victoria in a quick hello. "If you need more troops, I can have them in place within minutes."

"No," Adam said quickly. "Thank you for the supplies, but extra boots on the ground will create more danger. We have to go in light and quiet." Which might be the whole damn point. This was a setup. No question.

"Thanks for the ride," Kellach said.

"Understood. Call me." Dage zipped out of the room.

Alexandra's mouth pursed. "That is so weird."

"Right?" Victoria asked, stepping away. "I would've thought moving through dimensions would feel heavy. Or light. Or like something."

"Just air and nothing," Alexandra agreed.

Adam nodded at his brother. "Do we have any information on who took Jennie? It's somebody immortal, and they're working with Parker Monzelle." Could it actually be the manufacturer of the Apollo poison? "I see why he was sprung—or why we're supposed to think he's out, anyway—but I don't want to be right about who did it."

Alexandra spoke up before Kell. "You see why he was helped? Why? I don't get it."

Adam rubbed his chin, his arm itching to drag Victoria back to his side. So he put his hands in his pockets. "We took out Titans of Fire, and they were the main distributor of Apollo."

"Oh." Realization smoothed out Alexandra's features. "I get it. Our father has drug connections like no other, even after all this time in prison. The manufacturer of Apollo will need to get a new pipeline working, and fast. They'll need good old Dad for that."

Adam nodded. "Yeah. That's a simple guess."

"Fuck," Kellach said, catching his meaning.

Adam nodded. "Parker Monzelle is just another pawn."

"You donna really think the Council of the Coven Nine released a drug dealer and kidnapped an innocent woman just to flush us out?" Kellach asked.

Victoria gasped.

Alexandra frowned, her gaze hard.

"Maybe," Adam said, feeling the chess pieces move into place. "Getting you three under Parker's control again was probably just a bonus." Of course, Parker didn't just want to see them. He wanted to hurt them, and somebody powerful was helping him. "I'm sorry I didn't foresee this."

"It's okay." Victoria flashed him a smile, her shoulders going back. "Lexi can text him and say we're together. Then we go."

Adam stiffened, but Alexandra beat him to the words. "You're not going anywhere," Alexandra said.

Victoria turned on her sister, her wild hair flowing. "The hell I'm not. You heard what he said. He sees us both or he hurts Mom."

Alexandra's lips firmed into one long pink line. "I don't care. You're not trained, Tor. Period."

Anger swelled in Victoria so quickly Adam could feel the fury against his skin. "Too fucking bad, sister." Victoria put both hands on her hips. "That asshole has *my* mother, too. I'm going, and I'm helping. I've been practicing with guns, anyway."

Alexandra's eyes burned a much lighter hue than Victoria's sapphire ones. "I'm a cop, and the Dunnes are trained Enforcers. You will remain safe here, and I'll get back to you as soon as possible."

Adam stretched his neck against the uncomfortable feeling smacking into him. He didn't want Victoria anywhere near her psychotic father, but he really didn't like the hurt pouring off her. And he didn't appreciate her sister, cop or not, telling her what she could or could not do. "I'll cover her," he said mildly.

Alexandra jerked her attention toward him. "Excuse me?"

Man, she really did sound like a cop. Kellach watched the interchange, no expression on his hard face.

Adam moved his hands out of his pockets. "Victoria has been practicing with weapons, as she said. I've been training her. It's not fair to leave her here alone when her mother is in danger." Plus, the plan would work better if Parker saw both of them.

"You know it's a trap, right?" Alexandra snapped.

"Of course it's a trap," Adam agreed. "But if Victoria wants to go, she's going."

The look of gratitude Victoria shot him smashed right into his heart and spread out.

Alexandra pivoted toward her mate. "Do something."

Kell lifted an eyebrow. "Such as?"

"Stop him. Stop them both," she burst out, fear in her eyes.

Kellach sighed. "Sweetheart, I know you're scared for your mother and your sister. I get that. But she has a right to go, and if Adam is willing to cover her, there's nobody better."

Victoria reached for her sister's hand and took it. "I love you. Thank you for worrying."

Alexandra blinked twice. She frowned. "You know how to shoot?"

"Of course," Victoria said, cutting her eyes to Adam. "I get a green gun. They're the best."

Chapter 29

Tori shimmied into the bulletproof vest, mildly surprised by how heavy the damn thing felt. How had Lexi actually run through drug houses and shot people wearing such a thing? Tori pulled down her jacket and watched the world spin by outside. Their father had texted a meeting location a mere twenty minutes ago, and they'd all jumped into a borrowed SUV to head toward the warehouse district.

Dage had come through with weapons, vests, and the late-model SUV, which was probably bulletproof.

Adam drove, with Tori in the passenger seat. Kellach and Lexi were in the back, checking and double-checking guns. Lexi had finally agreed that Tori could go, even though she'd truly had no choice.

But Adam. He'd stood up for Tori. He'd faced both his brother and her stubborn sister and said she had the right to go. At that moment, he'd pretty much stolen her heart.

He believed in her.

Tension swelled in the vehicle, and her heart kept beating faster in response. She tried to keep calm and not mess with the engine. She was definitely getting better at controlling her strange gift. Concentrating on the vibrations from the two witches helped, and now even Lexi had a different signature—not as strong as her mate's, but definitely high and powerful.

Was this what it felt like before a raid? Tori didn't like it. Her skin felt too tight. Adam seemed just fine, though. She watched him drive from beneath her lashes. His face was a hard mask of concentration, while his capable hand controlled the steering wheel. Interesting, true. But what made him absolutely fascinating was the way his other hand worked the computer set into the console and brought up the schematics for the warehouse district, and one metal building in particular.

"Is that a satellite feed?" she breathed, leaning closer to the screen, her stomach doing somersaults.

"Aye," he said. "It's live." Glancing in the rearview mirror, he nodded at his brother. "I had to reposition the entire thing, so there may be fallout. If the Nine figures out it was me."

"It would have to be you," Kellach said. "I donna know anybody else who could do it. Well, anybody else who knows about the satellite's existence, anyway."

As darkness descended, clouds gathered across the sky and finished off what had been a fairly warm fall day, complete with sunshine. Tori shivered, even under the vest and jacket. Lexi had helped her to suit up, and she had a knife along her calf and a gun at her waist. She was much more familiar with the gun than the knife, and that wasn't saying much. She may have exaggerated her training a bit.

Did shooting at a couple of trees count as training?

She bit her lip.

Adam widened the screen. "Snipers in positions three and four." He took a sharp left turn.

His phone blared out the king's song, and he pressed a button in the dash. "Dage. What's up?"

"Got the video from Monzelle's escape," Dage said without preamble. "Definite immortal species, but I couldn't tell which one. Didn't use fire, enhanced abilities, or brain attacks."

Adam shook his head. "Just strength and speed?"

"Yeah. So they could be any species. I also don't recognize any of them but will forward you the video. Watch your backs. You're not just fighting humans tonight." The king clicked off.

"I know who hired them," Adam said quietly.

Kellach coughed. "If it's Gallagher, then he's somehow involved with the Apollo drug. The drug harms witches, so I always thought the manufacturer of Apollo was some other enemy. Maybe it's part of his grand power play for the Council."

Adam snorted. "Gallagher is a dickhead, that's for sure. But I don't see him being the grand mastermind behind the Apollo strike.

It's too dangerous and too focused. Somebody is pulling his strings, too. He came at us through politics, and that's where he dominates. Look what he's managed to do in a very short time."

"What has he done?" Tori asked, trying to keep track of the conversation.

Adam took another left turn just as a light rain began to fall. "He managed to clear the Council of two of our aunts and two of our cousins." He flicked on the windshield wipers. "Then he got three of the four Enforcers, all from our family, fired. I'm next."

Tori leaned back in her seat, her hands shaking so much she had to hide them. "Wow. That's quite the plan."

"Two more members of the Council were killed by Apollo darts, so that left only the current three," Adam continued, as if working it all through in his own mind. "Gallagher is definitely in charge, and Sal seems to be a yes-man. Nessa is the wild card, though she's young and inexperienced."

"And probably in danger if she votes against him again," Kellach said.

Adam nodded. "Agreed. When I meet with the Council, I'm thinking of locking her down somewhere safe."

"You're not meeting with the Council," Kell snarled.

"Of course I am," Adam said easily. "I have enough proof against Gallagher that the Guard will have to open an investigation."

Kell half leaned over the seat. "Then send it to them. You can't go into Council chambers. It's suicide. The Guard still answers to Gallagher."

Tori watched the interplay, noting how the more irritated Kell became, the calmer Adam grew. It was a hell of a way to fight—not getting emotional. She could learn a thing or two from him. Her cheeks heated. More than she'd already learned, that was.

He glanced her way. "You okay?"

She just nodded.

He turned his attention to the screen. "Listen, Kellach Gideon Dunne. We can fight about my plans after the current crisis, all right?"

"Fine," Kell said.

Lexi patted Tori's shoulder. "You can do this, Tor." When Lexi decided to get on board, she did it wholeheartedly.

"I know," Tori said. "Mom will be all right. She has to be."

Adam tapped the screen. "Besides the snipers, I see two men guarding the front entrance and two at the rear." He took another turn, this one down a long deserted street with abandoned buildings on both sides. "I'm guessing they can't patrol because they don't want to bring attention to the warehouse. They are armed and probably immortal."

Kellach leaned over the seat and studied the screen. "What's your plan?"

"I take out the sniper at position three, and you handle the guy at four. Then we go with the plan," Adam said levelly. He eyed Tori. "Are you still all right with the strategy?"

She nodded, the lump in her throat making it impossible to speak. Thunder cracked the sky above, and she jumped.

Adam rolled the SUV to a stop near a rusting metal building with a damaged roof. "We walk from here," he said.

Tori dutifully jumped out of the vehicle, her boots splashing water. The night took on a surreal haze. What was she doing? She wasn't a cop or an Enforcer. But her mother was in one of those metal buildings, and she was probably terrified. Tori lifted her shoulders and tried not to wince as the vest pulled against her breasts with a painful thud.

Adam took lead with Lexi behind him. Tori followed her sister, and Kellach took up the rear. There was no doubt they were keeping her protected, but Tori noticed Adam also keeping Lexi covered. Was she immortal yet? Man. Tori hadn't even had a chance to talk to her about the whole mating issue. What if Lexi wasn't immortal? She probably wasn't. God. If Lexi got shot, she could still die.

Tori bit her lip and tried to keep from screaming her head off. She could do this. She just needed to concentrate and keep the plan in her head. It was a good plan, because Adam had come up with it.

They finally reached a newly painted blue warehouse. Adam nodded for her and Lexi to hunker down. "We'll be right back."

Kellach gave Lexi a direct look, and something passed between them. Something oddly sweet. Then the Dunne men disappeared.

Water dripped down from the eaves. Lexi pulled Tori down in a crouch, her gun already out.

Tori followed suit, and for some reason, the gun felt heavier in her hand than it had earlier. Maybe because she was going to point it at people and not trees this time.

"Take a deep breath, count to five, and let it out, counting to seven," Lexi whispered, her gun pointed down the long area between warehouse buildings.

Tori nodded and breathed in and out, noting that the night came back into focus.

"Good. Now relax your shoulders, and tell yourself you can do this," Lexi said.

Tori rolled her shoulders, and the vest pulled again. Rain dripped down, plopping off quickly forming mud puddles and splashing the women. She grimaced. "I can't believe you do this for a living."

Her sister grinned. "I always loved a good raid."

The past tense caught Tori up short. "You're quitting." The tone had been there.

Lexi leaned against the building, her strong thighs keeping her easily in the crouch. "Bernie is retiring, and Kellach has to stay out of Seattle for a while."

Bernie was Lexi's partner and had pretty much become a father figure to them both over the years. Still, it was impossible to think that Lexi was leaving the force for a man. Even a man as manly mannish as Kellach. "So you're just going to follow Kell around?" That was not the sister she'd always known.

Lexi snorted. "Of course not. If we move somewhere else, I'll still get a job as a cop."

"If?" Tori asked.

Lexi breathed out and tugged her vest farther down, not taking her eyes off the alleyway at all. "This whole Council of the Coven Nine disaster has to break at some point. Either we're taking the war to them, or Adam will be able to prove Simone's innocence and get everybody their jobs back. If that happens, I'm thinking of the whole Enforcer bit."

"Huh." Tori could see that. "An Enforcer for the witch nation. Did you ever, in your wildest dreams, think that'd be a possibility?"

"No." Lexi cocked her head, stiffened, and then relaxed. "Can you believe witches exist?"

"Crazy, right?" Tori looked into the darkened night but couldn't see anything. "You love him, don't you? I mean, the real kind."

"Yes," Lexi said, without a second of hesitation. "With everything I am."

Wow. That was huge for Lexi. Definitely huge. "Um, about the mating. You're gonna live forever?"

Lexi looked pained. "Yeah, I guess." Her shoulders hunched. "It's weird. Don't tell anybody, but I've been trying to figure out who you and Mom can mate." She made a gagging sound. "Like I want to think about the two of you having sex with hot guys." She grimaced. "I thought maybe you and Adam would've just done it."

"Oh, we've done it plenty of times," Tori retorted, her chest aching a little at the thought.

"Ew," Lexi said. "Don't make me shoot him."

Tori forced a smile. "Does the mating hurt?"

"No, but there's a fucking brand." Lexi leaned to the side and tugged down her jeans. A beautiful Celtic knot, similar to but slightly different from the one on Adam's hand, showed on her smooth skin. "Like a cow."

Now Tori did bite back a real laugh. Oh, that had definitely pissed Lexi off. "Adam's brand is a little sharper at the edges."

Lexi stilled and swung her gaze toward Tori. "You've seen it?"

"On his hand," Tori said, heat filling her face.

"Oh. Just oh." Lexi checked her gun. "So, um. You guys are going to?"

"No." How could her sister even ask that? "We couldn't be more different. I mean, he's probably the smartest guy in the whole witch nation."

Lexi slowly turned her head back to Tori. "So?"

Geez. "So? I'm not."

"You're smart," Lexi protested.

"Right." The rain started falling harder and the spray shot wider. "I think he likes me, but that's about it." The words hurt to say.

Lexi nudged her with her shoulder. "You've fallen for the big bad witch, haven't you?"

Tori shrugged her shoulders but didn't answer.

A second later, a body fell from the rooftop with a sickening thud, and blood sprayed across the asphalt. Tori sucked in air and barely stopped herself from screaming. The man's head was turned toward her, and his eyes were blank in death. His neck was twisted awkwardly.

Adam landed next to the body in a low crouch, his descent silent and deadly. He shoved a knife into a pocket of his cargo pants. "He was human."

Tori gagged down bile and stood. "Um, okay."

He held out his hand. "Are you sure you can do this?"

No. Definitely no. She took his hand. "I'm sure."

Chapter 30

Tori's legs shook, but she stood facing the door to the warehouse, her stance wide. Her sister stood next to her in the same position. "I feel kind of like a badass in a Western," Tori whispered.

Lexi didn't answer. Her entire body was solid and her gaze focused. Once again, she impressed the heck out of Tori.

"We're here, old man," Lexi yelled.

Wind whipped into them, around them, scattering small rocks and spraying rain.

The door slowly opened, and a man Tori didn't recognize pointed a gun at them.

She swallowed. Adam was to the right with a weapon trained on the warehouse, and Kellach was up on the roof, looking for a way in. She kept her chest square with the door so the camera in her top button could capture everything.

The guy gestured with the gun.

"No," Lexi called out. "Let us see our mom, or we're not moving. And there are guns on you, asshole."

Tori just nodded. Their father had to know they'd bring backup. Why hide it?

A small scuffle sounded, and the guy stepped aside to show their mother. Her light blond hair was a mess, and there was blood on her fragile chin. Next to the man, she looked petite and helpless, her blue eyes wide. Before she could speak, she was yanked away.

"No," Tori yelled, moving forward.

Lexi grabbed her arm. "Wait."

"Come forward, or your father is going to kill her," the guy said. He was about six feet tall with bushy brown hair and dark eyes.

"Stay slightly behind me," Lexi said. "If I start shooting, you fucking run."

Not a chance. "Okay," Tori whispered.

They slowly approached the building. As soon as they got inside, the camera would reveal the location of all threats, and then Adam and Kell would come in, guns blazing. Tori's one and only job was to get her mother down and covered. She was fine with that.

They soon reached the door. The guy stood aside.

Lexi walked in first, and Tori peered around her. A folding screen decorated with exotic birds blocked their view of the rest of the warehouse.

The door clanged shut.

"Run," Lexi yelled, pivoting.

Tori turned, and the guy with the bushy hair grabbed her around the chest, manacling her arms. She struggled, fighting hard. He slapped the gun out of her hand, and it dropped harmlessly to the floor.

The screen was ripped away.

Lexi pivoted, and a gun instantly smashed onto her head. She dropped fast. Parker Monzelle stood there, a grotesque smile on his face.

Tori screamed.

The bushy-haired guy carried Tori over to an already running SUV and shoved her in the backseat. She landed next to her mother, who was handcuffed to a rod in the seat ahead of her. "Mom." Tears blurred her vision. She grabbed the cuffs and tried to loosen them, but they wouldn't give.

"Get out of here," her mother whispered, her voice hoarse.

It had all happened so fast.

Parker threw Lexi into the far back and slammed the door before jumping into the passenger seat. "Go, go, go," he ordered a darker-haired guy with a square diamond earring in his right ear.

The driver punched the gas just as a massive door opened at the opposite end of the warehouse. Tori had a moment to see a completely empty warehouse all around her as they sped the entire distance. So this was the trap.

They shot outside and into the rain, straight at Kellach. He leaped out of the way and rolled until she couldn't see him any longer. Tori's breath panted out, and her chest hurt. She turned to look into the far back, where Lexi lay in a motionless ball, blood seeping from her temple. "Lexi?" she whispered.

Her sister didn't move.

Tears slid down their mother's face. Her body shook violently as she looked over her shoulder. "Lexi? Sweetheart? Wake up."

Tori swallowed down bile. Neither she nor Lexi had their guns any longer. But the knife at her calf felt cold. She almost reached for it, but then she remembered Adam's words. *Stop and think . . . measure the timing.* He'd had a little time to train her before the mission.

Parker Monzelle turned around. "You stupid women thought you could outsmart me." He shook his head, his jowls moving. "Bringing the men you're fucking." He laughed, the sound grating. "I thought the six guards were a good touch."

Tori glared at him. "What is wrong with you?" There was more sadness than heat in her voice, but she didn't care.

"With me?" He turned and almost casually slapped her across the face.

Pain exploded beneath her eye, and her mother cried out, but Tori didn't make a sound. "You are such a fucking loser," she said quietly. "You deserved prison."

He glared. "I'm outta prison, in case you didn't notice. And I'm never going back."

Her own father. How was it possible her own father hated her so much? "Oh, I agree."

His eyebrows lifted. "How's that?"

"You're not going to make it back to prison." She held his gaze, even though her entire face was still aching. "You're definitely going to die this time. I promise."

The driver took a sharp right turn, and Tori fell against her mom. She righted herself.

Parker studied her. "Look who grew a pair. You think your boyfriend is gonna kill me? Or the guy who came with Lexi?"

"No," Tori said softly. "I'm going to be the one." She could do it, too. The man would always be a threat to them, and if he didn't kill them this time, he'd try again. "It'll be just like swatting a fly. You're nothing. You never were." Why had she spent her whole life feeling not quite good enough because he hadn't loved her? He wasn't worth it. The problem was inside him, not her.

"Oh, I'm going to enjoy teaching you a lesson," Parker spat.

The driver slowed down, but dark warehouses lined both sides of the street. They were still surrounded by warehouses, although they'd driven at least five minutes.

"Parker, you're all talk, you know that?" Tori sat back as if bored. She'd never again even think of him as her father. "Where exactly are we going?"

"To a place where it's hard to find the bodies," he said, his teeth flashing again.

Tremors shook her, but she hid her fear. She would die before she gave him that kind of satisfaction. "Who helped you escape the prison transport, anyway?" she asked, hoping the camera in her shirt button was still working.

"Friends," he said. "You wouldn't understand. You never had any."

She laughed then. "You are such a dick." She eyed the door nearest her.

"Go ahead," Parker said easily. "But you're leaving your mother and sister with me. I'll make them scream your name as they die."

Her lungs seized. She wanted to look down at the button and make sure it was still there, but then she'd give its existence away. She had to look elsewhere, so she focused on her mother. "Are you all right?" Reaching out, she smoothed her mom's hair away from her face.

Her mom nodded. A bruise marred her chin, and her face was pale, but her blue eyes were clear.

"We'll be okay," Tori whispered.

"I know," Jennie said. "Parker? Let the girls go. None of this is their fault. It's mine."

He turned, pure meanness in his expression. "You bet it's your fault they're both so disrespectful and weak."

"No. I meant it was my fault for marrying such a complete asshole like you," Jennie shot back.

Tori's mouth dropped open. "Go, Mom," she said.

Parker half turned, his fist already swinging. Tori jumped in front of her mom, taking the impact to her cheek. Pain popped behind her eye. "I can't wait to kill you," she hissed.

She settled back, her mind fuzzing. Lexi still hadn't moved. How badly had she been hit? Tori moved onto her knees and turned around, reaching for her sister's neck.

"Sit back down," Parker ordered.

Tori ignored him and felt for a pulse. Sure and steady. Good. But Lexi still didn't move.

Turning back around, Tori sat. Where were they going?

The second Victoria disappeared inside, Adam ran full bore for the entrance. The guy with bushy hair opened the door, spraying the street with an automatic rifle. Several bullets slammed into Adam's vest, and he threw himself to the side, rolling and coming up firing. The guy ducked back inside the building, blood dripping from his thigh.

Adam lunged to his feet, his gun out, his chest burning. He ran for the building again.

A screech of tires echoed, and then something roared.

He cleared the door and ran right into the guy, whom he tackled to the floor. Adam punched him in the face and hit him with the butt of his gun. The guy's eyes widened, and blue and red streaks were evident in them. The asshole was taking Apollo? Adam hit him again.

The guy roared, and fur shimmered up his arm.

Fuck.

Adam shot fast, right through the bear shifter's neck. Blood sprayed. Adam jerked away as the bear's head flopped twice and his eyes shut. He might be able to heal the throat wound, but it wasn't going to be soon.

Jumping up, Adam surveyed the empty warehouse. A gaping hole on the far side led to rain and darkness. "Kellach," he yelled.

Kellach limped around the corner, fury on this face, his gun down. "Get to the SUV!" he bellowed, turning back into the darkness.

Adam nodded and ran out the way he'd come in, going full speed around the several warehouses to the vehicle. He jumped in the front seat and was already backing out when Kellach yanked open the passenger-side door. God. Victoria. The bastard had her.

Kellach immediately punched up the GPS tracker on the screen to see a green blip moving quickly through the warehouse area. "Got it?" he asked tersely.

Adam took a good look, memorizing where Victoria was right that second. "Affirmative." He swung wide around a series of three smaller buildings. "Bring up the cameras." His stomach felt like a rock had pummeled into it along with the bullets he'd taken to the vest. There were at least five, and his ribs protested. But his only concern was Victoria Monzelle. "Fucker had a car ready."

"Aye," Kellach said, swiping his fingers across the screen. "We couldn't imagine every possibility, but we have them tagged, and the cameras will work."

"Unless he was expecting cameras and tags," Adam said grimly. What the hell had he been thinking, allowing Victoria into danger? He could've saved her mother another way. Somehow.

"He doesn't know us, Adam," Kellach said, his voice gritty. "He thinks Alexandra is on leave from the police department, which she is, and he has no clue who we are or what we do. He thinks his daughters are weak and scared of him, and the last thing he'd expect is this type of surveillance. Nobody would."

Adam breathed out. Okay. That was true. He punched the gas and fishtailed around another corner, spraying rainwater.

"Camera," Kellach said tersely. "It's Alexandra's."

Adam squinted. It was dark. Maybe carpet? "Where the hell is she?"

"Dunno." Kellach's voice deepened. "Let me switch to Tori's." He tapped the screen, and a full picture came into view. Tori's camera faced the front of an SUV. Parker was in the passenger seat, and a man with dark hair was driving.

"Maybe Lexi's camera fell off?" Adam asked.

"Maybe." Kellach pushed a series of buttons on the screen, and the video rolled backward. He reached a point where a gun came out of nowhere and Alexandra crashed to the floor.

So much tension filled the vehicle that Adam winced, his chest burning. "She's okay. She has to be."

Kellach punched the dash. Once, twice, and then a third time. The glove compartment clanged open and dropped to his feet, scattering papers.

Adam grabbed his brother's arm while taking another sharp turn. "She's strong and smart, Kellach." He tightened his hold and squeezed. "Victoria won't let anything else happen to her." Which was the absolute truth. Victoria would definitely put herself in harm's way to protect her sister. "You have to hold it together. Just until we get there."

Kellach didn't answer. His massive body shuddered. "I can't lose her."

"I know." Adam reached over and switched the screen to GPS again. "I need to see where they're going now." He watched the blip, memorizing the layout of the area. "I think they're staying within the warehouse district." They'd driven across a couple of sections, but Parker Monzelle's car seemed to be slowing down.

Kellach switched back to Alexandra's camera. Same view. Darkness, with maybe a hint of carpet. "She's out cold," he growled. "She has to be."

Adam nodded. If anything happened to Alexandra, his brother would lose his soul. "She's okay." There was no alternative. "You've been mated awhile, Kell. Her chromosomal pairs have surely increased already."

"We haven't been mated that long, and you know it," Kell said tersely. "That takes time."

Adam didn't answer because there wasn't anything to say. His brother was correct.

"What if he shot her?" Kellach asked, his voice shaking.

Adam shook his head. "No. We saw what happened. Parker knocked her out because she's trained and tough. He had to take her out, but he didn't want to finish her that fast." No, the asshole wanted to make them all suffer. "He didn't kill her, Kell. It was way too quick." The fact sucked, but might help his brother to focus.

Kellach nodded. "I know." His hand trembled when he reached to swipe the screen again to Victoria's camera. She was still looking ahead. Parker was saying something to her, raw hatred on his face and spittle flying from his mouth.

Rage swept Adam hotter and faster than any he'd felt during his long years on earth. "I am fucking going to kill that bastard."

"Not if I get to him first," Kellach said, death in his voice.

Chapter 31

Tori turned to check on her sister again. Nothing. Lexi had to be all right. What if she never woke up? No. That was impossible. Tears filled Tori's eyes, and she pushed them away. Strong. She had to be strong.

The SUV reached the back of a green warehouse, and the driver pushed a button in the roof of the vehicle. A double-wide door rolled up, and he manuevered the vehicle into the long metal building and cut the engine. As soon as they were inside, he pushed the button again. Tori turned and watched the door close. It impacted the ground, bounced, and then settled.

Silence slammed them from every side.

Parker exited the vehicle and opened her mom's door, quickly releasing the cuffs. He yanked her, and she flew out, her legs catching on the seat.

"Mom." Tori leaped after her, grabbing her waist before she could fall. She jerked her mom away from her dad. "Leave her alone."

Her mom regained her footing. "I'm okay, Tori." She turned. "Let's check on Lexi."

"No," Parker said, grabbing Jennie's arm. "You sit down." To the right of the vehicle was a cheap card table with four folding chairs. He shoved her into one.

She went down with a soft cry, grabbing onto the table to keep from falling.

Tori put herself between them, facing her father and quickly surveying the massive space. There were three men on the other side working along a wide table. Like the earlier warehouse, it was only one room, but several metal shelves made up one long wall. Tons of vials of gold liquid were lined up——thousands of them.

The three men barely looked up to acknowledge the newcomers, all working furiously at putting the liquid into capsules, using some odd machines.

Tori gasped. "Is that Apollo?"

"Sure is," Parker said proudly. "Do you have any idea how much money is sitting right there? And they need me——*me*——to move it all. To figure out how to get it onto the streets." His chest puffed out. "My distribution avenues are still the best, even after all of these years."

"That drug kills people," she spat, keeping her body between her mother's and his. "Burns them from the inside out."

Parker smiled wider. "All drugs kill people, you stupid bitch. But usually not until they're tapped out financially."

He really was an evil monster. There was no other way to look at it. "You are such a dick. Whoever is pulling the strings is just using you," Tori snapped.

"Wrong. They need me, and all I had to do was get you three women in the same place. Now I own the Apollo distribution monopoly in the States."

Tori caught her breath. The manufacturer of Apollo wanted her and Lexi in the same place? Why? Her head began to ache, and her stomach felt like she'd been kicked: *This isn't about us, you idiot.* This was about flushing out Adam and his brothers. Hell. She was just bait.

Another man came around the shelves, a clipboard in his hand. Wearing a lab coat, he was taller than the rest. With wild red hair and adult acne, he looked like a teenager. He gave Parker a short nod and then went back around the other side of the shelves, apparently cataloging.

She could get to the knife at her calf, but what about the driver of the SUV and the other workers? She couldn't take them all on with one knife, and Lexi was still out cold.

Parker pushed Tori in the chest, and she fell into the table, quickly straightening herself. "Sit the fuck down. Now," he ordered.

The other guy emerged from the back of the SUV, carrying an unconscious Lexi.

"Alexandra," their mom cried, partially standing.

Parker shoved Tori into her, and they both fell.

"What should I do with her?" asked the guy carrying Lexi.

Tori pushed off from the table. "I'll take her."

The guy waited for Parker.

"Put her on the floor," Parker said, with a careless sweep of his hand.

The guy looked at Parker and then shrugged, moving toward the table. He set Lexi down on the concrete floor, almost gently.

Tori rushed over and smoothed the hair away from Lexi's temple. A large purple bump was already forming. Tori felt her pulse. Slow but steady. Okay. Good.

Her father moved around her toward Lexi. "This isn't gonna be any fun if she doesn't wake up." He kicked her in the leg. She didn't move. He kicked her harder.

Tori saw red. Grabbing the knife from her boot, she lunged, jumping on his back and slashing as hard as she could. The knife went into his shoulder, and he howled, spinning around and trying to dislodge her. She tried to yank out the knife, shocked to find it embedded so well. Keeping her balance with her legs, she pulled it out with both hands and plunged it in again.

Hands grabbed her from behind, hauling her off Parker and throwing her. She hit the side of the SUV, and agony crashed through her shoulder. She thumped hard and fell to the floor, her nervous system on fire with pain. Oh God. Her shoulder hurt like it had been ripped off. Tears filled her eyes.

"Goddamn it," Parker roared, trying to remove the knife from his back.

The men on the other side of the warehouse looked up, surveyed the scene, and went back to work.

The guy who'd thrown Tori spun Parker around and pulled out the knife. He lifted Parker's shirt to look at his back. "You're going to need stitches," he said without inflection.

Parker took the knife and stomped toward Tori, a killing anger in his eyes and his face distorted with hatred. She faced him, knowing this was it. So she shoved to her feet, not willing to cower.

Her mom launched herself across the space, jumping on his back and pounding with her fist on his wound. She hit him so hard, blood sprayed every time she pulled back her arm.

He screamed again, shock in the sound.

Panic shot Tori forward, and she kicked as hard as she could, nailing Parker square in the balls. He made a sound like a pig being slaughtered and dropped to his knees, his eyes wide in surprise.

Tori pulled her mom off him and hurried her toward Lexi. "Go out the door. Run for help, Mom," she hissed, pushing Jennie toward freedom.

The driver of the SUV calmly leaned against the exit door and crossed his arms. He didn't seem interested in joining the fray, but his message was clear. Nobody was leaving the warehouse. The grips of two guns showed in his waistband, but he apparently felt no need to pull them out.

Jennie faltered and then turned around. In her mussed up white pants and torn pink shirt, she looked small and vulnerable. The bruise across her jaw only intensified the look.

Helplessness and fury consumed Tori. "Check on Lexi, Mom," she whispered, turning to face their biggest threat.

Parker Monzelle used the SUV tire and pulled himself to his feet, still partially bent over. He turned around, blowing out air, snot dribbling from his nose. "I'm going to rip out your throat." He stumbled toward her, his hand on his lower gut.

She set her stance again, ready for him once more.

"Gun," he bellowed, standing all the way upright.

The guy at the door pulled a gun and tossed it to him.

Parker caught it and pointed it at Tori's head.

She backed up, her hands out. "Let our mom go," she said, her voice barely shaking. "She doesn't deserve this. She was always true to you." Well, until Jennie had pounded on his knife wounds.

"No." He smiled, and there was blood on his teeth. Walking toward her, he forced her to walk backward to keep between Jennie and the gun. "In fact, you're about to learn a valuable lesson." His beefy arm swept out, and he shoved her to the side. His hand nailed her in the neck, and she coughed as pain slammed up into her skull. Then he drew in a breath and pointed the gun at Lexi, who still lay helpless on the floor. "Watch this," he muttered.

"No," Tori screamed, leaping toward her sister. She threw out every invisible wave she could, mentally attacking the gun in his hand, picturing the mechanism locking tight.

He squeezed the trigger.

Nothing.

Her eyes widened, and she landed next to her sister, blocking her. It had actually worked. She concentrated harder.

Parker shook the gun and then pointed it at Tori's face. "Fine. You go first."

Lexi finally stirred.

Parker paused.

Tori partially turned. "Lexi?" Her voice trembled.

Lexi sat up with a groan, using the floor to push herself up. She rolled and sat on her butt, her gaze slowly focusing. The purple bump seemed even bigger than before on her pale skin. Her blue eyes narrowed on Parker. "Well, fuck," she whispered.

He grinned. "You're just in time to see your sister die."

"Why?" Lexi asked, her voice soft, her gaze still cloudy.

Parker reared back. "Why what?"

"Why do you hate us?" Lexi asked, pulling her knees to her chest. "I've never understood. Still don't."

Tori wanted to comfort her sister, but she couldn't move. She looked at the man she would never love. "Yeah. Why?"

Something dark slithered in his eyes. "Neither of you are worth love. Stupid women."

Lexi stiffened and then snorted. The snort turned to a chuckle. Then the chuckle increased to a full-out laugh.

Tori turned her head, her mouth gaping at her sister. She was laughing? Really laughing. "Lexi?"

Lexi gasped for air, her hand on her diaphragm. "We're not worthy of love. Did you hear him? Really hear him?" She laughed again, merriment in her blue eyes.

Tori coughed. Then she grinned. The humor bubbled up from somewhere deep inside her, somewhere the asshole had never touched. She chuckled and then laughed. "Oh my. Yes. I heard him." And suddenly, it really was funny—the idea of Lexi or Tori or their mom not being worthy of love. They *were* love.

"Stop it," he yelled, shaking the gun. "It is so time you all died."

"Eh." Lexi swept out her arm, and fire flashed across Parker's knees.

He jumped back, yelling.

Lexi smiled. "I have a new skill." She wobbled next to Tori. "Shit. My head."

Then hell descended.

Kellach barreled through the far back door, instantly shooting one of the workers in the head. Adam rushed through the nearest door, sending the guy leaning against it flying to land hard on his face. Adam marched in, fire already dancing down his arms. He threw a ball across the warehouse to hit one of the workers, who was pulling out a gun just as Kell took out the third and final guy there.

Lexi rolled sideways and yanked the second gun from the driver's waistband, scooting back again.

Parker grabbed Tori and flipped her around, pressing his gun to her throat. She tried not to cry out from the pain, but her entire neck hurt.

Adam advanced, fury and death in his eyes. "Let her go."

Movement caught Tori's attention. "Adam," she yelled, just as the man in the lab coat skirted the shelves, firing an odd gun. Adam paused, looking right at the guy. What the hell was he doing? Two darts instantly stuck into Adam's neck, and he dropped.

Tori screamed. Why hadn't he jumped out of the way?

Adam backflipped and rushed the shooter, sweeping the dart gun to the side. Then he punched through the man's neck. The body fell.

Holy crap.

Adam yanked out the darts, his eyes morphing to a furious black. He advanced on Parker. "Let. Her. Go."

"And you won't kill me?" Parker spat. "Right." He looked toward the three dead workers as Kellach strode over from the far end of the warehouse. "What was that fire you had? I saw you with fire." His eyes widened. "You take Apollo."

The guy on the floor came to and lunged at Lexi, spinning the gun out of her hands. She turned and punched him in the throat, and he swept his hand out, throwing her sideways.

Kellach bellowed a battle cry and was across the entire span in a second, his knee connecting with the guy's neck and taking him down to the cement. Kell lifted his leg up and then shoved back down with his entire weight, fire lighting down his arms. The guy's neck broke with a sharp snap.

Adam's focus didn't move from Parker. "Release her. Now." His voice was low. Gritty. Threatening. The Apollo from the darts hadn't slowed him yet. God. Was he okay?

"No." Parker pulled Tori back, edging toward the SUV.

Jennie reached for the gun Lexi had lost and slowly stood. She used both hands and pointed it at Parker. "Let my girl go. Now."

Tori couldn't breathe. Her mom held a gun in her hands, and a deadly calm light had entered her eyes. In Tori's entire life, she'd never seen that look.

Adam edged toward her. "Jennie? Let me have the gun."

"No." Jennie didn't waver. "I swear to God, Parker. Let her go, or I'm going to blow off your fucking head."

Tori's breath stalled. "Mom," she whispered.

Kellach lifted Lexi to her feet and set her squarely behind him. "Monzelle? You're definitely surrounded. All your people are dead. Let her go, now."

"No." Parker's voice sounded wild. "I won't. You don't win. I win." As he spoke, he moved just enough.

Tori shot an elbow into his gut and followed with her fist in his balls. She let her body fall in a dead weight, and he wasn't fast enough to stop her.

Three shots rapidly rang out.

Parker's body jerked behind her, and blood sprayed out in front of her. Tori hit the ground, her gaze on her mother's gun. Jennie had shot him. Three times. She'd shot him.

Adam reached Tori in three steps, yanking her away from her father. Her entire body went numb. She turned to see Parker's mean eyes wide open in death. She coughed. Adam pivoted, pulling her into his body. "Don't look, baby." He moved her over to her mother and took the gun from Jennie.

Jennie's mouth was pinched, and her face pale, but her eyes were clear. She reached and enfolded Tori in a hug. "You're okay, my girl."

Tori didn't have any words. None. She looked toward Adam. She'd known he'd come. Every feeling in the world assailed her. Adam. She'd trusted him, and he'd come in on fire. Literally.

Shit. Adam had used all his powers. The Nine would be able to find them now. Without question.

He looked at the rows of Apollo on all the shelves and whistled. "That's a lot."

Kellach brought Lexi toward them, his arm over her shoulder, his eyes blazing. "What should we do with it?"

Adam's jaw hardened to what looked like solid rock. "Oh. We're gonna blow it up." He looked around. "Get everybody in the SUV. I'll just be a minute."

Kellach nodded and slipped his other arm over Jennie's shoulders. "Tori?"

She shook her head, careful not to look at her dead father. "I want to help Adam blow everything up." It was the perfect way to end her relationship with her asshat of a father. "We'll be right out."

Kell nodded and led the other two women away.

Adam reached Tori and ran a knuckle along her aching jaw. "Are you okay, sweetheart?"

His kind words brought tears to her eyes. "I am. I really am." She coughed. "Why did you let that man shoot you with darts?"

He looked at her through lowered lids. "Aren't you smart."

She blinked. "Huh?"

"Cameras."

She shook her head. The man wanted anybody watching to know he'd been hit? Weakened? "I don't understand."

"That's all right." He took her hand and led her over to where the workers had been making pills. "Don't look at the dead."

There were dead people around them. She swallowed down bile. Now that the fight had ended, her mind was starting to shut down. Once they reached the far wall, he set her away from him and then made fireballs in his hands. Taking aim, he blasted ball after ball at the liquid, breaking vials and jars along the entire length of the shelves. The liquid arched in every direction and covered the floor.

She watched it slide around. So now he wanted his powers to be known?

Then he grasped her hand and took her outside. "Watch this." Holding her with one hand, he formed a morphing ball in the other. Then he threw it to the center of the warehouse.

The entire floor, covered in the drug, ignited within seconds. Fire hissed and crackled.

He kicked the door shut and kept her hand, running into the rain. "Let's get to the SUV." They'd made it around two warehouses when he paused.

"What?" she asked, stopping. Rain smashed into them, and the wind bit into her skin. "Why are we stopping?"

Cars screeched. One helicopter and then two came into view, hovering what seemed like mere yards above them, their floodlights pointed at Adam. His shoulders went back. "Well now. They're exactly on time."

"Wh-what?" she asked. "The cops?" Three black SUVs careened toward them, stopping close with overbright lights.

"No." He growled. "It's the Guard."

Chapter 32

Adam barely kept his temper in check as they arrived at the private airport in the SUV. Thank God Kellach and Alexandra had gotten away.

The Guard soldiers hadn't said one word as they'd taken him hostage along with Victoria. He could feel the Apollo from the darts eating through his blood, so he combated it with healing cells the best he could. At some point, he needed to shut down completely. Not yet. He exited the SUV and held Tori's hand, walking her toward the plane and through the rain. Guns were trained on them from every direction, and even if he could see a target, he couldn't risk her life in a firefight with the Guard.

She pulled against him. "No. I can't. Adam. I really can't."

He paused, his vision hazing for a second. "Do you trust me?"

She stopped struggling, pure panic showing on her bruised face. "I do trust you."

Taking a moment, he leaned down and brushed her lips with his. "Then trust me right now. We're going to get onto that plane, and we'll be fine. Take the chance, Victoria. I've got you."

Her eyes were luminous in the stormy night. Almost numbly, she nodded.

Her trust, something he had no doubt she rarely gave, humbled him. "Good." He hurried her toward the stairs and climbed in first, just in case a gun waited.

A gun waited.

"Enforcer Adam Dunne," said a Guard lieutenant Adam hadn't met, his gun pointed. "I'm Jasper Marks. We finally found you."

"Aye." Adam kept his body between the soldier and Victoria. "The gun isn't necessary." He let himself sway in place.

"Those darts are taking effect, I can see." Jasper simply smiled.

"I am aware of that." Adam could feel Victoria trembling behind him. "How did you find us, anyway?"

"We've had feelers out for a week all over town. The second you used your powers to such a degree, you hit the grid. Finally." Jasper studied him. "Your signature was extremely strong."

That's because Kellach was using his as well. "I am a badass," Adam said easily, looking around, allowing his shoulders to slump just enough for Jasper to take notice and, hopefully, report back to the Council.

The plane had six wide seats and a private bedroom and bath in the back. "We just took out a huge shipment of Apollo and could use a rest. I'm assuming your plan is to lock us in the back?" he asked politely. God, he needed to rest and heal himself.

"It is," Jasper confirmed.

Adam drew Victoria with him down the aisle.

She stumbled. "Huh. I think I was already kidnapped once in this plane."

Adam pulled her into the large bedroom, and the door shut behind them with the audible click of a lock. He had no doubt Jasper would be facing the bedroom door during the whole journey, gun out and ready to shoot.

Victoria turned, panic on her face. "Adam, I can't—"

He pressed a finger to her lips. "You can. First, we are way away from the engines. Second, you are extremely capable and can control your gift. Third, I have every plan to distract you."

Interest deepened her eyes to the color of the sky right before midnight strikes. "You do?" she asked.

"Yes." He ran the pad of his finger across her lips and over to the bruise darkening her cheekbone right beneath her eye. He growled and tamped down his fury. "I do." The engines ignited, and she stiffened, so he leaned in and kissed each bruise marring her smooth skin.

She made a hum of appreciation. "I thought you were dizzy."

"Good. Hopefully, Jasper thought so, too." He tugged her shirt off and reached to release her from the bulletproof vest. They had just enough time to get her out of her head before he passed out.

Her sigh was pure relief as he tossed the vest into the corner. "I can't believe how heavy that thing is." She lifted his shirt over his head, and he ducked to assist her. "Do you think Lexi is okay? She really got hit hard."

Adam nodded, leaning in to kiss another bruise along her slender neck. If Parker Monzelle was still alive, Adam would take great pleasure in ripping him apart piece by piece, starting with his fingers. "Your sister will be fine. Kellach got her and your mother to safety, and if I had to guess, they're on their way to Realm headquarters right now."

Victoria stiffened. "My mom. My mom actually killed him." Wonder filled her voice. "I think that might screw her up a little."

Adam skidded his fingers down Victoria's ribs, counting each one, pleased there were no bruises. "The Realm shrink is one of the best. Her name is Lily." The prophet was also a little nutty, but she got the job done. "Your mom will get help, and before you know it, we'll be at headquarters with her."

Victoria lifted her head. "Do you really think so?"

"Aye," he said, meeting her gaze as his vision hazed a little. The last thing in the world he wanted to do was lie to her, but he needed her calm for the long flight. Avoiding a plane crash seemed like a good reason to tell a falsehood. "I'm sorry it took so long to get to you."

She tugged his belt free, pulling his jeans down past his cock. "You got there at the perfect time." She brightened. "I jammed his gun. Once, anyway."

"That's impressive." Adam slid a hand through her hair, cupping her precious head. "I need to know: Where are you hurt?"

She shook her head against his hand, her hair sliding like silk along his skin. "I'm fine. I thought my shoulder was broken, but it feels all right now. Just a little sore."

He turned her and bit back a curse at the raw purple bruise spreading from her shoulder blade. "Jesus. What happened?"

"My dad threw me into the SUV. Well, after I stabbed him

a couple of times." Pride filled her voice. "You know, a knife is a lot harder to get out of a person than I would've thought." Energy rushed from her and she hopped. "Then my mom, my actual mom, jumped on his back and hit him a bunch of times where I'd stabbed him."

Adam shut his eyes for the briefest of moments to calm himself. His blood boiled with the poison, but it was slow to spread. "When you were out of my sight, I thought I'd lose my mind," he whispered, the fear still holding him. He took a deep breath and focused on the bruise. "Let me help you." Concentrating on the air around them, he reshaped molecules and formed a reverberating deep green ball of fire.

She looked over her shoulder, and the glow reflected off her face. "Your fire is usually blue."

"This is different," he whispered, pressing the ball over her injury.

"Oh," she whispered, her body starting. The plane rose into the night.

He slid his other arm around her waist to hold her upright. "Just let it in." Closing his eyes again, he pushed the healing mass through her skin to reach tissue and muscle.

She sighed, her body going limp, healing energy rolling off her. "That's so nice."

He left the heat working inside her and removed her boots, jeans, and wet socks. Her bra was last, and instead of jarring her healing shoulder, he just burned the bra off without touching her delicate skin. She turned around, interest in her eyes. "I'm naked."

A smile tickled his lips. Tension of a different sort swelled in the small room. "I noticed."

She leaned in to survey his chest. "Oh," she gasped, gingerly touching one of the bruises from the spray of bullets. "Heal that."

"Yes ma'am." He sent cells to the bruises as the green fire inside her skin dissipated. He brushed back her hair and clasped her neck, kissing her with all the emotion he'd kept tamped down the last week.

She made a sound low in her throat and opened for him, letting him take her mouth. Both her hands reached to stroke him. His knees weakened, and his lungs filled. There was a delicacy to her, a sense of energy that seemed fractured.

He lifted her, kissing her deep, feeling her nipples pebble against his chest. Sliding his hand down, he heated her spine and then her ass. They needed to make this fast before he passed out. He could slow the poison inside him only for so long.

She gasped into his mouth, moving against him, already wet.

Gently, he turned them and fell back on the bed, keeping her pressed against him. Her knees fell on either side of his hips. "Adam?" she asked, desire thick in her voice.

"You get to be in charge," he said, trying not to smile. "For now, anyway."

"I want quick."

"Then take quick."

She levered herself up and positioned him against her sex and slowly slid down. Several times she had to stop and let her body adjust, and her arms shook with the effort. He planted his hands on her hips to steady her and take some of her weight. She tried again, taking her time, torturing them both. Finally, she sat on him, with his cock fully embedded inside her.

Her nails curled into his healed chest, and she arched her back.

Fire rushed down his spine and shot out, burning him from within. Yet he held himself in check. "Are you all right?" he asked.

She nodded, a bright flush across her face. "I knew you'd come for me tonight at the warehouse. I knew I just needed to hold everything together until you got there." Bending over, she kissed him, softer than any silk. "Thank you for coming."

"I'll always come for you," he said, in a vow he had no right to give. Definitely not now—considering what he was planning when he met with the Council.

She lifted her hips and moved down, torturing him with her wet heat.

His eyes nearly rolled back in his head. She was everything good in the world, and for this very brief moment in time, she was all his. Yet tension rode her, an emotion barely tapped. He reached between them, right where they were joined, and pressed his finger against her clit.

Vibrations shook her body, pulsing around his cock. He groaned.

She gasped and started to move, leaning down, her hands caressing his shoulders, so much sweetness in her his heart hurt. She was tougher than she realized, but her true strength lived in her sweetness, her gentleness and kindness. And she gave them all to him. "You make me feel like me," she whispered.

That easily, she sliced his heart in two. "Victoria." He cupped her head, taking over the kiss, unable to make any promises. The Guard was most likely going to try and kill him the second he set foot in Council chambers, and even in the best scenario, he'd end up on the run for eternities. So he deepened his kiss, gratified when her sex convulsed around him.

Her emotions were still raw, and he could think of only one way to help her. So he clamped his hands on her hips and started to move her faster, forcing her to use her knees for leverage and then pulling her down hard enough her pretty breasts bounced.

She partially sat up and threw her head back, her eyes shutting in pleasure.

He increased the movements, giving her the *quick* she'd wanted earlier. She met his speed, increasing her strength, so he released one hip and zeroed in to rub her clit.

She broke within seconds, her cry soft and her body shaking so hard he had no choice but to shudder hard with his own climax. As she came down slowly, her eyelids opened and her blue eyes focused. "Adam?"

He pulled her to the side and set them both beneath the covers, rolling her into his chest. He pressed her face to his neck. "It's okay, baby. The night was a rough one." He could feel her emotions as if they lived in his own skin, all fractured and confused yet physically satisfied.

Her first sob hurt him inside, but it was necessary. He rubbed down her back, providing comfort. "Let it out, Victoria. I've got you."

It was the promise of protection that made her break. She cried against him, a lost woman who'd seen her mother kill her father, who'd seen her sister almost murdered.

Who had just made love to a man who couldn't give her promises. As she wound down, she settled into a deep sleep. He started to follow suit as the Apollo poison weakened his limbs and sent dots across his vision. He'd fought it as long as he could, and now it had to run its course.

The plane hit turbulence, and he tightened his hold around her. God, he hoped that was turbulence.

Chapter 33

Ireland was pretty much the same as last time—guards with guns, secret drives through the city, blindfolds. Tori yanked off the offending silk the second she entered the same damn energy-riddled building as before. She followed Adam through a labyrinth of hallways lined with stone walls. A red carpet that looked old and expensive showed the path. Guards with guns were in front and behind them.

"Stay on the red carpet," Adam ordered, seeming all right after sleeping. "Weapons discharge from the walls if you don't."

"I'm starting to hate witches," Tori retorted.

Adam chuckled. "We get that a lot."

She couldn't believe she'd slept the entire plane ride. Well, after she'd had sex with Adam and then bawled all over him like a loser. Yet now she felt centered. In control. At peace. "Are they going to kill us?"

"No," he said.

She waited for an explanation. None came. Sometimes he seemed to say things just to put her at ease. There was probably a decent chance the Coven people would order their deaths since they hadn't mated. At the thought, her heart thumped like she'd been kicked by a horse.

Adam didn't want to mate her.

Sure, he liked her. He definitely liked sex with her. But not once had he even considered making it permanent. She glared at his back. To save his own life, you'd think he'd at least think about it. But no. He was all sweet and let her cry, but when it came to getting serious, the guy would rather have his head cut off than stay with her forever.

"Jerk," she muttered, trying to keep from crying again.

He stiffened but kept walking through the creepy underground tunnel. His movements were a little slower than normal. Was the Apollo still hurting him? "What?"

"Nothing." She fought the very immature urge to stick her tongue out at his too-broad, sexy, and muscular back.

He kept moving, and soon the guard in front rearranged a bunch of small rocks on the wall into a pretty design, and the wall slid open.

"I'm so tired of invisible doors," Tori groused.

Adam kept moving, his gait graceful. But she'd seen his eyes. They were bloodshot and streaked with an odd purple from the Apollo darts. "Are you healed?" she whispered.

He gave a short nod. "I'm fine. Sleeping on the plane helped."

They entered the same big stone chamber as before, and Adam led her over to the same big stone table. "Have you guys ever considered a decorator?" she mumbled.

Adam stood, his hands on the rock. Two armed guards took positions on either side of the chamber.

Yet another invisible door opened behind the wide raised bench, and the three judges walked in and took their seats. Tori studied the guy in the middle. Peter Gallagher had an arrogant tilt to his chin that she really didn't like. The Sal guy had big bags underneath his brown eyes, and he fiddled with his tie as he sat. The one woman, Nessa, looked at Adam with concern in her violet eyes.

This didn't look good.

Tori stiffened her back to keep from dropping to the floor. She was in witch land, and if they wanted her dead, she'd be dead. What she wouldn't give for a green gun right now.

Peter actually banged down an ancient-looking gavel. "Enforcer Adam Dunne. You have disregarded the orders of this Council and have assisted known fugitives in avoiding the law. You are hereby relieved of your duties."

Adam didn't so much as twitch.

Nessa held up a hand next to Peter. "Wait a minute. Adam is responsible not only for destroying an exorbitant amount of the Apollo drug but also for cutting off the distribution chain in Seattle. That has surely kept Dublin and our people safe for a while. His actions must be taken into account and acknowledged."

Peter cut her a harsh look. "As the newest and most inexperienced member on this Council, perhaps you should listen more than speak, Miss Lansa."

What a douchebag. "She has every right to speak," Tori piped up.

Adam cut her a harsh look.

She quelled and again fought the need to stick out her tongue. Girl power needed a serious lift in the Coven Nine. She leaned over to whisper. "Their tenors are odd. Gallagher's is kind of thick and dirty, while Nessa's is pure, if that makes sense."

Adam nodded. "He's lying while she's telling the truth, probably." His breath whispered against her ear.

Whoa. That was a good new talent to have. "I'd trust Nessa," Tori whispered.

Adam nodded.

"Stop whispering. In addition, you have not mated the human, as you promised," Gallagher said grimly. "I know you're a criminal, but I have to admit I'm surprised to see you break a vow."

Adam stood taller. A tremor went down his right arm, and Tori's eyes widened. He'd hidden it from the Council, but she'd noticed. How much Apollo was still in his system? "Adam?" she whispered.

He ignored her and continued facing the Council. His jaw was firm, and his shoulders back, giving no indication of the battle his body was fighting. "I have not broken any vow, as I did not agree to any arbitrary timeline. When I mate the human, it will be on a timeline that is none of your fucking business, Gallagher."

That was it. That was so it. Tori lost it. "You don't want to mate me. Don't sit here and call me a human and go on and on about damn timelines." Her temper burst through her so quickly she could barely breathe. "It's all complete bullshit."

He turned and seemed to forget all about the Council. "What in the hell?" he snapped, his eyes burning.

She planted both hands on her hips. As far as she was concerned, they were the only people in the whole stupid world. "I love you, Adam Dunne. Even though you're stubborn, difficult, and sometimes caught in the last century." She sucked in air. "But you're also strong, sweet, and totally trustworthy." She cut a glare at Gallagher, remembering the slimeball existed. "He'd never break a vow, you moron."

Adam stepped toward her. "Victoria—"

"No." She stomped her foot. "That's it. You've had the chance to mate me, and you didn't want to. I get it. You probably want a badass witch who has eaten crumpets with a queen or two. I get it. I'm from the wrong side of the tracks, and that's the truth."

"Crumpets?" He looked at her like she'd completely lost her mind.

She didn't care. "But you're wrong."

"I am?" he asked mildly.

His tone caught her off guard. Provided a sense of warning. Yet she couldn't stop. "Yes. Dead wrong. I'm the best thing that ever happened to you. I make you laugh. I make you see life in other terms than your rigid plans. And you like my music." She wound down, her heart hurting. "You always hold back, because you don't realize I can handle all of you. I *want* all of you."

"Victoria—" He reached for her, and a huge crash came from behind them. He pivoted, putting her to the side.

"What was that?" she whispered, as the air popped all around them. Magic was freakin' scary sometimes. Or physics. Hadn't Adam said it was really physics?

"I don't know." The muscles vibrated down his back.

Another crash, and the entire rock wall shimmered and rolled. What the hell?

Gallagher smashed his gavel down again. "Interlopers."

Tori bit back a totally inappropriate snort. Seriously. Who *used* that word? "What's happening, Adam?" She wanted to be brave, but being stuck underground where rocks collapsed sped the adrenaline through her.

He tilted his head. "It's familiar. Signatures." He breathed in through his nose. "You're fucking kidding me."

"What?" Tori asked, moving closer to him.

He shook his head. "Family. Damn it." He looked down at her, his eyes darkening and his lips pursing. "You said you could jam that gun?"

She nodded, her throat too dry to speak.

"Good." He pointed to the wavering wall. "If I had to guess, I'd say there's a cadre of witches on the other side, probably a vampire and demon as well, and they're trying to unravel the physics that keeps the wall in place. Why don't you help them?"

She blinked. "Me? Get rid of a wall?"

"'Tisn't really a wall," he said, crossing his arms. "It's not real at all. And there's a lot of power coming from the other side." Flames flowed naturally down his arms. "I'll aim high for the corners so I don't burn anybody, and you go for the center."

She gulped.

"Stop it. Stop this right now," Gallagher yelled from behind them. "Guards!"

Adam threw a fireball into the top right corner, and the wall morphed and stretched.

Tori shut her eyes and held out her hands, trying to focus all of herself into her fingers. A tingle started inside her. She pushed harder, energized by the now-familiar feeling.

"Kill them," Gallagher yelled.

Panic rushed through her, and she added it to her strength. Something shot from her fingers, something she felt like fire. A huge crash sounded, like windows upon windows of glass being shattered. She opened her eyes to see the wall collapse, hit the ground . . . and then disappear.

She swallowed air like it was water.

Kellach, Daire, Simone, and the king stood facing her, along with a dark-haired man with a scar along his jaw and another guy, this one blond with sharp black eyes.

"The cavalry?" Tori asked, her voice shaking.

"Aye," Adam said with a resigned sigh. "You know everyone except Zane Kyllwood, the leader of the demon nation"—he pointed to the large dark-haired man—"and Nick Veis, his second-in-command and Simone's mate." He nodded toward the blond.

Tori gave a weak wave. "Hi, demons."

"What the hell was that?" Kellach asked, twisting his neck to look where the edges of the wall had been.

"That was Victoria," Adam said proudly. "Now that's power."

Armed guards rushed in from both sides, guns pointed. Kellach started to form fire.

"Wait a minute," Nessa yelled.

Tori turned.

The stunning woman was standing, her face red. "Enough of this.

What is it with your family? You keep coming in and blowing up the Chambers." She shook her head, her dark hair spilling out of its knot. "You can't just keep showing up here with guns and blowing things up." Her arms gestured wildly. "We need better blooming protection." In full temper, the witch was truly gorgeous.

Adam held up a hand. "You're right. Everyone bank the fire, and let's talk."

"I sentence you to death," Gallagher thundered.

Nessa punched him in the arm hard enough to knock him sideways. "You, alone, can't pronounce that sentence. Now everyone relax, and let's figure this out." She retook her seat, regal as ever.

"I kinda like her," Tori murmured.

Adam turned to face the Council, and the group from the other side of the wall formed a barrier around him and Tori. "I have proof that Peter Gallagher was the person to set up Simone Brightston."

Nessa gasped. "Excuse me? Where is this proof?"

Adam faltered. "In the States."

"No it isn't." Kellach moved forward and tugged a manila file and a flash drive from behind his back. "Adam traced the money and the paper trail, and we found a couple of videos. The evidence is here, and it's damning."

Peter shook his head. "This is ridiculous."

Adam cleared his throat. "In addition, we've discovered that Peter Gallagher is working with or for the manufacturer of Apollo. We don't know why, but we do know he engineered the release of Parker Monzelle for the sole purpose of distributing the drugs."

"That is crazy," Peter yelled. "Why would I do that?"

Adam lifted a shoulder. "We don't have the motive as of yet, but I believe it's all about power. Whoever is behind Apollo promised you the world once the rest of the Council was taken out, now didn't they?"

Peter's face turned so red his eyes bugged out. "These are all lies. I'm innocent."

Nessa eyed him. "Yet we must investigate. I'll set our best investigators on the matter right now."

Rage distorted Peter's face. "That's your choice, and it's the wrong one." He turned back toward Adam, hatred in his dark eyes.

"Regardless of any investigation, I'm the head of the Council at this very moment, and our existing orders still stand. Guards? Take Kellach, Daire, Simone, and the human to cells to await death. Arrest everybody else."

Tori glared. "Stop calling me 'the human.' My name is Victoria Monzelle, and you can use it, dickhead."

Adam's lips twitched. "You're correct in that the current Council's orders stand while any investigation is taking place."

Gallagher shook his head, triumph lifting his weak chin. "There will not be a stay in the orders while we await any silly investigation."

"I'm no' asking for a stay," Adam said, his brogue out in full force.

"No?" Gallagher asked, his gaze narrowing.

"No. I, Adam Dunne, Enforcer for the Coven Nine, hereby challenge you for your seat on the Council of the Coven Nine, Peter Gallagher. The challenge starts now."

Kellach moved forward and grabbed Adam's arm. "You can't do this. The Apollo poison is still in your system. You're nowhere near full power."

Adam shrugged. "It's done."

Tori trembled, just from the tension emanating from the two men. "Wh-what does that mean? The challenge?"

Adam looked down at her, his face stoic and no emotion in his eyes. "It means we fight to the death. Right now."

Chapter 34

Adam faced Peter Gallagher, showing no emotion, although his left leg had gone partially numb. "Pete?" he asked.

Peter's head lifted, and his entire face hardened. "You're making a mistake."

Adam forced a smile. "You could avoid a fight and resign. If not, prepare to bleed." It truly was that simple.

Gallagher focused, his gaze narrowing and his forehead seeming to elongate. Although he was a diplomat, and a political genius, he came from a long line of warriors. The guy definitely had skills. "Last chance, Dunne. I've already read the report on your fight in Seattle. The poison in your blood will make it an easy kill for me." He jerked his head toward Victoria. "With your woman watching."

It was those words—those callous words about Victoria—that sent power surging through Adam. "Remember this second."

"Oh?" Gallagher asked, arrogance in every line of his body.

"Aye. The second I decided to kill you instead of just burn your powers away," Adam said, the battle songs of his ancestors singing through his blood.

Gallagher stood. "Challenge accepted."

With those words, the entire room came to life. Dimensional commands created centuries before took over, pushing all the spectators into a gallery area with a one-way mirror and pressing them to their seats. The stone bench and tables disappeared, and the wall that had just been destroyed reappeared, darker and thicker than even before.

A simple circular-shaped battle area with dirt floor and solid rock walls was all that remained on the other side of the mirror.

Magic and life whispered through the air, rolling with tension, peopled by souls from times past—magic and the application of psychics in configurations and spells that were long forgotten. Yet in this one second in time, in a battle for a Coven seat, they ruled.

Adam opened his hands at his sides, allowing the power in. Allowed it to lift him, to darken him.

Gallagher circled around, flames already morphing on his hands. Thick flames, a deep brown. "After I kill you, your woman is next."

Adam lifted an eyebrow, hoping she was all right behind the mirror. Oh, all he could see was a blank wall, but he knew how it worked, and he knew she could see but not hear what was going on. "Victoria has more power in her little finger than you've accumulated in two hundred years. My money is on her."

"Is that a fact?" Gallagher feinted left and then back.

"She'd kick your ass, Petey." The vision was still blurry in Adam's left eye, so he made sure to keep track of Gallagher with his right.

"We'll have to see," Gallagher said, forming a vibrating brown ball of flame.

If the guy was trying to motivate Adam, it was working. Without giving a hint of warning, he lifted his hand and arced pure blue fire at Gallagher.

The witch yelped and jumped out of the way, his gaze wild.

Adam smiled and followed suit with his other hand. This time, the fire caught Gallagher in the thigh before he could move far enough away. "Funny thing about being an Enforcer." Adam circle around, using his good eye. "You learn to throw fire without forming it first. Well, forming it outside your body."

"Good to know." Gallagher arced brown fire toward him.

Adam easily stepped to the side, just as three rapid fireballs came from Gallagher's other hand. One impacted Adam's ribs and burned right through his shirt, shooting pain to his spine. "Guess you already know that," Adam gasped.

"Guess so." Gallagher gracefully edged to the other side. "How's the pain? Your left eye isn't looking so good. Purple and all of that."

"Colored contacts. Matches Victoria's hair," Adam said, feinting left and right. "Your pants are still on fire."

Gallagher ignored the flames licking away his pants. "How good is the evidence you've found?"

"Excellent. Enough to put you away," Adam said.

Gallagher nodded toward the southern wall. "Not if I'm still on the Council. I'll bury it." He smiled. "You have to appreciate the architecture here."

"Stone walls and dirt floor? Definitely," Adam said, forcing pain away from his eye. Fucking Apollo.

Gallagher focused back on him. "No. The fact that people can watch the match, know what happens, but not hear a word." He gazed in appreciation at the magical walls. "It's the perfect confessional. Either for the killer or the one to die. A last time to state sins."

"You want to state your sins?" Adam asked, creating three smaller plasma balls on his right hand.

"No. I just like that I could," Gallagher said, sweeping his arm in a wide arc and throwing a furious plane of fire.

Adam ducked and rolled. The plane hit the wall and was smothered out. "How about one admission? Who are you working with?" Adam lobbed the three balls, throwing hard. The first hit Gallagher in the shoulder, the second in the thigh, and the third the wall behind him.

Gallagher dropped to the ground, hissing in pain, then leapfrogged back up, swinging three sharp plasma fireballs at Adam.

Adam jumped high and to the right. "Who?"

Gallagher shook his head and patted fire away from his shirt. The smell of burned skin filled the room. "Nobody. Do you really think I need help creating a false paper trail, especially for somebody like Simone? She hasn't exactly been careful through the years, and I truly needed her off the Council. Your whole family needed to be gone."

"Yeah, but you had council documents that you had to have gotten from somewhere. Give it up," Adam said. He held his empty hands out wide. "Unless you think you're going to lose."

Gallagher moved surprisingly fast and shot a narrow arc of fire right into Adam's chest.

Pain detonated in his solar plexus, winging out to every nerve. Adam fell back, his head impacting the wall with a thick thud. He could swear he heard a woman scream his name. Victoria? The vision in his left eye went completely black. He slid down, his ass hitting dirt, fire sparking uselessly from his fingertips.

Peter advanced, a kill ball in his hands. "Well, I guess I could confess now."

Adam's head lolled, but he managed to point his good eye toward Gallagher. The emotion coming through the wall, raw and fierce, almost stole his concentration, but he held on by a thread. "Let me guess. That traitor, Grace Sadler?"

Gallagher blinked. "You're not as dumb as you look."

Grace Sadler had been a council member removed from the bench, and she'd borne two sons, both of whom were recently dead after pursing a vendetta against the Dunne family. Adam blew out air, and real fire singed his mouth. "Tell me you're not involved in the Apollo trade."

"Of course not. Grace offered the documents, and I took them. That's it." Gallagher raised his hand high, preparing to strike down with the kill shot. "No idea about Apollo."

"Stop lying."

Gallagher sighed. "Fair enough. The manufacturer of Apollo has his own agenda, and while I don't agree with it, for now, being his ally suits my purpose."

"Of taking over the Council?" Adam gasped for air.

"Yes," Gallagher said. "After I'm in control, the real kind, I'll take care of the threat. It'll be my first true action in the new organization."

"Who is it?" Adam asked, his mind nearly blanking. He was running out of time.

Gallagher advanced, fire burning down his arms.

A woman screamed again, and this time Adam felt her fear in his chest. Victoria.

"You don't know who it is," Adam muttered, realization dawning.

Gallagher smiled. "Not yet. Good-bye, Adam Dunne." He pivoted back to throw a killing arc.

Adam lifted his left hand and shot a disk of razor-sharp fire. It sliced through Peter's neck and kept going. His eyes widened, and his mouth opened in a silent scream. The disk spun through and careened across the room to bounce off the wall. Peter's head fell down his back, and his body dropped straight down, landing on the knees and falling sideways.

Adam kicked him away. "If you'd read my complete dossier, you'd know I can do that. Moron."

The wall hiding the spectators shimmered and disappeared. The long raised dais reappeared, as did the stone tables on each side of the aisle. Victoria ran to him, sliding on her knees. "Adam?" She reached him a second before the king did.

Dage's fangs dropped, and he ripped open his own wrist, holding it to Adam's mouth. Blood poured inside Adam, tasting of something . . . grape? Power followed the grape taste, flashing through his limbs, returning his eyesight immediately. Adam gasped and pushed Dage's arm away.

"Thanks," Adam mumbled. Damn vampires had it good, now didn't they, to be able to heal with blood?

Victoria snuggled into his side, tears on her face. "Are you all right? Seriously?"

Power nearly shook him apart. Not only had Dage's blood helped, but he'd felt something move through him, something ancient and mighty, the second he'd killed Gallagher. "Aye, baby. I'm fine." He helped her to stand and then handed her to his brother. "I'll be right back." He strode up the steps of the dais, feeling the Apollo finally give up its hold on him.

He'd won Peter's position, which meant for the moment that he ruled the entire council. How convenient. When he reached Peter's seat, he sat down. Nessa and Sal took their respective seats.

Look at that. A nice gavel was already there. "Based not only on the evidence brought in earlier but on Peter Gallagher's own confession, I hereby vacate the death sentence imposed on Simone Brightston and reinstate her to her position on the Coven Nine." For good measure, Adam slammed the gavel. "I next reinstate Enforcers Daire Dunne, Kellach Dunne, and Moira Kayrs-Dunne, effective immediately." He slammed the damn thing again. "Finally, I reinstate the remaining council members who have been discharged temporarily of duty, especially Vivienne Northcutt as the head of the Council." He threw the gavel behind his head.

The people gathered in the room clapped, cheered, or looked on as if he'd gone crazy.

"Oh yeah." Adam stood tall. "The witch nation wants to realign itself with the Realm. Let's forget the withdrawal ever happened."

Dage gave one short nod. "It's already forgotten."

Nessa cleared her throat. "I, ah, am in agreement with such proclamation."

Sal looked on, his forehead dotting with sweat. "Agreed."

Adam eyed him. They needed to investigate the old witch. "Good."

Nessa looked around and nodded. "'Tis good. The Council is back and in control."

Adam took a deep breath. "I hereby resign as a council member and want my job as an Enforcer back. We have three council seats to fill, and I'm thinking maybe we should find people who aren't related to our family. Just to make things more balanced." Neither Sal nor Nessa was related, so that was a good start.

"Now." He focused on Victoria, who stood near Kellach, watching the entire show with wide eyes. "I believe you said you loved me and wanted to mate me."

She drew back. "I thought we were dying."

Oh, she was fucking adorable. "I also believe that you said you want all of me and am tired of my holding back with you." His heart started to beat faster, and the beast inside him roared wide fucking awake. He stood and bounded over the stone dais, landing squarely on his feet.

She took a step back, and the hunter inside him howled in joy. "Adam, I—"

"You also said you're the best thing that has ever happened to me, and that I should know it and want to mate you." He reached her and ran a gentle finger down her face.

She trembled. "Adam," she sighed.

"I do love you," he said. "With everything I am, and you can definitely have all of me."

Her smile started to spread.

He ducked and tossed her over his shoulder, turning toward the suddenly appearing doors.

"Where are you going?" Kellach called out.

"To fulfill my vow," he shot back, ignoring Victoria's panicked squeak. "On my time."

Chapter 35

Tori's head spun so much she couldn't catch one single thought as she rode on the back of Adam's bike through the rainy streets. Was it even Adam's bike? He carried her out of the Coven Nine headquarters and plunked her on the back of a Harley before starting it with fire from his hand.

Had he stolen the bike?

What the hell was going on? He'd said he loved her. *After* getting in a weird fire-throwing fight where he'd cut off Peter Gallagher's head.

Whatever had been in the king's blood had seemed to fully heal Adam from the Apollo darts. Or had he been healed after the fight? He'd seemed different—even stronger than before, if that were possible. His tenor, the vibrations, felt deadly. In a good way, if that made any sense at all.

Her arms were wrapped around his waist, and his heated body warmed her. The hard angles beneath her palms shortened her breath and softened her thighs. When they got to wherever he was driving, they needed to have a talk. A long talk to figure things out. The man had to stop tossing her over his shoulder every damn time he wanted to leave a room.

He drove up into the hills, and green surrounded them on both sides. Finally, he took a turn around a long bend, and an imposing rock house appeared on the top of a rolling green cliff. A river rushed below.

He jumped off the bike and took her with him.

"Where are we?" she asked, the wind chilling her.

"Wicklow Mountains, south of Dublin." He swept her up against his hard chest, striding around rocks to the door. There he rearranged stones, per usual, and the heavy door swung open. "It's my getaway."

"Oh." She wrapped her arms around his neck, looking at the stone fireplace in the corner fronted by living room furniture in a deep gray. Then the floor-to-ceiling windows caught her eye. Outside were rolling hills and water and rocks. Beautiful and barren. Lonely and stunning. "Put me down." They needed to talk.

"Gladly." He set her on her feet gently and ripped her shirt over her head—not so gently.

Her mouth went slack. "What are you doing?"

He kissed her then, going deep, driving her head back. She had no choice but to grab onto his nearly shredded T-shirt to keep from falling on her butt. His tongue swept inside, heated and insistent. Her head spun, and every nerve in her body flared wide awake and ready to play.

She jerked free. "Adam. Wait." She took a step back. Caution scored through her.

"Wait?" His hungry gaze nearly devoured her as he tracked her. "I've waited."

She held out a hand, as if that one simple act could ward him off. "I know, but—"

Her legs started backing her toward the windows on their own. Her nostrils flared like prey being stalked by a predator.

"I waited until we weren't under Council orders." Adam took a step toward her, muscles rippling beneath his jeans. "I waited until the threat was no longer over our heads." Two more steps. "I waited until I finally gained your trust." One long step, and her butt pressed against the chilled glass. "Finally, I waited until you accepted me. All of me." He reached her, his heat washing over her. His eyes glowed a violent hue. "Victoria?"

She swallowed. Barely. "What?" she whispered.

"I'm done waiting."

She blinked. There was nowhere to go. But she knew, she knew deep down, she couldn't make this easy on him. "Too bad," she whispered.

He smiled.

Then he flipped her around, lifting her arms and pressing her hands against the glass, high above her head. "Don't move," he whispered, his breath a burn against her ear.

She shivered. The glass cooled her front, while heat poured off the male behind her. He reached around and unzipped her pants, slipping his fingers inside to brush against her panties.

Her gasp left a round ring of condensation on the window. Her hands started to lower.

"No. Keep them there," he ordered. His fingers tapped along the top of her mound, sparking an electric bolt of pleasure to her clit.

She drew in a sharp breath, pushing her cheek against the glass. He moved her panties to one side, and then heat flared. Fire licked her thighs. Her jeans disintegrated as if they'd never even existed. Two seconds later, and her panties did the same.

"You can keep the boots on," he said, scraping his fangs over her bare shoulder.

She bit back a strangled moan. He slid his fingers, hotter than possible, over her already wet folds. Her knees trembled, and her hands started to lower.

"No." He plunged one finger inside her and pushed his groin against her bare butt. "You will obey me. Period." Another finger joined the first, and he stretched her, forcing pain into her pleasure. "Tell me you understand."

She gulped in air and kept her hands up where he'd put them, but she didn't reply.

"Not ready yet?" His chuckle made something clench inside her. He stroked her, his fingers playing her, his thumb rubbing against her clit. "All of this wet heat. The energy, the need. It's for me, isn't it?" He opened his mouth over the sensitive flesh where her shoulder met her neck and sucked, taking in the bite marks from last time.

Lightning bolted through her, and she moaned, pushing against his hand.

"You need to give up control, Victoria." He pressed hard on her clit, and her knees buckled. One arm bound her waist and held her upright. "And you will."

She blinked but couldn't focus on the amazing view. Only his fingers, his rough, velvety voice, his hard body existed.

"You wanted all of me. Here I am." Fire arced from the fingers inside her to her nipples.

She cried out, the heat of a thousand orgasms building. "That's not fair," she moaned.

He chuckled, scraping his teeth against her jugular. "I never play fair. Learn that now."

She opened her legs wider, giving him more access, needing more. The ease with which he played her body was matched by the ease with which he controlled her. His strength was so much more than hers. He could do anything he wanted, and something about that, the truth of her absolute trust in him, freed her in a way she'd never imagined. "I love you, Adam," she said.

"There it is." He bit her neck with regular teeth. Without warning, he grasped her hips and pivoted, shoving her over a long hand-carved dining room table. It was rough wood, ancient-looking, and he kicked the head chair across the room.

Her cheek rested against the wood, wood that slightly scratched her belly.

He leaned over her. "It feels rough, but I promise, no splinters."

Even now, caught up in the moment, he made sure to keep her safe. She closed her eyes.

"Hands," he ordered.

It took her a second, but she remembered, sliding her arms up and flattening her hands as she had on the glass. The position elongated her body and took away her ability to move quickly. When he grabbed her hips, she couldn't move at all.

"Good." His voice thickened with desire. Then he lifted her just enough that her feet no longer touched the rug on the stone floor.

Helplessness poured through her, right before a desperate need that made her groan out loud.

"You're being so good." He reached between her legs and petted her.

She arched and tried to give him better access. Her legs shook, but she couldn't reach the floor. He had her right where he wanted her. When he removed his fingers, her body shook in a violent refusal. She couldn't wait any longer.

Clothes rustled, and he returned to her, heating the back of her thighs with his skin. Slowly, he pushed inside her, this time going steady and not giving her time to accommodate him. The raw pleasure was edged with pain, and she struggled, but he planted a hand on her waist and held her easily in place.

He overcame her. In every real sense, he overwhelmed her. She was at his mercy, and in this moment, he didn't have any. At the thought, a mini-explosion rocked through her. Not enough. Not even close to enough. She trembled, needing more but not sure how to get it. She couldn't move.

"All you can do is take what I give you," he whispered at her ear, unerringly reading her mind. "Are you ready?"

"Yes," she all but sobbed.

"Good. I love you, Victoria." Then he lifted her hips even more, this time off the table, and pulled out to push back inside so hard she saw stars.

With her hands flat, her face turned, and her hips in the air, he truly did control every aspect of her. So she did as he'd ordered and took everything he had to give.

Adam Dunne was hers.

He moved hard and deep inside her, hammering with a fierce cadence. An orgasm rolled over her, and she barely had time to gasp before another one started to build, heating her, sparking out, stopping her breath. Air no longer mattered, only the feeling of him inside her, going so deep, hinting at all the pleasure he could create.

She jerked, her body poised on the cliff. Then she broke, crying out his name. A second later, as she was still riding the waves, a piercing pain ripped through her good shoulder.

His fangs.

Her mouth opened wide, but no sound came out. He bit her to the bone and then some, leaving his mark so she'd never be able to remove it. Tears gathered in her eyes, even as her orgasm increased in force, stealing even her will.

A scalding burn flared between her shoulder blades, and she stiffened. The marking. He'd marked her.

She came again, harder than before, her entire body shuddering with the unbelievable release. Finally, she came down and went limp, mumbling something that even sounded like Klingon to her.

He thrust once more inside her and released her shoulders, licking the wound closed.

She mumbled, her body done. Just done. Her mind done, too.

He licked her neck. "I love you."

She tried a grin. "I love you, too."

"Good. Let's spend the rest of the night in bed. Or maybe forever." He still rested against her. "How does forever sound?"

Her heart pretty much burst wide open. "Perfect."

Epilogue

Adam drank a beer in the corner of the opulent gathering room of his aunt Viv's house. The party was in full swing, with everyone in high spirits and drinking way too much alcohol. The Irish whiskey, the good stuff, had already made an appearance.

Nessa Lansa popped up next to him, a flush on her face. She looked pretty in a long blue skirt with a tight bodice. "Having fun?" she asked, a whiskey neat in her hand.

"I am." Adam looked for his mate, seeing her over by the fireplace with her sister. She looked stunning with the new brighter purple stripes in her hair, although she'd dressed in a lovely black skirt he couldn't wait to pull up to give him access. His pants got too tight, and he took a drink of his beer.

"Good," Nessa said, scoping the party. "I was hoping you'd give me some insight into Bear McDunphy."

Adam coughed. "Bear? Why?"

Nessa sighed. "Simone is blackmailing me into helping him." The young woman grinned. "Okay, maybe not blackmailing, but she's made me feel guilty enough about that former death sentence over her head that I promised I'd help him. Even though I voted no to death, by the way."

Adam frowned. "I think that's extortion, not blackmail."

"No, it's emotional blackmail." Nessa nodded. "Anyway, my people have a gift of healing. So she'd like me to help heal her brother, and then all is forgiven."

Adam studied the councilwoman. Her people had other gifts as well, and he knew it. They were bloodhounds on a case. "Is that the only reason you're heading to the States?" he asked.

Her violet-blue eyes widened. "Of course. Well, besides wanting some sort of adventure. I'm too settled here."

If anybody could unsettle her, it'd be Bear. Adam drank more of his beer. "The Council is doing well, right?" Everyone was back in place, and now they were conducting business as usual.

"Thanks to your taking out the main distributor and all of those vials of Apollo in Seattle, yes, we're good. Though the manufacturer . . ." she murmured.

"I'd like to go back to Seattle and hunt him down," Adam said thoughtfully.

"No," Daire said, coming up behind him. "You blew up Titans of Fire as well as the Apollo warehouse."

"Your mate blew up your Seattle penthouse. Twice," Adam shot back.

Daire nodded. "Exactly. There's too much heat on us in Seattle, and we have to stay off the human radar for a while. We can work the case from here and find the manufacturer. We're so close. I can feel it."

So could Adam.

Nessa smiled. "I shall be more than happy to investigate on your behalf while in Seattle."

"No," Adam said. "Sorry. Coven Nine council members don't investigate. In fact, we'll have to send members of the Guard with you."

Nessa chuckled. "I already resigned. My appointment was temporary until things returned to normal. But it was fun, yes?" She gracefully stood and moved toward the buffet table.

"What do you suppose she's up to?" Adam asked.

Daire shrugged, seeing his mate on the other side of the room receiving blueprints from their aunt. "Fuck. That had better not be blueprints to rob a bank." He strode quickly through the throng of bodies to reach his demoness.

Adam smiled.

"I love that sight," Victoria said, sidling up to him.

Everything inside him settled and calmed. "Then I shall do it more often, sweet mate." He pressed a kiss to her forehead.

"Good. Because about this whole mating thing . . ."

He lifted an eyebrow. "Aye?"

"I want the rest of it."

He studied her stunning eyes. "All right. What's the rest of it?"

"A wedding. Ring, proposal, on one knee, buddy." She bounced on her high-heeled boots.

He stiffened. "But we're mated. That trumps all of that other stuff."

Her eyes sparkled. "No, it doesn't. I want it all. Bridesmaids. Flowers. Cutting the cake. My mom can't wait." She snuggled into his side.

He sighed. Well, if that made her happy. "All right, Victoria."

She leaned up and kissed his chin. "See how easy you were to tame?"

He laughed out loud and ducked, tossing her over his shoulder. She yelped.

"No. Why don't you show me now?" he asked. Ignoring everybody, he made for the door and had her outside and at his bike before she could protest. He set her down, and all that glorious hair fell around her shoulders.

"I love you," she whispered.

"I love you forever." Aye. His entirely boring and logical life had completely changed. Thank God.

If you enjoyed WICKED KISS, don't miss

Coming next month!

"Fast-paced romance . . . very compelling. Highly recommended."
—*Library Journal*

As she hunts for a drug lord killing her fellow witches,
all Nessa Lansa's instincts point to the Grizzly motorcycle club.
That might be because their leader, Bear, is the strong,
silent shifter type: warm brown eyes and more muscle
and man than any woman can ignore. Which makes Nessa's plan
to seduce and betray him all the more dangerous . . .

Bear doesn't trust the curvy blue-eyed witch. But Nessa can heal
the injuries that sap his strength. And since he can't stop thinking
of her lush body and teasing smile, her plan to mate him to
reclaim her own power is highly tempting. Just one problem.
Once a desire this wild is loose, no one will ever control it . . .

And now you can binge read the first three
Realm Enforcers novels
with the Realm Enforcers Bundle

New York Times Bestselling Author
REBECCA
ZANETTI

THE
REALM
ENFORCERS

WICKED RIDE ● WICKED EDGE
●WICKED BURN●

Turn the page for a preview of the first novel
in the groundbreaking new series by Rebecca Zanetti!
Mercury Striking
Available now in paperback and e-book
from Zebra Books.

"Nothing is easy or black or white in Zanetti's grim new reality,
but *hope* is key, and I hope she writes faster!"
—*New York Times* **bestselling author Larissa Ione**

With nothing but rumors to lead her, Lynn Harmony has trekked
across a nightmare landscape to find one man—a mysterious,
damaged legend who protects the weak and leads the strong.
He's more than muscle and firepower—and in post-plague L.A.,
he's her only hope. As the one woman who could cure the disease,
Lynn is the single most volatile—and vulnerable—creature in this
new and ruthless world. But face to face with Jax Mercury . . .

Danger has never looked quite so delicious . . .

Chapter 1

Life on Earth is at the ever-increasing risk of being wiped out by a disaster, such as sudden global nuclear war, a genetically engineered virus or other dangers we have not yet thought of.—Stephen Hawking

Despair hungered in the darkness, not lingering, not languishing . . . but waiting to bite. No longer the little brother of rage, despair had taken over the night, ever present, an actor instead of an afterthought.

Lynn picked her way along the deserted twelve-lane interstate, allowing the weak light from the moon to guide her. An unnatural silence hung heavy over the empty land. Rusted carcasses of cars lined the sides, otherwise, the once vibrant 405 was dead, yet she trod carefully.

Her months of hiding had taught her stealth. Prey needed stealth, as did the hunter.

She was both.

The tennis shoes she'd stolen from an abandoned thrift store protected her feet from the cracked asphalt. A click echoed in the darkness. About time. She'd made it closer to Los Angeles, well, what used to be Los Angeles, than she'd hoped.

A strobe light hit her full on, rendering sight useless. She closed her eyes. They'd either kill her or not. Either way, no need to go blind. "I want to see Mercury."

Silence. Then several more clicks. Guns of some type.

She forced strength into her voice. "You don't want to kill me without taking me to Mercury first." Jax Mercury, to be exact. If he still existed. If not, she was screwed anyway.

"Why would we do that?" A voice from the darkness, angry and near.

She opened her eyes, allowing light to narrow her pupils. "I'm Lynn Harmony."

Gasps, low and male, echoed around her. They'd closed in silently, just as well trained as she'd heard. As she'd hoped.

"Bullshit," a voice hissed from her left.

She tilted her head toward the voice, then slowly, so slowly they wouldn't be spooked, she unbuttoned her shirt. No catcalls, no suggestive responses followed. Shrugging her shoulders, she dropped the cotton to the ground, facing the light.

She hadn't worn a bra, but she doubted the echoing exhales of shock were from her size B's. More likely the shimmering blue outline of her heart caught their attention. Yeah, she was a freak. Typhoid Mary in the body of a woman who'd made a mistake. A big one. But she might be able to save the men surrounding her. "So. Jax Mercury. Now."

One man stepped closer. Gang tattoos lined his face, inked tears showing his kills. He might have been thirty, he might have been sixty. Regardless, he was dangerous. Eyeing her chest, he quickly crossed himself. "Holy Mary, Mother of God."

"Not even close." Wearily, she reached down and grabbed her shirt, shrugging it back on. She figured the "take me to your leader" line would get her shot. "Do you want to live or not?"

He met her gaze, hope and fear twisting his scarred upper lip. "Yes."

It was the most sincere sound she'd heard in months. "We're running out of time." Time had deserted them long ago, but she needed to get a move on. "Please." The sound shocked her, the civility of it, a word she'd forgotten how to use. The slightest of hopes warmed that blue organ in her chest, reminding her of who she used to be. Who she'd lost.

Another figure stepped forward, this one big and silent. Deadly power vibrated in the shift of muscle as light illuminated him from behind, keeping his features shrouded. "I didn't tell you to put your shirt back on." No emotion, no hint of humanity echoed in the deep rumble.

The lack of emotion twittered anxiety through her abdomen. Without missing a beat, she secured each button, keeping the movements slow and sure. "I take it you're Mercury." Regardless of name, there was no doubt the guy was in charge.

"If I am?" Soft, his voice promised death.

A promise she'd make him keep. Someday. The breeze picked up, tumbling weeds across the deserted 405. She fought a shiver. Any weakness shown might get her killed. "You know who I am."

"I know who you say you are." His overwhelming form blocked out the light, reminding her of her smaller size. "Take off your shirt."

Something about the way he said it gave her pause. Before, she hadn't cared. But with him so close she could smell *male*; an awareness of her femininity brought fresh fear. Nevertheless, she unbuttoned her shirt.

This time, her hands trembled.

Straightening her spine, she squared her shoulders and left the shirt on, the worn material gaping in the front.

He waited.

She lifted her chin, trying to meet his eyes, although she couldn't see them. The men around them remained silent, yet alertness carried on the breeze. How many guns were trained on her? She wanted to tell them it would only take one. Though she'd been through hell, she'd never really learned to fight.

The wind whipped into action, lifting her long hair away from her face. Her arms tightened against her rib cage. Goose bumps rose along her skin.

Swearing softly, the man stepped in, long tapered fingers drawing her shirt apart. He shifted to the side, allowing light to blast her front. Neon blue glowed along her flesh.

"Jesus." He pressed his palm against her breastbone—directly above her heart.

Shock tightened her muscles, her eyes widening, and that heart ripping into a gallop. Her nipples pebbled from the breeze. Warmth cascaded from his hand when he spread his fingers over the odd blue of her skin. When was the last time someone had touched her gently?

And gentle, he was.

The touch had her looking down at his damaged hand. Faded white scars slashed across his knuckles, above the veins, past his wrist. The bizarre glow from her heart filtered through his long fingers. Her entire chest was aqua from within, those veins closest to her heart, which glowed neon blue, shining strong enough to be seen through her ribs and sternum.

He exhaled loudly, removing his touch.

An odd sense of loss filtered down her spine. Then surprise came as he quickly buttoned her shirt to the top.

He clasped her by the elbow. "Cut the light." His voice didn't rise, but instantly, the light was extinguished. "I'm Mercury. What do you want?"

What a question. What she wanted, nobody could provide. Yet she struggled to find the right words. Night after night, traveling under darkness to reach him, she'd planned for this moment. But the words wouldn't come. She wanted to breathe. To rest. To hide. "Help. I need your help." The truth tumbled out too fast to stop.

He stiffened and then tightened his hold on her arm. "That, darlin', you're gonna have to earn."

Jax eyed the brunette sitting in the backseat of the battered Subaru. He'd stolen the vehicle from a home in Beverly Hills after all hell had broken loose. The gardener who'd owned it no longer needed it, considering he was twelve feet under.

The luxury SUV sitting so close to the Subaru had tempted him, but the older car would last longer and use less gas, which was almost depleted, anyway. Hell, everything they had was almost depleted. From medical supplies to fuel to books to, well, hope. How the hell did he refill everybody with hope when he could barely remember the sensation?

The night raid had been a search for more gasoline from abandoned vehicles, not a search party for survivors. He'd never thought to find Lynn Harmony.

The woman had closed her eyes, her head resting against the plush leather. Soft moonlight wandered through the tinted windows to caress the sharp angles of her face. With deep green eyes and pale skin, she was much prettier than he'd expected . . . much softer. Too soft.

Though, searching him out, well now. The woman had guts.

Manny kept looking at her through the rearview mirror, and for some reason, that irritated Jax. "Watch the road."

Manny cut a glance his way. At over fifty years old, beaten and weathered, he took orders easily. "There's no one out here tonight but us."

"We hope." Jax's gut had never lied to him. Somebody was coming. If the woman had brought danger to his little place in the world, she'd pay.

Her eyes flashed open, directly meeting his gaze. The pupils contracted while her chin lifted. Devoid of expression, she just stared.

He stared back.

A light pink wandered from her chest up her face to color her high cheekbones. Fascinated, he watched the blush deepen. When was the last time he'd seen a woman blush? He certainly hadn't expected it from the woman who'd taken out most of the human race.

Around them, off-road vehicles kept pace. Some dirt bikes, a few four-wheelers, even a fancy Razor confiscated from another mansion. Tension rode the air, and some of it came from Manny.

"Say it," Jax murmured, acutely, maybe too much so, aware of the woman in the backseat.

"This is a mistake," Manny said, his hands tightening on the steering wheel. "You know who she is. What she is."

"I doubt that." He turned to glance again at the woman, his sidearm sweeping against the door. She'd turned to stare out at the night again, her shoulders hunched, her shirt hiding that odd blue glow. "Are you going to hurt me or mine?" he asked.

Slowly, she turned to meet his gaze again. "I don't know." Frowning, she leaned forward just enough to make his muscles tense in response. "How many people are yours?"

He paused, his head lifting. "All of them."

She smiled. "I'd heard that about you." Turning back to the window, she fingered the glass as if wanting to touch what was out of reach.

"Heard what?" he asked.

"Your sense of responsibility. Leadership. Absolute willingness to kill." Her tone lacked inflection, as if she just stated facts. "You are, right? Willing to kill?"

He stilled, his eyes cutting to Manny and back to the woman. "You want me to kill somebody?"

"Yes."

He kept from outwardly reacting. Not much surprised him any longer, but he hadn't been expecting a contract killing request from Lynn Harmony. "We've lost ninety-nine percent of the world's population, darlin'. Half of the survivors are useless, and the other half is just trying to survive. You'd better have a good reason for wanting someone dead."

"*Useless* isn't an accurate description," she said quietly.

"If they can't help me, if they're a hindrance, they're fucking useless." He'd turned off the switch deep down that discerned a gray area between the enemy and his people months ago, and there was no changing that. He'd become what was needed to survive and to live through desperate times. "You might want to remember that fact."

Her shoulders went back, and she rested her head, staring up at the ceiling. "I'd love to be useless."

He blinked and turned back around to the front. Her words had been soft, her tone sad, and her meaning heartbreaking. If he still had a heart. So the woman wanted to die, did she? No fucking way. The blood in her veins was more than a luxury, it might be a necessity. She didn't get to die. "Please tell me you're not the one I'm supposed to kill," he said, his heart beating faster.

Silence ticked around the dented SUV for a moment. "Not yet, no."

Great. All he needed was a depressed biological weapon in the form of a sexy brunette to mess with his already fucking fantastic daily schedule. "Lady, if you wanna eat a bullet, you should've done it before coming into my territory." Since she was there, he was making use of her, and if that meant suicide watch around the clock, he'd provide the guards to keep her breathing.

"I know." Fabric rustled, and she poked him in the neck. "When was your last injection?"

His head jerked as surprise flared his neurons to life. He grabbed her finger before turning and held tight. "Almost one month ago."

She tried to free herself and then frowned when she failed. "You're about due, then. How many vials of B do you have left?"

He tugged her closer until she was almost sitting in the front seat, his gaze near to hers. "Doesn't matter. Now I have you, don't I? If we find the cure, we won't need vitamin B." This close, under the dirt and fear, he could smell woman. Fresh and with a hint of—what was that—vanilla? No. Gardenias. Spicy and wild.

She shook her head and again tried to free herself. "You can have all the blood you want. It won't help."

"Stop the car," he said to Manny.

Manny nodded and pulled over. Jax released Lynn's finger, stepped out of the vehicle, and pressed into the backseat next to her.

Her eyes widened, and she huddled back against the other door.

He drew a hood from his back pocket. "Come here, darlin'."

"No." She scrambled away, her hands out.

With a sigh, he reached for a zip tie in his vest and way too easily secured her hands together. A second later, he pulled the hood over her head. He didn't like binding a woman, but he didn't have a choice. "In the past year, as the world has gone to hell, hasn't anybody taught you to fight?" he asked.

She kicked out, her bound hands striking for his bulletproof vest.

He lifted her onto his lap, wrapped an arm over hers and around her waist, manacling her legs with one of his. "Relax. I'm not going to hurt you, but you can't know where we're going."

"Right." She shoved back an elbow, her warm little body struggling hard.

Desire flushed through him, pounding instantly into his cock. God, she was a handful.

She paused. "Ah—"

"You're safe. Just stop wiggling." His voice was hoarse. Jesus. When was the last time he'd gotten laid? He actually couldn't remember. She was a tight little handful of energy and womanly curves, and his body reacted instantly. The more she gyrated against him, trying to fight, the more blood rushed south of his brain. He had to get her under control before he began panting like a teenager.

"No." Her voice rose, and she tried to flail around again. "You can't manhandle me like this."

If she had any clue how he'd like to handle her, she'd be screaming. He took several deep breaths and forced desire into the abyss, where it belonged. He wanted her hooded, not afraid. "If you were mine, you'd know how to fight." Where that thought came from, he'd never know.

She squirmed on his lap, fully contained. "Good thing I'm not yours, now isn't it?"

He exhaled and held her tighter until she gave up the fight and submitted against him. The light whimper of frustration echoing behind the hood sounded almost like a sigh of pleasure. When she softened, he hardened. Again.

Then he released his hold. "That's where you're wrong, Lynn Harmony. The second you crossed into my territory, the very moment you asked for my help, that's exactly what you became."

"What?" she asked, sounding breathless now.

"*Mine.*"

Dylan Patrick

New York Times and *USA Today* bestselling author REBECCA ZANETTI has worked as an art curator, Senate aide, lawyer, college professor, and a hearing examiner—only to culminate it all in stories about alpha males and the women who claim them. She writes contemporary romances, dark paranormal romances, and romantic suspense novels.

Growing up amid the glorious backdrops and winter wonderlands of the Pacific Northwest has given Rebecca fantastic scenery and adventures to weave into her stories. She resides in the wild north with her husband, children, and extended family who inspire her every day—or at the very least give her plenty of characters to write about.

Please visit Rebecca at: www.rebeccazanetti.com/
www.facebook.com/RebeccaZanetti.Author.FanPage
twitter.com/RebeccaZanetti

He remembers all her secrets...

TWISTED

USA Today Bestselling Author

REBECCA ZANETTI

"Paranormal romance at its best!"—Cynthia Eden

"Paranormal romance
at its best!"
—Cynthia Eden

POWER AND PLEASURE GO HAND IN HAND . . .

SHADOWED

USA Today Bestselling Author

REBECCA
ZANETTI

The wildest ride yet...

USA Today Bestselling Author

REBECCA
ZANETTI

TAMED

"If you want hot, sexy, dangerous
romance...this series is for you."
—Paranormal Haven

New York Times Bestselling Author

REBECCA ZANETTI

MARKED

New York Times Bestselling Author

REBECCA ZANETTI

WICKED RIDE

DARK PROTECTORS

THE WITCH ENFORCERS

Printed in the United States
by Baker & Taylor Publisher Services